Tales of Time and Space
Stories by Allen Steele

In-house editor: Ian Randal Strock

Fantastic Books
1380 East 17 Street, Suite 2233
Brooklyn, New York 11230
www.FantasticBooks.biz

ISBN 10: 1-62755-634-6
ISBN 13: 978-1-62755-634-7

First Edition

In memory of my sister,
Rachel Steele.

Table of Contents

INTRODUCTION:
PATTERN RECOGNITION

Someone wiser than me once noted that writing is a bit like competitive running in that, while novels are marathons that test the endurance and stamina of their authors, short fiction is more like fifty-yard dashes in which the writers expend their energy in quick bursts of energy and inspiration that carries them across the finish line.

That analogy makes a lot of sense to me. I write both novels and short stories, with novellas being the region between (novelettes are little more than a category created for awards purposes; in reality, they're just long short stories). Whereas a novel typically takes me nine or ten months to write—eighteen months or more with longer works like most of the Coyote novels—I can write a story in two or three weeks. Over the years, I've become accustomed to writing short fiction between novels as a way to recharge between the long fall-to-spring stretches in which I go into seclusion to produce another long work.

And just as a competitive sprinter moves from one track to another, the short stories and novellas I write are usually unrelated to one another (except, of course, when they're installments of a long-running series like Near Space or part of a mosaic novel like *Coyote*). In that case, I'm often working from notes I've jotted down or fragmentary ideas I've been carrying around in my head, waiting for the moment when I figure out what to do with them.

Unfortunately, the analogy breaks down when I gather the short fiction I've published lately to put together another collection. When that happens, I sometimes realize that I've been running a marathon of short sprints. That is, while the stories seem to be unrelated to one another, certain patterns begin to emerge once they're placed side by side.

Very often, these patterns indicate the sort of mindset I had at the time. For instance, one of my earlier collections, *All-American Alien Boy*, had an unusually high number of near-future stories set on Earth, specifically in St. Louis. In hindsight, it came clear that the reason for that was I'd become tired of writing about space, at least for a little while, and decided to use the city to which I'd recently moved as a setting.

This time around, though, I was at loss to explain what some of these patterns meant. For instance, of the twelve stories in this collection, eight are told by first-person narrators, and yet no two of these characters are exactly alike. A writer, a wilderness guide, a train conductor, an itinerant spacer, a former Navy airship crewman, a public relations spokesman, a valet, a harpooner-cum private detective... the identities are different, and even in the case of the stories which take place in my Coyote and Near Space universes, so are the locales. But I couldn't tell you why I put myself in the heads of those characters, other than the obvious narrative advantage of seeing things through their eyes.

It also occurred to me that, perhaps more than any other period in my writing career, I'd produced quite a few stories with historical settings. Yet while "Martian Blood" and "Locomotive Joe and the Wreck of Space Train No. 4" are alternate-history interplanetary adventures (with the former being set in an alternative *present*) and "The Observation Post" is a time-travel story, it's more difficult to describe "The Jekyll Island Horror" or "The Big Whale." They're hard to categorize, and I'm not sure I'd even call either one of them science fiction. Subconsciously, I think I was rebelling against the supposition that the future is the default setting for a science fiction story, and instead wrote stories that took place in the past. Even "Ticking" is pretty much set in the present day, if you ignore the fact that robots aren't yet ubiquitous to everyday life.

But the thing which I found most surprising, when I put together the acknowledgments page, is the fact that nine out of twelve of these stories were published in a two-year period... and indeed, if memory serves correctly, they were written in an eighteen-month stretch between late 2011 and early 2013. I know *how* I wrote this much short fiction in a relatively brief amount of time—a novel crashed on me, and so I turned to short stories for a while—but what eludes is me is *why*.

This was a rather stressful time in my life. I lost family and friends, almost always suddenly and with no warning, and a recurring medical condition put me in the hospital so many times the emergency room red-flagged me as a frequent patient: don't ask questions, just stick him in a bed and hook up him up to an IV. I won't go into details, but this put me in a dark and rather morbid frame of mind. I should have had a breakdown, but instead it appears that my response was to write a lot of short fiction... but why stories instead of, say, a 1,000-page novel?

It now occurs to me that, while this was going on, an anniversary crept up without me really realizing it. 2013 marked my twenty-fifth year as a published science fiction writer; while I wasn't looking, a quarter-century passed between my first widely published short story, "Live from the Mars Hotel," appearing in *Asimov's Science Fiction* (which has remained my home base ever since—three stories in this collection were first published there) and the appearance of most of the stories here.

I guess this makes sense. Although I've written nineteen novels over the past two and a half decades, the truth of the matter is that short fiction is my first love. When I set out as a teenager to become a science fiction writer when I grew up, my goal was to publish SF stories, not novels... and I guess it tells us something that nearly all of the awards I've received during my career have been for my short work, while only my first novel, *Orbital Decay*, has ever received any formal recognition (the *Locus* Award for Best First novel of 1989... and the late Charles Brown, the publisher of *Locus*, was too cheap to give me a plaque!).

On the other hand, it's entirely possible that I could be reading too much into this. There may not be any meaningful patterns to be divined here, only a set of coincidences. If so, these stories shouldn't be taken for anything other than what they are: tales of time and space, little excursions to other worlds and years. I've written brief introductions for each story in which I've talked a bit about their origins, but it's not necessary to read them, and you're invited to skip them if you're annoyed by this sort of thing.

I doubt I'll still be writing another twenty-five years from now. If I'm still alive by then, I probably will have long since retired from the keyboard. On the other hand, I'm a bit surprised that my career has lasted as long as it has. Barry Malzberg once wrote that a science fiction author's career, on average, usually lasts only twenty years. If this is true, then I've managed to beat the odds. So while I appreciate the editors who've bought and published these stories—their names are on the acknowledgments page, and I'll add to them Ian Randal Strock, the editor and publisher of Fantastic Books—my most sincere thanks go to my readers, who've allowed me to keep writing this stuff for all these years.

—Whately, Massachusetts
June, 2014

Except for Coyote, which I created myself, and the Moon, the world I've written the most about has been Mars. It was the setting of my first published story, "Live From the Mars Hotel," which eventually found its way to the actual planet aboard NASA's Phoenix lander—a long story in itself—and since then I've written about a half-dozen stories about the place, along with my novel Labyrinth of Night.

This one is a bit different from the others. It concerns the kind of Mars that was common in science fiction before the American and Russian probes of the 1960s revealed the world as being much less habitable than SF writers had imagined. I always loved the Mars depicted by Bradbury, Heinlein, Brackett, and Zelazny, so this is my homage to them. In its own way, it's quite accurate; my principal source was The Exploration of Mars *by Willy Ley and Wernher von Braun, published in 1956, with the place-names drawn from Giovanni Schiaparelli's maps from the late 1800s.*

This looks like alternate history, but that's not quite accurate. Cell phones, casinos, jeeps… this story is set in contemporary times. But I'm not sure this is a Mars any of us would necessarily want to visit. The natives are restless.

MARTIAN BLOOD

The most dangerous man on Mars was Omar al-Baz, and the first time I saw him, he was throwing up at the Rio Zephyria spaceport.

This happens more frequently than you might think. People coming here for the first time often don't realize just how thin the air really is. The cold surprises them, too, but I'm told the atmospheric pressure is about same as you'd find in the Himalayas. So they come trooping down the ramp of the shuttle that transported them from Deimos Station, and if the ride down didn't make them puke, then the shortness of breath, headaches, and nausea that comes with altitude sickness will.

I didn't know for sure that the middle-aged gent who'd doubled over and vomited was Dr. al-Baz, but I suspected he was; I hadn't seen any other Middle Eastern men on his flight. There was nothing I could do for him, though, so I waited patiently on the other side of the chain-link security fence while one of the flight attendants came down the ramp to help him. Dr. al-Baz waved her away; he didn't need any assistance, thank you. He straightened up, pulled a handkerchief from his overcoat pocket and wiped his mouth, then picked up the handle of the rolling bag he'd dropped when his stomach revolted. Nice to know that he wasn't entirely helpless.

He was one of the last passengers to step through the gate. He paused on the other side of the fence, looked around, and spotted the cardboard sign I was holding. A brief smile of relief, then he walked over to me.

"I'm Omar al-Baz," he said, holding out his hand. "You must be Mr. Ramsey."

"Yes, I'm your guide. Call me Jim." Not wanting to shake a hand that just wiped a mouth which had just spilled yuck all over nice clean concrete, I reached forward to relieve him of his bag.

"I can carry this myself, thank you," he said, not letting me take his bag from him. "But if you could help me with the rest of my luggage, I'd appreciate it."

"Sure. No problem." He hadn't hired me to be his porter, and if he'd been the jerk variety of tourist some of my former clients had been, I would've made him carry his own stuff. But I was already beginning to like the guy: early 50s, skinny but with the beginnings of a pot belly, coarse black hair going grey at the temples. He wore round spectacles and had a bushy mustache beneath a hooked aquiline nose, and looked a little like an Arab Groucho Marx. Omar al-Baz couldn't have been anything but what he was, an Egyptian-American professor from the University of Arizona.

I led him toward the terminal, stepping around the tourists and business travelers who had also disembarked from the 3 P.M. shuttle. "Are you by yourself, or did someone come with you?"

"Unfortunately, I come alone. The university provided grant money sufficient for only one fare, even though I requested that I bring a grad student as an assistant." He frowned. "This may hinder my work, but I hope that what I intend to do will be simple enough that I may accomplish it on my own."

I had only the vaguest idea of why he'd hired me to be his guide, but the noise and bustle of the terminal was too much for a conversation. Passenger bags were beginning to come down the conveyer belt, but Dr. al-Baz didn't join the crowd waiting to pick up suitcases and duffel bags. Instead, he went straight to the PanMars cargo window, where he presented a handful of receipts to the clerk. I began to regret my offer to help carry his bags when a cart was pushed through a side door. Stacked upon it were a half-dozen aluminum cases; even in Martian gravity, none small enough to be carried two at a time.

"You gotta be kidding," I murmured.

"My apologies, but for the work I need to do, I had to bring specialized equipment." He signed a form, then turned to me again. "Now… do you have a means of taking all this to my hotel, or will I have to get a cab?"

I looked over the stack of cases and decided that there weren't so many that I couldn't fit them all in the back of my jeep. So we pushed the cart out to where I'd parked beside the front entrance, and managed to get everything tied down with elastic cords I carried with me. Dr. al-Baz climbed into the passenger seat and put his suitcase on the floor between his feet.

"Hotel first?" I asked as I took my place behind the wheel.

"Yes, please… and then I wouldn't mind getting a drink." He caught the questioning look in my eye and gave me a knowing smile. "No, I am not a devout follower of the Prophet."

"Glad to hear it." I was liking him better all the time; I don't trust people who won't have a beer with me. I started up the jeep and pulled away from the curb. "So… you said in your email you'd like to visit an aboriginal settlement. Is that still what you want to do?"

"Yes, I do." He hesitated. "But now that we've met, I think it's only fair to tell you that this is not all that I mean to do. The trip here involves more than just meeting the natives."

"How so? What else do you want?"

He peered at me over the top of his glasses. "The blood of a Martian."

When I was a kid, one of my favorite movies was *The War of the Worlds*—the 1953 version, made about twelve years before the first probes went to Mars. Even back then, people knew that Mars had an Earthlike environment; spectroscopes had revealed the presence of an oxygen-nitrogen atmosphere, and strong telescopes made visible the seas and canals. But no one knew for sure whether the planet was inhabited until Ares I landed there in 1977, so George Pal had a lot of latitude when he and his film crew tried to imagine what a Martian would look like.

Anyway, there's a scene in the movie where Gene Barry and Ann Robinson have made their way to L.A. after escaping the collapsed farmhouse where they'd been pinned down by the alien invaders. Barry meets with his fellow scientists at the Pacific Tech and presents them with a ruined camera-eye he managed to grab while fighting off the attackers. The camera-eye is wrapped in Ann Robinson's scarf, which was splattered with gore when Gene clobbered a little green monster with a broken pipe.

"And this—" he says melodramatically, showing the scarf to the other scientists "—blood of a Martian!"

I've always loved that part. So when Dr. al-Baz said much the same thing, I wondered if he was being clever, copping a line from a classic movie that he figured most colonists might have seen. But there was no wink, no ironic smile. So far as I could tell, he was as serious as he could be.

I decided to let it wait until we had that drink together, so I held my tongue as I drove him into Rio Zephyria. The professor's reservation was at the John Carter Casino Resort, located on the strip near the Mare Cimmerium beach. No surprise there: it's the most famous hotel in Rio, so most tourists try to book rooms there. Edgar Rice Burroughs was having a literary renaissance around the time it was built, so someone decided that *A Princess of Mars* and its sequels would be a great theme for a casino. Since then, it's become the place most people think of when they daydream about taking a vacation trip to Mars.

Good for them, but I want to throw a rock through its gold-tinted windows every time I drive by. It's a ten-story monument to every stupid thing humans have done since coming here. And if I feel that way, as someone who was born and raised on Mars, then you can well imagine what the *shatan* think of it… when they come close enough to see it, that is.

It was hard to gauge Dr. al-Baz's reaction when we pulled up in front of the hotel lobby. I was beginning to learn that his normal expression was stoical. But as a bellhop was unloading his stuff and putting it on a cart, the professor spotted the casino entrance. The doorman was dark-skinned and a little more than two meters in height; he wore the burnoose robes of an aborigine, with a saber in the scabbard on his belt.

Dr. al-Baz stared at him. "He's not a Martian, is he?"

"Not unless he used to play center for the Blue Devils." Dr. al-Baz raised an eyebrow, and I smiled. "That's Tito Jones, star of the Duke basketball team… or at least until he came here." I shook my head. "Poor guy. He didn't know why the casino hired him to be their celebrity greeter until they put him in that outfit."

Dr. al-Baz had already lost interest. "I was hoping he might be a Martian," he said softly. "It would have made things easier."

"They wouldn't be caught dead here… or anywhere near the colonies, for that matter." I turned to follow the bellhop through the revolving door. "And by the way… we don't call them 'Martians'. 'Aborigines' is the preferred term."

"I'll keep that in mind. And what do the Mar… the aborigines call themselves?"

"They call themselves *shatan*… which means 'people' in their language." Before he could ask the obvious next question, I added, "Their word for us is *nashatan*, or 'not-people', but that's only when they're being polite. They call us a lot of things, most of them pretty nasty."

The professor nodded, and was quiet for a little while.

The University of Arizona might not have sprung for a grad student's marsliner ticket, but they made up for it by reserving a two-room suite. After the bellhop unloaded his cart and left, Dr. al-Baz explained that he'd need the main room, a large parlor complete with a bar, for the temporary lab he intended to set up. He didn't unpack right away, though; he was ready for that drink I'd promised him. So we left everything in the room and caught the elevator back downstairs.

The hotel bar is located in the casino, but I didn't want to drink in a place where the bartender is decked out like a Barsoomian warlord and the waitresses are dolled up as princesses of Helium. The John Carter is the only place on Mars where anyone looks like that; no one in their right mind would wear so few clothes outside, not even in the middle of summer. So we returned to the jeep and I got away from the strip, heading into the old part of town that the tourists seldom visit.

There's a good watering hole about three blocks from my apartment. It was still late afternoon, so the place wasn't crowded yet. The bar was quiet and dark, perfect for conversation. The owner knew me; he brought over a pitcher of ale as soon as the professor and I sat down at a table in the back.

"Take it easy with this," I told Dr. al-Baz as I poured beer into a tallneck and pushed it across the table to him. "Until you get acclimated, it might hit you pretty hard."

"I'll take your advice." The professor took a tentative sip and smiled. "Good. Better than I was expecting, in fact. Local?"

"Hellas City Amber. You think we'd have beer shipped all the way from Earth?" There were more important things we needed to discuss, so I changed the subject. "What's this about wanting blood? When you got in touch with me, all you said was that you wanted me to take you to a aboriginal settlement."

Dr. al-Baz didn't say anything for a moment or so. He toyed with the stem of his glass, rolling it back and forth between his fingers. "If I'd told you the entire truth," he finally admitted, "I was afraid you might not agree to take me. And you come very highly recommended. As I understand, you're not only native-born, but your parents were among the first settlers."

"I'm surprised you know that. You must have talked to a former client."

"Do you remember Ian Horner? Anthropologist from Cambridge University?" I did indeed, although not kindly; Dr. Horner had hired me as his guide, but if you'd believed everything he said, he knew more about Mars than I did. I nodded, keeping my opinion to myself. "He's a friend of mine," Dr. al-Baz continued, "or at least someone with whom I've been in contact on a professional basis."

"So you're another anthropologist."

"No." He sipped his beer. "Research biologist... astrobiology, to be exact. The study of extraterrestrial forms of life. Until now, most of my work has involved studying Venus, so this is the first time I've been to Mars. Of course, Venus is different. Its global ocean is quite interesting, but..."

"Professor, I don't want to be rude, but do you want to get down to it and tell me why you want the blood of a—" damn, he almost got me to say it! "—an aborigine?"

Sitting back in his chair, Dr. al-Baz folded his hands together on the tabletop. "Mr. Ramsey..."

"Jim."

"Jim, are you familiar with the panspermia hypothesis? The idea that life on Earth may have extraterrestrial origins, that it may have come from somewhere in outer space?"

"No, I've never heard that... but I guess that when you say 'somewhere,' you mean here."

"That is correct. I mean Mars." He tapped a finger firmly against the table. "Have you ever wondered why there's such a close resemblance between humans and Martian aborigines? Why the two races look so much alike even though they're from worlds over 70 million kilometers apart?"

"Parallel evolution."

"Yes, I expect that's what you've learned in school. The conventional explanation is that, because both planets have similar environments, evolution took approximately the same course on both worlds, the differences being that Martians... aborigines, sorry... are taller because of lower surface gravity, have higher metabolisms because of colder temperature, have significantly darker skin because of the thinner ozone layer, so forth and so on. This has been the prevalent theory because it's the only one that seems to fit the facts."

"That's what I've heard, yeah."

"Well, my friend, everything you know is wrong." He immediately shook his head, as if embarrassed by his momentary burst of arrogance. "I'm sorry. I don't mean to sound overbearing. However, several of my colleagues and I believe that the similarities between *Homo sapiens* and *Homo aresian* cannot be attributed to evolution alone. We think there may be a genetic link between the two races, that life on Earth... human life in particular... may have originated on Mars."

Dr. al-Baz paused, allowing a moment to let his words sink in. They did, all right; I was beginning to wonder if he was a kook. "Okay," I said, trying not to smile, "I'll bite. What leads you to think that?"

The professor raised a finger. "First, the geological composition of quite a few meteorites found on Earth is identical to those of rock samples brought from Mars. So there's a theory that, sometime in the distant past, there was a cataclysmic explosion on the Martian surface... possibly the eruption of Mt. Daedalia or one of the other volcanoes in the Albus range... which ejected debris into space. This debris travelled as meteors to Earth, which was also in its infancy. Those meteors may have contained organic molecules which seeded Earth with life where it hadn't previously existed."

He held up another finger. "Second... when the human genome was sequenced, one of the most surprising finds was the existence of DNA strands which have no apparent purpose. They're like parts of a machine that don't have any function. There's no reason for them to be there, yet nonetheless they are. Therefore, is it possible that these phantom strands may be genetic biomarkers left behind by organic material brought to Earth from Mars?"

"So that's why you want a blood sample? To see if there's a link?"

He nodded. "I have brought equipment that will enable me to sequence, at least partially, the genetic code of an aborigine blood sample and compare it to that of a human. If the native genome has non-functional archaic strands that match the ones found in the human genome, then we'll have evidence that the hypothesis is correct... life on Earth originated on Mars, and the two races are genetically linked."

I didn't say anything for a few seconds. Dr. al-Baz didn't sound quite as crazy as he had a couple of minutes earlier. As far-fetched as it may seem, what he said made sense. And if the hypothesis were true, then the implications were staggering: the *shatan* were close cousins to the inhabitants of Earth, not simply a primitive race that we'd happened to find when we came to Mars.

Not that I was ready to believe it. I'd met too many *shatan* to ever be willing to accept the idea that they had anything in common with my people. Or at least so I thought...

"Okay, I get what you're doing." I picked up my glass and took a long drink. "But let me tell you, getting that blood sample won't be easy."

"I know. I understand the aborigines are rather reclusive..."

"Now *that's* an understatement." I put down my glass again. "They've never wanted much to do with us. The Ares 1 expedition had been here for almost three weeks before anyone caught sight of them, and another month before there was any significant contact. It took years for us to even learn their language, and things only got worse when we started establishing colonies. Wherever we've gone, the *shatan* have moved out, packing up everything they owned, even burning their villages so that we couldn't explore their dwellings. They've become nomads since then. No trade, and not much in the way of cultural exchange..."

"So no one has ever managed to get anything from them on which they may have left organic material? No hair samples, no saliva, no skin?"

"No. They've never allowed us to collect any artifacts from them, and they're reluctant to even let us touch them. That outfit you saw Tito Jones wearing? It's not the real thing... just a costume based on some pictures someone took of them."

"But we've learned their language."

"Just a little of one of their dialects... pidgin *shatan*, you might call it."
I absently ran a finger around the rim of my glass. "If you're counting on
me to be your native interpreter... well, don't expect much. I know
enough to get by and that's about it. I may be able to keep them from
throwing a spear at us, but that's all."

He raised an eyebrow. "Are they dangerous?"

"Not so long as you mind your manners. They can be... well, kinda
aggressive... if you cross the line with them." I didn't want to tell him
some of the worst stories—I'd scared off other clients that way—so I tried
to reassure him. "I've met some of the local tribesmen, so they know me
well enough to let me visit their lands. But I'm not sure how much they
trust me." I hesitated. "Dr. Horner didn't get very far with them. I'm sure
he's told you that they wouldn't let him into their village."

"Yes, he has. To tell the truth, though, Ian has always been something
of an ass—" I laughed out loud when he said this, and he gave me a quick
smile in return "—so I imagine that, so long as I approach them with a
measure of humility, I may have more success than he did."

"You might." Ian Horner had come to Mars with the attitude of a
British army officer visiting colonial India, a condescending air of
superiority that the *shatan* picked up almost immediately. He learned little
as a result, and had come away referring to the "abos" as "cheeky
bahstahds." No doubt the aborigines felt much the same way about him...
but at least they'd let him live.

"So you'll take me out there? To one of their villages, I mean?"

"That's why you hired me, so... yeah, sure." I picked up my beer again.
"The nearest village is about a hundred and fifty kilometers southeast of
here, in an desert oasis near the Laestrygon canal. It'll take a couple of days
to get there. I hope you brought warm clothes and hiking boots."

"I brought a parka and boots, yes. But you have your jeep, don't you?
Then why are we going to need to walk?"

"We'll drive only until we get near the village. Then we'll have to get
out and walk the rest of the way. The *shatan* don't like motorized vehicles. The equatorial desert is pretty rough, so you better prepare for it."

He smiled. "I ask you... do I look like someone who's never been in
a desert?"

"No... but Mars isn't Earth."

#   #   #

I spent the next day preparing for the trip: collecting camping equipment from my rented storage shed, buying food and filling water bottles, putting fresh fuel cells in the jeep and making sure the tires had enough pressure. I made sure that Dr. al-Baz had the right clothing for several days in the outback and gave him the address of a local outfitter if he didn't, but I need not have worried; he clearly wasn't one of those tourists foolish enough to go out into the desert wearing Bermuda shorts and sandals.

When I came to pick him up at the hotel, I was amazed to find that the professor had turned his suite into a laboratory. Two flatscreen computers were set up on the bar, a microscope and a test-tube rack stood on the coffee table, and the TV had been pushed aside to make room for a small centrifuge. More equipment rested on bureaus and side tables; I didn't know what any of it was, but I spotted a radiation symbol on one and a WARNING - LASER sticker on another. He'd covered the carpet with plastic sheets, and there was even a lab coat hanging in the closest. Dr. al-Baz made no mention of any of this; he simply picked up his backpack and camera, put on a slouch cap, and followed me out the door, pausing to slip the DO NOT DISTURB sign over the knob.

Tourists stared at us as he flung his pack into the back of my jeep; it always seemed to surprise some people that anyone would come to Mars to do something besides drink and lose money at the gaming tables. I started up the jeep and we roared away from the John Carter, and in fifteen minutes we were on the outskirts of town, driving through the irrigated farmlands surrounding Rio Zephyria. The scarlet pines that line the shores of Mare Cimmerium gradually thinned out as we followed dirt roads usually travelled by farm vehicles and logging trucks, and even those disappeared as we left the colony behind and headed into the trackless desert.

I've been told that the Martian drylands look a lot like the American southwest, except that everything is red. I've never been to Earth, so I wouldn't know, but if anyone in New Mexico happens to spot a six-legged creature that looks sort of like a shaggy cow or a raptor that resembles a pterodactyl and sounds like a hyena, please drop me a line. And stay away from those pits that look a little like golf course sand-traps; there's something lurking within them that would eat you alive, one limb at a time.

As the jeep weaved its way through the desert, dodging boulders and bouncing over small rocks, Dr. al-Baz clung to the roll bars, fascinated by the wilderness opening before us. This was one of the things that made my job worthwhile, seeing familiar places through the eyes of someone who'd never been there before. I pointed out a Martian hare as it loped away from us, and stopped for a second to let him take pictures of a flock of *stakhas* as they wheeled high above us, shrieking their dismay at our intrusion.

About seventy kilometers southeast of Rio, we came upon the Laestryum canal, running almost due south from the sea. When Percival Lowell first spotted the Martian canals through his observatory telescope, he thought they were excavated waterways. He was half-right; the *shatan* had rerouted existing rivers, diverting them so that they'd go where the aborigines wanted. The fact that they'd done this with the simple, muscle-driven machines never failed to amaze anyone who saw them, but Earth people tend to underestimate the *shatan*. They're primitive, but not stupid.

We followed the canal, keeping far away from it so that we couldn't be easily spotted from the decks of any *shatan* boats that might be this far north. I didn't want any aborigines to see us before we reached the village; they might pass the word that humans were coming, and give their chieftain a chance to order his people to pack up and move out. We saw no one, though; the only sign of habitation was a skinny wooden suspension bridge than spanned the channel like an enormous bow, and even that didn't appear to be frequently used.

By late afternoon, we'd entered hill country. Flat-topped mesas rose around us, with massive stone pinnacles jutting upward between them; the jagged peaks of distant mountains lay just beyond the horizon. I drove until it was nearly dusk, then pulled up behind a hoodoo and stopped for the night.

Dr. al-Baz pitched a tent while I collected dead scrub brush. Once I had a fire going, I suspended a cookpot above the embers, then emptied a can of stew into it. The professor had thought to buy a couple of bottles of red wine before we left town; we opened one for dinner and worked our way through it after we ate.

"So tell me something," Dr. al-Baz said once we'd scrubbed down the pot, plates, and spoons. "Why did you become a guide?"

"You mean, other than getting a job as a blackjack dealer?" I propped the cookware up against a boulder. A stiff breeze was coming out of the west; the sand it carried would scour away the remaining grub. "Never really thought about it, to be honest. My folks are first-generation settlers, so I was born and raised here. I started prowling the desert as soon as I was old enough to go out alone, so…"

"That's just it." The professor moved a little closer to the fire, holding out his hands to warm them. Now that the sun was down, a cold night was ahead; we could already see our breath by the firelight. "Most of the colonists I've met seem content to stay in the city. When I told them that I was planning a trip into the desert, they all looked at me like I was mad. Someone even suggested that I buy a gun and take out extra life insurance."

"Whoever told you to buy a gun doesn't know a thing about the *shatan*. They never attack unless provoked, and the surest way to upset them is to approach one of their villages with a gun." I patted the utility knife on my belt. "This is the closest I come to carrying a weapon when there's even a possibility that I might run into aborigines. One reason why I'm on good terms with them… I mind my manners."

"Most people here haven't even seen an aborigine, I think."

"You're right, they haven't. Rio Zephyria is the biggest colony because of tourism, but most permanent residents prefer to live where there's flush toilets and cable TV." I sat down on the other side of the fire. "They can have it. The only reason I live there is because that's where the tourists are. If it wasn't for that, I'd have a place out in the boonies and hit town only when I need to stock up on supplies."

"I see." Dr. al-Baz picked up his tin cup and mine and poured some wine into each. "Forgive me if I'm wrong," he said as he handed my cup to me, "but it doesn't sound as if you very much approve of your fellow colonists."

"I don't." I took a sip and put the cup down beside me; I didn't want to get a headful of wine the night before I was going to have to deal with *shatan* tribesmen. "My folks came out here to explore a new world, but everyone who's come after those original settlers… well, you saw Rio. You know what it's like. We're building hotels and casinos and shopping centers, and introducing invasive species into our farms and dumping our sewage into the channels, and every few weeks during conjunction another ship brings in more people who think Mars is like Las Vegas only without as many hookers… not that we don't have plenty of those, too."

As I spoke, I craned my neck to look up the night sky. The major constellations gleamed brightly: Ursa Major, Draco, Cygnus, with Denes as the north star. You can't see the Milky Way very well in the city; you have to go out into the desert to get a decent view of the Martian night sky. "So who can blame the *shatan* for not wanting to have anything to do with us? They knew the score as soon as we showed up." Recalling a thought I'd had the day before, I chuckled to myself. "The old movies got it wrong. Mars didn't invade Earth… Earth invaded Mars."

"I didn't realize there was so much resentment on your part."

He sounded like his feelings were wounded. That was no way to treat a paying customer.

"No, no… it's not you," I quickly added. "I don't think you'd be caught dead at a poker table."

He laughed out loud. "No, I don't think the university would look very kindly upon me if my expense report included poker chips."

"Glad to hear it." I hesitated, then went on. "Just do me a favor, will you? If you find something here that might… I dunno… make things worse, would you consider keeping it yourself? Humans have done enough stupid things here already. We don't need to do anything more."

"I'll try to remember that," Dr. al-Baz said.

The next day, we found the *shatan*. Or rather, they found us.

We broke camp and continued following the Laestrygon as it flowed south through the desert hills. I'd been watching the jeep's odometer the entire trip, and when we were about fifty kilometers from where I remembered the aborigine settlement, I began driving along the canal banks. I told Dr. al-Baz to keep a sharp eye out for any signs of habitation—trails, or perhaps abandoned camps left behind by hunting parties—but what we found was a lot more obvious: another suspension bridge, and passing beneath it, a *shatan* boat.

The canal boat was a slender catamaran about ten meters long, with broad white sails catching the desert wind and a small cabin at its stern. The figures moving along its decks didn't notice us until one of them spotted the jeep. He let out a warbling cry—"*wallawallawalla!*"—and the others stopped what they were doing to gaze in the direction he was pointing. Then another *shatan* standing atop the cabin yelled something and everyone turned to dash into the cabin, with their captain disappearing through a hatch in its ceiling. Within seconds, the catamaran became a ghost ship.

"Wow." Dr. al-Baz was both astounded and disappointed. "They really don't want to see us, do they?"

"Actually, they don't want us to see them." He looked at me askance, not understanding the difference. "They believe that, if they can't be seen, then they've disappeared from the world. This way, they're hoping that, so far as we're concerned, they've ceased to exist." I shrugged. "Kind of logical, if you think about it."

There was no point in trying to persuade the crew to emerge from hiding, so we left the boat behind and continued our drive down the canal bank. But the catamaran had barely disappeared from sight when we heard a hollow roar from behind us, like a bullhorn being blown. The sound echoed off the nearby mesas; two more prolonged blasts, then the horn went silent.

"If there are any more *shatan* around, they'll hear that and know we're coming," I said. "They'll repeat the same signal with their own horns, and so on until the signal reaches the village."

"So they know we're here," Dr. al-Baz said. "Will they hide like the others?"

"Maybe. Maybe not." I shrugged. "It's up to them."

For a long time, we didn't spot anyone or anything. We were about eight kilometers from the village when we came upon another bridge. This time, we saw two figures standing near the foot of the bridge. They appeared unusually tall even for aborigines, but it wasn't until we got closer that we saw why: each of them rode a *hattas*—an enormous buffalo-like creature with six legs and elongated necks that the natives tamed as pack animals. It wasn't what they were riding that caught my attention, though, so much as the long spears they carried, or the heavy animal-hide outfits they wore.

"Uh-oh," I said quietly. "That's not good."

"What's not good?"

"I was hoping we'd run into hunters… but these guys are warriors. They can be a little… um, intense. Keep your hands in sight and never look away from them."

I halted the jeep about twenty feet from them. We climbed out and slowly walked toward them, hands at our sides. As we got closer, the warriors dismounted from their animals; they didn't approach us, though, but instead waited in silence.

When the owners of the John Carter hired a basketball star to masquerade as a *shatan*, they were trying to find someone who might pass as a Martian aborigine. Tito Jones was the best they could get, but he wasn't quite right. The *shatan* standing before us were taller; their skin was as dark as the sky at midnight, their long, silky hair the color of rust, yet their faces had fine-boned features reminiscent of someone of northern European descent. They were swathed in dusty, off-white robes that made them look vaguely Bedouin, and the hands that gripped their spears were larger than a human's, with long-nailed fingers and tendons which stood out from wrists.

Unblinking golden eyes studied us as we approached. When we'd come close enough, both warriors firmly planted their spears on the ground before us. I told Dr. al-Baz to stop, but I didn't have remind him not to look away from them. He stared at the *shatan* with awestruck curiosity, a scientist observing his subject up close for the first time.

I raised both hands palm out, and said, "*Issah tas sobbata shatan* (Greetings, honored *shatan* warriors). "*Seyta nashatan habbalah sa shatan heysa*" (Please allow us human travelers to enter your land).

The warrior on the left replied, "*Katas nashatan Hamsey. Sakey shatan habbalah fah?*" (We know you, human Ramsey. Why have you returned to our land?)

I wasn't surprised to have been recognized. Only a handful of humans spoke their language—albeit not very well; I probably sounded like a child to them—or knew the way to their village. I may not have met these particular warriors before, but they'd doubtless heard of me. And I tried not to smile at the mispronunciation of my name; the *shatan* have trouble rolling the "r" sound off their tongues.

"(I've brought a guest who wishes to learn more about your people)," I replied, still speaking the local dialect. I extended a hand toward the professor. "(Allow me to introduce you to Omar al-Baz. He is a wise man in search of knowledge.)" I avoided calling him "doctor"; that word has a specific meaning in their language, as someone who practices medicine.

"(Humans don't want to know anything about us. All they want to do is take what doesn't belong to them and ruin it.)"

I shook my head; oddly, that particular gesture means the same thing for both *shatan* and *nashatan*. "(This is not true. Many of my people do, yes, but not all. On his own world, al-Baz is a teacher. Whatever he learns from you, he will tell his students, and therefore increase their knowledge of your people.)"

"What are you saying?" Dr. al-Baz whispered. "I recognize my name, but…"

"Hush. Let me finish." I continued speaking the native tongue. "(Will you please escort us to your village? My companion wishes to beg a favor of your chieftain.)"

The other warrior stepped forward, walking toward the professor until he stood directly before him. The *shatan* towered above Dr. al-Baz; everything about him was menacing, yet the professor held his ground, saying nothing but continuing to look straight in the eye. The warrior silently regarded him for several long moments, then looked at me.

"(What does he want from our chieftain? Tell us, and we will decide whether we will allow you to enter our village.)"

I hesitated, then shook my head again. "(No. His question is for the chieftain alone.)"

I was taking a gamble. Refusing a demand from a *shatan* warrior guarding his homeland was not a great way to make friends. But it was entirely possible that the warriors would misunderstand me if I told them that Dr. al-Baz wanted to take some of their blood; they might think his intent was hostile. The best thing to do was have the professor ask the chieftain directly for permission to take a blood sample from one of his people.

The *shatans* stared at us for a moment without saying anything, then turned away and walked off a few feet to quietly confer with each other. "What's going on?" the professor asked, keeping his voice low. "What did you tell them?"

I gave him the gist of the conversation, including the risky thing I'd just said. "I figure it can go one of three ways. One, they kick the matter upstairs to the chieftain, which means that you get your wish if you play your cards right. Two, they tell us to get lost. If that happens, we turn around and go home, and that's that."

"Unacceptable. I've come too far to go away empty-handed. What's the third option."

"They impale us with their spears, wait for us to die, then chop up our bodies and scatter our remains for the animals to find." I let that sink in.

"Except our heads," I added. "Someone will carry those back to the city in the middle of the night, where they'll dump them on the doorstep of the nearest available house."

"Please tell me you're joking."

I didn't. The professor was scared enough already, and he didn't need any stories about what had happened to explorers who'd crossed the line with the *shatan*, or the occasional fool stupid enough to venture onto aboriginal territory without someone like me escorting them. I hadn't exaggerated anything, though, and he seemed to realize that, for he simply nodded and looked away.

The *shatan* finished their discussion. Not looking at us, they walked back to their *hattases* and climbed atop them again. For a moment, I thought they were taking the second option, but then they guided their mounts toward Dr. al-Baz and me.

"*Hessah,*" one of them said (Come with us).

I let out my breath. We were going to meet the village chieftain.

The village was different from the last time I'd seen it. Since the *shatan* became nomads, their settlements are usually tent cities which can be taken down, packed up, and relocated when necessary. This one had been there for quite a while, though; apparently the inhabitants had decided that they'd stay at the oasis for some time to come. Low, flat-roofed adobe buildings had taken the place of many of the tents, and scaffolds surrounded a stone wall being built to enclose them. But if the place had a name, I wasn't aware of it.

Dr. al-Baz and I were footsore and tired by the time we reached the village. As expected, the warriors had insisted that we leave the jeep behind, although they allowed us to retrieve our packs. They'd slowly ridden abreast of us all the way, only reluctantly letting us stop now and then to rest. Neither of them had spoken a word since we'd left the bridge, but when we were within sight of the settlement, one of them raised a whorled shell that looked like a giant ammonite. A long, loud blast from his horn was answered a few seconds later by a similar call from the village. The professor and I exchanged a wary glance. Too late to turn around now; the inhabitants knew we were coming.

The village seemed empty as we entered through a half-built gate and walked down packed-dirt streets. No one to be seen, and the only thing that moved were *hattases* tied up to hitching posts. The tent flaps were closed, though, and the narrow windows of the adobe houses were shuttered. No, the place wasn't deserted; it was just that the people who lived there had gone into hiding. The silence was eerie, and even more unsettling than the spears our escorts pointed at our backs.

The village center was a courtyard surrounding an artesian well, with a large adobe building dominating one side of the square. The only *shatan* we'd seen since our arrival peered down at us from a wooden tower atop the building. He waited until we'd reached the building. then raised an ammonite horn of his own and blew a short blast. The warriors halted their *hattases*, dismounted, and silently beckoned for us to follow them. One of them pushed aside the woven blanket which served as the building's only door, and the other warrior led us inside.

The room was dim, its sole illumination a shaft of sunlight slanting down through a hole in the ceiling. The air was thick with musky incense that drifted in hazy layers through the light and made my eyes water. Robed *shatan* stood around the room, their faces hidden by hoods they'd pulled up around their heads; I knew none of them were female, because their women were always kept out of sight when visitors arrived. The only sound was the slow, constant drip of a waterclock, with each drop announcing the passage of two more seconds.

The chieftain sat in the middle of the room. Long-fingered hands rested upon the armrests of his sandstone throne; golden eyes regarded us between strands of hair turned white with age. He wore nothing to indicate his position as the tribal leader save an implacable air of authority, and he let us know that he was the boss by silently raising both hands, then slowly lowering them once we'd halted, and saying nothing for a full minute.

At last he spoke. *"Essha shakay Hamsey?"* (Why are you here, Ramsey?)

I didn't think I'd ever met him before, but obviously he recognized me. Good. That would make things a little easier. I responded in his own language. "(I bring someone who wants to learn more about your people. He is a wise man from Earth, a teacher of others who wish to become wise themselves. He desires to ask a favor from you.)"

The chieftain turned his gaze from me to Dr. al-Baz. "(What do you want?)"

I looked at the professor. "Okay, you're on. He wants to know what you want. I'll translate for you. Just be careful… they're easily offended."

"So it seems." Dr. al-Baz was nervous, but he was hiding it well. He licked his lips and thought about it a moment, then went on. "Tell him… tell him that I would like to collect a small sample of blood from one of his people. A few drops will do. I wish to have this because I want to know… I mean, because I'd like to find out… whether his people and mine have common ancestors."

That seemed to be a respectful a way of stating what he wanted, so I turned to the chief and reiterated what he'd said. The only problem was that I didn't know the aboriginal word for "blood." It had simply never come up in any previous conversations I'd had with the *shatan*. So I had to generalize a bit, calling it "the liquid that runs within our bodies" while pantomiming a vein running down the inside of my right arm, and hoped that he'd understand what I meant.

He did, all right. He regarded me with cold disbelief, golden eyes flashing, thin lips writhing upon an otherwise stoical face. Around us, I heard the other *shatan* murmuring to one another. I couldn't tell what they were saying, but it didn't sound like they were very happy either.

We were in trouble.

"(Who dares say that shatan and nashatan have the same ancestors?)" he snapped, hands curling into fists as he leaned forward from his throne. "(Who dares believe that your people and mine are alike in any way?)"

I repeated what he'd said to Dr. al-Baz. The professor hesitated, then looked straight at the chieftain. "Tell him that no one believes these things," he said, his tone calm and deliberate. "It is only an hypothesis… an educated guess… that I want to either prove or disprove. That's why I need a blood sample, to discover the truth."

I took a deep breath, hoped that I was going to get out of there alive, then translated the professor's explanation. The chieftain continued to glare at us as I spoke, but he seemed to calm down a little. For several long seconds, he said nothing. And then he reached a decision.

Reaching into his robes, he withdrew a bone dagger from a sheath on his belt. My heart skipped a beat as the light fell upon its sharp white blade, and when he stood up and walked toward us, I thought my life had come to an end. But then he stopped in front of Dr. al-Baz and, still staring straight at him, raised his left hand, placed the knife against his palm, and ran its blade down his skin.

"(Take my blood)," he said, holding out his hand.

I didn't need to translate what he'd said. Dr. al-Baz quickly dropped his backpack from his shoulders and opened it. He withdrew a syringe, thought better of it, and pulled out a plastic test tube instead. The chieftain clenched his fist and let the blood trickle between his fingers, and the professor caught it in his test tube. Once he'd collected the specimen, he pulled out a tiny vial and added a couple of drops of anticoagulant. Then he capped the tube and nodded to the chieftain.

"Tell him that I greatly appreciate his kindness," he said, "and that I will return to tell him what I have found."

"Like hell we will!"

"Tell him." His eyes never left the chieftain's. "One way or another, he deserves to know the truth."

Promising the chieftain that we intended to return was the last thing I wanted to do, but I did it anyway. He didn't respond for a moment, but simply dropped his hand, allowing his blood to trickle to the floor.

"(Yes)," he said at last. "(Come back and tell me what you've learned. I wish to know as well.)" And then he turned his back to us and walked back to his chair. "(Now leave.)"

"Okay," I whispered, feeling my heart hammering against my chest. "You got what you came for. Now let's get out of here while we still have our heads."

Two days later, I was sitting in the casino bar at the John Carter, putting away tequila sunrises and occasionally dropping a coin into the video poker machine in front of me. I'd discovered that I didn't mind the place so long as I kept my back turned to everything going on around me, and I could drink for free if I slipped a quarter into the slots every now and then. At least that's what I told myself. The fact of the matter was that there was a certain sense of security in the casino's tawdry surroundings. This Mars was a fantasy, to be sure, but just then it was preferable to the unsettling reality I'd visited a couple of days earlier.

Omar al-Baz was upstairs, using the equipment he'd brought with him to analyze the chieftain's blood. We'd gone straight to the hotel upon returning to the city, but when it became obvious that it would take awhile for the professor to work his particular kind of magic, I decided to go downstairs and get a drink. Perhaps I should have gone home, but I was still keyed up from the long ride back, so I gave Dr. al-Baz my cell number and asked him to call me if and when he learned anything.

I was surprised that I stuck around. Usually when I return from a trip into the outback, all I really want to do is get out of the clothes I'd been wearing for days on end, open a beer, and take a nice, long soak in the bathtub. Instead, there I was, putting away one cocktail after another while demonstrating that I knew absolutely nothing about poker. The bartender was studying me and the waitresses were doing their best to stay upwind, but I could have cared less about what they thought. They were make-believe Martians, utterly harmless. The ones I'd met a little while ago would have killed me just for looking at them cross-eyed.

In all the years that I'd been going out in the wilderness, this was the first time I'd ever been really and truly scared. Not by the desert, but those who lived there. No *shatan* had ever threatened me, not even in an implicit way, until the moment the chieftain pulled out a knife and creased the palm of his hand with its blade. Sure, he'd done so to give Dr. al-Baz a little of his blood, but there was another meaning to his actions.

It was a warning… and the *shatan* don't give warnings lightly.

That was why I was doing my best to get drunk. The professor was too excited to think of anything except the specimen he'd just collected—all the way home, he'd babbled about nothing else—but I knew that we'd come within an inch of dying, and that ours would have been a really nasty death.

Yet the chieftain had given his blood of his own free will, and even asked that we return once the professor learned the truth. That puzzled me. Why would he be interested in the results, if the thought of being related to a human was so appalling?

I threw away another quarter, pushed the buttons and watched the machine tell me that I'd lost again, then looked around to see if I could flag down a princess and get her to fetch another sunrise. Dejah or Thuvia or Xaxa or whoever she was had apparently gone on break, though, because she was nowhere to be seen; I was about to try my luck again when something caught my eye. The TV above the bar was showing the evening news, and the weatherman was standing in front of his map. I couldn't hear what he was saying, but he was pointing at an animated cloud system west of Rio Zephyria that was moving across the desert toward the Laestrygon canal.

It appeared that a sandstorm was brewing in Mesogaea, the drylands adjacent to the Zephyria region. This sort of weather isn't uncommon in the summer; we call them haboobs, the Arabic name for sandstorms on Earth that somehow found its way to Mars. From the looks of things, it would reach the Zephyria outback sometime tomorrow afternoon. Good thing I'd come home; the last thing anyone would want is to be caught out in the desert during a bad storm.

A waitress strolled by, adjusting a strap of her costume bikini top. I raised my glass and silently jiggled it back and forth, and she feigned a smile as she nodded and headed for the bar. I was searching my pockets for another quarter so that she'd see that I was still pretending to be a gambler when my cell buzzed.

"Jim? Are you still here?"

"In the bar, professor. Come down and have a drink with me."

"No! No time for that! Come upstairs right away! I need to see you!"

"What's going on?"

"Just come up here! It's better if I show you!"

Dr. al-Baz opened the door at the first knock. Spotting the cocktail glass in my hand, he snatched it from me and drained it in one gulp. "Good heavens," he gasped, "I needed that!"

"Want me to get you another one?"

"No... but you can buy me a drink when I get to Stockholm." I didn't understand what he meant, but before I could ask he pulled me into the room. "Look!" he said, pointing to one of the computers set up on the bar. "This is incredible!"

I walked over to the bar, peered at the screen. Displayed upon it were rows of A's, C's, G's, and T's, arranged in a seemingly endless series of combinations, with smears that looked a little like dashes running in a vertical bar down the right side of the screen. A five-line cluster of combinations and smears was highlighted in yellow.

"Yeah, okay," I said. "Professor, I'm sorry, but you're going to have to..."

"You have no idea what you're looking at, do you?" he asked, and I shook my head. "This is the human genome... the genetic code present in every human being. And these—" his hand trembled as he pointed to the highlighted cluster "—are strands that are identical to the partially sequenced genome from the aborigine specimen."

"They're the same?"

"Exactly. There is no error… or at least none that the computers can detect." Dr. al-Baz took a deep breath. "Do you see what I'm getting at? The hypothesis is correct! Human life may have originated on Mars!"

I stared at the screen. Until then, I hadn't really believed anything that Dr. al-Baz had told me; it seemed too unlikely to be true. But now that the evidence was in front of me, I realized that I was looking at something that would shake the foundations of science. No, not just science… it would rattle history itself, forcing humankind to reconsider its origins.

"My god," I whispered. "Have you told anyone yet? On Earth, I mean"

"No. I'm tempted to send a message, but… no, I need to confirm this." The professor walked over to the window. "We have to go back," he said, his voice quiet but firm as he gazed out at the city lights and, beyond them, the dark expanse of the desert. "I need to get another blood sample, this time from a different *shatan*. If the same sequence appears in the second sample, then we'll know for sure."

Something cold slithered down my spine. "I'm not sure that's a good idea. The chieftain…"

"The chieftain told us that he wanted to know what we discovered. So we'll tell him, and explain that we need more blood… just a little… from one of his tribesmen to make sure that it's the truth." Dr. al-Baz glanced over his shoulder at me. "Not an unreasonable request, no?"

"I don't think he's going to be very happy about this, if that's what you're asking."

He was quiet for a few moments, contemplating what I'd just said. "Well… that's a risk we'll just have to take," he said at last. "I'll pay you again for another trip, if that's your concern… double your original fee, in fact. But I must go back as soon as possible." He continued to gaze out the window. "Tomorrow morning. I want to leave tomorrow morning."

My head was beginning to ache, dull blades pressing upon my temples. I shouldn't have had so much to drink. What I should have done was turn him down right then and there. But his offer to double my fee for a return trip was too good to pass up; I needed the money, and that would pay my rent for a couple of months. Besides, I was too drunk to argue.

"Okay," I said. "We'll head out first thing."

I went back to my place, took some aspirin, stripped off my filthy clothes, and took a shower, then flopped into bed. But I didn't fall asleep for quite a while. Instead, I stared at the ceiling as unwelcome thoughts ran an endless loop through my mind.

What would the chieftain do when Omar al-Baz informed him that *shatan* blood and *nashatan* blood were very much alike and that our two races might be related? He wouldn't be pleased, that much was certain. The aborigines never wanted to have anything to do with the invaders from Earth; as soon as our ships had arrived, they had retreated into the wilderness. This was the reason why they'd become nomads...

But they weren't any more, were they? The significance of what I'd seen at the village suddenly became clear to me. Not only had this particular tribe built permanent houses, but they were also erecting a wall around them. That meant they were planning to remain where they were for some time to come, and were taking measures to defend themselves. They were tiring of running from us; now they were digging in.

Until now, the human colonists had been content to ignore the *shatan*, thinking of them as reclusive savages best left alone. This would change, though, if humans came to believe that *Homo sapiens* and *Homo aresians* were cousins. Suddenly, we'd want to know all about them. First would come more biologists like Dr. al-Baz, more anthropologists like Dr. Horner. Maybe that wouldn't be so bad... but right behind them would be everyone else. Historians and journalists, tour buses and camera safaris, entrepreneurs looking to make a buck, missionaries determined to convert godless souls, real estate tycoons seeking prime land on which to build condos with a nice view of those quaint aborigine villages...

The *shatan* wouldn't tolerate this. And the chieftain would know it was inevitable the moment Dr. al-Baz told him what he'd learned. First, he'd order his warriors to kill both him and me. And then...

In my mind's eye, I saw the horrors to come. Wave upon wave of *shatan* warriors descending upon Rio Zephyria and the other colonies, hell-bent on driving the invaders from their world once and for all. Oh, we had superior weapons, this was true... but they had superior numbers, and it would only be a matter of time before they captured a few of our guns and learned how to use them. Ships from Earth would bring soldiers to defend the colonies, but history is unkind to would-be conquerors. Either we would be driven back, step by inexorable step, or we would commit genocide, exterminating entire tribes and driving the few survivors further into the wilderness.

Either way, the outcome was inevitable. War would come to a world named for a god of war. Red blood would fell upon red sand, human and Martian alike.

A storm was coming. Then I thought of a different storm, and knew what I had to do.

Two days later, I was found staggering out of the desert, caked with red sand from my hair to my boots save for raccoon-like patches around my eyes where my goggles had protected them. I was dehydrated and exhausted to the point of delirium.

I was also alone.

Ironically, the people who rescued me were another guide and the family from Minneapolis whom he'd escorted into the desert just outside Rio Zephyria. I remember little of what happened after I collapsed at their feet and had to be carried to the guide's land rover. The only things I clearly recall were the sweet taste of water within my parched mouth, a teenage girl gazing down at me with angelic blue eyes as she cradled my head in her lap, and the long, bouncing ride back into the city.

I was still in my hospital bed when the police came to see me. By then, I'd recovered enough to give them a clear and reasonably plausible account of what had happened. Like any successful lie, this one was firmly grounded in truth. The violent haboob that suddenly came upon us in the desert hills. The crash that happened when, blinded by wind-driven sand, I'd collided with a boulder, causing my jeep to topple over. How Dr. al-Baz and I had escaped from the wreckage, only to lose track of each other. How only I had managed to find shelter in the leeside of a pinnacle. The professor becoming lost in the storm, never to be seen again.

All true, every word of it. All I had to do was leave out a few facts, such as how I'd deliberately driven into the desert even though I knew a haboob was on its way, or that even after we saw the scarlet haze rising above the western horizon, I'd insisted upon continuing to drive south, telling Dr. al-Baz that we'd be able to outrun the storm. The cops never learned that I'd been careful to carry with me a pair of sand goggles and a scarf, but refrained from making sure that the professor took the same precautions. Nor did they need to know that I'd deliberately aimed for that boulder even though I could have easily avoided it.

I broke down when I spoke about how I'd heard Omar al-Baz calling my name, desperately trying to find me even as the air was filled with stinging red sand and visibility was reduced to only arm's length. That much, too, was true. What I didn't say was that Dr. al-Baz had come within three meters of where I was huddled, my eyes covered by goggles and a scarf wrapped around the lower part of my face. And yet I remained silent as I watched his indistinct form lurch past me, arms blindly thrust out before him, slowly suffocating as sand filled his nose and throat.

My tears were honest. I liked the professor. But his knowledge made him too dangerous to live.

As an alibi, my story worked. When a search party went out into the desert, they located my overturned jeep. Omar al-Baz's body was found about fifteen meters away, face-down and covered by several centimeters of sand. Our footprints had been erased by the wind, of course, so there was no way of telling how close the professor had been to me.

That settled any doubts the cops may have had. Dr. al-Baz's death was an accident. I had no motive for killing him, nor was there any evidence of foul play. If I was guilty of anything, it was only reckless and foolish behavior. My professional reputation was tarnished, but that was about it. The investigation was officially concluded the day I was released from the hospital. By then, I'd realized two things. The first was that I would get away with murder. The second was that my crime was far from perfect.

Dr. al-Baz hadn't taken the chieftain's blood specimen with him when he'd left the hotel. It was still in his room, along with all his equipment. This included the computers he'd used to analyze the sample; the results were saved in their memories, along with any notes he might have written. In fact, the only thing the professor had brought with him was his room key… which I'd neglected to retrieve from his body.

I couldn't return to his hotel room; any effort to get in would have aroused suspicion. All I could do was watch from the hotel lobby as, a couple of days later, the bellhops wheeled out a cart carrying the repacked equipment cases, bound for the spaceport and the shuttle which would ferry them to a marsliner docked at Deimos Station. In a few months, the professor's stuff would be back in the hands of his fellow faculty members. They would open the digital files and inspect what their late colleague had learned, and examine the blood specimen he'd collected. And then…

Well. We'll just have to see, won't we?

So now I sit alone in my neighborhood bar, where I drink and wait for the storm to come. And I never go into the desert again.

Some stories take a long time to produce. I'm not the sort of writer who gets an idea and runs straight to the keyboard... because, when it comes right down to it, I'm more interested in people than technology, so if I can't find people I'd like to write about, I'm not going to do a story that's just about a cool toy. The process of creating such characters takes time, though, so more often than not, story ideas gets jotted down in my pocket notebook and carried around for months or even years before I do anything with them. I prefer a slow-cooked meal to fast food, but sometimes the upstairs kitchen is really slow.

"Ticking" is a prime example. Back in 1992, I was a guest author at the annual Minicon science fiction convention. Minicon is held in a very large convention hotel on the outskirts of Minneapolis, and it was during that weekend when I got the brainstorm for this story. Between panels and readings, I roamed the hotel, making sketches of the layout and taking pictures with a disposable camera I bought in the gift shop—this was in the days before cell-phone cameras. I wrote the first scene in longhand Sunday afternoon at the airport while waiting for my flight home, and a few days later I transcribed it into my computer, believing that I'd complete it sometime in the next few weeks.

The story remained unfinished for the next twenty years. Very simply, I didn't know where to take it after that first scene; the two people in the first scene didn't interest me enough to build a story around them, and until I had characters I wanted to write about, the story wasn't going forward. I went at it again and again over the course of the next several months until, frustrated and impatient, I relocated the digital file to the "Unfinished Stories" folder, stuck the handwritten original in my file cabinet along with the photos and sketches, and walked away. And every now and then over the next couple of decades, I'd pull out the story, convert the text to the latest version of WordPerfect or MS Word I was using by then, and fiddle with it a little more, trying to find something to do with it. I went through several title changes, shifted from first-person to third-person, put characters in, took characters out, and even changed the locale and turned it into a screenplay that went unsold. Nothing seemed to work. I finally gave up, figuring that it would remain an uncompleted story like a half-dozen or so others moldering away in my files.

Then I read a magazine article about a new information-processing center in Utah, and then an online piece about the patterns of global *population growth over the past couple of centuries, and all at once everything seemed to come together. Suddenly, I knew what the story was missing... and no, I'm not going to tell you. Let it be a mystery that it took twenty years to solve.*

I pulled out the original handwritten manuscript, gave it a new title, and picked up where I'd left off in the airport two decades earlier. This time, the writing was effortless. I wrote the story in a couple of weeks, and wondered why it took me so long to finish the damn thing.

Maybe because it's a bit scary.

TICKING

Harold and Cindy were trying to find something to eat in the hotel kitchen when they were attacked by the cook.

Shortly after the refugees moved into the Wyatt-Centrum Airport, they'd divvied up the jobs necessary for their continued survival. Harold and the remaining desk clerk, Merle, had drawn the assignment of locating the hotel robots. That's all they had to do; just find them, then tell Karl and Sharon, the two Minneapolis cops who'd taken shelter at the Wyatt-Centrum when their cruiser died on the street outside. The officers had their service automatics and a pump-action .12-gauge shotgun they'd taken from their car; unlike most of their equipment, the guns weren't rendered inoperative. And they'd already discovered that an ordinary service robot could be taken out by a well-aimed gunshot; it was the big, heavy-duty ones that were hard to kill.

So Harold and Merle spent the second day after the blackout prowling the hotel's ten floors. Merle knew where the robots normally operated, so they only needed to confirm their positions while avoiding being spotted, and once they'd located all the 'bots Merle remembered, they returned to the pool and told the cops. Karl and Sharon made sure the barricades were secure, at least for the time being, then went up into the hotel and, moving from floor to floor, blew away all the 'bots the civilians had found.

This search-and-destroy mission netted ten housekeepers, five custodians, two room-service waiters, and two security guards. According to Merle, that accounted for the hotel robots; this didn't include the huge bellhop that killed two staff members and a guest before someone picked up a chair and used it to smash the robot's CPU. That happened on the first day; most of the guests fled after that, along with most of the remaining staff. After that sweep, everyone thought all the 'bots had been accounted for and destroyed.

By the end of the third day, the thirty-one people hiding in the Wyatt-Centrum's cathedral-like atrium were down to the last few cans of the junk food a couple of them had scavenged from a convenience store a few blocks down the street. Nobody wanted to venture outside, though—it had become too dangerous to leave the hotel—and the cops were reluctant to tear down the plywood boards they'd had nailed across the ground-level doors and windows. So when Cindy asked Harold if he'd mind coming along while she checked out the kitchen—"It can't all be fresh food," she'd said, "they must have some canned stuff, too."—she didn't have to twist his arm very hard.

Hunger wasn't the only reason why he went with her, though. Truth was, he wanted to get into Cindy's pants. Sure, she was at least twenty years younger and he was married besides, but Harold had been eyeing her for the past three days. Only that morning, he hadn't entirely turned his back when she'd taken a bath in the atrium swimming pool. As afraid as he was of dying, he was even more afraid of dying without having sex one last time. Such are the thought processes of the condemned. Perhaps he wouldn't get a chance to knock boots with her during this foray, but at least he'd be able to show off his machismo by escorting her through the lightness kitchen. That was the general idea, anyway… but before he got a chance to nail Cindy, that goddamn 'bot nearly nailed them instead.

Unfortunately, when Harold visited the kitchen earlier, he and Merle had neglected to check the big walk-in refrigerator. It wasn't entirely his fault; the two cooks they'd found attacked them the moment they pushed open the door, forcing a hasty retreat. Those were the first robots the cops had neutralized, and Merle believed they were the only ones in the kitchen. But he was wrong; a third 'bot had been trapped in the fridge when the lights went out.

The walk-in was located in the rear of the kitchen, just a little farther than Harold had gone the first time he'd searched the room. They'd found a carton of breakfast cereal, which would be good for the kids, and Cindy was hoping to find some milk that hadn't spoiled yet. She'd just unlatched the chrome door handle, and he was standing just behind her, when they heard the sound everyone had come to dread the last few days:

Tick-tick... tick-tick-tick... tick... tick-tick-tick...

"Watch out!" Harold yelled, and an instant later something huge slammed through the door. Cindy was knocked to the floor; falling down was probably the only thing that saved her from having an eight-inch ice pick shoved into her chest.

The cook was nearly as large as the bellhop. A Lang LHC-14 may seem harmless when it's stirring a vat of corned beef hash, but this one was hurtling toward them with a sharp metal spike clutched in its manipulator claw. And neither Harold nor Cindy was armed.

"Get back, get back, get back!" Harold yelled, as if she really needed any encouragement. Cindy scuttled backward on hands, hips, and heels while he threw himself away from the refrigerator, losing his flashlight in his haste.

Even if he hadn't dropped the light, though, he would have been able to see the cook. Red and green LEDs blinked across the front of its box-like body, the glow reflecting off the hooded stereoscopic lenses within its upper turret. As it trundled through the door on soft tandem tires, the turret swept back and forth, clicking softly as the lenses captured first Cindy, then Harold, then Cindy again. Mapping them, remembering their positions...

"Watch out! It's gonna charge!"

The turret snapped toward Harold as the 'bot determined which human was closer. At that moment, his groping hands found the cold metal surface of something that moved: a dessert cart, complete with the molding remains of several cakes. Torture wagons, his wife called these things, and he was only too happy to use one in a less metaphorical way. As the cook rushed him, he dodged behind the cart, grabbed its glass handle, and slammed it straight into the robot.

The impact dislodged the ice pick from the cook's claw. As it hit the tile floor, he wrenched the cart backward, then shoved it forward again, harder this time. Harold was trying to knock it over, but the 'bot had been designed for stability, bottom-heavy and with a low center of gravity. He was slowing it down, but he wasn't stopping it.

The situation was both dangerous and absurd. The cook would trundle forward, its arms swinging back and forth, and Harold would ram the cart into it. The 'bot would halt for a second, but as soon as he pulled the cart back, the machine would charge again, its claws missing his face by only a few inches. It might have been funny, but when Harold glanced over his shoulder, he saw in the shadowed illumination cast by the dropped flashlight that the cook was gradually backing him into a corner between a rack and a range grill. Dale was right: these things learned *fast*.

"Cindy! Get this friggin' thing off me!"

He didn't hear anything save for the incessant ticking, high-pitched whine of the 'bot's servos, and the loud clang of his cart ramming it again. A chocolate cake toppled off the wagon and was immediately pulverized by the cook's wheels. He had the wild, hopeless hope that the icing would somehow screw it up, make it lose traction…

"Cindy…!" Damn it, had she abandoned him?

All at once, the robot's turret did a one-eighty turn, its lenses snapping away from him as its motion detectors picked up movement from somewhere behind it. In that instant, Cindy dashed out of the darkness, something raised in both hands above her head. The robot started to swivel around, then a cast iron skillet came down on its turret and smashed its lenses.

Nice shot. Although the robot could still hear them, it was effectively blinded. While its claw lashed back and forth, trying to connect with one of them, Cindy beat on it with the skillet while Harold continued to slam it with the dessert cart.

"Hit it, hit it!"

"Get the claws!"

"Go for the top, the top!"

So forth and so on, until one last blow from Cindy's skillet managed to skrag the CPU just beneath the upper turret. The LEDs went dark and the cook halted. The ticking stopped.

When Harold was sure that the cook was good and dead, he came out from behind the cart. Cindy was leaning against an island, breathing hard, skillet still clutched in her hand. She stared at him for a moment, then dropped the skillet. It hit the floor with a loud bang that echoed off the stainless steel surfaces around them.

"Thanks." Harold sagged against a counter. "Tough, ain't it?"

"Built to last." Her cotton tank-top was damp with sweat, the nipples of her twenty-two-year-old breasts standing out. "You okay?"

"I'm good." Harold couldn't stop staring at her. "You?"

Cindy slowly nodded. She brushed back her damp hair, then looked up at him. Even in the wan glow of the dropped flashlight, she must have seen something in his eyes that she didn't like it at all.

"Fine. Just great." She turned away from him. "C'mon. Let's get out of here."

Harold let out his breath. Looked like he wasn't going to get laid after all, even if it was the end of the world.

Cindy tried to hide her irritation, but she was still quietly fuming when she and the other guy—what was his name? Harold?—returned to the atrium. She'd noticed the way he'd been watching her for the last couple of days, of course; men had been checking her out since she was fifteen, so she'd developed good radar for sexual attraction. Given the situation everyone was in, though, you'd think he'd have the common sense to put his impulses on hold. But for God's sake, they barely escape being killed, and what's the first thing he does? Stare at her tits.

Enough. Cindy had heard his dejected sigh as she picked up the carton of single-serving cereal boxes she'd found and left the kitchen. She could have cared less. It was times like these when she wondered whether she wouldn't be better off being a lesbian.

By the time they reached the pool, though, she'd almost forgotten the incident. As soon as she and what's-his-name walked in, the kids were all over them, jumping up and down in their excitement to see what she'd found. Cindy couldn't help but smile as she carried the carton to the poolside terrace and put it down on a table. There were a half-dozen children among the refugees, the youngest a four-year-old boy and the oldest a twelve-year-old girl, and none of them seemed to mind that they didn't have any milk to go with the Cheerios and Frosted Flakes she handed out. Even kids can get tired of Spam and candy bars if that's all they've had to eat for three days.

Once they'd all received a box of cereal, Cindy took the rest to the cabana room she was sharing with Officer McCoy. She'd never thought that she'd welcome having a cop as a roommate, but Sharon was pretty cool; besides, sleeping in the same room as a police officer assured that she wouldn't be bothered by any horny middle-aged guys who'd holed up in the Wyatt-Centrum.

Sharon was dozing on one of the twin beds when Cindy came in. She'd taken off her uniform shirt and was sleeping in her sports bra, her belt with its holstered gun, taser, and baton at her side. She opened her eyes and watched as Cindy carefully closed the door behind her, making sure that she didn't accidentally knock aside the pillow they'd been using as a doorstop. With the power out and even the emergency generator offline, there was nothing to prevent the guest room doors from automatically locking if they closed all the way.

"Find some food?" Sharon asked.

"A little. Ready for dinner?"

Sharon sat up to peer into the carton put down beside her. "That all? Couldn't you find something else?"

"Sorry. Didn't have a chance to look." Cindy told her about the cook. Sharon's expression didn't change, but Cindy figured that cops were usually poker-faced when it came to that sort of thing. And she left out the part about what's-his-name. No point in complaining about that; they had worse things to worry about.

"Well… anyway, I'm glad you made it back alive." Sharon selected a box of Cheerios, but didn't immediately open it. One of the hand-held radios the cops had borrowed from the hotel lay on the desk; their own cell radios no longer worked, forcing them to use the older kind. Sharon picked it up and thumbed the TALK button. "Charlie Baker Two, Charlie Baker One. How's everything looking?"

A couple of seconds went by, then Officer Overby's voice came over. *"Charlie Baker Two. 10-24, all clear."*

"Ten-four. Will relieve you in fifteen minutes. Out." Sharon put down the radio, then nodded to the smartphone that lay on the dresser. "What's happening there? Any change?"

Cindy picked up her phone, ran her finger down its screen. The phone would become silent once the charge ran down, but there was still a little bit of red on the battery icon. She pressed the volume control, and once again they heard the only sound it made:

Tick… tick-tick… tick-tick-tick-tick… tick… tick-tick…

Like a cheap stopwatch that skipped seconds. That wasn't what she immediately noticed, though, but instead the mysterious number that appeared on its screen: 4,576,036,057, a figure that decreased by one with each tick.

For the last three days, Cindy's phone had done nothing else but tick irregularly and display a ten-digit number that changed every second or so. What these things signified, she had no clue, but everyone else's phones, pads, and laptops had been doing the same thing ever since the blackout.

It started the moment she was standing on the curb outside the airport, flagging down a cab while at the same time calling her friend in St. Paul to tell her that she'd arrived. That was when the phone suddenly went dead. Thinking that her call had been dropped, she'd pulled the phone from her ear, glanced at the screen… and heard the first weird ticks coming from it.

She was still staring at the numbers which had appeared on the LCD display when the cab that was about pull up to the curb slammed into the back of a shuttle bus. A few seconds later, the pavement shook beneath her feet and she heard the rolling thunder of an incoming airliner crashing on the runway and exploding. That was how it all began…

Cindy glanced at her watch. Nearly 6 P.M. Perhaps the atrium would cool down a little once the mid-summer sun was no longer resting on the skylight windows. Unfortunately, the coming night would also mean that the robots would have an easier time tracking anyone still outside; their infrared vision worked better than their normal eyes, someone had explained to her. Probably Dale. He seemed to know a lot about such things.

Almost as if she'd read her mind, Sharon looked up from strapping on her belt. "Oh, by the way… Dale asked me to tell you that he'd like to see you."

Cindy was halfway to the bathroom; its door was closed against the stench of an unflushed toilet. She stopped and turned around. "Dale? Did he say why?"

"You said you're carrying a satphone, didn't you? He'd like to borrow it."

"Yeah, why not?" Cindy shrugged. "We won't get anyone with it. I've already tried to call my folks in Boston."

"I told him that, but…" Sharon finished buttoning her shirt. "C'mon. I'd like to see what he's got in mind."

Dale's cabana was on the other side of the pool. Like Cindy, he was rooming with a cop: Karl Overby, Sharon's partner. In his case, though, it was a matter of insistence. Cindy didn't know much about him other than that he worked for some federal agency, he knew a lot about computers, and his job was important enough that he requested—demanded, really—that he stay with a police officer. Dale was pleasant enough—he faintly resembled Cindy's old high school math teacher, whom she'd liked—but he'd been keeping a certain distance from everyone else in the hotel.

"Cindy, hi." Dale looked up from the laptop on his desk when she knocked on the room's half-open door. "Thanks for coming over. I've got a favor to ask. Do you…?"

"Have a satphone? Sure." It was in the backpack Cindy had carried with her on the plane. She'd flown to Minneapolis to hook up with an old college roommate for a camping trip in the lakes region, where cell coverage was spotty and it wasn't smart to be out in the woods with no way to contact anyone. "Not that it's going to do you any good."

Dale didn't seem to hear the last. "So long as its battery isn't dead—" a questioning look; Cindy shook her head "—I might be able to hook it up to my laptop through their serial ports. Maybe I can get through to someone."

"I don't know how." Sharon leaned against the door. "Internet's gone down. My partner and I found that out when we tried to use our cruiser laptop." She nodded at the digits on Dale's laptop. "We just got that, same as everyone else."

"Yes, well…" Dale absently ran a hand through thinning brown hair. "The place I want to try is a little better protected than most."

"Where's that, sir? The Pentagon?" Sharon's demeanor changed; she was a cop again, wanting a straight answer to a straight question. "You showed us a Pentagon I.D. when you came over here from the airport. Is that where you work?"

"No. That's just a place I sometimes visit. My job is somewhere else." Dale hesitated, then he pulled his wallet from his back pocket. Opening it, he removed a laminated card and showed it to Sharon. "This is where I work."

Cindy caught a glimpse of the card. His photo was above his name, Dale F. Heinz, and at the top of the card was NATIONAL SECURITY AGENCY. She had only the vaguest idea of what that was, but Sharon was obviously impressed.

"Okay. You're NSA." Her voice was very quiet. "So maybe you know what's going on here."

"That's what I'd like find out. Tonight, once we've gone upstairs to a balcony room."

Minneapolis was dying.

From the balcony of a concierge suite—the only tenth-floor room whose door wasn't locked—the city was a dark expanse silhouetted by random fires. No lights in the nearby industrial park, and the distant skyscrapers were nothing but black, lifeless shapes looming in the starless night. Sharon thought there ought to be the sirens of first-responders—police cruisers, fire trucks, ambulances—but she heard nothing but an occasional gunshot. The airport was on the other side of the hotel, so she couldn't tell whether the jet which had crashed there was still ablaze. Probably not, and if its fire had spread from the runway to the hangers or terminals, those living in the Wyatt-Centrum would have known it by now; the hotel was only a mile away.

A muttered obscenity brought her back to the balcony. Dale was seated at a sofa end-table they'd dragged through the sliding door; his laptop lay open upon it, connected to Cindy's satphone. He'd hoped to get a clear uplink once he was outside, and a top floor balcony was the safest place to do this. And it appeared to have worked; gazing over his shoulder, Sharon saw that the countdown had disappeared from the screen, to be replaced by the NSA seal.

"You got through." Cindy stood in the open doorway, holding a flashlight over Dale's computer. The satphone belonged to her, so she'd insisted on coming along. Sharon had, too, mainly because Dale might need protection. After the incident in the kitchen, there was no telling how many 'bots might still be active in the hotel, as yet undiscovered.

"I got there, yeah… but I'm not getting in. Look." Dale's fingers ran across the keyboard, and a row of asterisks appeared in the password bar. He tapped the ENTER key; a moment later, ACCESS DENIED appeared beneath the bar. "That was my backdoor password. It locked out my official one, too."

"At least you got through. That's got to count for something, right?"

Dale quietly gazed at the screen, absently rubbing his lower lip. "It does," he said at last, "but I don't like what it means."

He didn't say anything else for a moment or two. "Want to talk about it?" Sharon asked. "We've got a right to know, don't you think?"

Dale slowly let out his breath. "This isn't just any government website. It belongs to the Utah Data Center, the NSA's electronic surveillance facility in Bluffdale, Utah." He glanced up at Sharon. "Ever heard of it?"

"Isn't that the place where they bug everyone's phone?"

"That's one way of putting it, yeah. Bluffdale does more than that, though… a lot more. They're tapped into the entire global information grid. Not just phone calls… every piece of email, every download, every data search, every bank transaction. Anything that's transmitted or travels down a wire gets filtered through this place."

"You gotta be kidding." Harold appeared in the doorway behind Cindy, apparently having found the restroom he'd been searching for. He'd tagged along as well, saying that Sharon might need help if they ran into any more 'bots. Sharon knew that this was just an excuse to attach himself to Cindy, but didn't say anything. Her roommate knew how to keep away from a wolf… and indeed, she left the doorway and squeezed in beside Dale, maintaining a discrete distance from the annoying salesman.

"Not at all. There's two and half acres of computers there with enough processing power to scan a yottabyte of information every second. That's like being able to read 500 quintillion pages."

Harold gave a low whistle. "All right, I understand," Sharon said. "But what does that have to do with us?"

The legs of Dale's chair scraped against concrete as he turned half-around to face her and the others. "Look… something has shut down the entire electronic infrastructure, right? Electricity, cars, phones, planes, computers, robots… everything networked to the grid was knocked down three days ago. And then, almost immediately after that, every part connected to the system that's mobile and capable of acting independently… namely, the robots… came back online, but now with only one single purpose. Kill any human they encounter."

"Give me another headline," Harold said drily. "I think I might have missed the news."

"Hush." Cindy glared at him and he shut up.

"The only other thing that still functions are networked electronics like smartphones and laptops… stuff that runs on batteries. But they don't do anything except display a number and make a ticking sound just like the robots do. And that number seems to decrease by one every time there's a tick."

"Yeah, I noticed that, too," Cindy said. "It began the moment my cell phone dropped out."

Dale gave her a sharp look. "You were on the phone when the blackout happened?" Cindy nodded. "Do you happen to remember what the number was when it first appeared on your phone screen?"

"Sort of... it was seven billion and something."

"About seven and half billion, would you say?" Dale asked. She nodded again, and he hissed beneath his breath. "That's what I thought it might be."

"What are you getting at?" Sharon asked, although she had a bad feeling that she already knew.

"The global population is approximately seven and a half billion." Dale's voice was very low. "At least, that's about how many people were alive on Earth three days ago."

Sharon felt a cold snake slither into the pit of her stomach. A stunned silence settled upon the group. Her ears picked up a low purring sound from somewhere in the distance, but it was drowned out when both Cindy and Harold started speaking at once.

"But... but why—?"

"What the hell are you—?"

"I don't know!" Dale threw up his hands in exasperation. "I can only guess. But—" he nodded toward the laptop "—the fact that the most secure computer system in the world is still active but not letting anyone in tells me something. This isn't a cyberattack, and I don't think a hacker or terrorist group is behind it either." He hesitated. "I think... I think it may have come out of Bluffdale."

Sharon stared at him. "Are you saying the NSA did this?"

"No... I'm saying the NSA's computers might have done this." Dale shook his head. "They always said the day might come when the electronic world might become self-aware, start making decisions on its own. Maybe that's what happening here, with Bluffdale as the source."

The purring sound had become a low buzz. Sharon ignored it. "But why would it start killing people? What would that accomplish?"

"Maybe it's decided that seven and a half billion people are too many and the time has come to pare down the population to more... well, more sustainable numbers." Dale shrugged. "It took most of human history for the world to have just one billion people, but just another two hundred years for there to be six billion, and only thirty after that for it to rise seven and a half billion. We gave Bluffdale the power to interface with nearly everything on planet, and a mandate to protect national security. Maybe it's decided that the only certain way to do it is to…"

"What's that noise?" Harold asked.

The buzzing had become louder. Even as Sharon turned to see where the sound was coming from, she'd finally recognized it for what it was. A police drone, the civilian version of the airborne military robots used in Central America and the Middle East. She'd become so used to seeing them making low-attitude surveillance sweeps of Minneapolis's more crime-ridden neighborhoods that she had disregarded the sound of its push-prop engine.

That was a mistake.

For a moment or two, she saw nothing. Then she caught a glimpse of firelight reflecting off the drone's bulbous nose and low-swept wings. It was just a few hundred feet away and heading straight for the balcony.

"Down!" she shouted, and then she threw herself headfirst toward the door. Harold was in her way. She tackled him like a linebacker and hurled him to the floor. "Get outta there!" she yelled over her shoulder as they scrambled for cover.

They'd barely managed to dive behind a couch when the drone slammed into the hotel.

Afterwards, Harold reckoned he was lucky to be alive. Not just because Officer McCoy had thrown him through the balcony door, but also because the drone's hydrogen cell was almost depleted when it made its kamikaze attack. So there hadn't been an explosion which might have killed both of them, nor a fire that would have inevitably swept through the Wyatt-Centrum.

But Cindy was dead, and so was Dale. The cop's warning hadn't come in time; the drone killed them before they could get off the balcony. He later wondered if it had simply been random chance that its infrared night vision had picked up four human figures and homed in on them, or if the Bluffdale computer had backtracked the satphone link from Dale's laptop and dispatched the police drone to liquidate a possible threat. He'd never know, and it probably didn't matter anyway.

Harold didn't know Dale very well, but he missed Cindy more than he thought he would. He came to realize that his attraction to her hadn't been purely sexual; he'd liked her, period. He wondered if his wife was still alive, and reflected on the fact that he'd only been three hours from home when his car went dead on a side street near the hotel. He regretted all the times he'd cheated on her when he'd been on the road, and swore to himself that, if he lived through this and she did, too, he'd never again pick up another woman.

The drone attack was the last exciting thing to happen to him or anyone else in the hotel for the next couple of days. They loafed around the atrium pool like vacationers who didn't want to go home, scavenging more food from the kitchen and going upstairs to break into vending machines, drinking bottled water, getting drunk on booze stolen from the bar. Harold slept a lot, as did the others, and joined poker games when he was awake. He volunteered for a four-hour shift at the lobby barricades, keeping a sharp eye out for roaming robots. He saw nothing through the peep-holes in the plywood boards except a few stray dogs and some guy pushing a shopping cart loaded with stuff he'd probably looted from somewhere.

Five days after the blackout, nearly all the phones, pads, and laptop computers in the hotel were dead, their batteries and power packs drained. But then Officer McCoy, searching Cindy's backpack for an address book she could use to notify the late girl's parents, discovered another handy piece of high-tech camping equipment: a photovoltaic battery charger. Cindy had also left behind her phone; it hadn't been used since her death, so its battery still retained a whisker of power. Officer McCoy hooked the phone up to the recharger and placed them on a table in the atrium, and before long they had an active cell phone.

Its screen remained unchanged, except that the number was much lower than it had been two days ago. It continued to tick, yet the sound was increasingly sporadic; sometimes as much as a minute would go by between one tick and the next. By the end of the fifth day, a few people removed some boards and cautiously ventured outside. They saw little, and heard almost nothing; the world had become quieter and much less crowded.

Although Harold decided to remain at the Wyatt-Centrum until he was positive that it was safe to leave, the cops decided that their presence was no longer necessary. The hotel's refugees could fend for themselves, and the city needed all the cops they could get. Before Officer McCoy left, though, she gave him Cindy's phone so he could keep track of its ticking, slowly decreasing number.

In the dark hours just before dawn of the sixth day, Harold was awakened by light hitting his eyes. At first he thought it was morning sun coming in through the skylight, but then he opened his eyes and saw that the bedside table lamp was lit. An instant later, the wall TV came on; it showed nothing but fuzz, but nonetheless it was working.

The power had returned. Astonished, he rolled over and reached for Cindy's cellphone. It no longer ticked, yet its screen continued to display a number, frozen and unchanging:

1,000,000,000.

This is the first of two stories in this collection that take place within my Coyote *series and the spin-off novels set in the same universe, which has become my best-known work. It occurs very late in the chronology, after* Coyote Horizon *but before* Coyote Destiny, *and is loosely related to* Galaxy Blues *but it can be read on its own. This is also the first time Hex is mentioned, although I wouldn't get around to writing about that place until the novel* Hex *a couple of years later.*

But that's not what this story is about.

I think everyone has someone with whom they fall in love, only to have things not work out as they hoped they would. Heartbreak and regret is part of the human condition; we go through life wondering how things may have been if only you'd said or done the right thing at the right time. This story's title is taken from a traditional American spiritual, but somewhere out there is a girl—whose name isn't Jordan, by the way, although I once had a close friend with that name—whom I haven't seen since the night many, many years ago I said something to her that I shouldn't have said.

I doubt she'll ever read this, but if she does, I hope she'll consider this an apology.

THE OTHER SIDE OF JORDAN

Jordan and I broke up on the docks of Leeport, about as lovely a place as you can have for the end of an affair. It was a warm summer evening in Hamaliel, with sailboats on the water and Bear—the local name for Ursae Majoris 47-B—hovering above the West Channel. We'd gone down to the waterfront to have dinner at a small bistro that specialized in grilled brownhead fresh from the fishing net, but even before the waiter brought us the menu the inevitable arguments had begun. There had been a lot of those lately, most of them about issues too trivial to remember but too important to ignore, and even though we settled the matter, nonetheless the quarrel caused us to lose our appetites. So we skipped dinner and instead ordered a bottle of waterfruit wine, and by the time we'd worked our way through the bottle, she and I decided that it was time to call it quits.

By then, it had become apparent that we weren't in love. Mutual infatuation, yes. We had the strong passions that are both the blessing and the curse of the young, and Jordan and I never failed to have a good time in bed. Yet desire was not enough to keep us together; when it came right down to it, we were very different people. She'd been born and raised on Coyote, a third-generation descendant of original colonists; I was an émigré from Earth, one the gringos who'd managed to escape the meltdown of the Western Hemisphere Union before the hyperspace bridge to the old world was destroyed. She came from money; I'd been a working man all my life. She was a patron of the arts; my idea of a good time was a jug of bearshine and a hoot-and-holler band down at the tavern. She was quiet and reserved; I couldn't keep my mouth shut, even when it was in my best interests to do so.

But most important—and this was what really brought things to a head—she was content to live out the rest of her life on Coyote. Indeed, Jordan's ambitions extended no farther than inheriting her family's hemp plantation—where we'd met in the first place, much to her parents' disapproval, since I was little more than a hired hand—while having a platoon of children. I was only too willing to help her practice the art of making babies, but the thought of everything to follow made my heart freeze. After five years on Coyote—fifteen by Earth reckoning, long enough for me to have allegedly became an adult—I wanted to move on. Now that the starbridge had been rebuilt and the Coyote Federation had been tentatively accepted as a member of the Talus[1], humankind was moving out into the galaxy. There were worlds out there that no human had ever seen before, along with dozens of races whom we'd just met. This was my calling, or at least so I thought, and the last thing I wanted to do was settle down to a dull life of being a husband and father.

So we broke up. It wasn't hostile, just a shared agreement that our romance had gone as far as it could go, and perhaps it would be better if we no longer saw each other. Nonetheless, I said something that I'd later regret: I called her a rich girl who liked to slum with lower-class guys, which was how I'd secretly come to regard her. I'm surprised she didn't dump her glass over my head. But at least we managed to get out of the

---

1. Let me explain the Talus. In short, it's a loose alliance of the Milky Way's starfaring races—or at least those who've built starbridges—formed to promote diplomacy, trade, and cultural exchange. Sort of a galactic club, so to speak, with humankind as the members who've only recently paid their dues.

restaurant without causing a scene; a brief hug, but no kisses, then we went our separate ways.

The next morning, I quit my job at the plantation—her father couldn't have been more pleased—then went back to my apartment to pack my bags and turn in the key to the landlady. By the end of the day, I was aboard the Leeport ferry, on my way to the New Brighton spaceport.

I thought I was done with Jordan, and that I'd never see her again. But some women cast a spell that can't easily be broken.

It wasn't hard to land a job as a spacer. The Federation merchant marine was always looking for a few good people, so long as you were smart enough to fill out the application form, were reasonably fit, and didn't have any outstanding arrest warrants. No experience necessary; you trained on the job, although the wash-out rate was high enough that the probation clause of the employment contract was invoked more often than not. But the pay was good, and the benefits included full health coverage, two weeks paid vacation, performance bonuses, and even a retirement plan.

When Starbridge Coyote was destroyed[2], it was at the height of the refugee crisis, with as many as a dozen ships arriving from Earth each and every day. After the starbridge went down, those ships were effectively stranded in the 47 Uma system, with no way home. The Coyote Federation laid claim to those vessels and reflagged them, and once the starbridge was rebuilt—with the technological assistance of the *hjadd*,[3] whose emissaries had been marooned on Coyote as well—the Federation now had in its possession a merchant fleet consisting of everything from passenger ships and freighters to a wide assortment of landers and shuttles.

---

2. I'll explain starbridges, too. They're a means of getting from one place in the galaxy to another, very fast, by using zero-point energy generators to create artificial wormholes within giant rings. You have to have one at your departure point, though, and another one at your destination, for you to get from here to there. A religious fanatic blew up the first one we humans built in the 47 Ursae Majoris system because he didn't like aliens. Leave it to a nutjob to screw things up for everyone else.

3. The *hjadd* were the first extraterrestrials our people encountered, and also our primary sponsors in the Talus. They're from a planet in the Rho Coronae Borealis system and look a little like giant tortoises, only standing upright and without shells. Nice folks, albeit a little persnickety. Oh, and they eat marijuana the way we eat oregano. Go figure.

Yet when the *hjadd* offered a helping hand, they'd carefully attached a string or two. Although they'd come to respect the humans on Coyote, they were also aware that the individual who'd caused the starbridge's destruction was from Earth, and this was just one more reason for them to regard the cradle of humanity with considerable distrust. So they made a major stipulation: the rebuilt starbridge could be used for travel to any world in our corner of the galaxy *except* Earth. Or at least until the High Council of the Talus, to which the *hjadd* belonged, determined that Earth no longer posed a threat to other starfaring races. And if the Federation didn't like it, the *hjadd* could always withdraw their ambassadors, shut down their embassy on New Florida, and leave Coyote once and for all, slamming the door into hyperspace behind them. They'd reconstructed the starbridge, sure… but they also knew how to disable it so that no ships could pass through it without their permission.

To be sure, quite a few people objected to being cut off from Earth. Yet a surprisingly large majority supported the *hjadd*'s decision. Ever since the unexpected arrival of the first Western Hemisphere Union starship, four years after the *Alabama* party set foot on Coyote, and the military occupation that followed, Earth had been little but trouble for the colonies. The refugee crisis had been only the latest example of how the folks back home were using and abusing the new world, with little but a supply of trade goods to show for it. But if the Talus was willing to make up for this shortfall with a new source of vital materials… well, why bother with Earth at all?

So Coyote had become the latest partner in a galactic network of commerce and cultural exchange, with vessels constantly coming and going through the starbridge, bound for distant worlds whose very existence had been unknown until only a few years ago. And those ships needed crews. The fleet already had plenty of captains and first officers and navigators and engineers; those guys had come with their vessels, and their jobs essentially remained unchanged. But someone had to load cargo, repair hull plates, scrub decks, cook meals, clean toilets, and otherwise perform all the menial tasks to go with running a starship… and that's how guys like me earned our paychecks.

After I passed through a four-week boot camp and earned my union card, I became a Payload Specialist Third Class, which is a polite way of saying that I was a cargo rat. My first billet was aboard the *Lady Amelia*, a jovian-class freighter that made regular runs out to a planet in the HD 114386 system, locally known as… well, I'm not going to try to spell the name of the place; you couldn't pronounce it anyway. The inhabitants called themselves the *arsashi*, and they had a use for the mountain briar our loggers cut in the highlands of Great Dakota. So I spent a couple of days loading lumber aboard a pair of payload containers, and once the containers were lifted into orbit and attached to the *Lady Amelia*, off we went to the Puppis constellation.

I didn't see much of the *arsashi* homeworld. A small planet the color of ear-wax in orbit around a white dwarf, its atmosphere had too much ammonia and too little nitrogen for it to be habitable by humans—which is, indeed, the case for most worlds of the Talus. Yet the natives were friendly enough for a race of eight-foot tall, bug-eyed yeti; once my fellow rats and I unloaded five tons of wood, the *arsashi* did their best to make Amelia's crew as comfortable as possible, even putting us up for the night in a small dome suitable for humans. Their food was indigestible, but at least we had a nice view of a nearby shield volcano. Which, so far as I could tell, was the only thing on their planet worth seeing.

I stayed aboard *Amelia* for the next six months, Coyote time, long enough to make five more trips to HD 114386. By then, I'd ended my probation period and had been promoted to Payload Specialist Second Class. I was tired of the *arsashi* and their dismal little wad of a planet, so after that last run, I gave up my billet to another spacer and went in search of a new job.

This time, I lucked out: the next available post for a cargo rat was aboard the *Pride of Cucamonga*, the freighter that made history by undertaking the first trade expedition to Rho Coronae Borealis. Word had it that, if you were fortunate enough to crew aboard the *Pride*, then you could get a job anywhere in the fleet. As things turned out, the *Pride*'s cargomaster was about to take maternity leave, and Captain Harker— himself a near-legendary figure—needed someone to fill her position. I was barely qualified for the job, but the letter of recommendation that the *Lady Amelia*'s captain had written on my behalf went far to ease his reluctance. So I managed to get one of the choice jobs in the merchant marine.

Cargo for the *Pride of Cucamonga* was *cannabis sativa*, but that wasn't the only thing we brought with us. The Talus races opened trade with Coyote for our raw materials, yet it wasn't long before we learned that they were willing to pay better for something else entirely. Not our technology; with the exception of seawater desalinization, for which the *sorenta* gave us negative-mass drive, anything humans had invented, the aliens had long since perfected.

To our surprise, what they liked the most about us was our culture.

The *nord* enjoyed our music. They didn't think much of Mozart or Bach, and thought jazz was boring, but they liked bluegrass and were absolutely wild about traditional Indian music; apparently both the banjo and the sitar sounded much like their own instruments, only different. The *sorenta* were fascinated by our art, the more abstract the better, and didn't mind very much if what we brought them were copies of Pollock, Kandinksy, or Mondrian. The *kua'tah* were interested in nature films; Coyote's surface gravity and atmospheric density meant that they'd never set foot on our world, but they loved seeing vids of the plants and animals we'd found there.

As for the *hjadd*… the *hjadd* were intrigued by our literature. They'd learned how to translate most of our major languages long before humans actually made contact with them—a long story that I shouldn't need to repeat—so they read everything we brought them, from Shakespeare, Milton, and Shelley to 20th Century potboilers to *The Chronicles of Prince Rupurt*. So not only was the *Pride of Cucamonga* carrying five thousand pounds of cannabis to Rho Coronae Borealis, but also a comp loaded with novels, stories, and poems by authors as diverse as Jane Austen, John D. MacDonald, Edward E. Smith, and Dr. Seuss… all as another payment for the sophisticated microassemblers that had enabled us to transform log-cabin colonies like Liberty and New Boston into cities the likes of which had never been seen on Earth. Our nanotech was primitive compared to theirs… but then again, there's nothing else in the universe quite like *Green Eggs and Ham*.[4]

We never actually landed on Hjarr, of course. No non-*hjadd* ever had, with the sole exception of the chaaz'braan, the Great Teacher of the Sa'Tong. Instead, the *Pride* once again docked at *Talus qua'spah*, the

---

4. Seriously. There isn't. I know it's a children's book, and quite old at that, but if you haven't yet read *Green Eggs and Ham*, stop reading this story *right now* and go find a copy. Come back when you're done. You'll thank me for it.

immense space colony in orbit above Hjarr that served as one of the major rendezvous points for the Talus races. This was the first time I'd visited the House of the Talus, the place from which I'd embark on a journey that would eventually bring me to Hex.

But before then, I'd send a letter home.

After I left Jordan, I told myself that she was just another girl with whom I'd had a brief affair, and that I'd miss her no more than any other woman I've slept with. She was gone. No regrets.

As time went by, though, I gradually discovered that I was wrong. I *did* miss Jordan, and I *did* regret the things I'd said to her. It wasn't as if I was lacking female companionship. I'd had a brief fling with *Lady Amelia's* com officer, and on those occasions when another merchant marine vessel was docked at *Talus qua'spah*, I could always count on a one-night stand with another Federation spacer. But these dalliances were nothing more than sexual exercise, and more than once I woke up in a bunk with a woman whose name I barely knew, to find myself thinking, if only for a moment, that it was Jordan who was curled up beside me.

Yet when I tried to get in touch with her, those times when I was back on Coyote between flights, I discovered that she'd taken measures to cut me out of her life. Her pad number had been changed, and when I tried calling her house, her folks would immediately disconnect, leaving me talking to a dead phone. Mutual friends informed me that she was still in Leeport and hadn't yet taken up with someone else; on the other hand, she never mentioned my name, or seemed to miss me in any way.

Nonetheless, I wanted her back. And so, during my third trip to *Talus qua'spah*, I wrote her a letter.

In order to send mail across the galaxy, one relies on hyperspace communication links. Once a message was encrypted and addressed to its recipient, it's sent to a network of transceivers maintained by the Talus, which in turn relays the letter to its intended destination. Unfortunately, that means that it's theoretically possible for the message to be intercepted, decrypted, and read anywhere along the line. One has to be able to translate the written language of an alien race in order to do that, of course, and while I doubted that anyone would have much interest in what I had to say to my former girlfriend, nonetheless I didn't want others to read my mail.

So I opted for a slower means of communication. I hand-wrote my letter on pages ripped from my logbook, sealed them in an envelope, and addressed it to Jordan's home. A friend of mine who was heading back to Coyote aboard another ship offered to carry my letter for me. An old-fashioned way of doing things, sure, but at least I'd be a little more assured of privacy.

In that letter, I let Jordan know where I was and what I was doing, then went on to apologize for the things I'd said to her. I told her that I missed her very much, and that I wanted to see her again. I also attached a recent picture of me standing watch on the *Pride*'s bridge, the galaxy-trotting spacer and all that. After adding the ship's hyperlink suffix—no sense in her going through the same rigmarole if she didn't want to—I gave the letter to my buddy. And then I went about my business, and tried not to be too anxious about when I'd get a reply.

None came.

A couple of weeks later, the *Pride* returned to Coyote to drop off cargo and take on another load of weed and books. Just before we left for Rho Coronae Borealis again, Captain Harker informed me that the regular cargomaster had successfully delivered her baby and that she would soon be coming back to work. After this trip, I'd have to find another ship. So I sent a second letter to Jordan in which I informed her of my change of plans before reiterating everything I'd written in my first letter.

I waited. Still, no response.

At *Talus qua'spah*, I happened to run into an old acquaintance, another guy who'd gone through training at the same time I did. His ship was the *Texas Rose*, a long-range merchanteer that didn't come and go between just two planets, but instead traveled among the Talus worlds on year-long voyages, carrying freight from one planet to another. My friend had done two of these circuits, and he'd seen enough of the galaxy; the time had come for him to go home.

I spent the night getting drunk and having a long talk with my heart. The following morning, still nursing a hangover, I went to see Captain Harker and asked permission to leave the *Pride* and take a job that had just opened up on the *Rose*. Ted was willing to do this, and so was the *Rose*'s captain, and so my friend and I swapped billets; he returned to Coyote aboard the *Pride*, while I...

Let's be honest. I told myself that I was fulfilling my ambition to see the stars, but the truth of the matter was that I was running away from a woman who, through her silence, had told me that she wanted nothing more to do with me.

But still, I continued to write to her. It had become a habit, a way of passing time when I was off-duty. I had no idea whether Jordan was receiving my letters, let alone reading them, but nonetheless it was something I had to do.

For the next year, I visited worlds that were once beyond my reach. At Tau Bootis, I walked upon the shores of a methane sea beneath the ruddy glow of a variable star. At HD 150706, in the Ursa Minor constellation, I found myself on the moon of a superjovian whose orbit about its primary was so eccentric that its summers were hot enough to boil mercury, while the carbon dioxide of its atmosphere froze solid during the winter; no indigenous life was possible in such a hellhole, but the *kua'tah* had established a mining outpost there, and so the *Texas Rose* took on a load of iron ingots in exchange for vids of ice medusae. From high orbit above the *sorenta* homeworld in the HD 73256 system, I saw one of the wonders of the galaxy: a continental mountain range, larger and higher than even the Andes, which primitive *sorenta* had spent countless generations carving into the likeness of the god that they'd worshipped in ancient times, until it resembled a vast, somber face perpetually staring up into the sky.[5]

All these worlds, and many others, I told Jordan about in my letters. For even though I'd tried to run away, I couldn't escape my memory of her. I traveled hundreds of light-years, visited nearly a dozen planets, and yet every night I lay awake in my bunk and wished that she was there with me.

And then, at the farthest point in the *Rose*'s circuitous route, we arrived at Hex.

Humans didn't learn about Hex until we made contact with the *nord*, and even then it wasn't until after their homeworld was destroyed when a rogue black hole passed through its system at HD 70642. The *nord* met our people at *Talus qua'spah*, and when they found that we had

---

5. I'm told that the *sorenta* went to all the trouble to do this because they wanted their god to come down from the sky and pay them a visit. Which raises the obvious question: if their god had never visited them before, how did the *sorenta* know what it looked like? I cannot figure out religion...

something they wanted—did I mention that they really loved bluegrass? —they offered to reveal to us the starbridge coordinates of the place where they'd gone after they evacuated Nordash. At first, we were only politely curious... but then a Federation Navy ship went there, and realized that this information was worth its weight in banjos.[6]

HD 76700 is a G-class star located in the Volans constellation, about 194 light-years from Earth. It's also the home system of the *danui*, a rather reclusive race that, although capable of interstellar travel and hence a member of the Talus, wasn't much interested in visiting other worlds. Instead, the *danui* did exactly the opposite: they made something that would guarantee that other starfaring races would visit them instead.

They built Hex.

Once, several millennia ago, HD 76700 was home to a fairly modest solar system, with a couple of terrestrial-size planets in stable orbits within its habitable zone and a small gas giant in close proximity to the star itself. Except for the hot jupe,[7] those planets no longer exist; the *danui* dismantled them—don't ask how; no one knows, and the *danui* aren't telling—to construct the largest artificial habitat in the entire galaxy.

Picture a geodesic sphere—the technical term is geode, or "twisted dual geodesic dome"—comprised of hexagons, with empty space at the center of each hex. Now, make that geode 186 million miles in diameter, with a circumference of 584,337,600 miles; the legs of the individual hexagons are hollow cylinders 1,000 miles long and 100 miles wide, with a total perimeter of 6,000 miles. Construct this enormous sphere around a small yellow sun at the radial distance of one a.u., leaving the hot jupe where it is in order to furnish the hexes near the equator with an eclipse once every four days. Rotate the entire thing so that centrifugal force provides gravity within each cylinder, ranging from 2 g's at the equator to nearly zero-g at the poles; the top half of each cylinder is a transparent roof comprised of a some polymeric substance that provides radiation protection while also retaining atmospheric pressure.

---

6. And let me tell you: that's a hell of a lot of banjos.

7. "Hot jupe": hot Jupiter. An old-time name that spacers still use for jovians that are way too close to their suns. Not nice places to visit. And, yes, we are weird... but fun, once you get to know us.

The result is a habitat the size of a planetary system, comprised of nearly 100 trillion cylinders, each with its own individual environment.

The *danui* did this. And then they opened the doors and invited their neighbors to move in.

Why go to such effort? Damned if anyone knew, except that they liked company but hated to travel. But what everyone agreed upon was that only the *danui* would even conceive of such a thing, let alone pull it off. As a race, they had what, in a human, would be diagnosed as Asperger syndrome. Shy, inept at communication, and ugly as sin—they looked like gigantic tarantulas with enormous, lobster-like heads—the *danui* nonetheless were genius engineers, capable of focusing their entire attention on a single goal and working at it obsessively until it was brought to completion. At some point in their history, they'd decided to pull apart their homeworld, along with its closest neighbor and a nearby asteroid belt, and turn it into Hex.

That's what humans called the place. The other races of the Talus, of course, had their own names for it. And nearly every one of them had accepted the *danui* invitation to establish colonies within individual hexes. There was no reason for anyone to push or shove—plenty of room for everyone, and then some—and the *danui* were willing to help newcomers transform their hexes into miniature replicas of their native worlds. The only stipulation was that the inhabitants live together in peace.

Which was an easy thing to agree to; wars are fought over territory, after all, and who'd go to war over a place where there's more elbow room than anyone could possibly want? Besides, the other Talus races had already seen what had happened to the *morath* when they'd attempted to invade the *kua'tah* hex: the *danui* had simply sealed off the *morath* hex, then jettisoned it into space, toward the sun. It had taken nearly three months for the *morath* colony to fall into HD 76700, and the few survivors were told to leave Hex and never return.[8]

Humans were only the latest race to stake out land on Hex. Our six habs were located about halfway up the northern hemisphere where the surface gravity was about .7-g, less than Earth's but just a little more than

---

8. Last footnote, I promise... but this is just one example of why war is nearly non-existent within the Talus. Some of the member races are just too damn powerful for anyone to screw around with.

Coyote's. The *Texas Rose* entered a spherical node between habs One and Two; a mile in diameter, it was spacious enough to hangar the entire Federation fleet, and indeed, two other vessels were already docked there. Our ships had been coming to Hex for over a year now, bringing materials necessary to turn our hexagon into a little version of Coyote. Now that the *Rose* had completed its circuit, about half of our cargo would end up here, most of it various items we'd acquired in trade with other races.

So far, only Hab One—christened Nueva Italia by those who lived there—was settled, and even so its population was still less than a thousand. Not many people on Coyote were willing to pull up roots and relocate so far away from others of their own kind. A small town, Milan, had been built near the western end of the cylinder, not far from the tram station that connected Nueva Italia with the other habs in our hex. The dwellings were prefab faux-birch yurts shipped from 47 Uma, but it was hoped that, once sufficient forestland was cultivated, the colonists would have their own supply of lumber.

I spent the better part of my first day on Hex driving a forklift, hauling pallets, crates and barrels from the tram to an open-sided shed where the supplies were stockpiled, so I didn't get much of a chance to look around. Indeed, I was trying hard not to; I'd seen many strange things during my tour of the galaxy, but even this minuscule corner of Hex was mesmerizing. It took an effort to not become distracted by a landscape that lacked a discernible horizon, but instead curved upward on both sides and at either end until it merged with a barrel-shaped sky where a sun perpetually stayed in the same place, never rising or setting.

Even so, the day on Nueva Italia did eventually come to an end. The *danui* had programmed the window panes to gradually polarize over the course of hours until a semblance of nighttime came upon Milan. A collection of yurts in the center of town served as a bed-and-breakfast for travelers, and nearby was a small tavern. After knocking off work, I joined the rest of my crew at the tavern. Hex marked the end of our long voyage, and the captain was feeling generous; he told the barkeep that he'd pay the tab for everyone at our table, and so we settled in for a night of drinking.

I was on my third or fourth pint of ale when I became aware of something tugging at my left foot. Looking down, I found a young woman kneeling beside me; the laces of my work shoes had come undone, and she was retying them for me. Her head was bowed, so the only thing I saw at first was the top of her scalp; light brown hair fell around her shoulders, hiding her face from me. I started to tell her that I could tie my own shoes, thanks anyway, but then she looked up at me.

"Do I know you?" she asked.

"Yes… yes, I think you do."

"You should be more careful. If you walk around with untied shoes, you might trip over them and hurt yourself."

"Good advice. I make mistakes like that sometimes."

"People are like that. They do things they don't mean to do."

"Umm… yeah, you're right. Sometimes you don't…"

"Hush." Jordan reached up to take my face in her hands. "I forgive you."

She'd received my letters. That was my first question; any others were unnecessary, or at least just then.

In time, she would tell how she'd thought about responding, but decided instead to maintain an aloof silence while waiting to see what I'd say or do next. And when she'd heard enough to convince herself that my apologies were sincere and that I really did love her, she left her family and caught the next ship to Hex, knowing that the *Rose* would eventually make its way there. And then she'd waited for me to show up, to tell me…

"I got your letters," Jordan said, once she'd kissed me. "I read every one of them. And I'm sorry, too."

"You don't have to be." She was sitting beside me at the table, her hands in mine. The rest of my crew, realizing that we needed to be left alone, had quietly moved to another side of the room. "Anything you said, I don't…"

"No. That's not what I mean. Your letters… I'm sorry, but I don't have them any more."

"What did you…?"

"I had to get here somehow, and my family didn't want me to… well, you know how my parents feel about you. So I sold your letters to buy passage out here."

"I don't understand. Who would buy my letters? Who'd even want to read…?"

"Who do you think?"

Who, indeed?

Of course, I forgave her for this. Love is a matter of forgiveness, if nothing else. Since then, we've had a very happy life together, here on Hex, where the sun never sets and we have plenty of neighbors to keep us company.

All the same, we try to avoid the *hjadd*. They know enough about us already. How our story ends is none of their business.

This is the last Coyote story… I think.

I spent eleven years writing the Coyote series, along with the novels set in the same universe and associated stories such as this, and although I had a great time, it was never meant to be the only *thing I'd write for the rest of my life. In fact, considering that* Coyote *was originally intended to be a stand-alone novel, I'm amazed that it led to a trilogy, a duology, three spinoffs, a book-length novella, and a handful of short stories.*

But it was only inevitable that the day would come when I'd realize that I'd said all that needed to be said, and if I carried the series any further it would become redundant and mediocre. So I stopped work on a sequel to Hex *that was becoming rather silly, told my editor and my agent that enough was enough, then filed away all my notes and maps and turned my attention to other things.*

I thought this was the end. A couple of months later, though, I went to Orlando, Florida, to attend the 100 Year Starship Conference, a gathering of scientists, futurists, and science fiction writers during which plausible near-term scenarios for interstellar travel were discussed. During the conference, my old friends Greg Benford and his brother Jim approached me about writing a story for an anthology, Starship Century, *they were co-editing as a product of this conference. They wanted me to write what would amount to the anthology's keynote story, so I decided to set it at the conference itself… and somehow, it became not only a new Coyote story, but also both a prelude and a coda to the series as a whole.*

Will there ever be a new Coyote novel? I don't think so. On the other hand, I've said that before, right after I finished Coyote Frontier, *so I'm hedging my bets a little. But for now…*

CATHEDRALS

Florida Ballroom 5 was a ballroom in name only; Frank doubted that it was large enough for even a half-decent foxtrot. He found himself envying Orange Ballroom D just down the hall, where the keynote speeches had been held; it had a couple of thousand chairs, with screens big enough to be seen from the back of the room. But the conference's breakout sessions—as many as five occurring at any one time—had been scheduled for these smaller rooms where there were only a few dozen seats, often forcing many of the attendees to stand along the walls or sit on the floor.

At one of yesterday's sessions, Frank had heard John Cramer call the conference "Woodstock for nerds." Frank had missed Woodstock—in 1969 he'd been at Marshall Space Center, helping NASA plan those last two Apollo missions that the Nixon administration killed—but he supposed that the analogy was as good as any. Sure, the conference didn't have tents, mud, brown acid, or Jimi Hendrix playing the "Star Spangled Banner" at sunrise, but nonetheless there was a sense of freewheeling, wide-eyed possibility that a hippie would have grooved on. He smiled at the thought. Did anyone still say groovy? Or was he just showing his age?

At the podium beside him, Jim Benford was wrapping up his introduction for this afternoon's session on breakthrough propulsion systems. Frank shuffled his notes as he pretended not to notice that the room was half-empty. Only about thirty or so people had shown up to hear him speak. Which wasn't bad, really—before he'd retired from Stanford, his lectures typically had only a dozen or so grad students—but this morning's talk on faster-than-light travel had been standing room only. Once again, he scolded himself for being a bit reserved in his choice of title for his presentation. "Warp Field Mechanics" sounded a little more intriguing than "Quantised Inertia and FTL," but wasn't anywhere near as interesting as "Terraforming Planets, Geoengineering Earth" or "Hostile Journey and Destination—Yes, But Weapons?" And none of them rocked—oh, yeah, that was the word that replaced groovy—like "Did Jesus Die for Klingons, Too?" Frank had no idea what that was about, other than it belonged to the program track for philosophical and ethical considerations, but he had little doubt that it had jammed Florida Ballroom 7.

His thoughts were interrupted by scattered applause from the audience, and he looked up to see Jim stepping away from the podium. Frank picked up his notes, pushed back his chair, and sauntered toward the podium, exchanging a brief smile and a nod with Jim as they walked past each other. He laid his notes upon the podium and picked up the wireless remote used to operate the projector in the back of the room. Half of the conference speakers had run into trouble with the damn thing—apparently it used a version of PowerPoint few of them were familiar with—and he prayed that he wouldn't embarrass himself, at least not that way.

Never mind that now. The next twenty minutes were his. Frank glanced at the longhand notes he'd written on a yellow legal pad—an explanation of the Alcubierre metric; a discourse on the problems inherent in generating a warp bubble within spacetime; speculation on the creation of boost shells within pseudo horizons; the possibility of constructing a toroidal capacitor ring as a means of harnessing negative energy—and realized that it wouldn't be wise to jump straight into his presentation's most technical material. This wasn't Stanford; if he wanted to keep his audience from wondering what Jesus might say to a Klingon, he'd better open with something a little more compelling than equations.

A remark someone said to him over breakfast that morning came back to him. Frank wasn't above cribbing from his colleagues, so he stole it.

"You know," he began, "I've been thinking about how we should go about interstellar travel, and it occurs to me that we do this much the same way the great cathedrals of Europe were built…"

As he spoke, his voice was amplified by the podium mike, while his image was caught by the Sony digital camera mounted on a platform in the back of the room. Both fed straight into one of the half-dozen or so DVD recorders saving the conference's sessions for posterity.

The camera softly purred as it focused upon him, capturing the projection screen in the background…

When Karen Cho's grandfather died, his passing was newsworthy enough to be mentioned on the front page of the *Liberty Post*: DAVID CHO, ORIGINAL ALABAMA COLONIST, DIES. The story went on to explain that Dr. Cho was one of the fabled "d.i.'s" who hijacked the URSS *Alabama* in 2070 and was therefore among the 109 people who, after a 230-year journey, reached the 47 Ursae Majoris system to establish the first colony on Coyote.

The reporter who'd written the story apparently thought his readers needed a history refresher, because he went on to reiterate—rather unnecessarily, in Karen's opinion—what every child who had been born and raised on Coyote had been told since their first days of school: how a small group of conspirators led by Captain R.E. Lee had managed to substitute half of the ship's military crew with d.i.'s who had been arrested and were on their way to a government re-education camp. The article went on to explain that one of them had been Karen's grandfather, an engineer who'd worked for the Federal Space Agency until his questionable loyalty to the United Republic of America had caused him to be branded as a dissident intellectual—the term for those who hadn't toed the Liberty Party line—and dismissed from his job. Nonetheless, Dr. Cho had been among those responsible for the design of humankind's first starship, and so when Captain Lee and his closest associates hatched the conspiracy, he and her grandmother (who'd died before Karen was born) had been among the civilians who were smuggled aboard the *Alabama*.

Karen knew all this, of course. She'd grown up hearing the stories, from both her parents and from her grandfather himself. However, what she'd been told as a child had exaggerated her grandfather's role in the hijacking, making it seem as if he'd charged aboard the ship, fighting Federal Service soldiers shoulder-to-shoulder with heroes like Capt. Lee, Tom Shapiro, and Jorge Montero. It wasn't until years later that she understood how this was an embroidered version of how things actually happened. The hijackers hadn't taken *Alabama* by storm, but instead had come aboard rather quietly, using subterfuge rather than force. There had been no fight in the main airlock, as legend has it, and her grandparents had done nothing more than go to their berths, strap in, and wait for others in the command center to usurp control of the ship's computers and engage the launch sequence. Indeed, it was this discovery that led Karen to become a historian; she decided that she'd rather know banal reality than glorious fantasy.

All the same, she'd honored and respected her grandfather, and after her own parents were killed in a ferry accident on the Great Equatorial River, she'd cared for the old man during his last years. By then, Gran'pa barely remembered Earth at all, and even had trouble recalling the details of how he'd come to Coyote. Unfortunately, this sort of senescence wasn't uncommon among original colonists; doctors at the University of New Florida believed that degeneration of neural tissue was a long-term aftereffect of the centuries-long biostasis they had endured aboard *Alabama*. Even Marie Montero, the younger sister of former Coyote Federation president Jorge Montero, had been afflicted by this.

So Karen had brought Gran'pa into her home while she finished her graduate studies at the university, and it was shortly before she received her master's that the old man quietly passed away while taking an afternoon nap. Karen had been expecting this for quite some time, and although she grieved at the death of the last member of her immediate family, there was comfort to be taken from the fact that Gran'pa's death had been peaceful and without pain.

His memorial service was remarkably well-attended, even if she didn't recognize many of those who showed up. Gran'pa had few friends left, and although Karen had her own supporters, she suspected that most of the people there simply wanted to pay respects to one of the *Alabama* colonists. Karen spoke for a few minutes, and then David Cho's shroud-wrapped body was placed upon a wooden bier and set afire. The service was followed by a wake, but Karen showed up just long enough to accept a few condolences before going home.

As her grandfather's sole survivor, it fell to her to settle his final affairs. Gran'pa had left everything to her, so it became mainly a matter of going through his belongings and deciding what to discard, what to give away, and what to keep. This was a sad but rather mundane chore until she came upon a small nylon bag among the things he kept in his desk.

The bag was threadbare, dusty, and obviously quite old. When Karen opened it, she discovered that it contained a thin plastic cartridge with a plug and a serial port at one end. It took a few minutes for her to recognize what it was: an antique backup drive, the sort once used to store digital information.

Karen realized that this was an artifact from Earth that Gran'pa had carried with him aboard the *Alabama*. For a historian such as herself, such a find was priceless; there was no telling what might be stored on it. The technology was obsolete, of course, but the University's history department possessed a 21st Century computer, itself another *Alabama* relic, which was carefully maintained for the express purpose of reading such data caches when they were found.

A few days later, once she had the time, she took the old drive to the University, where she showed it to the history curator and asked if he could find out what it contained. After warning her that it was entirely possible that its memory might have decayed to the point of uselessness, the curator carried the backup drive to a dust-free room where an impossibly old comp stood upon a table. He ran a cable from the comp to the drive, then carefully typed instructions into the brittle keyboard that opened the drive's file directory.

As it turned out, the curator's warning had been correct. Of the dozens of files contained on Gran'pa's drive, all but a few had eroded over time, leaving behind only a list of filenames—*notes.doc, SPsched, phonelist,* and so forth—which offered nothing but tantalizing clues as to what they'd been about. Yet among those still readable was one with an intriguing name: *100YrSS—Grandfather*.

Karen asked the curator to open this one. Instead of text, they discovered that it contained an old-style video wavefile. Was this something Gran'pa had once recorded? This was Karen's first thought, until she realized that her grandfather would have never referred to himself as such. And what did "100YrSS" mean? "100 Year" was the most likely interpretation for "100Yr", but the letters "SS" were mysterious.

The chronometer indicated that the wavefile had once been a little more than twenty minutes long, but what had survived was much shorter than that: less than two minutes had survived. When the curator played it, they saw:

An elderly gentleman, wearing a dark sport coat and necktie of late 20th Century style, stood before a podium. The word *Hilton* was visible on a plaque attached to the front of the podium, but this was less obvious than what projected on the large video screen beside him: *100 Year Starship*, the words superimposed upon a stylized celestial compass, obviously a logo of some sort. The video was apparently shot from a camera located in the back of a meeting room. At the bottom of the screen were the backs of a dozen or more heads; at one point a young woman briefly walked in front of the camera, obscuring the image for a second.

"You know," the man at the podium said, *"I've been thinking about how we should go about interstellar travel, and it occurs to me that we should do this much the same way the great cathedrals of Europe were built. Not as a short-term project, with goals that can be achieved only within a few years and everything else pushed back to a hazy and not well-conceived timeline, but rather as a long-term initiative that may not be completed until our children's or even grandchildren's time. When we currently think about the logistics of space exploration, such as returning to the Moon or going to Mars, we tend to fall into a pattern that we used during Project Apollo. That was good for putting men on the Moon within a decade, but it's not so appropriate when confronting the challenges of sending a vessel to another star system a hundred years from now, if not sooner…"*

He raised his left hand toward the screen, fumbled with something he was holding. The logo disappeared, replaced an instant later by a diagram which looked like a pair of parabolic curves placed against each other on either side of a horizontal line. *"Indeed, the technology for building a practical warp-drive engine may not come into existence for another couple of generations. However, because we can project with some degree of confidence just what such a drive might entail, we don't necessarily have to push this into our grandchildren's laps. We can begin thinking about it now. The Alcubierre Metric, for example, postulates using negative energy to generate a field, or warp bubble, around a spacecraft which would it allow it to..."*

The video came to an abrupt end. The curator tried to salvage the remaining data, but was unable to retrieve anything more than harsh static and a few grainy images. The rest was lost to time.

What little they saw, though, was enough to cause Karen to stop breathing for nearly two full minutes. For in those few precious moments, she realized that the man at the podium wasn't her grandfather, but rather *his* grandfather, and that he was speaking to her from across a gulf of nearly 400 years.

"There's not much family resemblance, is there?" Sitting up in bed, Arturo studied the image of Karen's great-great-grandfather which her data pad had projected on a wall screen. He smiled as he glanced at her. "You're sure he's related to you?"

"I'm sure." Karen sat on the edge of the bed, wrapped in a hemp bathrobe and drying her damp hair with a towel. "You told me yourself... Dr. Frank O'Connell, Ph.D., professor of physics, Stanford University, and NASA." She frowned. "That's the National Aeronautics and Space Agency, isn't it?"

"National Aeronautics and Space Administration. Otherwise, yes, you got it... that's what I found when I double-checked the historical records." He gazed at the image again. "I'm just saying, he doesn't... he didn't... look a lot like you."

"The Asian bloodline hadn't entered my family's gene pool quite yet." Karen laid down the damp towel, then picked up a brush and began combing out her long, black hair. "From what I remember of my family history, my great-grandmother married a guy from Seoul. That's how Koreans came to belong to an otherwise Irish-American family." She nodded toward the holo. "I see the resemblance. You just have to look hard, that's all."

"Hmm… I suppose." The smile reappeared, a little more coy this time, as Arturo's hand slid across the bed. "Perhaps I should make a more thorough investigation," he said, taking hold of the sash that held closed the front of her robe.

"Quit." Karen gave his hand a gentle slap. The two of them had been sleeping together for the past several months, having met at the University, but this was the first time she'd felt comfortable having Arturo share her bed. Because she didn't want to have her grandfather hear them from the next room, they'd always made love at his place instead. "I'm serious. I know so little about him. That's why I asked you to look into it for me. So you found out his name and that he'd worked at Stanford and NASA…"

"Sure. That was easy enough." Arturo let go of her sash, picked up her pad and used it to expand the image until the 100 Year Starship logo filled the wallscreen. "Once I knew where the vid was recorded, I just had to dig into the history archives until I found the proceedings of the conference. And there he was, listed right there on the agenda. 'Warp Drive Mechanics', F. O'Connell… 12:50 P.M., Florida Ballroom 5."

"And the date was…?"

"Saturday, October 1, 2011." He ran a hand through his dark brown hair. "Can I use the shower next? I'd like to freshen up a bit, too."

"Let's talk first." Karen laid down her comb. She wanted to get dressed, but she was afraid that if she removed her robe, Arturo would get distracted and… well, they'd never get through this. "So you got his name, and from his biography in the published proceedings you got the rest."

"Uh-huh." He lowered an eyebrow and stared at her intently, an expression that she'd learned to recognize as inquisitive puzzlement. "I don't understand. How can you realize that he was your ancestor, but know so little about him? His name, for instance?"

"My grandparents left Earth with almost nothing but the clothes they were wearing. Everything they owned was left behind, and the government of United Republic of America confiscated all that once they were gone. So what little I know about my family has been pretty much what I've been told."

"I understand," he said. "Same sort of thing happened to my family."

Arturo's parents had come to Coyote only about twenty years earlier, during the second great immigration wave following the collapse of

Earth's major governments which occurred in the wake of the global environmental catastrophes that made humankind's homeworld all but uninhabitable. It wasn't quite the same thing—those immigrants had been able to bring a few belongings, at least—but Karen wasn't about to argue the point with him.

"Sure," she said. "Anyway, Gran'pa used to tell me that *his* grandfather had been one of the first scientists to work on interstellar travel, and that his work had led to Project Starflight, which in turn led to the construction of the *Alabama*."

"But since that was all hearsay, you had no way of knowing for certain." Arturo nodded. "All right, I understand. So now you do..."

"No, I don't... not completely, I mean." Karen let out her breath in a frustrated sigh. "Look, I know there's not much here, but from what I can tell, my great-great-grandfather didn't have anything to do with the *Alabama* or Project Starlight. He was involved in something else entirely, the theoretical development of a warp drive... and that's not what was used by the *Alabama*."

"No, it wasn't." Stretching luxuriously beneath the sheets, Arturo folded his arms behind his head. "*Alabama* used a RAIR engine... a ram-augmented interstellar rocket. Sort of a variation on a Bussard ramscoop. The designers decided on that because no one yet knew how to build a warp engine... those were still many years away from being built or perfected... and starbridges were only a vague possibility." An ironic chuckle. "You know what's funny? Of all the possible propulsion systems discussed during that conference, Bussard rams were not among them. I don't know why, but..." He shrugged.

"Then my great-great-grandfather didn't contribute anything." Karen's voice echoed her disappointment. Another story about her family debunked. All of a sudden, she wondered if Gran'pa had been little more than a free-loader who'd managed to get aboard the *Alabama* simply out of blind luck.

"I wouldn't say that." Arturo shook his head. "Warp drive was eventually developed, wasn't it? Maybe it wasn't used by the *Alabama*, but the sub-sequent ships sent by the Western Hemisphere Union used that technology."

"The Millis-Clement Drive, sure. But my great-great-grandfather..."

"Might have had something to do with it. Who knows? I'd be willing to bet that, if you were to investigate the history of its research and development, you'd find citations to theoretical work by Dr. Frank

O'Connell. And even if not… well, consider him one of the cathedral's anonymous bricklayers."

She looked at him askance. "Come again?"

"Think about what he said, when he compared building a starship to building a cathedral." Pushing aside the sheets, Arturo swung his legs over the side of the bed. "The cathedrals of Earth… the ones built in Europe during the Renaissance, I mean… were the result of generations of labor. Those who built them had to work with the available technology of their time, which was not much more advanced than bricks and mortar, ropes and pulleys. So the ones who started work on cathedrals like Notre Dame knew that their work probably wouldn't be finished in their own lifetimes, but probably by their children or grandchildren. And they were content with that."

"You think so?" Karen couldn't help but watch Arturo as he rose from bed. She enjoyed seeing him nude. "I mean, to spend your life working on something, knowing that you won't benefit from it yourself…"

"I don't know about you, but I think it would give my life purpose. I think that's what people like your ancestor were doing when they went to that conference… starting something which they intended to be finished by their children or grandchildren, if not themselves. Like a cathedral."

"You make it sound almost religious."

"Faith doesn't need religion. Just the ability to believe in something greater than yourself." Arturo stood up, started to head for the bathroom. "Does that make sense to you?"

"Umm-hmm." She couldn't take her gaze off his buttocks. "It does, I suppose."

"Good." He glanced back at her, then paused in mid-step. "But I think we were talking about something else before then. Family resemblances? Expanding the gene pool? That sort of thing?"

She felt a smile coming to her face. "Yes, we could have been."

Arturo turned around to walk back to her. She stood up from the bed, and he began untying the sash of her robe. "Maybe we ought conduct a little experiment of our own…"

After he finished his talk, Frank was given about five minutes to take questions from the audience. There were only a few, but nonetheless they were worth answering, giving him a chance mostly to explain a few of the more technical aspects of his presentation. Then Jim reminded everyone that they were scheduled for a fifteen-minute break before the next sessions began, and there was a brief smattering of applause before everyone stood up to leave the room.

All the sessions let out at the same time, and the convention center mezzanine was filled with attendees, each with laminated name badges dangling around their necks. Frank took a Coke from one of the beverage carts the Hilton staff positioned in the mezzanine during breaks, and stood off to one side, decompressing from the efforts of the last half-hour.

A knot of people stood in front of the British Interplanetary Society table, examining their exhibit on Project Icarus. Over here, Jill Tartar chatted with people who'd been at her talk. Over there, Douglas Trumbull was deep in conversation with another person. A group of science fiction writers—instantly recognizable as such because nearly all of them had beards and were losing their hair—were clustered together, perhaps discussing what they were managing to learn from these sessions that they would later use in their stories. Frank had just spotted Stewart Brand walking by when the cell phone in his coat pocket purred.

He dug out his Android and glanced at the screen: L. Cho 415-555-0994. Smiling, he ran his finger down the screen, then held the phone to his ear. "Hello, Lisa," he said, raising his voice a little so he could be heard above the crowd around him.

"Hi, Dad. How's the conference going?"

"Pretty well. I just finished my presentation a few minutes ago."

"Great! How did it go?"

"Umm… not bad. Could have used a few more people in the room, but there's a lot going on here, so I had a lot of competition."

"I'm sure they were all there for you."

Frank grinned. That was his daughter: always trying to be optimistic. "Yeah, well… how's things with you this weekend?"

"Good. Kim went off to the gym, so I'm taking care of David this morning. We're going to the zoo in a little while."

"Sounds like fun." It had taken Frank a few years to get used to the fact that his daughter had married an artist from South Korea, but Kim Cho seemed like a nice enough fellow. He spent a lot of time working out at the Y, though. "I'm sure Davy will like the zoo."

"Yeah." A sigh of motherly exasperation. *"I'm know he will… he insists on going at least once a month."*

"Maybe he needs to expand his interests. Couldn't you take him to the science museum instead?"

"He's four, Dad… give him time. Anyway, when are you flying back tomorrow? Kim and I were thinking about picking you up at the airport, then going out for dinner after that."

"That would be great. I'd like that." Frank rubbed his forehead, trying to remember his flight schedule. "Umm… I think I get in around 4:30 P.M. your time. Is that too early for you?"

"Not at all. Once we get through traffic, it'll be about time to eat."

"All right, then. If you'll pick me up outside the United baggage claim area, we can…"

A child babbled from somewhere in the background. *"Oh, all right,"* Lisa said, voice a little distant, then she returned again. *"David wants to talk to you."*

Frank grinned. "Put him on, by all means."

He heard hands fumbling at a distant cell phone, then a small boy's high-pitched voice. *"Gran'pa!"*

"Hello, David," he said, turning away and placing a hand over his left ear so that he could hear better. "How are you?"

An uncertain pause. *"Fine."*

"Good, that's good. I hear you're going to the zoo today."

Another pause. *"Yeah."*

"Oh, that's good. I'm sure you'll enjoy that. Do you know where I am?"

A couple of seconds passed. *"No."*

"I'm in Florida, talking about starships."

For a second or two, he was unsure whether David had heard him. Then his grandson piped up again. *"What's a starship?"*

Frank smiled. "Well, then… I suppose I'll have a lot to tell you when I see you tomorrow."

There's already a foreword to this story, but like the story itself, it becomes counterfactual about halfway through; that is, while based on true facts, it is untrue. Some might call this alternative history, but I don't think that really describes what's going on here: in this instance, I decided to play with the reader's head by telling a story which isn't entirely a work of fiction.

I am a great fan of pulp fiction of the 1930s and 1940s. It's my opinion that the pulp era was one of the great periods of American literature. Although it's usually ignored or dismissed by academia, it can't be denied that some of the best American writers of the 20th Century—from Dashiell Hammett and Raymond Chandler to H.P. Lovecraft and Ray Bradbury, among many others—made their first appearances in ten-cent magazines with covers that were lurid beyond belief and back-page ads for rupture belts. So this story is a tribute to the pulp writers of the 1930s, and the people who published them.

THE JEKYLL ISLAND HORROR

Foreword

The following story is not my own but someone else's, one which was passed to me under unusual circumstances.

In March, 2008, my wife and I drove to Jekyll Island, Georgia, to attend my niece's wedding. One of the "Golden Isles" on the Atlantic Coast just north of the Florida state line, it's also—among other things—a wildlife sanctuary. My niece is an avid birdwatcher, so she'd been there many times, and for that reason she'd decided to be married in this place. I was looking forward to a family reunion and also a break from last days of a hard New England winter, but anticipated nothing else.

Because the bridegroom wanted to have a traditional Jewish wedding, the ceremony was scheduled to begin at sundown Saturday evening. That gave my wife and me plenty of time to wander around. I'd visited Jekyll Island several years earlier, when I was a guest author at a science fiction convention held at one of the island's seaside resort hotels, and thus was already familiar with the place and its history. Linda had never been there before, though, so we spent the morning exploring the historic district on the mainland side, where the State of Georgia had preserved the "cottages"—small mansions, really—built at the turn of the last century by the millionaires who'd once claimed the island as their winter retreat.

These second-homes lay inside a fenced-in compound that surrounded the sprawling manse of the Jekyll Island Club. In its heyday, the Jekyll Island Club had been one of the most exclusive in America, its roster limited to one hundred members and including such notables as John Pierpont Morgan, William Rockefeller, Marshall Field, Joseph Pulitzer, William Vanderbilt, and Cyrus McCormick, Jr. Their cottages, usually echoing the Victorian architecture of the clubhouse but sometimes also modeled after Swiss chateaus and Spanish haciendas, line the white gravel footpaths that wind through the surrounding pine groves. The club had its own indoor and outdoor tennis courts, swimming pool, eighteen-hole golf course, and other luxuries, and the compound's isolation was assured by the lack of permanent residences elsewhere on the island. Most of Jekyll Island was uninhabited when it had been the preserve of the wealthy and powerful, and because the first bridge to the mainland wasn't built until the mid-twentieth century, the only way to get there was aboard a small private steamer from Brunswick, where the winter residents would arrive by train at the beginning of the season.

After walking around the compound for awhile, Linda and I paid a visit to the island's only bookstore, located in what had once been the club's private infirmary. As usual, I checked to see if any of my novels were there, and was pleasantly surprised to find a couple of them on the shelves. Since I'm in the habit of signing my books when I'm on the road, I took them to the front counter, where I introduced myself to the proprietor.

This turned out to be a gentleman in his late sixties, George Hess. He was only too happy to let a visiting author autograph his books, and as I did so, Mr. Hess and I got to talking. He told me that he'd been born and raised on the island, and that his late father—who'd also written a few SF stories himself, during the pulp era—had once been the valet of a New York magazine publisher who'd joined the Jekyll Island Club in the early 1930s. His father remained on Jekyll Island after the club closed down during World War II, where he married a former servant who'd once worked at the club.

Our conversation then took an interesting turn. Mr. Hess asked if I thought there was intelligent life beyond Earth. As a science fiction writer, this is a question I've heard more times than I like to remember. Suppressing a sigh, I responded that, yes, I considered this to be a very strong possibility, and indeed would be surprised if there were no other races inhabiting our galaxy. But when he asked if I thought aliens had ever visited Earth, I shook my head. No, I replied, I rather doubt that; UFOs are little more than modern myths, if not outright hoaxes, and theories of so-called "ancient astronauts" are usually misinterpretations of legends and archeological artifacts. In any case, there is no indisputable proof that extraterrestrials have been to our world, now or in the past.

Mr. Hess politely heard me out, but I couldn't help but notice his wry smile. What sort of evidence would you need to make you change your mind? *he asked.* It would have to be pretty strong, *I said.* Stronger than anything I've seen so far, at least.

By then, Linda had returned to the counter with a biography she'd heard about. While I bought it for her, we briefly discussed where to have lunch. Mr. Hess recommended the Jekyll Island Club; now a resort hotel, its restaurant was open to the public, and he said that we'd probably enjoy the menu. Linda and I decided that this would be our next stop, so we left the bookstore and walked across the compound to the hotel, where we got a table on its courtyard terrace.

We were just finishing our Cobb salads when our waiter came to the table and asked if I happened to be Mr. Steele. Since my family didn't know exactly where Linda and I were, my first thought was that there had been some sort of emergency and that they were desperately trying to find me. But then he produced a thick manila envelope and explained that it had been dropped off at the club's front desk, with instructions that it be delivered to me. The waiter didn't know where it had come from or who had brought it to the restaurant; there was no name on the envelope, or any clue as to its origin.

Opening the envelope, I discovered a typewritten manuscript, its ink fading on paper already yellow with age. There was a breeze upon the terrace, so I didn't examine it then and there, but instead took it back to my hotel, where I read it that afternoon before getting dressed for the wedding. Because Linda and I had to leave early Sunday morning to begin the two-day drive back to Massachusetts, I didn't get a chance to return the manuscript to the bookstore, where I have little doubt it came from. I suspect, though, that Mr. Hess didn't want to get it back. Apparently he'd waited a long time for someone like me to come along, and the fact that subsequent attempts to contact him have been met with silence reinforces my opinion that he wishes to have this document made public.

I've inserted footnotes for the sake of clarity, but have otherwise left the manuscript unedited. I don't know whether to believe this story; that, I'll leave to the reader.—AMS

I. The Millionaire

My name is Solomon Hess, and I was once the personal valet of William Apollo Russell. It was in this capacity that I witnessed the terrifying events of March, 1934, on Jekyll Island, Georgia, which have never been made public... until now, by my own hand.

As I write, twenty years later,[9] few people remember my former employer. His name has been largely forgotten, save by historians of American popular culture. In his day, though, William A. Russell was one of the most successful New York magazine publishers. Apollo Publications, Inc., which he established in 1919 upon the foundation of his late father's printing business, produced more than a dozen magazines every month. Although a few were respectable periodicals like *The American Liberty* and *Apollo Monthly*, most of them were cheap fiction magazines that catered to the masses: *Private Eye Mystery*, *Fascinating Science-Fiction*, *New York Romance*, *Silver Star Western*, and its bestselling title, *The Gang Buster*.[10]

It was from these "dime novels" that William A. Russell had become a wealthy man. In his late-thirties, trim and athletic, with a high forehead beneath jet-black hair, he was a fixture of Manhattan high society, regularly seen in its more exclusive clubs and bistros. His residence was a townhouse just off Gramercy Park, where he regularly entertained the rich and influential, and among his possessions were a private Pullman

---

9. The manuscript wasn't dated, but judging from this remark, I believe that it was written in 1954.

10. During the 1930s, Apollo Publications was the second-largest publisher of pulp fiction, rivaled only by Street & Smith.

sleeper car for when he travelled by rail to his 1,500-acre horse farm in the Berkshires. His financial assets were nearly bottomless, or so it seemed to anyone who knew him.

Yet William Russell was not without liabilities. His wife, Edith Russell, was a heavy drinker, and she wasn't entirely faithful to her husband. She was often spotted in various "speak-easies" on the lower East Side, usually in the company of younger men of less than sterling reputation, and Mr. Russell spent considerable time and money keeping her name out of the gossip columns. It was rumored that he hadn't gained his fortune entirely from the magazine business, but rather that he'd made an arrangement with a certain crime syndicate to allow them to smuggle liquor into the country inside rolls of paper trucked in from Canada. Indeed, one of the reasons why Apollo Publications produced so many titles was to deter suspicion from the vast amounts of pulp-stock it brought in from north of the border. Furthermore, it was also the subject of hearsay that William Apollo Russell wasn't the name on his birth certificate, but instead one that he'd adopted in order to conceal his Jewish ancestry, which he apparently considered to an impediment to acceptance within certain New York social circles.[11]

But perhaps my employer's worst problem was money: namely, how to keep it. Almost no one knew it at the time but, contrary to appearances, by the winter of 1933 Mr. Russell's financial situation had become rather precarious. He had invested heavily in the stock market, and while the crash of 1929 wasn't quite the disaster to him as it had been to others, nevertheless he'd lost a considerable amount of money. Since the repeal of the Eighteenth Amendment also caused the loss of his Prohibition-era income, that meant his fortune had come to rely solely upon his magazine empire. And Mrs. Russell's lifestyle was costly to maintain, although it could hardly be said that Mr. Russell was frugal himself.

I was aware of all these things because of my close proximity to him. Someone such as William A. Russell may be able to conceal the truth from friends, business associates, and even the IRS or the FBI, but there's little that he can hide from his "gentleman's gentleman." And while I

---

11. This is true. According to Arthur Thomas's biography of William Apollo Russell, *American Pulp* (Prentice-Hall, 1983), he legally changed his name from Werner Aaron Rabinowitz in 1919, shortly after his father's death.

can't consider myself to have been his confidante, there wasn't much in his household that I didn't see.

How I came to be Mr. Russell's valet is worth noting. It wasn't my intent to be hired as such when I first visited the midtown offices of Apollo Publications in the summer of 1931. I was eighteen years old then, a recent graduate of DeWitt Clinton High in the Bronx, and it was my life's dream to become a writer. My family couldn't afford to send me to college, though, so I couldn't afford the benefits of a higher education. Thus I hoped to land a job at Apollo Publications, perhaps as an editorial assistant, and eventually work my way into the position of being a staff writer for *The American Liberty*.

A letter of introduction from my high school principal, a hand-me-down suit from an older cousin, and stack of clips from the school's literary magazine managed to get me an interview with William A. Russell. He greeted me cordially enough, but gave my stories and poems from *The Magpie* only a brief perusal before informing me that his company had no job openings, not even in the mail room. However, he himself needed someone: a personal valet, a manservant who would lay out his clothes, remind him of appointments and social engagements, greet dinner guests at the door, bring him a cup of hot chocolate at bedtime, and all the other things for which a busy person needed assistance. I seemed to be a bright and eager young lad: would I be willing to take this job?

It wasn't what I was expecting, to be sure, but I immediately accepted the offer. My father was a tailor, so making sure that a man's clothes fit him well wasn't beyond me. The salary was generous, and since the job also included room and board in his Gramercy Park townhouse, I was intrigued by the prospect of rubbing elbows with New York's social elite. And I had my own private agenda as well. I believed, perhaps naively, that if I did well for Mr. Russell, he might be impressed enough by my performance to reward me with that position at *The American Liberty* I so dearly wanted.

In hindsight, though, I believe the real reason why Mr. Russell hired me to be his valet had less to do with what I could do than with who I was. If he was, indeed, a Jew himself, then my background mirrored his own. Although one might suspect that he was fulfilling some unconscious desire to have a young Jewish kid from the Bronx whom he could boss around, I rather believe that he simply wanted to give me a leg up in the world. Mr. Russell could be arrogant on occasion, but he was never capricious or unkind, or at least not to me. At the very least, he treated me with far more respect than Mrs. Russell, whom he'd come to regard as little more than a hopeless drunk.

Indeed, I think her "delicate condition" was the reason why Mr. Russell joined the Jekyll Island Club. Climbing the social ladder was not something he had to worry about; he'd already been accepted into New York high society, and regularly saw many of the club's members in the salons and grilles of Manhattan. Instead, I believe that he simply wanted to get away from her. By then, he and Mrs. Russell were married in name only; they no longer slept in the same room, let alone the same bed, and it was only the likelihood of a costly and very public divorce that prevented him from throwing her out of the house. But Mrs. Russell hated to travel—unless it was to Paris, where she'd spend her days buying expensive outfits that she'd wear only once, and her nights at the cabaret —and she was horrified by the prospect of wintering on some mosquito-infested island. Which suited my employer just fine; he'd go down south to Jekyll Island, while she… well, Mrs. Russell didn't know it at the time, but her husband had plans for her.

During the 1920s, the Jekyll Island Club was still exclusive enough that it would have never admitted William A. Russell as a full member. By 1933, though, the situation had changed; most of its founding members had either died or were too old to travel, and the Depression had taken its toll on the fortunes of others, causing many to resign. So when its Board of Directors quietly announced that it would begin accepting applications for "associate memberships"—that is, people of wealth and means who were not necessarily among the hundred richest men in America—my employer leaped at the chance.

There was no question as to whether his application would be accepted. But just as he thought he'd have to settle for a clubhouse apartment, he chanced upon an opportunity that he couldn't ignore. Riverside, the waterfront cottage that had been the winter home of Manhattan bank magnate Eliot Sloan, came up for sale following his death earlier that year. His family no longer wanted his place on Jekyll Island, and although the asking price of $180,000 was a severe pinch on Mr. Russell's finances, he dug deep into his bank account and bought the house virtually sight-unseen. Next to that, his membership dues of $700 was little more than pocket change.

So while Mrs. Russell was sent off to Connecticut for a winter vacation,[12] Mr. Russell and I packed up his wardrobe and boarded his private coach for the long train ride to Brunswick. I was his only servant to go with him; the rest stayed behind in New York. We arrived in the first week of January, 1934, where we boarded the club's private launch, the *Sylvia*, for the final leg of our journey, a quick trip across St. Simons Sound and down the Jekyll River to the club's boat dock. A Ford flat-bed truck was waiting for us there —one of very few automobiles on the island—and its colored driver loaded our trunks and suitcases before carrying us the short distance to Riverside.

II. The Compound

As it turned out, Mr. Russell had gotten a bargain for his money. The cottage was built in the Cape Cod style, white-painted and quite handsome, with bay windows, an enclosed wrap-around porch, and a third-floor widow's walk. There was a lovely old willow tree in the front yard, its limbs draped with Spanish moss, and from the living room windows we could see the Jekyll River just a couple of hundred yards away. The house had come completely furnished, and although most of the couches, chairs, and tables were unfashionably Victorian, Mr. Russell was charmed by their quaint luxury. However, upon visiting the kitchen, he made a point of reminding me to acquire the new Sears catalog: the fixtures were embarrassingly out-of-date, including an old-fashioned ice box instead of a modern refrigerator.

Once he settled in, though, it wasn't long before Mr. Russell became a fixture of the Jekyll Island social scene. He kept up with his business by mail and telephone; his mornings were usually spent in long-distance conversations with his associate publisher and various editors,[13] and every

---

12. Hess is being discrete here, but Russell's biography tells the whole story. In December, 1933, a New York judge ordered Edith Russell to six months in a Connecticut sanitarium, where she underwent treatment for alcoholism and nymphomania. This court-mandated stay, of course, was arranged by her husband.

13. The Jekyll Island Club participated in the first transcontinental "party line" phone conversation, in a ceremony held on January 15, 1915, that included President Woodrow Wilson phoning in from the White House, Alexander Graham Bell calling from New York, his assistant Thomas Watson talking in San Francisco, and William Rockefeller speaking to everyone from the clubhouse.

day I'd visit the island post office, sending letters to New York and picking up the same in return. Mr. Russell would knock off work around noon, at which time he'd leave me with the household chores and walk up the road to the clubhouse for lunch. His afternoons were devoted to one of any number of activities. When the weather was fair, he'd join a foursome on the club golf course, located a short distance inland from the compound. When it rained, he'd play tennis in the indoor courts or find partners for a few hands of bridge in the recreation center. Once the weather grew warm enough, he swam laps in the club pool; although he wasn't a hunter, a couple of times he joined a party that would venture into the wooded marshlands in search of deer, quail, or even the occasional alligator unfortunate enough to be in the wrong place at the wrong time.

Late in the day, Mr. Russell would return to Riverside. A brief nap, then I'd help him into his tails for dinner at the club (white-tie was always required in the main dining room). Once there, he'd take a seat at his assigned table with other associate members, where they would dine on oysters, sea turtle soup, venison, grilled steak, and fresh greens from the club's vegetable garden, to be followed by brandy and cigars in the drawing room. Once or twice a week, he would have dinner at the cottage; he'd hired a couple of part-time cooks from the club's staff, a young Negro by the name of Robert and his wife Lilly, both of whom were wizards in the kitchen, and he'd invite over a few friends for an informal get-together.

For the most part, though, once he returned from the club, it was to spend a quiet evening at the cottage: smoking, reading, listening to the radio. By then, I had finished my chores for the day, and would use the time to pursue my own interests—that is, writing short stories on the Remington portable typewriter Mr. Russell had recently given me as a holiday present. Over the course of the last three years, I'd gradually come to realize that my prospects of joining *The American Liberty*'s editorial staff were slim or none, and that my best chance of "breaking in" was to write stories for his pulps. Besides, I'd lately come to enjoy reading and writing science fiction; perhaps I wasn't destined to become the next Robert Benchley, but maybe I could share a contents page with Edward E. Smith or Jack Williamson. So I worked in my little room next to the pantry, sitting on the edge of my bed with my typewriter on a folding table.

I had no intentions of showing my work to my employer—frankly, I was a bit embarrassed by the space adventures I was now writing—but he gradually became interested in what I was doing, and finally asked to see my stories. Mr. Russell was a businessman, but I think that he fancied himself to be an editor as well; although he admitted that he didn't like science fiction very much, and had started *Fascinating* only because "that junk" made money, he read my work and offered critiques that, while not always valuable, nevertheless gave me an insight as to what he wanted from his writers. This continued to give me hope that he'd eventually come around to giving me an editorial job, even though he seemed to be more impressed by my talent at ironing his shirts.

In this way, the winter of 1934 was passed in a state of blissful indolence. Picnics on the beach, tennis matches on the outdoor courts, card games at the club; for the privileged few who made the island their second home, it was easy to pretend that life was free and easy, and forget that men and women were standing in line outside soup kitchens or a fanatical regime had risen to power in Germany. For a few months, Mr. Russell was as happy as I'd ever seen him; sometimes he even spoke of moving to Jekyll Island permanently, even though he knew that the club closed down after Easter, at which time all his friends would return to New York, Chicago, and Boston. But I think that he was relieved to be away from the burdens of both a struggling business and a failing marriage, if only for a short time.

I didn't share any of Mr. Russell's pastimes, of course. Servants weren't allowed in the clubhouse, save for the club's own employees, nor did we have permission to enjoy its facilities. The servants and staff members lived in what was called Red Row, a collection of cabins and boarding houses located in the rear acreage of the compound. Practically a village in itself, it included a one-room school and playground for their children, along with its own general store and laundry. Once I got to know Robert and Lilly a little better, they invited me over to their place for dinner. The club's seasonal employees were a mixed bag of colored people, white Southerners, and working-class Irish from the cities of the North, so the lines of segregation were observed on Red Row, but nonetheless no one made an issue of a white man visiting a Negro home. And I found that they had their own simple pleasures, such as employee picnics during their days off, and it wasn't long before I was invited to join them when Mr. Russell didn't need me.

It was during one of those picnics that I met Elizabeth Marley, an unmarried young woman whose family had escaped the Kansas dustbowl to resettle in Georgia. Elizabeth—or Betty, as she preferred to be called—worked as a housekeeper at the club, and lived by herself in the women's dormitory. She was very shy about me at first, until I let her know that I had harbored no dishonorable intentions, and she was the most beautiful girl I'd ever met. It wasn't long before I fell in love with her.

In that, I was more fortunate than Mr. Russell. From time to time, while on one errand or another that would take me through the clubhouse grounds, I'd spot him in the company of women. There were a few single ladies among the members of the Jekyll Island Club, most of them the elder daughters of wealthy families but also the occasional gay divorcee, and Mr. Russell saw them regularly on the tennis courts or at the poolside. Yet he was all too aware of the fact that he couldn't pursue any of them seriously, or even indulge in a furtive affair. Many of the club members were from the same social circles as the ones he belonged to in New York, and gossip travels as fast as a telegram among such people. If it became known that William A. Russell was courting another woman, it would only be a matter of time before the news reached his estranged wife. Mrs. Russell may have been a drunk, but she knew a few prominent lawyers, and the inevitable divorce would deprive him of what remained of his fortune. So however much Mr. Russell might have liked otherwise, I can attest that he always went to bed alone, and never spent a night away from Riverside.

So he and I spent our winter months on Jekyll Island in a relaxed sort of way, far from the cold streets of New York. And our sabbatical may have ended as little more than a memorable vacation were it not for the strange occurrences of one Saturday night in last weekend of March, and the horror that soon followed.

III. The Mystery

I was walking back to the cottage from Red Row when it happened. It was a warm evening, and Mr. Russell had let me off work early so that I could have dinner with Betty at her dorm. We'd sat out on one of the picnic tables for a little while afterward, but since she had to get up early the next morning for her job at the club, I'd kissed her goodnight before heading back to Riverside. So I was outside, and thus saw the whole thing.

An abrupt boom from somewhere high above caused me to stop and look up. My first thought was that it was thunder, yet the sky was clear, with no signs of an approaching storm. As it so happened, I was on one of the footpaths between the cottages, out from beneath the trees that would have otherwise interfered with my view, and thus I was able to see the fireball that raced across the starlit sky.

I'd seen meteors before, of course, on those rare times when my family escaped from the city for a weekend in the Catskills, yet what I saw was nothing like that. Larger and brighter than any falling star, it raced westward across the heavens. In less time than it takes to tell, the object vanished behind the trees… and yet, in the instant before I lost sight of it, I had the distinct impression that it slowed down, almost as if it was somehow braking its descent.

From somewhere nearby, I heard voices raised in astonishment. I'd barely realized that I wasn't the only person to witness this phenomenon when, in the far distance, another sound reached my ears: a second boom, not as loud as the first but nevertheless quite audible, as if something had impacted the Atlantic Ocean on the other side of the island. Then nothing, save for a soft, warm rush of air that stirred the tree limbs, as if the object had caused a strange wind to fall across the island.

Again, I heard voices. Looking down, I noticed for the first time a number of people standing in the gardens of the nearby Crane Cottage. Apparently the incident had drawn the attention of those attending an outdoor party. Against the cottage's lighted windows, I saw several silhouetted figures gazing up in amazement, with some pointing to the sky.

Yet I thought little of what I'd seen, other than to consider myself lucky to have spotted a larger-than-normal meteorite on its way to the earth. I made a wish—that Betty and I would somehow stay together, as I recall—then continued my walk back to Riverside. At least I'd have a story to tell Mr. Russell when I saw him again in a few minutes.

Once I reached the cottage, though, I found that my employer wasn't around. His hat and coat were missing from the rack by the front door, so I figured that he must have stepped out for the evening. Perhaps he was at the party I'd seen. So I puttered around in the kitchen for a few minutes, straightening up a bit, then fetched a bottle of beer from the brand-new refrigerator and took it to my room. The night was still young, and I decided to write a couple of pages before Mr. Russell came home, when he'd want his customary hot chocolate before bedtime.

Yet I'd barely written more than a few paragraphs when I heard the front door bang open, and a moment later Mr. Russell rushed into my room. Wild-eyed and out of breath, it appeared as if he'd run all the way back to the cottage.

"My God, Sol," he exclaimed, "did you see that?"

I didn't need to ask what he meant. "I certainly did, sir," I said, calmly smiling at him from behind the typewriter. "Wasn't that a hoot?"

"A hoot?" He regarded me with astonishment, as if I'd just witnessed a herd of wild elephants stampeding down Fifth Avenue and could only say, *Well, isn't that a stitch?* "Is that all you…?" Then he shook his head as he cast his eyes around the room. "Never mind. Isn't there a flashlight around here?"

"Yes, sir… in the utility closet." I pushed aside my folding table. "I'll find it for—"

"I'll get it myself." He turned away from me, darting in the direction of the closet where I kept the household tools. "Go upstairs and pull out my outdoor clothes. That includes the swamp boots and my cap. Hurry!"

I'd seldom seen him quite so impatient, not even when running late for some social event. And never before had he ever rushed out at this late hour, save perhaps the time Mrs. Russell had been found by the New York police sitting astride one of the Public Library lions with a bottle of Scotch in hand. But it wasn't my place to ask why, though, only to do what I was told. So while he turned the utility closet upside-down searching for the flashlight, I went up to his bedroom and laid out the canvas trousers, denim shirt, waterproof knee boots, and fisherman's cap that he wore when he went hunting. I'd scarcely placed them on the bureau when he jogged up the stairs and, throwing off his evening clothes, put on the outdoor gear as hastily as if the house was on fire.

When he sat down on the bed to pull on his boots, I ventured the obvious question. "Mr. Russell, if I may ask…?"

"It came down on the other side of the island," he snapped. "Of that, we're quite positive. You mean you didn't see… I mean, hear… it?" Before I could respond, he went on. "Renny, Phil, and I are going out there at once. If it's a meteorite and it hit the beach, we may be able to locate it while the tide is still low."

I couldn't help but smile when he said that. Perhaps I hadn't gone to college, but I'd learned enough about meteorites during my high school science classes to know that their chances of finding a newly-fallen space rock were remote at best. Even if the meteorite had hit dry land, and not simply been swallowed up by the ocean, in all likelihood it would be so small as to be indistinguishable from any other random object one might find on a beach.

Yet I didn't say anything. Mr. Russell and his friends—Arleigh Renwick, Philip Sidwell, perhaps a few other club members he'd neglected to mention—were obviously spoiling for an adventure. Over the last few months, they'd whiled away the time with golf games and tennis matches, and perhaps they'd become bored with all that. So here was something new: a late-night sortie to the island's uninhabited Atlantic side, in search of a trophy more exotic than another buck head. Far be it from me to ruin their fun with some inconvenient facts.

An automobile horn honked just outside the cottage. Mr. Russell yanked his left boot the rest of the way on, then snatched up the flashlight and bolted from the room. "No need to wait up for me, Sol!" he yelled over his shoulder as he dashed down the stairs, taking the risers two at a time. "I'll be back late!"

"Very good, sir," I replied, but I don't think he heard me before he charged through the front door. When I went down to close it behind him, I caught a glimpse of the headlights of Mr. Renwick's old Model-T "island car" heading down Riverview Drive.

I went to bed shortly after that, and didn't hear Mr. Russell return. But when I rose early the next morning, I found him in the living room. He'd fallen asleep on a couch, still wearing his clothes; his boots were caked with moist sand, as were the knees of his trousers. He'd apparently been too exhausted to go upstairs to bed, so I lay a blanket across him, then went to the kitchen to make coffee.

He slept through the better part of the morning, and when he finally woke up, he said very little to me, but instead went upstairs to take a bath. I had just made a late breakfast of bacon and eggs when he reappeared. Wearing only his robe, he took a seat at the dining room table and wolfed down his food. He said nothing about where he'd gone or what he'd done. Figuring that he was in one of his moods, I went about my chores without trying to make conversation.

I'd just collected his soiled clothes and was about to add them to the laundry hamper when he stopped me. "Don't bother," he said. "I'll be wearing them again today."

"Very well, sir." I turned to carry them back upstairs, then my curiosity got the better of me. "Did you find the meteorite you were searching for?"

Mr. Russell said nothing for a moment. "Sol… how well can I trust you?"

That stopped me. This was something he'd never asked before, perhaps because he'd never had reason to question my loyalty. In the four years that I'd lived and worked in his household, I'd become privy to most of his secrets: his underworld connections, his wife's bad behavior, the rocky state of his finances, even the rumor that he was actually a Jew. But I'd never revealed anything that I'd learned about his private life, and there was an unspoken agreement among us that I never would. So it was odd—and, yes, a bit of an insult—that, after all this time, he'd actually come right out and ask whether he could trust me.

"Explicitly, Mr. Russell," I replied, looking him straight in the eye. "You should know that by now."

He slowly nodded, apparently satisfied by my reply. "I thought so," he said. "I think…" Another pause, as if he had some final reluctance that he needed to overcome. "I think I need your assistance," he went on. "A matter of a rather… well, unusual nature."

My curiosity became greater. "The meteorite, sir?"

The slightest of smiles. "There was no meteorite. We found something else entirely. I'm going back there today, and I'd like you to come with me. I think you may… ah, be able to offer certain insights as to what we've discovered."

He wouldn't tell me more, though, but instead asked me to put his outdoor clothes back where I'd found them, and instructed me to dress in the same fashion. So I returned his clothes to his room, then went to put on the clothes I usually wore for cutting the grass or trimming the hedges. I'd just put together a picnic lunch when he came back downstairs, again dressed the same way as he had been before. As an afterthought, he added a notebook and a couple of pencils to my picnic basket, and then we left the cottage.

I'd assumed that Mr. Renwick would be picking us up in his car, so I was surprised when we set out on foot instead. An unpaved automobile road led across Jekyll Island to the Atlantic side, but once we reached the golf course, we left the road and cut across the fairways. At one point, we spotted a couple of club members on the ninth hole green; although Mr. Russell recognized them, he quietly insisted that we cut through the woods to avoid being seen. I followed him through the thickets until we reached a bridal path that eventually brought us to the dirt road that ran parallel to the beach.

Noticing fresh tire tracks, I figured that this was the way Mr. Renwick had driven the night before. But Mr. Russell didn't say anything about this as we followed the road for a couple of miles, heading toward the island's remote southern tip. We'd almost reached Jekyll Point when the tire tracks abruptly left the road, leading into the scrub-covered dunes that bordered the beach. We followed the tracks, and fifty feet from the road came upon two automobiles—Mr. Renwick's Model T and a Chrysler roadster I recognized as belonging to Cecil Hadley—hidden behind a dense wall of brush.

"Damn," Mr. Russell murmured upon seeing them. "The others are already here." He turned to me. "Remember, Sol… no matter what the others may say, you're with me. You're here as a consultant, not as my valet. Understand?"

Mystified, I nodded. "Understood, sir."

He hesitated. "And one more thing… what you're about to see is a secret of the highest order. You're to never, ever, speak or write about this without my express permission. Can I count on you to be quiet about this?"

"Yes, sir, you can."

He must have noticed the nervous tremor in my voice, for a smile crossed his face. "If this works out, your silence will be amply rewarded." I nodded again, and he gave me what was meant to be a reassuring pat on the shoulder. "Very well, then… come with me."

IV. The Horror

Following the footprints left behind by the others, we made our way through the dunes until we came to the beach. About sixty yards away, several men had gathered around a enormous object that lay at the water's edge. Dark gray, about seventy feet in length, it rested upon the white sand like some giant mollusk that had been washed ashore by the morning tide.

My first thought was that it was a beached whale, but as we came closer, I saw that it wasn't that at all.

It was a creature, all right, but unlike any that I'd ever seen before. Lying prone on the beach, with its head and forequarters upon the sand and its feet and tail in the surf, it resembled some prehistoric beast that had emerged from time's abyss after a long sleep of countless millions of years. Its long arms lay at its sides, exposing long-fingered claws large enough to seize a full-grown man, while its legs were muscular and forward-jointed, obviously capable of standing upright. Rising from the great hump of its back was a serrated dorsal fin that tapered off at its long neck, at the end of which was a triangular, serpent-like skull, with a lipless mouth beneath a blunt snout and small eyes—both closed, thankfully—set deep within a ridged forehead.

In all, the creature looked a bit like a tyrannosaur... and yet, as soon as I saw it, I knew that it hadn't evolved on our world. Perhaps it was only intuition, but I realized that no paleontologist had ever discovered fossil remains of anything like this in the Black Hills of North Dakota. Whatever this thing was, it wasn't from Earth.

The men who'd come here earlier had brought one of the club's picnic tents with them. They had erected it a short distance up the beach from the monster; a couple of lawn chairs were set up within its shade, and it appeared that they'd brought their own wicker basket as well. Someone had even gone to the trouble of collecting driftwood for a small bonfire, although it hadn't been lit yet. A half-dozen club members stood around the creature; dressed in seersucker jackets and straw boating hats, they could have been having a midday clam bake. As Mr. Russell and I approached them, Mr. Sidwell raised his hand in greeting while the others simply stared at us.

"For God's sake, Bill," Mr. Renwick said once we joined them. "Didn't we agree to keep our mouths shut about this?"

He didn't look directly at me as he said this, but I had no doubt that I was the object of his disapproval. The others glared at me; it was obvious that a lowly manservant was the last person they wanted to have join their party.

"Relax, Renny." My employer favored him with an easy-going smile. "Sol has been sworn to secrecy. He has certain expertise in such matters, and I thought it wise to bring him in."

I almost laughed out loud when he said this. My formal education had ended with a high school diploma; I was an expert only in how to knot Mr. Russell's dinner tie. Before I could say anything, though, Mr. Russell put his arm around my shoulder. "Gentlemen," he said, addressing the group as a whole, "if you haven't met him before, this is Mr. Solomon Hess. Sol's presently employed as my valet, yes, but he's also a writer, and I've read enough of his work to know that he's an astute thinker in subjects of a speculative nature."

Which was a roundabout way of saying that I wrote science fiction. Yet it seemed to disarm the men standing before me, because they each stepped forward to shake my hand, albeit reluctantly. I was already familiar with them, of course—Renwick, Sidwell, and Hadley, and also George Collier, Lester Smith, and Byron DuMont—but until then I'd been an invisible man, someone beneath their notice. Yet if Mr. Russell was willing to vouch for me, then they had little choice but to acknowledge my presence.

"Well then, Sol," Mr. Hadley said, once the introductions were made, "perhaps you can shed some light on our little mystery."

His words were pleasant enough, but he was obviously testing his friend's claim that I was some sort of great scientific thinker. From the corner of my eye, I could see Mr. Russell watching me expectantly, perhaps hoping that I wouldn't embarrass him in front of his friends. *I don't know what it is either* was the truthful response, but it was also the one that simply wouldn't do.

I didn't respond at once, but instead approached the creature. It lay inert upon the beach, with no visible movement whatsoever, yet as I came closer, I noticed something peculiar. Although seagulls and terns wheeled about it, squawking as they pirouetted overhead, never once did they alight upon its head or back.

"You found it last night?" I asked.

"Just as you see it." Mr. Russell stepped away from his friends to join me. "We thought at first it may have been a meteorite, but when we got close to it…" He grinned. "Well, it's no meteorite, that much is certain."

"And it hasn't moved since then… um, sir?"

A couple of smiles from Mr. Collier and Mr. Hadley; they hadn't missed the deferential way in which I'd addressed Mr. Russell. "No, not at all," he said. "Don't worry. It's quite plainly dead."

I looked up at the circling birds. "I don't think so. If it were, then the gulls would be all over it."

No one said anything, but I couldn't help but notice that a few of the men took a nervous step back. Mr. Hadley remained skeptical. "I don't care what it looks like," he said. "It's not an animal, either dead or alive. See for yourself... place your hand on it."

I was reluctant to do so. If this thing had come from outer space, then there was a chance that it might be radioactive. But there was no Geiger counter available, and I was being put on the spot, so I had little choice but to walk up to the creature and gently lay my palm against its side. I was surprised to find not the warm flesh of a mammal, or even the cool skin of a reptile, but instead a cold surface that was flexible yet nonetheless vaguely metallic. And when I peered more closely at the creature, I noticed what appeared to be seams between its shoulder and biceps, and also at its elbow; the same for its lower neck, and also the hinge of its jaw.

At the time, I hadn't yet encountered industrial-grade plastics; in hindsight, that may have been what it was made of. The fact that the thing had distinct junctures at its joints hinted that it was not organic in nature. And yet, as my hand lay upon its side, I felt a faint, almost rhythmic vibration from deep within its body, much that which I would expect from a slumbering animal. Despite what Mr. Hadley said, I had the distinct impression that this was a living machine.[14]

"Well?" Mr. Russell stood behind me, awaiting my verdict. "What do you think, Sol?"

I stepped away from the creature. "I'm not sure, but this may be some sort of robot." Noticing his uncomprehending expression, I tried to explain what I meant. "An automaton, that is... a device deliberately built to resemble a living creature."

"Really?" Mr. Hadley remained skeptical. "If so, who the devil would build such a thing? Not only that, but where did it come from?"

"The Germans, most likely." This from Mr. Smith, who stood near the creature's snout, examining its closed eyes. "Probably brought here by submarine, and left to baffle whoever found it."

---

14. It appears Hess was trying to describe a biomechanism, but lacked the modern-day terminology for it.

A derisive snort from Mr. DuMont. "Oh, come now, Lester… you think the krauts are behind everything."

"I have to agree," I said quietly. "I don't believe this is from Germany… or anywhere else on Earth, for that matter."

They fell silent, each of them staring at me in astonishment. Judging from their expressions, I realized that what I'd said was beyond the reach of their imaginations. These men perceived the world in ordinary terms; for them, there was little that couldn't be explained by actuarial charts or departmental reports or the *Wall Street Journal*. They'd never been called upon to see past the here-and-now, save perhaps next-quarter projections. And here I was, asking them to consider the possibility of life beyond our world.

"Poppycock," Mr. Smith said at last. "This is nothing but an elaborate hoax."

Mr. Russell cleared his throat. "Gentlemen, you're looking at this entirely the wrong way. It doesn't matter where this thing came from, really… only that it's here, and that it presents an opportunity that we'd be foolish to miss."

"Hear, hear!" Mr. Renwick stepped to Mr. Russell's side. "Listen to what he has to say. I think he's onto something." He clapped a hand on his friend's shoulder. "Go on, Bill."

"As I was saying, we've found something here that could be quite profitable, if handled correctly." Speaking to the others as if they were seated in a corporate boardroom, Mr. Russell clasped his hands together as he stood before the creature. "Since this object washed upon our island, it rightfully belongs to us…"

"The state of Georgia might argue with that," Mr. Collier murmured.

"And my attorneys might argue with the state of Georgia," Mr. Russell replied, and this earned smug laughter from the others. "Be that as it may, once we arrange for its transportation, I believe that we could exhibit it commercially. Perhaps license it to someone in the entertainment business."

"The Barnum circus!" Mr. DuMont exclaimed.

"Perhaps." Mr. Russell nodded his head. "Or maybe someone in Hollywood would be better suited. Whatever the venue may be, though, I propose that the seven of us form a partnership to exploit this to our best advantage. My magazines would be the logical starting point, of course, but there's also potential for radio and motion pictures, not to mention…"

As he spoke, understanding slowly dawned upon the faces of the other men. They might not think much of the possibility of extraterrestrial life, but they knew a great deal about money and its acquisition. No doubt they'd all been hurt by the Depression, or that they'd all been searching for new investment ventures. They began to see the scenario that Mr. Russell painted for them: the creature, loaded onto a railroad flatbed car, making a cross-country tour of carnivals and state fairs where curious locals would pay for the privilege of stepping into a circus tent to view the abomination with their own eyes. The tour would be promoted by magazine articles, newsreels, and radio stories, with profits further maximized by the sale of souvenir pamphlets, postcards, and pennants, tin-toy replicas, jig-saw puzzles, or whatever else could be brought to market.

By much the same token, though, I knew at once that proper scientific examination was the farthest thing from anyone's mind. In time, perhaps. researchers would be given a chance to study this mysterious thing. Only if were willing to pay for the privilege, though; these men would be smart enough not to let anyone see it for free.

By the time Mr. Russell was finished, his friends were practically dancing with glee. The creature itself would have to be a closely-guarded secret until everything was in place, of course, but no one was worried about that; it wouldn't be the first time that club concocted a private business deal.[15] The island's ocean side was uninhabited, so the creature could be covered by tarps until the time came for it to be removed by barge and carried to the mainland.

Then Mr. Renwick had a flash of inspiration. Walking over to the tent, he opened the picnic basket he'd brought with him and produced a bottle of Champagne and a Kodak Brownie. After popping the cork and giving the bottle to Mr. Sidwell, he had the others stand in front of the creature; what they needed to commemorate their discovery, he said, was a group photo. The gentlemen were only too happy to comply, but it was Mr. Russell who'd insist on having the most prominent place in the picture. With assistance from Mr. DuMont and Mr. Hadley, he climbed atop the

---

15. A reference to a secret conference held at the Jekyll Island Club in 1910, when a small group of members, along with Rhode Island Senator Nelson Aldrich and several economic experts, met to plan the restructure of the American banking system. The Federal Reserve System was the result of this meeting.

creature's head. Arms crossed, feet planted just above its eyes, his pose was that of a man who'd conquered a monster.

Once everyone was ready, Mr. Renwick handed the camera to me. Its plate was already loaded; all I'd need to do was aim, focus, and press the shutter. It was then that I realized what my role in all this would be. Despite Mr. Russell's promise, I wasn't to be a partner but only a servant, as invisible as always. It wasn't my place to protest, though, so I made sure that the men were properly lined up before I raised the camera and peered through the viewfinder. It was then that I noticed that the creature's eyes were open.

At first, I thought it was only an illusion, an odd reflection caused by sunlight falling on the camera lens. Where there had once been closed eyelids, two oyster-white orbs now stared straight at me, its gaze unnoticed by the men who stood with their backs turned toward the creature.

For a moment, I was too stunned to speak. Yet I'd just looked up from the camera when Mr. Russell suddenly lost his balance. "Good heavens," he exclaimed as he struggled to stay on his feet, "I think this thing just...!"

And then the creature's arms moved from its sides, pulling forward to plant its claws against the sand. Mr. Sidwell turned to see this, and he yelled a warning to the others. An instant later, Mr. Russell toppled from his perch; arms flailing, he fell to the ground, landing on his back.

By now, the rest of the party were aware that the creature was waking up. As it began to rise, they broke ranks and began to run, falling over themselves and each other in their haste to get away. I turned to run as well, but then I looked back and saw that Mr. Russell still lay where he'd fallen. Apparently frozen in terror, he watched with astonishment as the creature slowly pushed itself upward on its arms, its feet and tail emerging from the surf as it started to rise.

I dropped the camera and ran to my employer. From behind me, I heard the loud report of gunshots. Glancing over my shoulder, I saw that Mr. Renwick had pulled a small revolver from his coat pocket and was firing at the thing. If his shots had any effect, though, I didn't stop to see, for in the next second I was at Mr. Russell's side, grabbing him by the lapels and hoisting him to his feet.

Beneath the startled cries of men behind me, I heard a faint, almost mechanical sound: a whirring and clinking, as if servomotors within the creature were putting its armored joints into motion. Looking around, I saw the thing now stood erect; hunched forward, with its long tail raised to counterbalance the rest of its body, it towered above the beach, the blank orbs of its eyes studying the men with malevolent intent.

By then, Mr. Renwick had run out of bullets. Apparently realizing that he hadn't stopped the creature, he dropped the gun and started to back away. But then he noticed the Brownie where I'd dropped it. A moment of hesitation, then he darted for the camera. Perhaps he thought I'd managed to take the picture and wanted to save it. I'll never know the reason for his rash and foolish action, because he'd barely snatched up the camera when the creature lunged forward.

I barely had time to be amazed by how quickly the monster was capable of moving before it hurled itself upon Mr. Renwick. He didn't even have a chance to scream before the creature's clawed right foot came down on him. A sickening crunch, then a gout of blood rushed from his mouth as he was crushed beneath the monster's enormous mass.

The camera had fallen aside, apparently undamaged... and then the creature did something that haunts me to this day. Ignoring Mr. Renwick's corpse, it turned its head to peer at it. A second or two passed, and then it deliberately lifted its right foot again and brought it down on the camera, obliterating it as easily as it had its owner. It was as if the monster knew what it was, and didn't want to leave behind any evidence of its existence.

The rest of the group had taken cover behind the dunes, but they hadn't left the scene entirely; I could hear them shouting to Mr. Russell and me, begging us to run for our lives. But when the creature attacked Mr. Renwick, it put itself between us and the dunes. There was only the ocean behind us now, and I immediately knew that the cold blue waters of the Atlantic wouldn't hide us from the thing's murderous rampage.

As if remembering that two men were still remained on the beach, the creature turned toward Mr. Russell and me. We stood next to each other, transfixed by the monster towering above us. For a timeless moment it stood silent and still, swaying slightly upon its haunches as its awful eyes studied us. I had the impression that it was trying to make up its mind which of us to kill next. If that were so, then only one of us stood even the slightest chance of escape...

Apparently the same thought occurred to Mr. Russell, because in the next second, I felt two strong hands plant themselves against my back and shove me forward.

As I fell to my hands and knees, Mr. Russell sprinted in the opposite direction. Stunned by the realization that he'd betrayed me, I could only watch as he ran down the beach. Yet, even though I was easy prey, the creature regarded me for only a brief second before it turned to race after him.

Hearing the monster's heavy footfalls behind him, Mr. Russell glanced back over his shoulder. Crying out in terror, he started to run faster, and for a second or two I thought he might actually get away. Yet the creature easily caught up with him. Reaching forward with its left arm, it knocked him off his feet with one swipe of its claws, ripping the back of his shirt and sending him sprawling across the sand.

At first, I thought Mr. Russell's back was broken, but then I saw rise to his hands and knees. Although stunned by the blow, he retained enough of his wits to try to crawl away. Yet the creature wasn't about to let him escape. Moving forward to plant its immense feet on either side of him, it bent over him, its mouth agape.

Thinking that he was about to be eaten alive, I screamed in horror. But then something rushed from the creature's jaws: milk-white fluid, thick and almost gelatinous, that completely covered Mr. Russell. He cried out again and tried to rise, but he was totally inundated by the fluid. Sticky tendrils still dangled from the monster's mouth, and as I watched, its jaws expanded the way a Burmese python's does when it's about to swallow its prey.

And then, with a grotesque sucking sound, the creature seemed to inhale the fluid, and as it did so, it pulled Mr. Russell from the ground. He was still alive; I could see him thrashing against the material that had ensnared him. But the fluid was too thick for him to fight against; within seconds, he was pulled into the creature's mouth.

Closing its jaws, it lifted its head and straightened its neck as if to swallow him whole. For a moment, I thought I still heard Mr. Russell, howling like a madman from deep within the monster's gullet, but then this sound was lost to me as creature turned in my direction.

Still on my knees, knowing that any attempt to flee would be futile, I waited for creature to come for me. Yet it only regarded me with what seemed to be indifference before turning away again, this time to stomp back up the beach to where Mr. Renwick lay. Bending over again, it reached down with its left claw to pluck his pulverized corpse from the sand. And then, clutching the limp body against its massive chest, it pivoted on its hind legs and stalked away, heading for the water.

I'll never know why the creature ignored me as it went by. From the dunes, I heard the loud crack of a rifle; I'd later learn that Mr. Hadley had run back to his car to retrieve the hunting rifle he kept in its trunk. If any of his bullets actually hit the creature, though, there was no indication, for the monster paid no further attention to me or anyone else as it marched into the surf. It remained visible for only the few seconds it took for it to reach the deeper waters a dozen yards out, then it abruptly lurched forward and disappeared beneath the waves.

And then it was gone.

V. The Sentinel

As I wrote at the beginning of this account, it's not until now that I've committed my recollections to paper. There's a reason for this: I've been sworn to secrecy, first by the club members who witnessed the events, and later by others.

When it was all over, there was no real evidence that the creature had ever been there; all that it left behind was a destroyed camera, some enormous footprints, and a bloodstained patch of sand. Even before they left the beach, the others came to the conclusion that no one else would ever believe them; the story was just too incredible. Not only that, but they agreed that the consequences of trying to make anyone believe them were potentially devastating. Hadley, Sidwell, DuMont, Collier, and Smith all had much to lose, and they feared the loss of wealth and reputation.

Thus they decided, then and there, to invent a more believable explanation for the disappearances of William Russell and Arleigh Renwick. During a beachside picnic, Mr. Renwick decided to go for a swim, but he went too far out from shore and was caught in a riptide. Mr. Russell swam in to rescue him, but he suffered the same fate as well. Both were swept out to sea, never to be seen again.

I refused to go along with this at first, until I was told, in no uncertain terms, that if I attempted to reveal the truth, the others would disavow me. Furthermore, they would claim that I'd murdered both Mr. Russell and Mr. Renwick, weighting their bodies with heavy rocks and casting them into the ocean, and then come up with this outlandish tale as an attempt to cover my crime. In the end, it would be my word against theirs; if I didn't end up in the electric chair, then I'd spend the rest of my life in an insane asylum.

I had little choice but to go along with them. Truth to be told, I was angered by Mr. Russell's cowardice, at the way he'd been willing to sacrifice my life to save his own. The lie made him seem more heroic than he actually was. On the other hand, the truth was something none of us were ready to admit, even to ourselves. So while I didn't argue very long or hard with Mr. Russell's friends, I privately vowed never to trust any of them again.

As it turned out, they couldn't be trusted even amongst themselves, because one of the five apparently did speak with someone in authority. Only a day after the tragic story of Mr. Russell's and Mr. Renwick's untimely deaths appeared in the newspapers, I was paid a unexpected visit.

I was still on Jekyll Island, packing up Mr. Russell's belongings, when two men appeared at the cottage's front door. Although they wore civilian clothes, they produced credentials identifying themselves as belonging to U.S. Army intelligence, whereupon they let me know that they knew what had really happened two days earlier. They spent the afternoon interviewing me, and once they had my side of the story, they made me an offer that I dared not refuse.

The island has been my home ever since.

The Jekyll Island Club closed during World War II. By then, Betty and I had gotten married, and for a few years we worked as the club's custodians, taking care of its shuttered and unvisited buildings. But the club didn't reopen after the war, and eventually the property was purchased by the state of Georgia, with the nearby cottages either sold or simply abandoned. Indeed, once Mrs. Russell inherited her husband's estate, one of the first things she did was sell Riverside. She retained ownership of her late husband's publishing company, but eventually Apollo Publications went bankrupt, killed by the wartime paper shortage and the changing tastes of the public. The last I heard of her, she was still living off William A. Russell's money, her Gramercy Park townhouse lined with bottles and boys.[16]

_____

16. Edith Russell died in New York in 1959.

I still write on occasion, although my ambitions to become a noted author are a thing of the past. For a time, I contributed stories to a variety of science fiction magazines; all were published under a pseudonym,[17] though, and none allude to that terrible day. This is the first and last time I'll ever write about what I saw. I intend for it to remain locked in my file cabinet until my death, when it'll pass to my heirs. Perhaps then my son George, who is still only a teenager, will decide one day to let it become public. For his own sake, though, I hope that he will wait until such a time comes when he believes disclosure will be in world's best interests.

For the most part, I abide by my agreement with the government. Every month, I receive a generous check from Uncle Sam that allows me to live in reasonable comfort. In return, I keep quiet about what I witnessed. And every day, I visit the ocean, where I look for any indications that the creature may have returned.

I don't know where it came from, or why it was here, or where it has gone. Only William A. Russell ever learned these things. The creature must have had its reasons for taking him, and the possibilities of what they were are what keep me up at night. In my nightmares, I still hear him screaming.

The creature has never returned. Nonetheless, I'm afraid that it may come back one day, and that it may not come alone.

---

17. I've attempted to learn the pseudonym Solomon Hess used, yet this information isn't available in any of the standard literary references.

Another counterfactual tale, this one more far-fetched than the last, but also with a seed of truth at its core. Dr. Goddard's space train is based on two things: the illustration that accompanied the Worcester Gazette *story mentioned herein, and a late 1950's proposal for a lunar lander by astronautical designer Kraft Ericke, who came up with dozens of fascinating spacecraft, although so far as I know none of them actually flew.*

When my friends Tom Easton and Judith Klein-Dial asked me to contribute something to their anthology Impossible Futures, *I knew at once that I had to give them a story about a space train. Here it is… and anyone who tries to nitpick it for "scientific accuracy" needs to get a clue.*

LOCOMOTIVE JOE AND THE WRECK OF SPACE TRAIN No. 4

The space trains are gone now, of course. The wreck of the No. 4 did them in, way back in '39. Since then it's been step-rockets and spaceplanes, which everyone agrees are safer and more reliable, although perhaps not as much fun. But whenever the guys who used to work the trains get together—not so often these days; there's only a few of us left— we talk about the good old days when we'd fly these things to the Moon. And inevitably, we tell the story of Locomotive Joe and how he saved the lives of everyone aboard the *Tycho Express.*

I was a conductor aboard the No. 4, so I was there when it happened. That's important, because the story has been embellished so many times over the years that the truth is now buried beneath the legend. And I knew Joe Welch, of course. His nickname didn't come 'til later, and that's part of the legend, too. Everyone considers him to be a hero, and I suppose he was; who am I to argue? But I can tell you with absolute certainty that courage and bravery were only part of the story. There was something else, too.

Young people today don't know much about the space trains. Those things belonged to their grandparents' and great-grandparents' time, and so what little they've learned about them generally comes from old movies, and sometimes not a lot even then. So I'm going to have to assume that things have to be explained to you if you're younger than… oh, say, 70… and ask that you be patient with an old codger like me.

(It's called knowledge, kids, not infodumps. Explanations used to be respected. Then computers came along and reduced everyone's attention span to that a puppy. Let's see if you're smarter than a eight-month-old terrier with a tennis ball. Sit down and shut up and let an old man talk.)

Anyway... the space trains were the first passenger-carrying spacecraft, the ones built by the Goddard Rocket Company back in the '30s. Almost as soon as Bob Goddard launched his first liquid-fuel contraption from his Aunt Effie's farm in Massachusetts, people started clamoring for rocketships that would carry them into space. When the *Worcester Telegram* published a front page story saying that rockets would be carrying people to the Moon within ten years, Dr. Goddard suddenly began getting offers from investors who wanted to put money into this, and never mind the fact that the *Telegram* story was total horse poop. But ol' Doc knew a good buck when he saw it, so once he patented his work and raised investment capitol from his pals Slim Lindbergh and Harry Guggenheim, he moved from Mass to New Mexico and started the Goddard Rocket Company.

From the get-go, it was Dr. Goddard's idea that a rocket's engine should be placed forward, not aft, of the payload. Cars do it, planes do it; why not spaceships, too? Some people think he got the notion from the illustration that accompanied the Worcester newspaper story, which itself bore a certain similarity to a picture in the original French edition of Jules Verne's *From the Earth to the Moon*. But it doesn't matter. Rocket up front, passenger compartment dragged behind it; that was the way the Lord and Robert Goddard intended.

Further study showed, though, that this design was inadequate for achieving escape velocity. So Doc had to... well, let's say borrow... an idea from the Germans, who were also beginning to do the same sort of thing, and build a big booster rocket that would act as a first stage. The booster wouldn't make the whole trip, of course. It would be ditched as soon as the ship penetrated the atmosphere. But it got the rest of the ship off the ground, and that's what the Goddard Rocket Company ended up building.

No. 1, aka the *Comet*, was launched from Roswell in 1933. It wasn't very large and carried only four people: Doctor G, his wife Esther, Harry Guggenheim, and their pilot, Charlie Lindbergh himself. But it made big screaming headlines after it circled the earth a couple of times and came back safe and sound, and that meant the money started pouring in from those still well-heeled enough after the stock market crash to afford a joy-ride into space. Once they had a few more million dollars to play with, the Goddard Rocket Company scaled-up the *Comet* design and proceeded to build its space trains.

The *Tycho Express* was the fourth one built, and it was a monster: two hundred feet tall on its launch stand, with a massive first-stage booster capable of sending the locomotive and its 22,000-pound Pullman car into orbit. Once the booster was dropped into the Gulf of Mexico, the passenger car would be extended back from the locomotive upon four 1,000-foot tow cables, then the big gasoline and liquid oxygen engine would fire, and the whole thing would be on its way to the Moon. The engine would ignite again every now and then to correct its course, but most of the time the train would coast along on its own momentum, the crew and passengers enjoying zero-gravity weightlessness. About two and a half days later, it would swing around the Moon, letting everyone aboard get a good look at all the green cheese down there—just kidding; they never saw anything except rock and sand—then the locomotive would fire up again and the train would return home. Once it reached Earth, the car would be detached from the locomotive, fire retro-rockets, enter the atmosphere tail-first, open its parachutes, and splash down just off the Atlantic coast, where a steamship would pick it up and carry the passengers to New York. The locomotive would break up when it made an uncontrolled re-entry, and probably kill a whale or two when its remains crashed in the ocean, but that was okay; the rockets were cheap and the company could always make more.

The trains carried ten people: four crewmembers—a pilot, a copilot, an engineer, and a conductor—and six passengers. I was recruited by the company in '38. I was only 21 at the time, but my family had been working the rails for three generations, and I'd been a Pullman conductor since I was 17. The company needed experienced railroad men to take care of their customers and I wanted to go to the Moon, so we were a natural fit for each other. Six months training, including a couple of orbital flights on ol' No. 1, and then they put me on No. 4, the *Tycho Express*.

The train had a good crew. Floyd Simmons was a great pilot and Rich Sneed a terrific second officer, but our engineer, Joe Welch, was the one who stood out. Joe knew the ship backward and forward; there wasn't a rivet he was unfamiliar with, and I swear he could have taken the locomotive apart and put it back together without checking the blueprints. But that wasn't all. Joe was frustrated that the space trains weren't designed to actually land on the Moon. No one had done that yet, and it made him mad that the company had very little interest in doing so. So even though the *Tycho Express* would come within sixty miles of the lunar surface, all he could do was peer out the window and watch longingly as the mountains and craters swept by, so close and yet so far.

Me, I was too busy. Looking after six people—six very rich people at that—for five days was hard work. The easy part was getting them safely strapped into their couches just before take-off and cleaning up after them when they inevitably threw up after we reached orbit. Once the train was in zero gravity, you'd have to teach the simplest things—how to get out of bed, use the toilet, get dressed, eat, so on and so forth—and assist them if they couldn't or wouldn't learn. There were three double-occupancy staterooms on the car's lower deck, so I had to clean them every day, including changing the hammock liners, putting away personal belongings before they floated away, and scrubbing the commodes. And there were always hassles. Unruly children. Fussy parents. Unmarried men who wanted to induct single women into the so-called 240,000 Mile Club (I didn't mind, so long as they closed the door and didn't make a lot of noise). The occasional idiot who wanted to smoke a pipe or fool around in the airlock. I have a theory about the rich: if you make more than a million dollars, the universe compensates by dropping your I.Q. fifty percent.

There was never a problem, though, that I couldn't handle. Or at least not until April 9, 1939, the day the Goddard Rocket Company had its first—and last—major accident.

That morning, the *Tycho Express* took off from its launch depot. It was the train's sixth trip to the Moon, my fourth as its conductor. The first part of the flight was business as usual. After it dropped the booster in the drink, the locomotive lowered the car, then fired the main engine; it shut down about ninety seconds later, once the train reached low orbit. A quick swing around the planet so that Floyd and Rich could make their final calculations and the passengers could get their first look at Earth from space (and finish losing their breakfast), then Floyd pointed the train toward the Moon and fired the main engine.

That was how things usually went.

What went wrong was that the engine didn't shut down again.

To this day, no one knows exactly why that happened. The instruments worked fine, there were no shorts in the wiring, and before you ask, no, there wasn't any indication of human error. The best theory is that a valve stuck in the locomotive's primary ignition chamber, causing the engine to keep firing even after the pilot sent a signal up the wire for the engine to shut down.

We'll probably never know for sure. Whatever the reason, it remains one of three unsolved mysteries behind the wreck of the No. 4.

I realized we were in trouble when the train remained under thrust longer than it should have. I'd ridden the train enough times to know that there's a distinct series of events that must occur during a successful flight, and if any of them doesn't occur when it's supposed to, it means that something is seriously screwed up. So when we still had 1-g in the car after the sixty-second period of the translunar engine burn, I unsnapped my seat harness and skedaddled up to the control room.

Floyd, Rich, and Joe were all over the instrument panels when I came in. No one was panicking—they were too well-trained for that—but they weren't taking it lightly either. So I grabbed a safety rail and watched as they tried to correct the problem, until Floyd finally managed to engage the stand-by system and shut down the engine.

By then, it was too late. The locomotive had been firing for just over three minutes, and thus our velocity was almost sixty percent higher than it should have been. That meant two things. First, the fuel reserve was depleted by nearly one-quarter; we'd reach the Moon, but we wouldn't have enough fuel to get home. Second, our higher speed would cause us to reach our destination sooner than anticipated... and when Rich pulled out his slide ruler and ran the numbers, his recalculations showed us that the train would no longer slingshot around the Moon, but hit it straight on.

Fortunately, this sort of accident had been anticipated. The operations manual laid out the abort procedure: uncouple the car from the locomotive, then use the retro-rockets to send it back to Earth for emergency re-entry. Floyd radioed back home to tell them what was going on, and he hit the switch that would detach the tow cables and release the car.

And nothing happened.

This is the second unsolved mystery: why did the release mechanism fail? A lot of people think that it can't be a coincidence, and over the years I've heard quite a few conspiracy theories. Everyone from the Germans to rival space companies to alien invaders have been blamed. Personally, though, I don't believe sabotage was involved. Bad luck happens sometimes, not just once but twice.

In any case, we still needed to uncouple the locomotive, and there was only way left to do that. Someone would have to put on a vacuum suit, go out through the airlock, and do the job manually, from the top of the car. Floyd and Rich couldn't leave the control room, though, and I just didn't have that kind of experience. But Joe had been spacewalking a couple of times already, and as I said, he knew the train like no one else.

It wasn't a matter of picking a short straw, which is one part of the legend that's untrue. This was his job, and he went about it without argument or complaint. Joe and I went down below, where I helped him suit up while telling the passengers to remain in their cabins and stop asking silly questions. Once he'd put on the airtight rubber garment and sealed the deep-sea diver's helmet, he entered the airlock. The last I saw of him was after I closed the inner hatch and dogged it tight; he waved to me through the window while I turned the wheel to depressurize the compartment.

At first, everything went just as it was supposed to. As soon as the outer hatch was open, Joe clipped his safety line to the outer hull, then attached the magnetic soles of his boots and began to slowly walk up the side of the car. Those old Mark I spacesuits didn't have their own radios, but from inside we could hear the steady *clunk-clunk-clunk* as he made his way to the roof.

When he got there, Joe began to make his way around its circular edge, approaching each stanchion where the tow cables were attached, and using a monkey wrench to unfasten their big lug nuts. He was halfway around the circumference when he suddenly stopped. When he didn't move for a minute or two, Floyd went to the little porthole in the control room ceiling and peered out to see what was going on.

What he saw made him cuss out loud. Joe's safety line had become wrapped around the radio mast, and rather than spend precious time untangling it, he'd simply detached the line from his suit. Which was dangerous as hell. If his boots lost their grip, he'd float off and there would be no way to save him. But no one could tell him not to take this risk, so all Floyd could do was hold his breath and pray that Joe kept both feet firmly planted.

Which he did, right up until the moment he set free the fourth and final tow cable. And that's when the third mysterious thing happened.

The locomotive drifted away from the car, and Joe went with it.

Some people think he just made a mistake, and grabbed hold of the cable thinking that it was his safety line. But I know different, and so did the pilots. Joe was too smart to do something like that. Besides, his safety line was a dozen feet away, at least.

You want to know what I think happened? Joe saw his chance to go to the Moon and he took it. That's why he grabbed the cable. The locomotive was going the way he wanted to go, so he went along for the ride. Sure, it was suicide, but... well, who knows what was going on inside his head? In any case, the last anyone saw of Joe Welch and No. 4, they were falling toward the Moon, our chief engineer a small white figure clinging to a tow cable.

We got the rest of the train safely back to Earth and managed to make an emergency splash-down in the Indian Ocean. That was the last time a space train left the ground. The newspapers called Joe Welch a hero— some reporter called him Locomotive Joe, and that's how the nickname got stuck—but the government decided that trains were too dangerous and laws were passed against them being used again. By the time the Goddard Rocket Company went bankrupt, I was back to my old job, punching tickets on the Long Island Railroad.

Did Joe make it to the Moon? I doubt it. He didn't have enough air in his tanks, and when the locomotive's wreckage was located many years later in the Mare Imbrium, his body was nowhere to be found. All the same, moonwalkers in that region will occasionally report spotting someone in a Mark I suit who doesn't respond to comlink hails.

Locomotive Joe's ghost? Perhaps that's another unsolved mystery.

This is the first of four stories from my Near Space series to appear in this book… which makes me feel rather guilty, because the last collection I published, the expanded second edition of Sex and Violence in Zero-G, *was subtitled "The Complete Near Space Stories." And almost as soon as it was published, what did I do but go out and write a handful of new stories in the series, thereby making the subtitle less than accurate.*

It wasn't my intent to deceive anyone. This isn't the first time I've ended a series, only to return to it later, and I doubt it will be the last. I go where my imagination takes me, and so long as my readers or editors have no objections, I'm just as happy to do so. Consistency is overrated.

This story has its genesis in a couple of adventures my wife and I had in 2012. We had our 25th anniversary that year, and since Linda was also having a significant birthday, we celebrated with a vacation trip to France. I underwrote the expenses in part by doing a little research for my novel V-S Day, *but it was while visiting the royal palace at Versailles that I got the notion for this story. When I saw the Mars Vase, I realized at once that I'd later want to put it in a story, I took pictures and made notes, and it appears here exactly as described.*

I was still playing with the idea later that summer when, on the day of our anniversary, we took the zipline tour of a mountainside at the Berkshire East ski resort in western Massachusetts. Riding a zipline is described pretty much as I experienced it… I just moved the action to Mars. Who says research can't be fun?

SIXTEEN MILLION LEAGUES FROM VERSAILLES

Louis XIV lived in splendor beyond imagination. Far from the squalor of the Paris streets, the royal palace at Versailles possessed an opulence that bordered on the grotesque. From the ornate fountains and statues of its vast gardens to the marble pavement of the courtyard, from the ceiling frescoes of its dining rooms to the elaborate murals and sculptures of its bed chambers, Versailles was a gilded world in which the Sun King spent his days surrounded by luxury unmatched by any other monarch of the 18th Century.

One of the palace's more important rooms was the Council Study. Located just off the Hall of Mirrors, this was where Louis XIV met

Sundays and Wednesdays with the Council of State, and Tuesdays and Saturdays with the Council of Finances. During these meetings, the monarch sat at a table beneath an immense crystal chandelier. Behind him was black marble fireplace upon which rested a golden clock. Two matching vases stood at either end of the mantle; one was a tribute to Minerva, the goddess of wisdom, the other to the war god Mars.

Long after the Sun King's great-great-great-grandson, Louis XVI, placed his head upon the guillotine, the twin vases remained in Versailles, just two of the palace's many treasures. And then one day the vase on the right was removed from the mantle, carefully placed in a specially-made container, and sent to a world even Louis the Great couldn't have imagined…

And vanished.

Baynes was supervising repairs to Arsia Station's solar farm when Jenkins called him to the office. He would have rather stayed with the work crew—the dust storm that swept across the Martian equator the day before had caused considerable damage—but the general manager insisted that he join him inside, so he returned to the Hab 1 airlock, took off his suit, and headed for the office the two men shared next to the operations center.

"Hi, Will," Jenkins said as he walked in. There was a young woman sitting across from him: small and slender, with boyishly-cut black hair and a pleasant but solemn face. "Let me introduce you, if you haven't already met. This is Camille Bacquart, a curator from the Museum and National Estate at Versailles. Ms. Bacquart, this is Will Baynes, our associate general manager."

"Pleased to meet you, Ms. Bacquart." Baynes stepped past her to sit down at his desk. The office had just enough room for both Jenkins and him. With a visitor, it could be crowded, but Camille Bacquart was so petite that they were able to sit next to each other without having their knees touch.

"Dr. Bacquart," she said pointedly, with just enough of a pout to embarrass him.

"Sorry… Dr. Bacquart." As soon as Jenkins told Baynes who she was, he knew why she was there. "And I'm also sorry for the loss of the cargo lander. I wish it hadn't happened, but…" He fumbled for words. "Well, it just did."

The pout deepened into an angry glare, and he realized at once that he'd said the wrong thing. "It shouldn't have 'just happened,' Mr. Baynes," she replied, the edge in her voice just slightly sharper than her dark brown eyes. "I'm hoping that you and Mr. Jenkins—" Murray's last name rolled off her tongue, becoming *Zhenkins* "—will be able to rectify matters."

There's nothing like the displeasure of a pretty woman to make a man feel like a jerk. If he hadn't been Arsia's second-in-command, Baynes might have excused myself and retreated to the Mars Hotel for a nice, stiff drink. But Camille Bacquart had every right to be upset, so he kept his mouth shut and simply nodded.

"Dr. Bacquart came in on the *Bradbury* a couple of days ago," Jenkins said. "She was sent to escort the Versailles exhibit back to France. Fortunately, she was scheduled fly up with everyone else on the next shuttle, so she wasn't aboard the lander when it went down."

"That's lucky." Baynes looked at her again. "There's a reason why we send cargo and passengers into orbit on separate craft, y'know. Cargo has more mass than people, generally speaking, so it takes more fuel to get it into low orbit. More fuel means bigger engines, and big engines are more prone to failure. When we lose a spacecraft... it doesn't happen very often, but sometimes it does; that's what I was trying to say... it's usually been the cargo boat that goes down. And we'd sooner lose freight than people."

"I understand what you're saying, but..." Letting out her breath as a long sigh, Bacquart shook her head, a gesture that barely disturbed her boyishly cut black hair. "Forgive me to saying so, but the Mars vase is more valuable than mere human life. People can be replaced, but this... this is a priceless piece of history."

When Bacquart said this, Baynes' feelings for her changed. Like many colonists, he had originally come to Mars on a short-term contract, but after those two years were up he'd decided to remain a permanent resident. The planet sometimes did that to people. Yet life here was challenging and often dangerous, and he'd seen people die enough times to know that nothing could replace a friend who'd been lost. He didn't care how valuable the vase was; it wasn't worth dying for.

"Perhaps." Seeing the look on Baynes' faces, Jenkins tactfully cleared his throat. "Did you get a chance to see the vase while it was here, Will?"

"No. I've been busy with a lot of stuff lately." He didn't add that museum exhibits had little appeal to him, even those which had travelled more than seventy-eight million kilometers.

"Maybe you should see what we're talking about. Camille…?"

She'd already pulled out her pad and opened it. Moving a finger across its screen, she interfaced with the holo projector above the general manager's desk. The three-dimensional map globe which perpetually hovered there vanished, to be replaced by the artifact. A covered urn about sixty centimeters tall, it was made of dark blue porcelain trimmed with bronze filigree. Four maidens in Roman togas supported its lid, upon which sat Mars, plumed war helm on his head and an oval shield draped across his right arm.

Baynes had to admit that it was beautiful. The vase had been the centerpiece of a special exhibit, "The Mars Room of Versailles," which had been brought here two years ago by the *Bradbury* during the cycleship's last voyage. Some time ago, ConSpace's board of directors had become concerned that, although the Mars colonies had grown and were now self-sufficient, their inhabitants were becoming culturally deprived, their children having little or no knowledge of the world their parents had come from. Someone who'd recently visited France lit upon the idea of asking the French cultural ministry if they'd be willing to put together a travelling exhibit which would feature one of Versailles' more interesting features, the Mars Drawing Room where chamber quartets had often performed for Louis XIV's entertainment. Since the room had originally been built for the palace guards, its motif was classically military… hence its name and décor, which was principally red and featured elaborate murals of the God of War.

The exhibit had featured a scaled-down representation of the drawing room which visitors could walk through, showing them what they'd see if they visited the real palace at Versailles. Since none of the room's furniture could be sent to Mars—it was both too big and too delicate—it was decided that another artifact would be included. True, the Mars vase belonged in a different room entirely, but at least it shared the same theme. And it would be a tangible object that people could see as an authentic museum piece.

Over the past two years, the exhibit had travelled across Mars, spending a few months at a time at each of the Seven Colonies. After leaving Zubrinville it had returned to its starting place at Arsia Station. By then the *Bradbury* had come back, and the vase had joined the mural reproductions and holo projectors in the cargo lander.

But then a foolish decision was made. Although a violent dust storm was grinding its way eastward across the Tharsis region west of Arsia Station, the lander had been launched anyway. It should have stayed put until the storm was over. However, the *Bradbury* would be in orbit for only a few days, and its window for the return flight to Earth wouldn't last very long. So the lander was sent up, and less than a minute after it left the ground, a strong gust of wind from the storm's leading edge caught the spacecraft broadsides, throwing it off its bearings and sending it careening into the Valles Marineres west of Arsia.

At least the lander was unmanned; there weren't any pilots aboard, so no one was killed. Yet its instruments indicated that, although the emergency parachutes had automatically deployed, they hadn't been done so in time to prevent a catastrophic crash landing. There was little doubt that the lander had been destroyed on impact, and with it…

"Dr. Bacquart—" Baynes hesitated "—what makes you think that the vase survived the crash? When we lose a lander during a launch or landing accident, there's usually not much left."

"The museum anticipated that something like this was possible, even though we'd been assured that it wouldn't happen." Again she gave him an accusatory look, which Baynes chose to ignore. "Its container was specially designed for just this sort of occurrence. Not only was its interior padded by gelatin cells, but its outer shell was fitted with airbags which had their own shock-detection system. The airbags were supposed to inflate the moment the system detected a sudden change of motion, like that of a spacecraft about to make an uncontrolled descent. Before it left Earth, we tested the container by placing a replica of the vase inside and dropping it from an airplane at six kilometers. The vase was intact when we opened the container."

Baynes nodded. He was still unconvinced that there was anything left of the vase except pretty bits of porcelain and bronze, but she'd made a good argument otherwise. "The GPS transponder remained functional until impact," Jenkins said. "It appears that it came down somewhere in the Ius Chasma. Ever been there?"

"I've flown over it. Rough country, but it could be worse. I take it you want me to go out there and see if…"

"If there's anything at all, we need to have it brought back. And you won't be travelling alone. Camille will be going with you."

Baynes winced. The last thing he wanted to do was bring along someone who had no marswalking experience. "I've worn a skinsuit before, if that's what you're thinking," Bacquart said. "And I've done quite a bit of hiking in the Alps."

"That's not…"

"Camille, will you please excuse us a moment?" Jenkins asked.

Bacquart frowned, but she got up from her chair and left the office without another word. Jenkins waited until she closed the door behind her, then let out his breath. "Look, I know she's a pain, but it can't be helped. Like it or not, we're responsible for what happened to the lander. It's up to us to help her recover the vase."

"Yeah, well…" Baynes stretched out his legs. "I'd bet my next paycheck against your next paycheck that she won't find enough to glue back together."

"You're probably right, but that's not for us to decide." Jenkins paused. "I want to send someone with you who has outback experience. Someone who knows the Valles Marineris like the back of his hand. Do you know Lincoln McGrath?"

Baynes closed his eyes. "Murray, please… not him."

A wry smile. "Oh, so you have met Link…"

"I can handle one pain in the ass. Not two."

"Oh, I agree… he's as obnoxious as they get. But he's the best guide in the colonies, and he's also spent more time in the Valles Marineris than anyone else. If there's anyone who can get you to the wreckage in time…"

"In time?" Then Baynes realized what Jenkins was saying. "Oh, right… the *Bradbury* is still in orbit, isn't it?"

Jenkins nodded. "It's scheduled to break orbit in about seventy-four hours—" approximately three days by Mars reckoning "—but I've spoken with the captain, and she's willing to delay departure a little to accommodate us. But that means you have to get there and back again in four days, max, or the ship leaves without Dr. Bacquart. I don't think she's going to be very happy staying with us until the next ship comes six months from now, though, and we're already in enough trouble with the front office."

"Got it." Baynes pushed back his chair and stood up. No time to waste; he'd have to leave this morning. "I'll get us packed and ready to go.

Where do I find McGrath?" Then he saw Jenkins' smile. "Oh, hell… you called him already, didn't you?"

"Uh-huh. He should be at the airfield by now, waiting for you and Camille." The smile became a wide grin. "Good luck."

The Valles Marineris stretched out before them like an unhealed scar across the face of Mars. From an altitude of one hundred and fifty meters, the Noctis Labyrinthis of its western end passed beneath the airship gondola as a scarlet maze of gorges, buttes, and box canyons. The morning haze had burned off several hours earlier, but even the midday sun couldn't penetrate the shadows that lay upon its narrow floor. There was a good reason why this region was called the Labyrinth of Night; gazing into its depths, Baynes was just happy that this wasn't where the lander had gone down.

"Oh, yeah, it's a mess down there… major mess," Lincoln McGrath said. "Hell of a place to get lost, lemme tell you. Couple'a years ago, I took a *National Geographic* team through it. One of those guys was a big-shot writer… what's his name, I can't remember, wrote a book about it later… and he thought he was ready for it 'cause he'd climbed K2 and been down the Amazon and all that, and I thought he was gonna crap in his suit when one of our air recyclers went on the fritz and we lost track of where we were. But we got out of there all right, of course. I was with them."

As he spoke, McGrath half-turned around in his seat next to the pilot to peer at Camille Bacquart again. The airship had left Arsia Station about four hours ago, and he hadn't shut his mouth the entire time, delivering a non-stop prattle of travelogue, trivia, and tall tales while his gaze constantly returned to the young woman seated behind him. Like everyone else, she'd made herself comfortable in the pressurized cabin by unzipping the front of her skinsuit and pulling its top half down around her waist. She wore a black tank-top beneath her EVA gear that she filled out nicely, and McGrath couldn't seem to be able to take his eyes off her.

Again, Baynes wondered why Jenkins couldn't have found someone —anyone—else to guide them on this trek. McGrath was a familiar type to him, one of those guys who'd come to Mars because he wanted to pit his machismo against the red planet. Most of the time, they either went home after a couple of years, having discovered that they weren't as tough as they thought they were, or they got themselves killed in one stupid accident or another that they usually brought upon themselves. Somehow, McGrath had beaten the odds. Almost too big for a skinsuit, with curly black hair tied back behind his neck and a thick beard framing a heavy-featured face, he looked like he would have been comfortable aboard a pirate ship. The only thing out of place were the rimless glasses perched on the bridge of his flat nose; they made him appear a little wiser than he actually was.

Camille paid little attention to him. She was focused almost entirely upon the false-color topographic map she'd pulled up on her pad. "The valley where the lander crashed... it's quite deep, isn't it?"

"Miles and miles, sweetheart, miles and miles. It's..."

"Depends where it actually came down." Baynes was tired of McGrath dominating the conversation. Leaning forward in his seat, he placed a fingertip on the pad and moved it sideways, causing the map to scroll across the screen. "On average, Ius Chasma is only about three kilometers deep, although in places the floor can be six klicks down. But it's over 900 kilometers long, and it's also the most narrow part of the Valles Marineris. So even though we've got a rough idea of where the crash site is, getting there is going to be tough."

"No problem." McGrath shook his wooly head. "Once we reach Base Camp Three, the rest will be easy. We've already got a couple of rovers parked down there, and if the transponder signal wasn't off too much, the crash site is only about a hundred kilometers east of the camp."

"A rover," Camille repeated, and both Baynes and McGrath nodded. "I don't understand. Wouldn't it be quicker simply to fly straight to the crash site? This airship..."

"I won't take you into Ius Chasma." Emil D'Oro, the pilot, spoke up for the first time. "The wind patterns can be unpredictable. We once lost an airship down there. I don't want to be the next one."

"Then a spacecraft..."

"Nope." McGrath shook his head again. "No can do." His eyes narrowed as they turned toward Baynes. "You can thank the colonial government for that."

Bacquart looked at Baynes in disbelief, and he fought an urge to snap at McGrath. "What Link means is that the colonies have strict rules against using rocket vehicles to explore the Valles Marineris. The canyon floors contain native microorganisms which are quite vulnerable, and rocket exhaust could wipe out habitats which have been there for thousands of years. Even using a rover is taking a risk. We may have to stop the vehicle and go the rest of the way on foot, if we come upon a cryptogam field on our way to the crash site."

"Goddamn nuisance, if you ask me." McGrath peered at him over the top of his glasses. "I swear, guys like you, there's times when I wonder whose side you're on… ours or Earth's."

Baynes had heard this sort of thing before. There was a strong sentiment among many settlers that the Seven Colonies should declare independence from Earth and join the Pax Astra, the interplanetary alliance which had been formed among the lunar and orbital colonies. One of their chief complaints was that ConSpace and the Earth governments that supported it had imposed too many rules and regulations upon the Martian settlements, some of which were impediments to the colonies' economic growth.

This was the first time, though, that he'd heard this charge leveled against an environmental regulation that almost everyone agreed to as being common sense. Was McGrath one of the secessionists, or even a sympathizer?

"I didn't know that there were two sides," he said. "Why do you think there are?"

For a moment, it appeared that McGrath was going to argue with him. He merely shrugged, though, as he turned back around his seat. "I'm just sayin', that's all," he murmured, then he rocked back his head and closed his eyes. "Gonna take a nap for awhile. Wake me when we get to the descent station."

At least he'd finally shut up. But once again, Baynes wondered if Jenkins had made the wrong choice for the guy who'd take him and Bacquart into the canyons.

Descent Station Three was one of six scattered around the rim of Valles Marineris.

Located midway up a long, narrow gorge on the northern side of Ius Chasma, it wasn't until the airship came in for landing that Baynes saw the base for what it was, little more than an elevated steel platform projecting out over the gorge.

He was surprised to see a rover parked beside the dome. Three figures in skinsuits waited for the airship to touch down. As D'Oro dropped the mooring lines, they trotted forward to grab the ropes and haul them to iron posts hammered into the ground. Once the men signaled the pilot that the lines were secure, D'Oro brought the airship the rest of the way down.

By then, everyone had put their helmets on and closed their suits. A final check to make sure that they'd not forgotten to pressurize their suits, then D'Oro depressurized the cabin. A minute after the single fat tire of the airship's landing gear bounced across the rocky ground, the pilot popped the portside hatch. Baynes pushed it the rest of the way open and lowered the ladder, then climbed down from the gondola, Basquat and McGrath behind him.

"Hello, there," he said to one of the men who'd acted as ground crew. "We weren't expecting to find anyone here. Thanks for the help."

"No problem." He was a young guy, a two-day beard visible through his helmet faceplate. "We were on a survey job when we spotted your ship coming in. Thought you could use a hand."

"Much obliged, amigo." McGrath put down the canvas equipment bags he'd carried off the airship, stuck out his hand. "Link McGrath, from Arsia Station." He didn't bother introduce his companions, Baynes was annoyed to notice.

The other man hesitated before shaking his hand. "Smith, from Wellstown." He didn't introduce his friends either. "Where're y'all going?"

"Into the gorge, then up the valley." Baynes stepped forward. "I'm Will Baynes, and this is Camille Bacquart. Did you say you were from Wellstown?"

"Uh-huh," Smith replied. "Out on a water survey, saw your ship, decided to come over and pitch in."

His story sounded innocent enough, but nonetheless Baynes became suspicious. True, Wellstown was the nearest place for these men to have come from, a large settlement in the southern part of the Lunae Planum, yet it was over a hundred kilometers from this part of the Valles Marineris. Survey missions undertaken by rovers usually didn't venture that far from home; beyond seventy-five kilometers, airships were used instead. And the subsurface aquifers which the colonies depended upon for drinking water were seldom, if ever, found in this region; the ancient rivers which helped create the Valles Marineris were long gone, and the last remaining water on Mars was located beneath the rocky terrain of the northern tundra.

Then there was the fact that Smith's skinsuit lacked a name patch. There was a bald spot on his chest where one appeared to have been recently removed. Why would he want to conceal his identity? Barnes wondered if Smith was even his real name.

"Well, we appreciate it. Thanks." Baynes turned to McGrath. "I imagine Emil wants to get home before dark, so let's hurry up and get the gear unloaded."

McGrath nodded, but he didn't move from Baynes' side. "So what're your plans?" Smith asked. "I mean, what are you going into the valley for?"

"We're searching for—" Bacquart began.

"Microfossils." Baynes interrupted her before she could tell the truth. "Dr. Bacquart is an astrobiologist from the Sorbonne in Paris. She's hoping to find something in the eastern end of the Noctis Labyrinthis that earlier expeditions may have overlooked."

He hoped this sounded more plausible than the story Smith had told him. Call it instinct, intuition, or outright paranoia, but nonetheless he had a gut feeling that Smith and his crew shouldn't know the truth. The Labyrinth of Night lay behind them, in the opposite direction from where the lander was thought to have come down. If he could mislead them into believing that this was just a routine scientific expedition...

"Oh, all right," Smith said. "I was just wondering if you might be looking for the lander that came down yesterday. We heard about that, and kinda thought y'all might be going down there to hunt for it."

Baynes felt something cold in his stomach. News travels fast in the colonies, and for once he regretted it. "Nope," McGrath said before he could muster a reply. "Just lil' bitty Martians, that's all."

"'Cause if you were," Smith went on, "me and my boys would be happy to lend a hand."

"Thanks, but that's not necessary." Baynes tried to maintain a casual and friendly tone. He glanced at the airship. Its outboard props were still slowly turning; D'Oro was keeping the engines at idle, preparing for an immediate lift-off. "Anyway, if you don't mind..."

"Sure, sure. You got things to do." Smith stepped back. "Anyway, nice to meet you. And if you run into any trouble, give us a shout. We'll be monitoring the emergency channel."

"Will do, thanks." Baynes turned to McGrath and Bacquart. "C'mon, let's get the rest of our gear. We need to get into the valley before dark."

The three of them turned away from Smith and his men. By the time they finished unloading their remaining equipment from the airship and released the lines, the Wellstown men had climbed back into their rover and driven away. Baynes watched as it trundled away, its six wheels causing a plume of red dust to rise behind it. It was headed west, he noted, a direction which would take it further along the valley rim, not back toward Wellstown.

"Why didn't you tell them where we're going?" Bacquart asked. "They offered to help us."

"I don't think that's what they had in mind," Baynes replied, but he didn't take time to explain. Besides, there was always a chance that his suspicions were wrong.

There were two ways of getting down into the gorge. The first was a man-made trail that meandered its way down the steep, alluvial slopes to the narrow floor two kilometers below. McGrath assured Baynes and Bacquart that it would take nearly four hours for them to make the hike; by the time they reached the bottom, there would be no daylight left, and they'd be forced to travel the rest of the way to the base camp in the dark.

The other way was the zipline.

"No, no. I won't do it." Standing on the platform, Camille stared at the elevated steel cable that descended into the gorge. "I can't do it… I just can't."

"Sure, you can." McGrath knelt before her, tightening the straps of the girdle-like harness that wound between her legs and around her waist. "It's perfectly safe, I promise. Hell, it's fun."

"But this thing goes straight down…"

"No, it doesn't." Standing up, the guide attached a carabineer to the long strap hanging from the harness center. He gave it an experimental tug that yanked her slightly closer to him. "There's seven more platforms just like this one, and the farthest distance between them is only half a klick. We'll go from one to the next until we reach the bottom. All you have to do is hang onto this strap and enjoy the ride."

Baynes gazed down the length of the zipline. As McGrath said, the next platform was only two hundred meters away, its support posts sunk into an outcropping that protruded from the gorge wall. Suspended from masts erected at the center of each platform, the steel cable continued downward in a zigzag line, its angle never more than forty-five degrees.

"Looks simple enough," he murmured, trying not to sound nervous.

"Done it myself dozens of times. Believe me, when we're down there, you're gonna wish this thing worked uphill, too."

McGrath pulled three pulleys from a small bag strapped to his waist. He handed two of them to Baynes and Bacquart, then used his own to show them how to clamp its two tandem wheels to the cable and attach the carabineer at the end of the center strap to the pulley. He warned them not to touch the pulley or the carabineers at any time, but just to hang onto the strap. If they wanted to go faster, they could curl up into a ball; if they wanted to go slower, all they had to do was spread apart their arms and legs.

"We'll send down the equipment first," he said as he attached three more pulleys to the cable and ran their straps to the harnesses they'd wrapped around the containers they'd taken off the airship. "I'll go next, so I can be there to catch y'all when you come in. Doc, you follow me. Boss, you bring up the rear. After we get to each platform, I'll reattach the pulleys to next length of cable, then we'll repeat the whole thing. Got it?"

Bacquart was staring down into the gorge. "What if we fall?" she whispered, her voice barely audible through the comlink.

"You won't. It's never happened. Trust me."

Trust wasn't something Baynes was easily inclined to give Link McGrath, but he had to admit that he'd never heard of anyone dying while using the Valles Marineris ziplines. He helped McGrath carry the aluminum containers to the platform's lip and, one at a time, push them over the side. They shot down the wire, and he watched as they were caught by the nylon net on the platform below. McGrath snapped his strap's carabineer to his pulley, yanked it a couple of times to make sure it was on tight, and looked back at him and Bacquart.

"See you soon," he said, grinning at them from within his beard. Then he grabbed the top of the strap, yelled "Geronimo!" and ran straight off the platform.

Dangling from the strap, the guide raced down the zip-line, legs tucked in for speed. In less than ten seconds, he reached the next platform. He took a couple of minutes to switch the container pulleys to the next cable and send them on their way, then he looked back up at him and Camille. "Okay, Doc… ready for you. C'mon on down."

"I can't do it," Bacquart said as Baynes clipped her pulley to the cable and checked her straps and carabineers. "I'll walk down. You can wait for me. I won't take…"

"I'm sorry, Dr. Bacquart. Please forgive me." And then Baynes pushed her off the platform.

She screamed all the way down, but she made it to the next platform. She was still cursing Baynes, some of it in French, when he made his own leap of faith. The strap yanked the harness tight against his groin and his stomach felt as if he'd suddenly gone weightless. He dared not look down, but he barely had time to become scared before his boots touched the edge of the next platform and McGrath reached out to grab him.

"See?" McGrath asked. "Fun, ain't it?"

Baynes caught the cold glare Bacquart gave him, and knew that if he hadn't been wearing a helmet, the palm of her hand would have smacked his face. Oblivious to all this, McGrath was already attaching his pulley to the next length of the zip-line. The third platform lay several hundred meters below; the containers were already there, and within minutes they followed them.

Gliding from one platform to the next, the three of them made the descent into the gorge. McGrath was right; it *was* fun, once Baynes got used to the initial jump and the high-speed ride that followed. He didn't think Bacquart ever enjoyed herself, but at least she stopped screaming. As the floor of the gorge came closer, though, the distance between platforms became longer, and it wasn't until they'd nearly reached the bottom that they reached the most harrowing part of the journey.

The next to last two platforms stretched all the way across the gorge itself, travelling from the west wall to the east. McGrath explained that the team who'd built the zipline had been forced to do it this way because the sandstone near the base of the west wall was too loose to allow for safe anchorage of a platform. So the cable was pulled across the gorge; here, the distance was nearly half a kilometer, with a maximum height of almost a hundred meters.

"This is the best part of all," McGrath insisted. "Check out the view as you cross. You're gonna love it."

By then, Bacquart was beyond protesting. She merely nodded, resigned to the inevitable. Yet she didn't appear to look anywhere except straight ahead as she soared across the abyss, and when Baynes took his turn, he almost did the same thing. Yet he'd learned how to twist the strap so that he could turn his body from one side to another, so as he made the long crossing, he did as McGrath suggested. The gorge spread out beneath his feet as a v-shaped expanse of red rock and sand, and in the distance lay the lowlands of the Valles Marineris, its southern walls tinted golden by the late afternoon sun.

In all the years he'd spent on Mars, he'd seldom felt a moment of awe as he did just then.

He almost regretted reaching the platform on the opposite side of the gorge.

The final platform was only a short distance away, erected in the center of the canyon floor. They detached the pulleys for the last time and took off their harnesses, then picked up the containers and carried them down a short flight of stairs. At the bottom of the tower was the trail leading from the gorge to Base Camp Three, a couple of kilometers away. Before they started walking, though, they peered up at the massive bluffs rising above them.

"Still want to make that hike, Doc?" McGrath pointed to where the narrow path traced a nearly invisible line up the canyon's western wall. "There it is."

Bacquart stared at the path. "How are we going to get the vase all the way up that?"

"Guess we're gonna have to carry it." McGrath looked at Baynes. "Unless you persuade someone to bend the rules a little and send an airship down here."

Baynes didn't reply. He wasn't looking forward to carrying a heavy artifact uphill either. On the other hand, he doubted this would be an issue. The vase was probably destroyed. This trip was just to convince Camille Bacquart of the truth.

They reached Base Camp Three around dusk, as the last light of day was dimming in Ius Chasma. The base was a large, inflatable dome with its own toilet, air generator, and solar array. There was no point in trying to go any further that day, so they entered the dome, switched on the heat, settled in for the night. Dinner was freeze-dried stew from their supplies, rehydrated and warmed. They took the opportunity to recharge their suit batteries and CO_2 filters, then unfolded the cots stored in the dome. It had been a long day, so they went to bed early, although Baynes was kept awake for awhile by loud snoring from the other side of the small room. McGrath, of course.

Next morning, Baynes and McGrath checked out the two rovers parked beside the dome. Both were protected by tarps, which in turn were covered by sand from recent dust storms. They swept away the grit, removed the tarps, and inspected each vehicle. Both were usable, but one was a bit less battered than the other. Baynes switched on its solar collector and let it bring the batteries to full charge while they loaded their gear aboard, and by mid-morning they were ready to go.

It wasn't the first time anyone had driven through these parts. Tire tracks led east along the valley's north wall, just visible through the most recent deposit of wind-blown sand. It would have been convenient to simply follow the tracks, hence avoiding the countless rocks and boulders that threatened to obstruct their way, but Baynes was careful not to succumb to temptation. Although it was the narrowest part of the Valles Marineris, Ius Chasma was still wide enough that they could easily miss the lander if they hugged the valley walls.

Baynes took the first shift at the wheel, with McGrath sitting beside him. The rover had a small observation dome just behind the front seats; Bacquart stood within it, bracing herself with one hand while using a pair of binoculars to search the terrain. Once they cleared a small mesa squatting in the middle of the valley not far from the base camp, Baynes steered to the right, taking them out of the tire tracks and toward the valley's midline. Soon the towering north wall no longer spread its shadow upon them, while the ridgeline that ran down the Ius Chasma's center loomed to their right as an irregular row of jagged peaks.

The trip was rough. The rover had six fat wheels mounted on an independent suspension system, but they didn't save its passengers from the constant bumping and jouncing that came with every rock and pothole they rolled across. It was all Baynes could do just to keep the wheel steady; he let the other two look for the lander while he concentrated on avoiding as much debris as possible. He'd hoped to make good time, but soon discovered that he was doing well if he managed twenty kph; at times, he was forced to slow to a crawl that a man on foot would have outpaced.

Around midday, they stopped to take a lunch break and change drivers. By then they'd put seventy-three kilometers between them and the base camp. Not bad, but not very good either.

Bacquart had taken the worst abuse during the ride. At least Baynes and McGrath had the benefit of seat belts. She'd stood the entire time, and as a result she'd bruised her shoulders and bashed her head a couple of times against the observation dome; her legs were stiff and sore when she finally sat down. Baynes volunteered to take her place at the dome, and once they'd finished their sandwiches and taken turns visiting the small chemical toilet in the back of the rover, he reluctantly planted his feet where she'd stood and prepared him for the ordeal to come.

Just as McGrath started up the rover again, though, Baynes happened to glance back at the way they'd come. Far in the distance, almost at the visible horizon, he spotted something odd: a small plume of hazy red dust swirling up from the center of the valley, almost exactly where they'd been only about an hour earlier.

"Hold it!" he snapped. "I think I see something!"

McGrath stepped on the brakes just as the rover began to move. Bacquart turned around. "The lander?"

"No... the other direction." Baynes used the binoculars to peer more closely at the plume. It base was too far away for him to make out, and it seemed to diminish even as he watched it. "I could have sworn... I don't know, but it looked like another rover."

"The one from the camp?" McGrath asked, and chuckled when Baynes nodded. "Don't let your eyes fool you, boss. It's a dust devil."

Baynes was unconvinced. "I still think it's..."

"Naw, I've seen those down here before. Wind plays tricks down here. Bounces off the walls, spins around, kicks up sand... looks like another rover, but it ain't." McGrath pushed the gearshift forward again. "Dust devil. Take my word for it."

Baynes looked back once more. The plume had reappeared, but he had to admit that McGrath could be right. It might well be a natural phenomenon, not the sign of another vehicle following him. All the same, he couldn't help but remember their encounter with the men from Wellstown, and how Smith had insisted on joining them.

Were they following them? It was possible, but it was just as likely that his suspicions were only getting the better of him. Baynes told himself that there was no sense in worrying. He needed to pay attention to where they were going, not what lay behind. So he kept his eyes trained on the way ahead and tried not to let himself get bounced around too much.

It was just as well that he didn't let himself get distracted, for only an hour and a half later they found the lander.

The glint of sunlight reflecting off metal was what drew Baynes' eye. He spotted it from almost a kilometer away and immediately told McGrath to veer left. He hoped it wasn't a mirage, and it wasn't. The reflection grew brighter as they approached its source, and within a few minutes they found the crash site.

The lander had come down hard, yet somehow remained upright, although listing slightly to one side. Its cylindrical engine module resembled a barrel crushed underfoot by a giant, with twisted hull plates scattered in all directions. The conical payload module had a big dent in one side but was otherwise intact. The emergency parachute had deployed, which was probably what saved the vehicle from total destruction; a ripped candy-cane shroud fluttering in the errant breeze was evidence that its lines had probably snarled during the descent, limiting its effectiveness. If the lander had been a manned vehicle, everyone aboard probably would have been severely injured or killed on impact.

Even before the rover came to a halt, Baynes told the others to put on their helmets and seal their suits. McGrath decompressed the rover, and he popped the hatch as soon as he put on the brakes. Bacquart nearly shoved Baynes out of her way in her haste to get out, but he begged her to be patient until he made sure that the lander was safe to approach; any fuel still leaking from the ruptured tanks might pose a hazard.

The hazmat detector he'd brought with him found only trace amounts of liquid oxygen and hydrazine; most of it had already evaporated. So he and Bacquart unloaded their equipment and carried it to the wreckage. McGrath remained in the rover to call Arsia Station and report their success.

Baynes was in luck. The recessed rungs of the access ladder hadn't been damaged, with the lowest ones within reach. He took a few hand tools from one of the equipment cases and slipped them into the skinsuit's thigh pockets, then carefully scaled the ladder. The payload hatch was badly dented and couldn't be easily opened; after working it over with a wrench and screwdriver, he asked McGrath to fetch the cutting torch they'd brought with them.

The guide emerged from the rover with the torch's carrying case in hand. Watching him from atop the lander, Baynes wondered what had taken him so long. His most immediate concern was getting the hatch open, though, so he had Bacquart toss up a nylon rope. He looped one end through the hatch's hand rung, then dropped the other end to the ground and told McGrath to fasten it to the torch. Once he had it in hand, Baynes adjusted the portable laser's focus, then aimed it at the hatch and switched it on.

It took about ten minutes to cut through the hatch's ruined lock. Once that was done, he was able to finally swing the hatch open. Switching on his helmet lamps, he peered inside. As he'd expected, everything was thrown around. Crates and boxes had snapped their tie-down lines and fallen against one another, their lids bursting to spill their contents; everything from bagged mineral samples to underwear lay in a jumble.

On hands and knees, Baynes pushed aside the junk, searching for what he knew to be the largest object in the module. It took him several minutes to find it: a large, octagonal sphere, its panels draped with the deflated sacks of its airbags. He'd just located it when he heard a hollow thump; twisting around, he saw that Bacquart had climbed up the ladder and crawled into the payload module behind him.

"There it is!" she shouted. "Open it, quickly!"

"Just a minute. Hold on." Baynes had to look hard to find the panel marked ACCESS OPEN. It was sealed with lug nuts; he used a rotary hex wrench to unfasten them, then lifted the panel away. Its interior was filled with gelatin capsules; as Bacquart crowded in beside him, he used his hands to scoop them out and drop them on the deck around their feet.

Suddenly, there it was. Within the beams of their helmet lamps lay a large and decadently ornate vase, the figurine of a war god perched on its lid regarding them with an impetuous gaze as if to say, *Well, what took you so long?* Not broken. He was glad that Jenkins hadn't taken that bet he'd made.

Bacquart sighed with relief, murmured something in French. "You and me both," Baynes replied, even though he didn't understand what she'd said. "You were right… the container did its job."

"I thought it would." Her voice was choked. When Baynes looked at her again, he saw tears on the other side of her faceplate. "*Merci... merci beaucoup.*"

He didn't know whether she was thanking him, the container's designer, or a higher power, but it didn't matter. "Don't be too thankful," he said. Withdrawing his hands from the container, he slapped a hand against its side and gave it a quick once-over. "Here's the bad news... there's no way we're going to get this thing out of here. Not without the forklift they used to put it in here in the first place."

"We can't take the container?"

"Uh-uh. Just the vase." He gave her a reassuring smile. "It's not all bad. We can put together another container once we're home. Maybe not with all the safety features this one had, but good enough to get it back to Versailles."

Bacquart hesitated. "All right, but we'll have to be careful. Perhaps there's something here...?"

"My thoughts exactly."

Squatting on his thighs, Baynes rummaged through the stuff which lay around them until he found what he was looking for, an aluminum crate about the size of a beer cooler which had broken open during the crash. Dark blue stains and broken bottles attested to what had once been in it: Martian sauvignon noir, probably from the famed hydroponic vineyards of the DaVinci colony, to be shipped to a wealthy wine collector back on Earth.

"This will do, I think," he said, and he was right. The crate was large enough to hold the vase. Working together, Baynes and Bacquart delicately removed the vase from the shipping container and lay it down in the crate, padding it at the top, bottom, and around the sides with gelatin capsules. The crate's lock was damaged but still usable; they could seal it later with duct tape.

"We'll have to carry it all the way uphill once we get back to the gorge," Baynes said, "but I think we can manage." He patted one of the handles attached to either end of the crate. "If you'll get me the rope I used for the torch, please...?"

McGrath was standing at the bottom of the lander when they finally emerged from the payload module. He watched as Baynes and Bacquart pulled the crate through the hatch and, each holding the rope, carefully lowered it to the ground. Baynes noticed that he was unusually quiet, but it wasn't until he and Bacquart reached the ground that they discovered the reason why.

Another rover was stopped a short distance away, on the other side of the lander where it couldn't be seen from anyone inside the lander. Baynes immediately recognized it as the second one from the base camp. It must have arrived only a minute or so earlier, because three men were walking toward them.

Smith and his friends. And they were carrying guns.

Firearms were uncommon on Mars. There had never been much need for colonists to have guns; no threats from native animals, and disputes among settlers were generally settled through peaceful arbitration or, if that failed, marshals carrying nonlethal weapons.

In recent years, though, guns had begun to make their way from Earth. The separatist movement was responsible for this. Believing that revolution was inevitable, political extremists had begun smuggling handguns and rifles to the colonies, albeit only two or three at a time, in expectation that they would use armed force to take control of settlements during an insurrection. So when Baynes saw Smith and his companions were armed, he knew at once who they were and what they had in mind.

"You're not getting it," he said, stepping between them and the crate.

"Wanna bet?" Smith hadn't yet raised the .45 semi-auto in his right hand, but the two men following him did. "Make it easy on yourself. Step away from the box and no one has to get hurt."

Baynes glanced at McGrath. The guide stood quietly nearby, neither coming to Baynes' aid nor lifting a hand to help Smith. Not that Baynes believed for a moment that he wasn't involved. McGrath must have seen the other rover approaching while he and Bacquart were inside the lander, yet he hadn't warned them. Just as he'd known that the plume Baynes had spotted a couple of hours earlier wasn't really a dust devil.

"I'd do as he says," McGrath said. "I know this guy. He means business."

"Funny that you neglected to tell me that earlier," Baynes growled. "When did you get in touch with him? Before we left Arsia, so he'd be there when we arrived at the descent station?"

McGrath didn't reply, but he looked away when Baynes said this. "I don't understand," Bacquart said. She stood beside the crate, staring in disbelief at Smith and his men. "Why would they want the vase? They can't possibly sell it or have any use for it."

"Sell it, no. But use it, yes. They're secessionists... part of an underground movement that wants to liberate the colonies and join the Pax Astra." Baynes gestured toward the crate. "I'm guessing that they see some advantage in stealing a valuable artifact."

"You got it, chief." Smith's grin was visible through his helmet faceplate. "I got the idea when it was being shown in Wellstown. Pretty piece of junk like this must be worth something to somebody. Maybe you can't sell it, at least not out there, but you can sure hold it for ransom. Guns, supplies... or maybe just hold on to it as a bargaining chip for when the time comes for some... y'know, forceful negotiations."

"So why didn't you just steal it in Wellstown when you had a chance?"

"It was under lock and key most of the time, and there wouldn't have been any way to hide it even if we did get it. Out here, though..." Smith shrugged. "Anyway, you get the idea. Let's stop wasting time." He turned to the two men standing behind him. "Go on, go get it. They're not going to stop you."

"No," Bacquart said. "You may not have it."

Smith laughed again. "Lady, you ain't got no choice." He raised the gun in his hand. "Stand aside, Frenchie, or take a bullet. Up to you."

"Then I *do* have a choice, don't I?" Her voice was tight. "Very well, then..."

She sat down on the crate.

Baynes stared at her, utterly surprised by what she'd just done. "Camille, are you out of your mind?"

"Very possibly, *oui*." Sitting bolt upright, she placed her hands on her knees. "Nonetheless, I will not be moved. They will have to shoot me first."

Smith's men stopped. They too were stunned by what she was doing. "Dude..." one of them began, looking helplessly at their leader.

"Look, lady, I'm warning you." Taking a step closer, Smith grasped his gun with both hands and took aim straight at Bacquart. "Get off the box. Now."

Bacquart didn't move. "No."

For a second, Baynes had an impulse to rush Smith, perhaps tackle him and rip the gun from his hand. But he was standing too far away and his finger was within the trigger guard; any sudden action would be fatal, either to him or Bacquart. Yet Smith wasn't tightening his finger on the trigger. He had a dead bead on her, but it seemed as if he was hesitating. Perhaps…

"C'mon, guys." Taking one hand from the gun, Smith impatiently waved his men toward her. "Drag her out of the way."

"You heard what she said." Before anyone could stop him, Baynes took a seat on the crate beside Bacquart. "The lady says no… and so do I."

Smith's men halted in midstep. Pulling a defenseless woman away from the crate was one thing; doing the same to two people was another. Baynes felt the crate's aluminum lid bend slightly beneath him; he tried not to put his full weight upon it as he curled his right arm within her left elbow. Now they were inseparable, or at least not without the combined efforts of all three Wellstown men. And Smith would have to put down his gun if he wanted to help his partners.

"What the hell do you think you're doing?" Smith was no longer sure of himself. He pointed the gun at Baynes. "Get off that thing! I mean it!"

"Sorry, no." Baynes's mouth was dry, his heart hammering against his chest. "You'll just have to shoot us both. That's all there is to it."

"Smith…" McGrath let out his breath. "Give it up."

"Like hell!" Smith's voice rose, becoming higher in desperation. "If they don't get off that thing, I'm gonna…"

"You know what'll happen if you kill 'em. The boss is the second-in-command at Arsia, and the doc is a VIP from France. If they wind up dead…" He paused meaningfully, giving them a moment to think about it. "You and your guys will become wanted men. Even the movement will disown you. No one will rest until you're caught… and you'll get the airlock when they do."

"Then you're gonna help us." Smith's gun turned toward McGrath. "You're part of this, too, y'know."

"Nope. I didn't sign up for this." McGrath pointed toward the second rover. "Now go on… get out of here. The vase won't do you any good now."

Smith didn't say or do anything for several moments, and neither did his two accomplices. Baynes waited for whatever was going to happen next, still half-expecting the next breath he took to be his last.

Smith muttered an obscenity. He relaxed his grip on the gun and let his arm fall to his side, then he looked at the other two men. "All right," he said quietly, "let's go."

Without another word, the three of them turned and walked back to the rover. Baynes waited until they climbed in and drove away, heading back up the valley the way they'd come, before he dared let out his breath.

"That was... that was close," he said softly.

"Yeah, well... they just hadn't thought things through." McGrath said nothing for a second. "I guess you're going to have to report this to Jenkins."

Baynes considered the situation as he stood up from the crate. His knees felt stiff, as if he'd been sitting there for hours. He still didn't trust Link McGrath, or even particularly like him, but the fact remained that he owned him one.

"I don't think anyone has to know what happened here," he said at last. "No harm, no foul... so long as you stay out of trouble, I mean."

"If by 'trouble' you mean the movement..." McGrath shook his head. "Sorry, boss, I can't make that promise. I agree with the motives, not the methods."

"Yeah, okay... whatever." Baynes was too relieved to argue with him. So far as he was concerned, he was just happy to still be alive and to still have the vase in his possession.

He turned to Bacquart. She'd stood up from the crate and had opened it, peering inside to make sure that the vase was undamaged. "I have to tell you, that was the bravest thing I've ever seen."

"If you say so." She didn't look up from the vase.

"One hell of a bluff, doc," McGrath added. "I am impressed."

She closed the crate, locked it again. "I wasn't bluffing."

Baynes was about to object, then he remembered what she'd said to him in Jenkins' office about how she considered the vase, with its place in history, to be more precious than mere human life. No, she hadn't been bluffing. She'd meant every word.

"I believe you." He reached down to wrap a hand around one of the crate handles. "Okay, then... let's get this thing home."

I'm fascinated by eccentrics, particularly those who go to great lengths to be left alone. Although I'm not maniacally reclusive, in this era where privacy has allegedly come to an end, I've discovered there's something to be said for what the late, great Warren Zevon called "splendid isolation." So my phone number is unlisted, my mail comes to a post office box, I don't blog or tweet, and my arm had to bent before I surrendered to the inevitable and started a Facebook page.

Still... I think you can take being a hermit just a little too far.

ALIVE AND WELL, A LONG WAY FROM ANYWHERE

When Jerry Stone died, exactly three minutes and thirty-six seconds went by before anyone on Earth knew he was gone. That was the time it took for the med bracelet on his left wrist to register his final heartbeat and relay that information to the Stone House's main computer, which in return transmitted an automatic signal across the 40,362,000 miles that currently lay between asteroid 2010 TK7 and Earth.

JSTONE LIFE FACTORS TERMINAL. That was the text of the message, as terse and coldly factual as only a computer could express it. I was asleep when someone minding the graveyard shift at a deep-space communications center in Texas called to tell me the news. I'm embarrassed to admit that the first thing to enter my mind wasn't that Jerry Stone, my boss for the last forty-two years, was dead, but rather the fact that there's a two-hour time difference between Houston and Reno, and that the kid who called from Texas hadn't taken a moment to consider whether an old guy like me might still be in bed at 5 AM.

How rude of Jerry to pass away at such an inconvenient hour.

I got up and made coffee, then went to my desk to read the report sent me via encrypted mail. It wasn't until I saw that terse message from the Stone House, followed by the flatlined biofeedback from Jerry's bracelet, that the truth sank in. I don't know how long I stared at the desk screen, only that my coffee was cold when I picked it up again.

Jeremiah Edward Stone, age 72, was dead. The founder and CEO of ConSpace, once the largest private space corporation, was no longer among the living. Not that anyone would have noticed. It had been more than four decades since Jerry Stone had rubbed elbows with the rest of the human race. Since December 23, 2063, his only companions had been the packs of fogzes he'd raised. Indeed, I was one of few people who'd spoken to him in many years.

Now he was gone, and I didn't know how I was supposed to feel. Sadness, relief... I was tasting a bit of both, and something else as well: anger. A mystery had surrounded Jerry Stone for all those years. He'd never revealed its answer to anyone. I'd always hoped that he'd tell me, but he never did, and now it appeared that he never would.

"Jerry." I closed my eyes, let out my breath, and sank back in my chair. "Jerry, Jerry, Jerry... sometimes you really piss me off."

Then I straightened up, activated the desk's keyboard, and did what I'd always done for him. I wrote a press release.

Everyone in the world—no, scratch that; everyone in the solar system —knew Jerry Stone. Or at least they thought they did. That's the price of fame. Your face and voice are familiar to all, but the realities of your everyday existence—what you have for breakfast, your favorite colors, the little things you like or dislike—are trivialities very few people know and which probably wouldn't interest them even if they did. The greater your celebrity, the more you become a caricature of yourself, until you vanish as a person and simply become a media image.

These are the public facts about Jerry Stone. Born in 2027 to a middle-class family in Decatur, Georgia, he began building his fortune at age 12, when he started using part of his weekly allowance to invest in penny stocks. From his bedroom, Jerry played the stock market the way other kids played computer games; he was a child prodigy when it came to the venture capital investment, and could have taught a Wall Street trader a few tricks. He was making more money than his parents by the time he turned 16, and was already a millionaire when he graduated high school.

For someone like him, college wasn't necessary. He went anyway, if only because it was a great way to meet girls. In three years he'd graduated from the Yale business school with a Skull and Bones ring on his finger and more women than he could handle. At 21, he was one of the world's youngest billionaires.

By then, humankind had established itself as a spacefaring civilization. Solar power satellites were in geosynchronous orbit above Earth. Industrial bases had been built on the Moon, mining its regolith for

helium-3 and rare-earth minerals. Multi-national companies had
established colonies on Mars. The first efforts to mine main-belt asteroids
had begun. Even distant Jupiter was on its way to being exploited for its
vast reserves of He^3. The solar system was the new place to make serious
money, and Jerry was among the many major investors who'd bankrolled
companies like Skycorp and Uchu-Hiko. But Jerry wasn't just another
entrepreneur looking to score big bucks from space development. In an
interview for *Fortune*, he said that he'd been fascinated by space since
childhood, when he'd seen images of the first expedition to reach Mars;
indeed, he pointed out that the first stock he'd ever bought was for a small
company which manufactured solenoids for orbital satellites. Jerry put
money into everything from cars to chickens, but space was always his
primary interest; a percentage of the profits he made from the other stuff
was sunk into the space industry, and as always he had an uncanny ability
to predict which companies were worth the investment.

Sometimes his prescience was scary. No one else foresaw that the
major space companies would go bankrupt after the Descartes Station
lunar colony declared independence and formed what would eventually
become the Pax Astra. Even as the lunar revolution was heating up, Jerry
secretly met with other major space investors and laid out the facts as he
saw them: if the revolution was successful, it would eventually grow to
include the Mars settlements, and anyone who tried to compete with them
was doomed because the lunar and Martian colonies would hold all the
cards. So the smart thing to do would be to wait until companies like
Skycorp were about to fold, as it inevitably would, then sell their stock for
whatever it was worth, take the money, and start a new corporation which
would do business with the Pax Astra.

The other investors paid attention to Jerry. Most of them, at least.
Those who didn't found themselves holding worthless stock when his
predictions turned out to be correct. The investors who knew better than
to argue with a 25-year-old *wunderkind* became the Board of Directors of
ConSpace, the phoenix that rose from the ashes of the old establishment.
Naturally, they elected Jeremiah Edward Stone as its President and CEO.
They had no choice; Jerry was also the majority shareholder.

A number of financial sages, from New York to Hong Kong, said that
ConSpace was a gamble. Certainly it was, but it wasn't a crap-shoot; Jerry
knew what he was doing. Once the Mars colonies joined Descartes Station

to form the Pax Astra, they discovered that they still needed to do business with Earth if the Pax was going to survive. And since ConSpace had already established itself as the main interplanetary transport company, the Pax had no choice but to contract with ConSpace.

As CEO, Jerry deferred an annual salary in exchange for a percentage from the cost-per-pound surcharge for every payload that went to or from Earth. A number of people thought he was crazy, but he knew exactly what he was doing. By the time he turned 35, Jerry Stone was one of the wealthiest men alive. No one except he and his accountants knew the extent of his assets, but it was estimated to be as much as $100 billion.

Jerry was hardly a recluse in those days. Far from it. He was almost always in the news. One day he was escorting a famous supermodel down the red carpet of a Hollywood premiere. A few days later, he'd be sighted on the aft deck of his ninety-foot yacht, warming himself beneath the Mediterranean sun while another beautiful woman rubbed oil on his back. A week later, he was on the Moon, joining a hiking party to walk the length of the Straight Wall. And then it was back to Earth, to cut the ribbon of another children's hospital.

Jerry Stone was a man all men aspired to be: billionaire, philanthropist, adventurer, lover, hero. I'm not sure, though, that he truly enjoyed his life. When I saw pictures of him—at the cotillion, at the European race track, at the president's inaugural ball—it always seemed to me that his smile was just a little too wide, his eyes gleaming just a little too brightly, as if he was consciously forcing himself to be happy, and not quite succeeding.

There were also peculiar aspects of his personality. The fact that he always wore the same outfit—black long-sleeve shirt, black trousers, black socks, black shoes—was obvious, of course, but accepted as a minor eccentricity; indeed, quite a number of guys emulated his style. And it was well-known that Jerry was a strict vegetarian who was revolted by the very sight of meat.

Yet only those close to him knew about his oddest tendencies. He showered at least twice a day, three times if he wasn't too busy, and washed his hands constantly. One of the women who went to bed with Jerry told me that he insisted upon turning off all the lights before anyone took off their clothes, and that sex was brief, mechanical, and unsatisfying. After a while, he stopped dating women entirely. And once Jerry had enough money that he could set the rules of engagement, his business partners soon found that they almost never had personal meetings with him. Jerry preferred to speak with them via video hookup, even when he was in the same building as the persons who'd made appointments to see him.

Something happened to him. Exactly what, we'll probably never know. One thing about having money and power: no one can tell you what to do, even when it's for your own good. In fact, it's hard to find anyone honest enough to tell you that you need help... and Jerry was known to have a quick temper, particularly when it came to criticism. A psychiatrist told me that, based on the available evidence, he believed Jerry had developed a social phobia that manifested itself in a number of obsessive compulsive disorders. But since Jerry refused to see anyone, voluntary psychiatric examination was unlikely.

At any rate, his public appearances became increasingly infrequent, until he was rarely seen anymore. He lived either on his yacht, which no longer went anywhere but instead became permanently anchored in the San Diego harbor just off Coronado, or in his chalet in the Swiss Alps, which he'd reach by suborbital shuttle from a private spaceport in southern California. Models and movie stars were no longer his consorts, and drop-in visits to four-star restaurants became a thing of the past. ConSpace rolled right along, making money like no other company in the 21st Century, but its founder and CEO became a recluse only occasionally seen on some vice-president's wall screen.

Someone like Jerry doesn't withdraw from the public eye without questions being asked, and it wasn't long before his behavior became the subject of media speculation. The talking heads spent countless hours wondering what was going on; their theories ran from him having some hideous disease, perhaps a form of skin cancer that had permanently disfigured him, to the bizarre notion that he was dead, a victim of an accident that had taken his life, and that ConSpace was covering up his demise by carrying on the pretense that he was still alive. Photographers staked out his yacht, his chalet, even the spaceport, but all their long lenses ever caught was a distant figure, wearing a black overcoat and a slouch hat, who disappeared almost as quickly as he was spotted.

One of those blurred snapshots had appeared on a gossip site the morning I received a request to meet with ConSpace's executive vice-president. I had just sat down at my desk in the company's public relations department when I opened the red-flagged email. I stared at the brief message for a minute or so, wondering what I had done that would cause me to be summoned to Alberto Diaz's office. Was it a press release I had written? Coming back late from my lunch breaks? Was I about to be laid off only eight months after going to work for ConSpace? I had no idea. The email told me to come at once, so I put on the tie I kept in my desk drawer, left my cube without telling anyone where I was going, and took the elevator up to the top floor.

I thought I was about to be fired. I wasn't, but had I known what was about to happen, I would have quit right then and there.

Diaz's assistant was apparently expecting me. A perfect smile and a lilted request to wait just a moment, then she levitated through the oak door behind her. I had just enough time to admire the Chinese silk tapestries before she reappeared. Mr. Diaz would see me now, and would I like coffee?

You're usually not offered coffee just before you're fired, so I relaxed a little as she ushered me into Diaz's office. My entire department could have been relocated to that one room; the carpet alone was probably worth more than my salary. Alberto Diaz was seated behind an antique chestnut desk in front of floor-to-ceiling windows; Houston skyscrapers formed a backdrop behind him. He stood up as I walked in. A brief handshake, then I took a seat in a leather armchair across the desk from him.

I'd never met Alberto Diaz before. When I'd been interviewed for my job, the person who eventually hired me was the PR department's senior manager. This was my first visit to the executive suite. So I sat nervously and sipped the coffee Diaz's secretary brought me while her boss studied his desk screen. There was a cryptic smile on his face as his eyes moved back and forth, and every now and then he made a satisfied grunt. Alberto Diaz was in his mid-sixties, overweight, and losing his hair. Something about him bespoke a lifelong bully who'd learned how to imitate a gentleman.

"Lauderdale," he said at last, still not looking at me even as he said my name. "Paul Lauderdale... very, very interesting." He nodded to the screen. "Undergraduate degree in journalism, University of Missouri. Postgrad studies at Columbia University, no degree. Three years at the

Times, then you left journalism and went to work as a press secretary for Representative Joanna Robeson of New York…"

"Yes, sir. I…"

Diaz's eyes flitted toward me; he didn't say anything, but his expression told me that I wasn't to speak until given permission to do so. I shut up, and his attention returned to his screen. "You remained her press secretary for eight years, following her as she went from the House to the Senate, and left in… yes, I see, 2060." He was quiet for a moment. "That was the year she was involved that scandal, wasn't it? The one about payoffs to key House and Senate members?"

"Yes, sir."

His eyes turned toward me again, and this time they didn't move away. "Were you still working for her when she was indicted?"

"Yes, sir, I was." This wasn't something I'd told my boss during the job interview. Until now, no one at ConSpace knew about this chapter of my career. Alberto was pretty swift, picking up on something I'd tried to keep hidden.

"Uh-huh." He slowly nodded. "When did you quit?"

"About three weeks before she resigned."

"Why?" When I hesitated, a knowing smile crept across his face. "Don't worry. You're not going to lose your job. I just want to know why you decided to stop being press secretary for one of the most influential senators in Washington."

I let out my breath. "I got tired of lying for her, that's all." He seemed to be waiting, so I went on. "She was guilty, and she and I both knew it, but still I had to go out there every day and tell the press things that I knew to be untrue. After awhile, I realized that I was about to be dragged down with her, so I quit."

"I see." Again, Diaz slowly nodded. "So you know how to lie."

"Yes, I do. But it doesn't mean I like—"

"Tell me a lie."

"What?"

"Tell me a lie. Tell me something that isn't true."

"I… I don't know what you…"

"How's your wife?"

Diaz's eyes glittered when he said that. I decided then and there that I didn't like him. Nonetheless, I gave him an answer. "She's fine. We're doing great. Happy as a pair of clams."

He didn't even glance at the desk screen. "She divorced you three months ago. Court papers say she got full custody of your daughter. That was about five months after you went to work for us, isn't that right?"

"I said we're happy. I didn't say we're still married. And you didn't ask about our daughter."

He stared at me for a moment, then laughed out loud. "Oh, well done! Outstanding! A lie and the truth at the same time!" He was genuinely amused; I forced a smile and waited for him to go on. "So... an experienced journalist and former Capitol Hill press secretary, now a staff writer for our public relations department. What brings you here?"

I didn't know whether or not he wanted another lie, so I played it safe and told him the truth. "I've always been interested in space, and I was sick and tired of politics, so when I left Washington I looked for a job in the industry. ConSpace seemed to be the natural place to go. An old Mizzou classmate who used to work here gave me a referral, so... well, here I am."

"And here you are." Diaz rocked back in his chair. The smile remained on his face as he regarded me for a few seconds. "Sort of a waste of your talents, isn't it?" he said at last. "First a *Times* reporter, then a senior staff member for a U.S. Senator... and now you're churning out press releases. I'd think it would be a bit of a come-down."

"I think this job offers plenty of opportunity for career advancement." An automatic response, the very same thing I'd said during my interview.

Diaz shook his head. "No... no, it doesn't. Oh, your salary may go up a little, and if you play your cards right you may even get your boss's job when he retires. But that's as far as you'll ever go. Ten years from now, twenty years, thirty, you'll still be doing the same thing... writing press releases and handling media conferences."

Had he been anyone else, I might have argued with him. One look at Alberto Diaz's beefy face, though, and I knew that he was telling the truth. My job at ConSpace was a dead-end. I was destined to become nothing more than a flack, a corporate stooge doomed to a boring eight-to-five task, day after day, until someone came along and told me that the time had come for me to clean out my desk. Not the life I'd imagined for myself.

"Umm..." It seemed like I was supposed to say something. "Well, I..."

"That doesn't have to be the way it's going to be," Diaz said, rescuing me from whatever ineffectual response I was about to make. "I have a better job for you, one that's more suitable for someone of your talent and experience." A smile hovered at the corners of his mouth. "Particularly your ability to be honest and untruthful at the same time. That's a true gift, my friend, and I have a use for it."

I didn't like the way he called me "my friend," nor the fact that he considered lying to be an enviable gift, but I tried not to show it. "What do you...?"

Again, his eyes hardened, and I took that as a silent cue to shut up. "You're familiar with our CEO, aren't you? Jerry Stone?" I nodded and he went on. "Well, Mr. Stone needs a personal media representative... someone who will act as a go-between in his relations with the public at large."

"Someone to write press releases for him," I said.

Diaz shook his head. "Oh, no. You may be doing some of that, of course, but the person he needs will do far more than the usual PR. He wants someone who will act as his public persona. Someone to speak for him, taking his statements and giving them a face and a voice acceptable to the outside world."

"A spokesman, you mean."

"Yes... but more than that, I think." Diaz hesitated. "In many ways, Paul, you'll be closer to him than anyone else. He may say things to you that he won't share with any of the board members... not even me. Of course, we'll want you to report such matters to us, but... well, that's something we'll have to work out."

"I see." I was becoming intrigued. "So... does this mean I'll be meeting with Mr. Stone on a regular basis?"

"No." Diaz shook his head. "Not in person, if that's what you mean. His dealings with you will be... um, a bit distant." He must have noticed the look on my face, because he leaned forward in his chair. "Mr. Stone will soon be... ah, shall we say, making some lifestyle changes... that are rather unusual. Because of this, he wants someone who will act as an intermediary. As I said, a spokesman, but more than that."

"I see," I replied, even though I didn't. "And when would I begin this job? Next week?"

"No, not for a month or two. For the time being, you'll continue your present tasks. But if everything goes according to plan, we'll be asking you to assume your new position in about eight weeks." Another smile.

"Believe me, it will be much more interesting than your current position. You'll have your job for as long as you want it… unless Jerry says that he wants someone else, of course, at which time we'll find another position for you in the company. And your pay will be commensurate with your new responsibilities."

I asked what my new salary would be, and he gave me a figure that made me realize that I would never again worry about the mortgage. Even Sen. Robeson hadn't taken home that much dough before she got caught with her hand in the cookie jar.

"Well… all right then," I said. "I'll take the job."

"Very good." Diaz's smile remained fixed; he made a small, dismissive gesture with his hand, shooing me to the door. "We'll call you when we need you.

Diaz eventually made good on his promise. But long before he called —only a couple of days after our conversation, in fact—I heard from someone else.

I had just gotten home from work when the phone buzzed. I was about to touch the VIEW button when I noticed the blinking yellow light telling me that the call was voice-only; the holo was disabled and the display read PRIVATE UNLISTED.

The only person who called me that way was my ex. Expecting another nag about late child support payments, I snatched up the receiver. "Yeah, what is it?"

"Hello?" A young-sounding male voice. *"Is this Paul Lauderdale?"*

"Yeah, what do you want?" I'm not normally that abrupt, but my former wife had really been getting on my nerves lately. Whoever was calling me, he sounded rattled by the way I'd picked up the phone. Figuring that he was another lawyer, I wanted to keep him that way. The sooner I got rid of him, the sooner I could have a drink and make dinner.

"My apologies for the intrusion. I just wanted to…"

"Who is this?"

"Jerry Stone."

"Uhh… pardon me?"

"I'd like to, but you're making it difficult."

The voice was his; once he identified himself, I recognized him immediately. My mouth opened, closed, opened again. I discovered that it's possible to remain standing upright after your heart stops beating; it's not easy, but it can be done. "I... I... I..."

"Yes, Paul? You'd like to say something?" Faint amusement in his tone.

"Mr. Stone, I'm... I'm sorry. I'm so, so sorry." I managed to find a seat somewhere besides the floor. "I didn't know... I mean, I thought you were..."

"Your ex. Either that, or her lawyer."

Not a question, but a statement of fact. For half a second, I wondered how he would have known this, then I remembered to whom I was speaking. Jerry Stone had information assets that probably matched the world's best intelligence agencies; he could have probably told me not only the name of my first-grade teacher, but also whom she'd been dating.

"Yes, sir, that's who I thought you..." I took a deep breath. "Sir, I know that's not a good excuse. Please pardon me for..."

"No reason to apologize. I called in a manner usually done by your former wife's attorneys. No wonder you mistook me for one of them." A brief chuckle. *"Actually, I'm impressed. If you're going to be my personal spokesman, there may be times when I'll want you to be rude. The press in particular will have questions that you and I can't or won't answer, and telling them to go to hell may be our only option. Do you understand?"*

This was not something I looked forward to doing, but I wasn't about to say so. "Yes, sir. I understand."

"Good." A short pause. *"Anyway, I just wanted to give you a quick call and take a moment to say hello. Alberto believes you're the perfect person for this job. I've looked at your record and I think he's right."*

"Thank you, sir."

"I should warn you, if Al didn't, that this may be a long-term relationship. I'll be absent for quite some time, and circumstances will have it that you may be my sole means of contact with just about everyone else. So I'm expecting you to remain a ConSpace employee for many years. Do you think you can do this?"

This was not part of the agreement I'd made with Diaz, but I had little doubt that, if Jerry Stone was making this a condition of my employment, ConSpace would probably have me sign legal documents which would assure that I couldn't suddenly quit and walk away. If I said yes, the contract would be on my desk by tomorrow morning. On the other hand, the money was pretty damn good. And in the present economy, it would give considerable peace of mind to know that my job wasn't going to disappear any time soon.

"Yes, sir, I can," I said at last.

"Excellent. I'm pleased to hear this." A dry laugh. *"Well, then, I'll let you get back to what you were doing."* I waited for him to ask me what I was having for dinner, but apparently that didn't interest him… or he already knew. *"It will be a while before we speak again, so until then…"*

"Sir… Mr. Stone?"

"Call me Jerry, please."

I wasn't ready to do that. "Could I ask a question, please?" No reply; he was waiting for me to go on. "When you said you were going to be absent for quite some time… what did you mean by that?"

"You'll find out soon enough. Good night, Paul." And then he hung up.

I said nothing to anyone about my new job. In fact, the only person who had an inkling that my life had changed was my ex-wife's lawyer, who called to thank me for sending the child-support payments on time. This discretion wasn't entirely my choice. As I expected, my promotion had come with a contractual agreement; Page 7, Paragraph 14 was a clause prohibiting me from revealing confidential information about my employer. I had no idea what Jerry was planning, but it would be unwise to make it a topic of water cooler conversation.

However, only a few days after I spoke with Jerry, I had a hint of things to come. That morning, the PR office sent out a press release about an upcoming test program. Since I wrote the release myself, I knew the details better than most people.

Over the past decade, ConSpace had been developing an experimental propulsion system which combined the best features of solar sails and lasers. The hybrid involved a very large solar-cell array, built on the lunar farside near Daedalus Crater, which used laser amplifiers to focus photons through a series of lenses, then fire them as a high-power beam which could aimed almost anywhere. Its target was a spacecraft with a 3,280-foot diameter solar sail and a 1,000-ton payload module tethered at its center. The photon beam would push against the sail, and the beamship would be carried away. Once the vessel arrived at its destination, another beam projector would fire at the sail from the opposite direction, thus braking the ship and allowing it to enter orbit.

ConSpace hoped that, if the test program proved out, beamships would eventually replace the nuclear-powered cycleships that traveled between Earth and Mars, with photon projectors erected on Deimos sending the ships back to Earth as well as decelerating them. The advantage was obvious; since beamships wouldn't have to carry their own fuel, their payload mass could be used almost entirely for passengers and cargo. It was also calculated that beamships could cut the average travel time between Earth and Mars from five months to one, thus allowing more ships to make the crossing at a fraction of the cost.

Before attempting anything so ambitious, though, the company had to make sure that the system actually worked. So ConSpace decided to send a prototype beamship to a target not quite as far from Earth as Mars, but even harder to reach: asteroid 2010 TK7.

2010 TK7 is an anomaly among near-Earth objects. Only about 1,000 feet in diameter, it occupies a Lagrange point about 60 degrees further along Earth's heliocentric orbit, making it a tiny companion that precedes Earth as it travels around the Sun. Such Trojan asteroids are also located near Mars, Jupiter, and Neptune, but not until the early 21st Century was it found that Earth had one of its own. Unlike other near-Earth asteroids whose orbits periodically take them behind the sun, though, 2010 TK7 is never totally invisible from Earth. It always remains within sight, although its low albedo made it difficult for astronomers to find in the first place.

Even for a Trojan, 2010 TK7 is unusual. As it revolves around the Sun, the asteroid spirals around its orbital plane, with each oscillation taking a little more than a year to complete. Furthermore, this spiral is inclined about 21 degrees above and below the solar plane of ellipse. Imagine an old-fashioned Slinky toy that's been stretched out, pulled into a loop, then had its coils tilted sideways, and you get a rough idea of the asteroid's movement around the Sun.

This weird orbit means that the asteroid's distance from Earth varies greatly over time. During a 390-year period, 2010 TK7 is between .8 AU and 1.19 AU from Earth. Thus, its delta-v—the factor for its change of velocity—is about 9.4 kilometers per second. For those of us who don't talk like rocket scientists, this means that a ship would have to use up a lot of fuel to get there. Enough, in fact, to make a round-trip prohibitive.

Since a beamship doesn't carry its own fuel, though, this wouldn't be a issue. The photon projector on the Moon would automatically track the asteroid, adjusting its aim so that the ship would remain on course. Once the ship arrived at the asteroid, its crew would erect an identical projector on its surface, thus allowing the vessel to return home the same way.

There wasn't much about 2010 TK7 that seemed to make the trip worth the effort. It appeared to be no more than a wad of rock; although there seemed to be ice deposits beneath the surface, spectral analysis hadn't revealed any metallic traces which would have lured asteroid miners. However, it was an ideal site for ConSpace to test its prototype beam-propulsion system, which was why the company was sending an experimental beamship, the *Achilles*, out there.

I sent the press release to the usual newsites and scheduled a press conference for the next day. Only three reporters showed up, and they were probably there for the coffee and doughnuts. I couldn't blame anyone for their lack of interest. An experimental propulsion system was hardly home-page news, no more or less important than anything else the company was doing at the time.

Achilles launched from lunar orbit on November 11, 2063, and arrived at 2010 TK7 about a month later. The beamship furled its sails, then fired descent engines and made a soft landing, firing pitons into the rocky terrain to anchor itself. Its five-member crew sent back a photo of themselves standing on its cinder-black surface, with Earth a small blue-green orb hovering above the close horizon. The shot appeared on a couple of newsites as filler between that day's man-bites-dog stories. Another landmark in the human exploration of space. Whoopie.

Achilles remained on 2010 TK7 for almost two weeks. I wondered why the expedition stayed so long—someone in the engineering division told me that the beam projector and its solar array were largely preassembled and would only take a few days to erect—but I figured that the science department had some experiments that they wanted the crew to conduct. However, I noticed that the control center where the mission was being monitored was kept closed, with no one but a handful of personnel allowed inside. Not only that, but precious little information about the expedition being sent to the PR department. It was as if the company didn't want the public to know what was happening on 2010 TK7.

Which, in fact, they did not. It wasn't until after *Achilles* lifted off from the asteroid, though, that only a few people knew why.

I was one of the first to learn the truth. I was at my desk when Alberto Diaz called. Would I please come upstairs? This was the first time I'd heard from him in a couple of months, and I was beginning to wonder if he'd forgotten about me. Better late than never, though. I put down what I was doing and took the elevator to the top floor. His assistant was waiting for me; another offer of coffee, then she escorted me to an oak-paneled executive boardroom.

Alberto was seated the far end of a long table, the only person in the room. Well, not exactly; he was only person *physically* in the room. Behind him was a massive wall screen, and on the screen, bigger than life, was Jerry Stone.

Jerry seemed to be staring straight at me, an amused smile upon his face. "We received this about twenty minutes ago," Diaz said, and that was when I realized that Jerry's image was a vid frozen in replay. "Sit down. You need to hear this."

I took a seat across the table from him. Diaz waved a hand above an embedded remote, and Jerry came to life. *"Hello, Paul. I assume Al has asked you to hear this, and that he obeyed my instructions to keep you in the dark until he heard directly from me. So now that you're here, let me tell you what's going on."*

Jerry's hand moved forward; apparently he was sitting on a camp stool in front of a camera he was operating himself. The image pulled back a little, and now I saw that he was in a pressurized compartment: burnished steel walls, a couple of control panels, a ceiling handrail. A hardsuit dangled from a rack, its helmet upon a shelf above it.

"Yes, I'm in space," Jerry said, *"but I'm not where you might think I'd be. Can you guess where? I'll give you a hint... I'm so far away that two-way conversation is impossible unless you'd care to wait about fifteen minutes to hear me reply to anything you might say."* His smile became playful. *"And, no, I'm not on Mars."*

From the corner of my eye, I saw Diaz watching me expectantly. I looked at him. "If he's not on Mars, then he must be..." And then I remembered *Achilles*. "Oh, no. You can't be serious. Tell me he's not..."

"That's right." Jerry was keeping up his end of an imaginary conversation, but nonetheless I had the eerie feeling that he'd heard me.

"I'm on 2010 TK7. After I spoke with you, I left Earth the very next morning and boarded the Achilles *two days later. No one except Alberto, the ship's crew, and a few ground controllers knew I was aboard. I didn't tell anyone else, not even the company directors. And in case you think this is a hoax..."*

Jerry stood up. There was just enough gravity to keep him seated so long as he remained still, but the momentum of getting up from his stool was enough to cause him to float upward. The camera tracked him as he rose to the low ceiling above him. *"See? Not a gag. And if you're still not convinced..."*

Still grinning, he grabbed hold of a handrail and pulled himself toward the camera. He disappeared behind it; a moment later, the image jiggled a little, then there was a soft snap as Jerry detached the camera from its mount. The image blurred as Jerry carried the camera toward a small porthole set in the center of a pressure door. His face was reflected in the glass for a second, then the view through the porthole sharpened as he focused the lens. Now we could see the asteroid surface; in the foreground were several cargo containers, apparently left behind by the *Achilles* before it left, and farther away were the solar array and parabolic dish of the beam projector.

"Here's my new home," Jerry continued, off-camera. *"I'm in the airlock, the only part that's above the surface. Before they left, I had the crew excavate the first four rooms of the underground shelter where I'll live. They left the laser drills and other excavation equipment, along with plenty of building material, so I'll be able to complete the project. It'll take a while to finish, but I'm calling it the Stone House."*

The camera jiggled again as Jerry reattached it to the mount, then he reappeared. *"They've left me enough food, water, and air to keep me alive for a couple of months, and I've arranged for unmanned beamships to regularly bring supplies from the Moon."* His expression became a little more serious. *"I don't want any visitors. I mean it. No one, repeat, no one has permission to come out here. If any other ships comes out this way, I won't give permission for it to land or let anyone through the airlock."*

Jerry didn't sit down, but instead stood in front of the camera. *"How long am I going to be here? I don't know. Maybe I'll be back in a few months. Maybe a few years. Or maybe never."* He shrugged. *"Believe me,*

I haven't done this without studying it carefully. If all goes well, I should be able to live here indefinitely. As for the obvious question…"

He paused, looking away for a moment. *"Well, that's a little hard to explain. Let's just say that I'm sick of people and I want to get away for awhile. I'm rich enough that I can do whatever I want, and this is what I want to do."*

The smile suddenly returned. He looked straight at the camera again. *"Anyway… well, there it is. Write a press release, call a press conference, do whatever you need to do. Any further communications will come straight from me to you. Your job is to be my surrogate… my eyes, ears, and mouth. If you or anyone else has questions, send me either a memo or a vid, and I'll get back to you as soon as I can. Alberto will take care of business while I'm gone, but you'll be my voice. Got it?"*

The smile faded. *"I guess that's about all for now. Let me know what the media says about all this…"* An abrupt laugh. *"No, on second thought, don't. They're a big reason why I'm doing this."* Another shrug. *"Keep in touch, all right? Merry Christmas, and so long…"*

He reached toward the camera. The screen went dark.

I let out my breath, then looked across the table at Diaz. Arms folded across his chest, he gazed back at me, his expression implacable. "You knew he was going to do this?" I asked, and he slowly nodded. "Why?"

"You heard him. He wants to get away from people." He shook his head. "It's his money, his life. If that's what he wants to do…"

He didn't finish the thought. He was curiously indifferent; apparently he thought Jerry's move was only temporary and that he'd return in a month or two. "Yeah, well—" I pushed back my chair— "maybe I better get started on that press conference. The media is going to love this."

"I'm sure they will." Diaz watched as I stood up. "Just one thing… the next time you hear from him, let me know what he says before you go public with it, okay?"

"Sure. But why…?"

"Maybe it's best that you do." He hesitated. "Don't tell anyone I said this, but I'm not sure Jerry is still sane."

That's what a lot of people said after the story broke.

The *Achilles* expedition had been minor news before I heard from Jerry, but it jumped to the big-font headlines after I put out the release. So many people showed up for the press conference, we had to move it to an auditorium, and forget the coffee and sinkers.

No one was interested in photon beam propulsion or even 2010 TK7. What they wanted to know was why one of the world's richest men decided to become a hermit on an asteroid so far away that a Tibetan monastery would have been a Park Avenue penthouse by comparison. Jerry Stone had always been a figure of interest, but in recent years he'd faded from view; that changed the moment ConSpace revealed that he'd taken up residence on 2010 TK7.

As Jerry's spokesman, I was careful with what I told the media. I struck to the essential details, giving them the first four of the five w's— who, what, when, and where—while staying clear of the fifth—why—as much as possible. I assured them that Jerry was still the company's president and CEO, and that he would continue being involved with both day-to-day operations and long-range decision making. I showed them an edited portion of the vid he'd sent from the asteroid, carefully leaving out the part where he became vague about his return plans, and said that he was tired of dealing with the human race.

Alberto Diaz was in the room. He quietly stood off to one side, leaning against the wall as he silently watched me field questions from the press. I'd offered Alberto a chance to speak, but he didn't take it. He seemed content to let me be Jerry's ombudsman, and I was glad that he did. I hadn't yet made up my mind about Jerry's mental health, but I sure as hell didn't want a senior executive who thought the boss had gone off the deep end to be talking to the press.

The story hit the news sites and became an instant sensation. Across the entire width and breadth of webspace, everyone weighed in with their opinions, informed or otherwise. By then, I'd moved to a new office, this time on the top floor, complete with my own window and a door I could shut whenever I pleased. I was no longer a cube gnome, but I paid for my newfound status with an increased workload; the first week, all I did was take care of interview requests. Those were easy to handle; Jerry wasn't interested in talking to anyone except me. What was more difficult was telling reporters why no one would be able to visit him even if they tried to hire a spacecraft pilot to carry them out to 2010 TK7. Try explaining orbital mechanics to someone who barely understands Newton's third law, and see how far that gets you.

Did people think Jerry had flipped out? Yep. In fact, that was the general consensus: Jerry Stone had gone mad, nuts, bonzo, bull goose crazy, or however you want to say it, and that was why he'd moved to a remote asteroid. I relayed the most pertinent commentary to the Stone House, yet Jerry didn't respond. No matter how stupid or unkind the remarks were, he kept himself above the fray, which was exactly what he should have done.

As usual, the story faded after about ten days or so. A movie star got caught in bed with someone who was neither his wife nor the legal age of consent, and the celebrity kick-me sign was removed from Jerry's back. I still received the occasional interview request, but otherwise, my job became easier.

I was still Jerry's point man, though, which meant that all communications between him and ConSpace's various directors, division heads, and senior managers filtered through me. On a daily basis, I received an average of two dozen memos—at least half of them flagged *Urgent*—which needed to be sent to 2010 TK7. I'd forward them to the operations center, which would transmit them to ConSpace's deep-space communications network, which in turn would relay them to Jerry... and then everyone would sit back and wait for a reply. If we were very lucky, we'd get a response within half an hour. That meant Jerry was reading his email and considered the issue to be important enough to warrant an immediate reply. Most of the time, though, we would have to wait hours, even days, to hear back from him... if at all. After a while, Jerry developed his own method of dealing with stuff he didn't consider to be worth his attention: cold silence. I'd ping him a couple of times, reminding him that he hadn't responded to a particular message, and then I'd have to go back to the person who sent the original memo and tell them that the boss wasn't interested in anything that they had to say. Think that's fun? Get your ear chewed off a few times by someone who obviously thinks you're an uppity little roadblock, and let me know if you still do.

Most of the time, Jerry's communiqués took the form of written memos, each signed with his digital signature. On occasion, though, I'd receive a vid, relayed straight to my office from the ops center. About three weeks after he moved to the asteroid, Jerry startled me by shaving his head; he explained that having hair was a nuisance in 2010 TK7'S almost non-existent gravity, so he'd decided to get rid of it. Jerry had always been a rather charismatic person, but it was surprising to find just how much that depended on a full head of hair: bald, he looked like a monk. I tried to keep those pictures from going public, but they inevitably did, and they convinced a lot of people that Jerry had lost his mind.

His changed appearance was only his first surprise. The second came during the sixth vid he sent me. That was when a fogz showed up.

Jerry was in the midst of answering a question from the company's propulsion lab when a fuzzy red-and-white object floated between the camera lens and him. At first I thought it was a sweater, then it twisted around and I found myself staring at two brown eyes that mischievously regarded me from above a short canine muzzle.

It was a fox. Or at least that's what I thought it was. Startled, I recoiled from the screen at the same time that Jerry gently grabbed the animal by the long, soft-looking fur at the back of its neck.

"Reynard! Behave!" Jerry pulled the fox away from the camera. Its mouth stretched into a wily, sharp-toothed grin as it settled into the crook of Jerry's arm, its long white-tipped tail curling around his neck. *"Sorry 'bout that,"* he said apologetically. *"Sometimes they get in the way."* Then he realized that I'd probably have no idea what he was holding. *"This is Reynard. He's one of three fogzes I've brought with me as companions. I kept them in biostasis until a few days ago. I wanted to make sure that the Stone House's life-support system was adequate for all four of us before I woke up Ren and Sylva as well."*

"That's nice," I murmured. I'd lately started talking to Jerry even though he couldn't hear me. "What the hell is a fogz?"

Reynard bent forward to lick Jerry's cheek. For all the world, he could have been a puppy. *"Thanks, pal,"* Jerry said, his grin matching his pet's, as he shifted Reynard from one arm to the other. *"In case you're wondering... a fogz is my invention. Well, sort of. I asked the guys at a bioengineering company I own if they could give me a pet that would be suitable for microgravity. They chose the domesticated Russian fox. A little tinkering with its genome, and they came up with these guys. We call 'em fogzes... short for zero-g foxes."*

He let Reynard go, and I noticed for the first time that the fogz's legs were stunted while its tail was longer and bushier. Reynard kicked off from Jerry and flagellated its tail to propel itself across the compartment.

"I've got two males and a female," Jerry said as he watched it go. *"None of them are neutered, so I expect that it won't be long before Sylva has kits. I'd offer to send you one… they're really sweet… but I don't think he or she would be happy on Earth. Too much gravity. But at least I'll have plenty of friends to keep me company."*

I was glad to hear that Jerry wasn't entirely alone out there. However, the fact that he was committed to raising generations of fogzes made me realize that he'd been fudging things a bit when he said that he might come home soon. This, and the fact that an unmanned cargo beamship was already scheduled to be launched from lunar orbit, hinted that Jerry was going to be out there longer than a few months.

This worried me, so I called Charles David, his personal physician. Charlie came over later that day, and I showed him the vid I'd just received. He didn't say anything until it was over, then he sat back in his chair and let out his breath.

"How long has Jerry been out there?" he asked. "Be specific, if you can."

I checked my calendar. "Four months, two weeks, three days, and… um, call it twelve hours." I thought about it another moment, then added, "That's not counting the month or so it took the beamship to get him there."

"Okay… almost six months, total. That's not so bad. It takes cycleships six months to get to Mars, and their carousels don't spin the entire time. And the old American and Russian spacers used to live on the first space stations for up to two years, although they were usually in sad shape when they came home." He frowned. "But still… I'm worried about him."

"I was afraid you might say that." I glanced at my office door to make sure it was closed. "If he stays out there too long…"

"It's going to affect his long-term health, yeah. Do you know if he's exercising regularly? I told him that he needed to spend at least an hour a day on the treadmill."

"I don't know. He's never mentioned it to me." In fact, in all the vids he'd sent me, I'd never seen a treadmill anywhere in the background. Perhaps one had been sent with him, but he'd never unpacked it.

"If he's not exercising daily, and he doesn't come home in another month or two, he'd need significant rehabilitation before he can walk again." Charlie hesitated. "And if he remains out there much longer than that, then his cardiovascular system will undergo significant deterioration. Bone calcium loss, muscle atrophy... sure, he may be able to stay alive indefinitely so long as he remains in low gravity and doesn't expose himself unnecessarily to cosmic radiation. But coming back to Earth could be fatal."

I didn't say anything for a second or two. In none of his memos or vids had Jerry had given me any indication that he planned to leave 2010 TK7 any time soon. In fact, only the other day he'd sent me the final list of things that he wanted to be placed aboard the cargo ship. Along with a larger industrial-grade excavation drill and several pallets of building materials—he was planning to expand his subsurface living quarters, including an addition to his greenhouse—he'd requested sufficient food, water, and compressed air to get him through another six months. And aside from a modified powersat construction pod that he could use for station repair, he didn't have a spacecraft out there, or at least one capable of bringing him home.

"I'll remind him of that," I said. Charlie David might be Jerry's doctor, but I didn't want to risk telling him anything that might go public. One of the sleazier newsites had a standing offer of $50,000 for juicy info about Jerry—that's how the shaved-head pictures got out—and even a physician's confidentiality can be bought.

"Do that, please. At the very least, remind him to wear his biomonitor bracelet. I've tried to keep tabs on him, but he forgets to put it on in the morning."

Jerry went halfway with me. He began wearing the bracelet constantly. Returning to Earth, though, was another matter entirely.

The months went by, and Jerry Stone didn't come home. The months became a year, and Jerry stayed where he was. A year became two years, then three, then more... and by then it was obvious that 2010 TK7 had a permanent resident.

My place in ConSpace's upper management had become permanent as well. I was Jerry's proxy, his mouthpiece, his mannequin. My status was clarified by none other than Alberto Diaz, who abandoned his pretensions of civility shortly after I moved to the top floor. At first, when he visited my office, he'd begin by saying, "The next time you hear from

Jerry, tell him…". After a while, though, it became, "Tell Jerry…". Eventually he rarely mentioned Jerry's name at all, instead simply speaking to me as if I was Jerry's eyes and ears and somehow expecting his message to be telepathically communicated to the boss. The next time I saw Alberto, he'd be expecting an answer: "What about that problem I talked to you about yesterday? Have you decided what to do yet…?"

Ironically enough, Jerry still had an office just down the hall. He'd seldom visited it even before he left Earth for the final time, but nonetheless it was the place where his executive assistant answered his mail, sent out memos in his name, and otherwise maintained the illusion that he was going to come strolling in any minute now. She was eventually transferred to another department, but the office was still there; its door was closed but not locked, and every so often a custodian would come by to dust the place. If you walked in, you'd see evidence of his former presence. His pictures were on the walls, his mementoes were on the shelves, and there was even a sport coat hanging from a hook on the other side of the door. But the desk was clear of everything except an empty notebook and a phone, and its drawers contained nothing but company stationary and a few pens.

Jerry himself was gone. He'd literally disappeared from the face of the Earth, and as time went by, I heard from him less and less. I dutifully forwarded to him personnel memos, departmental reports, and the minutes of the annual stockholder meetings, and sometimes I'd get a response and sometimes I wouldn't. When he replied, it was usually a terse memo of his own, addressed either to an individual or a group, which I would then relay through the proper channels. As time went by, contact between Jerry and the company he'd founded became increasingly tenuous. ConSpace went about its business as usual, with its CEO an unseen oracle living in a temple on some faraway island.

Meanwhile, history moved on. There had always been rivalry between the Pax Astra and its independent competitors, the Transient Body Shipping Association, over economic control of the asteroid belt and the newly-established Jovian colonies. The TBSA and the Jovian colonists eventually formed a secret alliance, the Zodiac, which began preying upon Pax vessels operating in the outer solar system. This caused political turmoil in the Pax, with the democratic New Ark Party losing control to neo-monarchists during a bloodless *coup d'etat*. The Mars colonies seceded from the Pax shortly after Queen Macedonia's coronation, and formed the Ares Alliance. War talk was in the air.

All this had an enormous impact on ConSpace. Its commercial alliance with the Pax Astra had relied upon the Mars colonies belonging to the Pax and the Pax remaining a democracy. When the Zodiac started attacking Pax spacecraft in the belt, it was ConSpace who had the most to lose; the majority of those ships belonged to the company. And because the monarchists never liked the cozy relationship between the Pax and ConSpace, one of the first things that Queen Macedonia's prime minister, Sir Lucius Robeson, did upon gaining power was to tear up all the existing contracts. This left the Ares Alliance and a handful of independent near-Earth space companies as ConSpace's major clients, and it was anyone's guess how long the Mars colonies would continue doing business with a corporation that had begun to bleed as badly as ConSpace did.

Things may have been different if Jerry was still around. He might have been able to negotiate a new agreement with the Pax monarchists, or even use back-channels to get in touch with the Zodiac and work out a truce with them. But he ignored all memos and reports telling him that everything was going to hell in a bucket, and the few times I spoke to him—which came down to about once every few weeks, and only when he called me—he preferred to chat about things like the wonderful roses he was cultivating in the greenhouse, or how Sylva had just given birth to another litter of fogzes. He was happy, I'll say that for him… happier than he'd been in his last years on Earth. So long as the Zodiac didn't raid the Stone House—highly unlikely; 2010 TK7's eccentric orbit assured his privacy—he didn't seem to care what happened to his company.

His indifference wasn't mutual. The morning after a ConSpace freighter en route to Ceres was destroyed by a Zodiac raider, Alberto Diaz marched into my office. He didn't bother to knock, but instead dropped a folder on my desk. Before I had a chance to pick it up, he sat down in a chair across from me.

"Tell Jerry he's fired," he said.

"Pardon me?"

"He's fired." Alberto propped his feet up on my desk and regarded me with smug little eyes. "The board of directors met this morning and took a vote, and they decided to replace him. He's no longer CEO… I am."

I stared at Alberto for a moment. So far as I could tell, he hadn't indulged himself in a martini breakfast, so I picked up the folder and opened it. Inside was a corporate resolution, signed by the board of directors and notarized by the company's legal council, formally dismissing Jerry Stone as president and chief executive officer of ConSpace.

"You can't do this," I said. "Jerry's the majority stockholder…"

"Not any more, he's not." Alberto propped his chin upon his hand in the amused gesture of a chess master who'd just pulled a cunning move against an inexperienced novice. "Jerry's cash flow has become a bit tight lately. All the stuff he needs, the expense of shipping out there… it takes a lot of jack. He finally had to sell a few shares of company stock. Just enough to make ends meet, but—" a sly grin "—as soon as it came on the market, a friend of mine who works on Wall Street tipped me off and…"

"You bought him out."

"Yes, I did." He shrugged. "It wasn't much, really… but just enough that, once I added it to my portfolio, I was able to make a deal with the board's other principal shareholders. They're just as tired of putting up with him as I am, and we think we can turn the company around before it goes into the toilet."

"Maybe you can, or maybe you can't, but—"

"No, no… no 'buts' about it. Jerry's out. Tell him to pack his bags, we're bringing him home. Keeping him on that rock is a major drain on company finances, and it's not earning us a dime." His smile became mean. "Then you can start cleaning out your desk, too."

"What? I…"

"You don't get it, do you?" Alberto still had his feet crossed on my desk; he deliberately shifted his right foot, toppling a ceramic mug my daughter had made for me that I used as a pen holder. The mug fell over, spilling pens and pencils across my desk. I reached forward to grab the mug before Alberto could kick it off my desk, and he snickered. "If he doesn't have a job here anymore, then neither do you. So pack up, you little worm. You're outta here."

I didn't respond. Anything I could have said would have only satisfied him. I'd pegged Alberto Diaz the moment I met him; he was a playground bully who'd never grown up. Maybe he'd been planning this the entire time, waiting for a chance to oust Jerry so that he and his cronies could take over ConSpace. Now his time had come… and I knew that, if I wasn't careful, firing me would be only the first way he'd punish me for being loyal to Jerry.

So I waited until Alberto left, and then I opened a direct line to the Stone House. It took about ten minutes to tell Jerry what had just happened; when I was done, I flagged the vid *Urgent* and sent it on its way, and hoped that Jerry wasn't too busy playing with his fogzes to check his messages.

He wasn't. When I returned from the mail room with a couple of empty cardboard boxes, a red light was flashing on my desk screen: an incoming message from Jerry. I shut the door, sat down at the desk, and typed in my password. What I found was an encrypted text message, utilizing a private code that we used for high-priority business messages. I entered in a second password that deciphered the code, and an instant lster the unscrambled message appeared on my screen:

Paul—Sorry this has happened. Hate to say it, but I've been expecting this for awhile.

Never really trusted D. Figured he'd stick a knife in my back sooner or later. Couldn't fire him from the board, though, because he has too much support (politics… ugh! one more reason why I left).

Anyway, I prepared for this. Go to my office and find my safe. It's behind the Mars painting. Enter the combination: Rats Live On No Evil Star. There's a minidisk in there. Don't read it. Just take it to BK. He'll know what to do.

Sit tight. Don't worry. Everything will be fine.—J

I deleted the message and erased it from the memory buffer, then got up and, as casually as I could, sauntered down the hall to Jerry's office. Several empty boxes were stacked beside the door—Alberto obviously wasn't wasting time—but no one was inside.

Hanging above the couch was an original Eggleton of a Martian landscape that Jerry had once purchased in a Sotheby's auction. I'd often admired the painting, but never dreamt that it might hide anything. Yet it did; the painting was mounted on a hinged door that opened silently when I moved the frame, revealing a wall safe with an alphanumerical keypad recessed within its chrome steel door.

I typed in the first letters of the palindrome and the safe popped open. Inside were stock certificates, several letters, a small metal box that I didn't open, and enough bundled cash to pay a CEO's kidnap ransom. The minidisk lay on top of the cash.

I have to admit, for a moment or two my own loyalty was tested. I could have taken the money and trashed the minidisk, and no one would have been the wiser. What could have Jerry done—fire me? Any temptation I might have felt to betray Jerry, though, lasted only a second. Jerry had always been good to me, while Alberto had screwed both of us the first chance he had. So I slipped the disk into my shirt pocket, closed the safe, and covered it with the painting again.

BK was Benny Klein, Jerry's personal attorney and also one of his closest friends. His office was only four blocks away; I caught a rickshaw cab and was there in fifteen minutes. I didn't call ahead—it was possible that Alberto might have the company security team tapping my phones—but Benny let me see him without an appointment. I handed him the minidisk, told him what was going on at ConSpace and how Jerry had instructed me to deliver the disk to him, and then left.

I had no idea what was on the disk. All I knew was that Benny had made good use of it. By the end of the day, Alberto Diaz was gone, as were three members of the board of directors. All four resigned immediately, after issuing a joint statement saying that they were leaving to pursue new careers outside the space industry.

However, Alberto's attempted palace coup was successful to some degree. A week after it happened, Jerry sent me a brief memo, announcing that he'd decided to step down as president and CEO of ConSpace.

I asked him why, of course, but his response was brief and uninformative: *Because I want to* was the gist of it. When Jerry didn't want to answer a question, that was the best reply one was likely to get; silence was his usual response.

I did as I was supposed to do. I called Alberto's successor, another board member who'd not been jettisoned during the purge, and let him know that he was in for another surprise. This fellow convened the remaining directors in the executive board room, where I gave them Jerry's memo. Once they picked themselves off the floor, they sent Jerry a letter demanding an explanation.

Jerry must have been waiting for them to call back, because his reply was received within minutes. This time, he sent a vid. He was seated in his greenhouse, wearing a linen dashiki and surrounded by tomato vines and green algae tanks, a silver-and-black fogz nestled in his arms. Although his head was still shaved, lately he'd let his beard grow out. To me, he appeared to be his normal self—relaxed, smiling, unconcerned with such trifles as the leadership of a major corporation—but when I looked at him through the eyes of the board members, I saw a wealthy eccentric whose mind had slipped its last tenuous grip on sanity.

"Good day, gentlemen," he said, gently stroking the fogz in his arms. *"I appreciate your prompt response to the memo I sent Paul earlier today. I also appreciate your concern, especially since it follows hard on the heels of last week's misadventure."*

Some of the directors looked askance at each other. The company had undergone a major crisis, and he called it a "misadventure." Jerry went on. *"However, recent events have led me to realize something that I've suspected for awhile now… that my absence has become detrimental to the company's future, and that ConSpace needs a chief executive who is actually on Earth, if not in Houston."*

The fogz—Ren, if I wasn't mistaken—yawned indolently as Jerry's hands continued to stroke his plush fur. *"However, I have no desire to return to Earth. My home is here, and I don't wish to leave it. So I'm willing to make an agreement with the board. I will step down as president and CEO, and also sell all but ten percent of my remaining stock in the company. In return, the company will respect my status as founder and president emeritus by continuing to support my residence here on 2010 TK7, including sending any necessary supplies that I may need…"*

He suddenly snapped his fingers, as if remembering something. *"Oh, yes… another thing or two. I wish to remain alone and undisturbed… but I'd like to have Paul Lauderdale continue as my private spokesman, with the company paying his salary."* He smiled. *"Over the last few years, I've come to rely on Paul, and the events of last week have proved that my trust hasn't been misplaced.….unlike a few other individuals I could mention, that is."*

A couple of people coughed while others averted their gaze. Although Alberto and three other directors had been the instigators of the attempted coup, the fact remained that everyone in the room had signed the declaration that attempted to terminate Jerry's employment. I didn't know why they were still there—maybe because Jerry didn't have anything on them—but I was the only person present who hadn't stood by while Alberto and his cohorts tried to stick a knife in his back. I was suddenly proud of myself for not succumbing to temptation. My conscience was clear, even if theirs was not.

"In any case, I'm no longer interested in running ConSpace, and I wish to hand over the reins to someone who is. I'll leave it up to you to choose my successor and arrange for the legal transfer of corporate authority." A quiet smile. *"I'm looking forward to hearing from you soon."*

The vid ended. There was a long moment of silence. And then everyone sitting around that long oak table breathed a collective sigh of relief.

The board of directors agreed to Jerry's terms, of course. Which they did as soon as Jerry put his electronic signature on a stack of forms. Not surprisingly, the new boss was one of their own, a likeable but unimaginative drone who promised not to take any risks while leading ConSpace back to its glory days.

The company also agreed to keep me on retainer as Jerry's spokesman. My salary remained the same, and my only duty would be to keep open lines of communication between ConSpace and its founder. But the new CEO soon made it clear that he no longer wanted me in the executive suite; I could keep my position, but not my office.

It was just as well that the company let me go. Within a few years, ConSpace was bankrupt. The Pax Astra had no further need for them and neither did the Ares Alliance. The new CEO's patter about fresh approaches was empty talk; now its visionary-in-residence was gone, the company had nothing new to offer. ConSpace's stock was eventually bought by a holding company, which carved up the assets and sold them off at fire-sale prices.

I often wondered whether Jerry saw this coming. I wouldn't be surprised if he had.

Fortunately, his severance agreement remained legally binding, as did mine. By then, I'd moved to Reno, bought a place in the mountains overlooking the city, and set up a boutique public-relations consulting firm. My ConSpace pension was sufficient that I really didn't need any other clients, yet I had to have someone other than Jerry to keep me busy.

In time, I repped everyone from artists to scientists—no politicians; I was done with them—but Jerry remained my primary concern.

With ConSpace no longer part of his life, Jerry became less indifferent to messages from home. I remained his gatekeeper, but he began to send more letters back to Earth, most of them private email to friends and family he'd left behind. He and I talked more frequently as well. We'd learned how to cope with the long radio delay by jotting down notes about what the other person was saying, cribbing from those notes while transmitting a reply, then puttering around for a few minutes while the other guy repeated the cycle at his end. The same system was used when we started playing board games. Chess was our favorite pastime, but we also learned how to play Battleship and Monopoly the same way, with games sometimes lasting several weeks.

I never had the impression that Jerry was lonely. He'd picked this way of living with his eyes wide open, and although he never spoke openly of his reasons for becoming a hermit, it was obvious that he'd become tired of the human race and wanted to have little to do with anyone besides his fogzes. But it wasn't hard to tell that, at times, he suffered from homesickness. He'd speak of suiting up and going out the airlock, just to stand on the asteroid surface and look at Earth, a bright blue orb that hung in the star-filled sky as 2010 TK7's eternal companion. He could easily cover Earth with an outstretched thumb, but he didn't; that would have been like blotting out everyone and everything that he'd left behind, and he didn't want to do that.

Yet there was no question that his exile had become permanent. Even if he wanted to return to Earth, going back was no longer an option. He'd been on the asteroid for so long that Earth's gravity would have killed him, and even if he'd tried to take up residence in a lunar colony, he would have been little more than a cripple. We briefly discussed the idea of him relocating to a space station in Earth orbit, but he didn't like the prospect of spending the rest of his life, as he put it, "kicking around in a tin can."

On 2010 TK7, he'd made a good life for himself. Over the years he gradually expanded the Stone House's underground maze of tunnels and rooms until it had almost as much square-footage as any of the homes he'd owned on Earth. Once he'd tapped into subsurface ice deposits and installed pumps, filters, and pipes, he had an almost-inexhaustible supply of fresh water. And his greenhouse was amazing; his vegetable gardens could have fed a dozen guests, and in low gravity the ivy and honeysuckle vines he'd cultivated had spread outward into the tunnels, clinging to the rock walls and lending his home a leafy appearance much like the walls of a country manor.

A writer for a prestigious and well-established magazine—print, not electronic—approached me to ask if he could interview Jerry for a profile. By then, Jerry had been living on 2010 TK7 for nearly 25 years. ConSpace was long gone, and even Alberto Diaz was dead, having suffered a fatal stroke a few years earlier. I took the writer's proposal to Jerry, and after some discussion he agreed to an in-depth interview. Charlie David was still Jerry's doctor, though, and he was concerned that his patient might no longer have natural immunity to any germs or viruses the reporter might carry into Jerry's home. So the interviews were conducted long-distance, although Jerry cheerfully agreed to carry a camera around the Stone House so that the writer could see where he lived.

The interviews were conducted over three days, and the writer touched on just about everything, from how Jerry had made his fortune to his former playboy life to the possible social anxiety disorders which led him to seek solitude. Jerry was as candid as I'd ever known him to be, perhaps even more. He even addressed a persistent rumor that he wasn't, in fact, in space at all, but instead was living on a remote island in the south Pacific and had been faking the whole asteroid thing the entire time. Jerry settled that by turning upside-down, pulling a small rubber ball from his pocket, and playing fetch with a couple of fogz kits.

Yet he remained evasive about why he'd moved to 2010 TK7 when, as the writer pointed, it would have been easier for him to build a private habitat on the far side of the Moon. When that question came up, Jerry's smile became enigmatic. *"I came out here because I could,"* he said. *"I had my reasons... let's just leave it at that."*

The article that came out of the interviews was published a couple of months later. It was a good piece that earned the writer a Pulitzer nomination, but it was also the last time Jerry spoke publically. He clammed up again after that, and stayed that way.

If Jerry had returned to Earth, or at least Earth orbit, he would have witnessed the changes that occurred during the last seventeen years of his life. He would have seen Queen Macedonia's death and King Lucius's coronation, and his subsequent declaration of war against the Ares Alliance. He would have watched as the System War raged from Venus all the way to Titan, not ending until the Treaty of Ceres ceded Callisto to the Pax Astra and Saturn's moons to the Alliance. He would have seen the rise of *Homo superior*, the so-called googles, and how they came to dominate the outer solar system. He would have seen the mysterious Pasquale Chicago transform another asteroid, 4442 Garcia, into a generation ship, its flight beyond our solar system commencing just after the turn of the new century. And in 2102, he would have outlived King Lucius and, if he'd cared to do so, celebrated the collapse of the Pax Astra.

Jerry was around for all this, but I don't think he noticed anything that happened beyond his own little rock. I sent him a news digest every day, but I think he seldom opened it, let alone read it. When he spoke to me, he spoke as an old man whose outlook hadn't changed in decades. So far as I could tell, he'd stopped paying attention to… well, just about everything… around 2085, and didn't give a damn anyway.

It might have been just as well that he'd remained a recluse all the way to the end. The truth of the matter is, Jerry Stone no longer had anything to contribute. The age of the space tycoon was over. Humankind had not only come to inhabit most of the solar system, but had also made the first steps to the stars beyond, and the 22nd Century had no place for either emperors or entrepreneurs. Even his most daring innovation, the beam-propulsion system, was a relic of the past, a technology that never went into mass production.

Jerry Stone had nothing left to offer anyone. Or so it seemed.

I spoke to him less and less during his last years. I made sure that he continued to receive regular cargo shipments even though he told me that he was completely self-sufficient, and occasionally sent him a letter telling him what I was doing now that I was retired and enjoying the life of a geriatric desert rat. I didn't get much from him in return, but I'd come to expect that. For me, he became just another old guy I knew, just a little more crazy than most.

And then one morning, I got a call from the deep-space communication center in Texas that I'd hired to monitor Jerry's bracelet, informing me that all his vital signs had flatlined. I'd been anticipating this day for quite some time, so I wrote his obituary and sent it to all the major news sites, and then I had a shot of whisky in honor of my dead friend.

That might have been the end, but it wasn't. A few days later, I got a call from an attorney in Benny Klein's old law firm. Benny was long gone, of course, but his firm was representing Jerry's estate. I was told that Jerry's relatives were planning to hire people to travel out to 2010 TK7 and retrieve his body. They weren't doing this just to give him a decent funeral; in order to properly execute Jerry's will to the satisfaction of the probate court, they needed to have someone come along who could identify the corpse and ascertain that it was Jerry's. Since I was the only person who'd been in regular contact with him during the last years of his life, I was the obvious choice.

I agreed to make the trip. The Stone family was offering generous compensation—after all, they had much to gain from Jerry's estate, which was still worth billions—but that wasn't the only reason. I figured that I owed it to my friend to see that he was treated well. And besides, I was curious. What had he been doing while living without physical human contact for more than forty years? I wanted to know.

A doctor gave me a thorough examination and pronounced me fit a long space voyage, provided that my vessel provided me with artificial gravity for most of the journey. So an old Mars cycleship was refitted with a solar sail, then launched via photon beam toward 2010 TK7. I endured the voyage about as well as could be expected for a 70-year-old guy who'd left Earth only twice in his life, and a little more than four weeks later the ship rendezvoused with the Trojan asteroid.

Once we decelerated and made orbit with the asteroid, I joined the three crewmen who boarded an orbital ferry. After a reconnaissance fly-by, we located the airlock node installed by the original construction crew. Ironically, this was the same place from where Jerry had sent his first transmission. The pilot was able to dock directly with the node, and once he ascertained that there was an atmosphere on the other side of the hatch, we entered the airlock. This was the front door of Jerry's home; I couldn't help but feel as if we should have rung a doorbell, or at least wiped our feet on the mat.

A half dozen fogzes were waiting for us on the other side of the hatch. A couple of them growled and bared their teeth, looking for all the world like guard dogs wary of unexpected guests, but the others yip-yapped and spun their tails in joy. Apparently they had some means of feeding themselves without Jerry's help. For a second, I was afraid that they might have been dining on their master's body, until I remembered that they were vegetarians and that Jerry had once mentioned having rigged an automatic dispenser for their kibble.

A couple of surprises awaited us as we made our way through the underground habitat. One was that there were more fogzes here than I'd ever suspected. Every time we entered a room or tunnel, another two or three animals were already there. I tried to keep count, but gave up after awhile; eventually, we'd discover that two dozen fogzes lived in the asteroid. The air had a canine reek barely masked by the sweet smell of honeysuckle, but I suppose you could get used to it after awhile, particularly if mutant foxes were your only companions for 37 years.

The other surprise was just how large the Stone House had become. We went in there expecting a handful of rooms and a large hydroponics greenhouse, not to mention maintenance facilities. What we found instead was room after room after room carved out of solid rock, dozens in all, connected to one another by a labyrinthine network of tunnels. The tunnels were bored deep into the mantle and seemed to lead in all six axial directions, and were lighted by fiberoptic cables which brought underground sunlight captured on the surface. Honeysuckle had spread through the tunnels and into the rooms, clinging to the rock walls as a dense, leafy shroud. It was easy to get lost in there, so mazelike the asteroid's interior had become.

This was what Jerry had spent four decades doing: using laser drills to carve out the inside of 2010 TK7, the way a worm chews through the inside of an apple while leaving its skin intact. There were more rooms than any one person could possibly use; in fact, only the four rooms originally made for him by the *Achilles* crew had ever been inhabited. The rest were vacant except for fogzes, who played among the vines like happy children.

Except for the largest room. That was where we found Jerry.

In death, he floated in the very place where gravity would have no hold upon him: at the asteroid's core, within the center of a spherical chamber sixty feet in diameter. The fiberoptic light, filtered by the honeysuckle vine, cast autumnal shadows across the body that hung in midair, arms and legs limp, head slightly bowed. Jerry had let his hair grow out in the last years of his life, and like his beard it had gone a very pale shade of grey. He'd become mummified, but otherwise he was well preserved.

When I found him, I saw that his eyes were open, and he seemed to gaze in sightless wonder at something which, in his last moments of life, had given him reason to smile every so slightly.

I had little doubt that he'd come here to die. Fogzes played around us as I gazed at him for a very long time, all too aware that, after all these years, this was the first time we'd ever met face to face. *Hello, old friend*, his expression seemed to say. *How good to meet you at last.*

Jerry had become sick of people, but he'd never given up on the human race. So he'd left us to go off and make a world of his own, then spent the rest of his life turning his home into a place we could inhabit when he was gone. His fortune went to his relatives, but the Stone House was bequeathed to everyone on the distant world he could always see but would never walk upon again. This was stipulated in his will; the Stone House is inhabited to this day, mainly by eccentrics—writers, artists, sculptors, dreamers—who just want to get away for a while.

Was he a madman or a visionary? For some people, I'm not sure there's really a difference.

I love space opera.

Once upon a time, that's an admission that would have gotten a serious writer of science fiction in a lot of trouble. After all, the term itself was originally derived from "soap opera" as a name for a low-brow form of science fiction. This has changed over the last couple of decades, though, and now it's perfectly acceptable for a SF author to write space-op without being dismissed as a hack.

The Near Space series isn't space opera, but rather more or less realistic space fiction; there's a subtle difference between the two which would take an essay to thoroughly explain. Even so, every now and then I've let the series veer into space-op, particularly when it concerns one of my favorite recurring characters, who makes an appearance here. This is the first time the Crew shows up, though, and I think I'd like to write about them again one day.

THE HEIRESS OF AIR

"Tell me about the job."

Red couldn't see the one who spoke to him. The voice came from the other side of the cone of light surrounding the chair in which he sat; it wasn't unfriendly, but neither was it particularly kind. Two men stood behind him, menacingly silent. They might be told to offer him lunch or drag him to the nearest airlock; it all depended on how he answered the questions given to him by the unseen figure seated just out of sight.

"I think you know that already." Red started to casually cross his legs, then decided against it; he didn't want to come off as insolent. "I mean… not to be obtuse about such things, but if you don't, then why am I here?"

"You were caught taking something that doesn't belong to you."

"Well, no. Not exactly." Red tried not to smile. "We were taking back something that belongs to someone else. Besides, she doesn't belong to anyone, not even her father. And you didn't catch me… I'm here of my own free will." He quietly hoped that hadn't been a mistake.

A moment of silence. "All true," the man on the other side of the lights admitted. "Which makes the situation even more interesting. If you could have avoided us, then why have you…?"

"I want to try to work things out." This time Red smiled. "It's not smart to get on your bad side. Everyone knows that. And if the Crew had known you had anything to do with this, we wouldn't have taken the job in the first place."

A quiet laugh. For an instant, Red caught a glimpse of a face white as comet ice, eyes the color of the Martian sky. Then the face retreated back into the darkness. "No, I'm not someone to be trifled with, Captain McGee. And that brings us back to my original question. The job…"

"The job was to find Cozy and bring her home. That simple. Her father hired us. Finding her wasn't a problem. But getting her back—" Red let out his breath "—well, I guess that's why I'm here, isn't it?"

It only made sense that the men who'd kidnapped Cosette Trudeau would head for Ceres. There were few other places they could have gone once they'd left the Moon. Cislunar traffic control hadn't reported any vessels on an earthbound trajectory during the time-frame in which the abduction occurred that matched witness descriptions of the one that had lifted off from the Trudeau family's private estate just outside Descartes City. Mars was currently at opposition on the other side of the Sun from Earth; Jupiter was too far away, and no one but the mad and the desperate go to Venus. Ceres was in conjunction, though, making it conveniently accessible for a deep-space craft fleeing for the outer system, and as the largest port between Mars and Jupiter, Ceres Station is the jump-off point for the rest of the belt.

So it made sense that the kidnappers would dock at Ceres Station, wait for its orbit to take it within distance of their ultimate destination— wherever that may be—then make the final sprint to whatever rockhound hideaway was awaiting them.

Unless, of course, Antoine Trudeau decided to pay the one million lox ransom the kidnappers had demanded in the laser transmission received by the Lunar Air Company twenty-four hours after three heavily armed men took the girl from her crater home. By then, *pere* Trudeau had already made that very decision. His people got in touch with the Crew and told Red McGee that he was willing to pay an identical sum to have his daughter brought back to him, plus expenses.

"I wonder why he didn't just pay the ransom," the voice behind the lights said. "It would have been easier."

"But he'd lose face that way, wouldn't he?" Red replied. "Money's not a problem for someone like that, but reputation…well, that's another matter, isn't it? If it got out that one of the wealthiest men in the system could be horned out of a million lox by a bunch of lowlifes..." He shrugged. "So of course he'd rather hire someone to retrieve his little girl."

"Of course. Go on. You figured out they were headed for Ceres..."

And wasted no time getting there. In fact, *Wormtown Sally* reached Ceres Station just hours after its traffic control center reported the arrival of a light-cargo freighter christened the *Olympus Dreamer*. Full thrust at 1-g had seen to that. Indeed, *Sally* could have even overtaken the *Dreamer* if Red had known for sure that it was the ship they were chasing, but it wasn't until a friendly source at Ceres Traffic informed him that the freighter's crew hadn't left their vessel but instead were still inside that Red was certain—reasonably certain, at least—that the *Dreamer* was the right ship. And besides, rendezvousing and docking with another spacecraft is nearly impossible when both ships are under thrust.

So *Wormtown Sally*—itself another converted freighter, albeit with upgraded gas-core nuclear engines and with plasma-beam cannons concealed within its forward hull—quietly approached Ceres and, with the cooperation of the friendly trafco guy ("who received a nice finder's fee for his tip," Red added), slid into berth adjacent to the *Dreamer*. And even before the massive outer doors closed behind *Sally*, the Crew was getting ready to earn its pay.

There were four men in the Crew: Red, Raphael Coto, Jack Dog Jones, and Breaker. Tough guys. Hardasses. Red, Raphael, and Jack Dog were Pax Astra Royal Navy vets, while no one knew any more about Breaker's background than they did his real name. They suited up in the airlock ready-room—body armor fitted with holo projectors, straps stuffed with tear gas and stun grenades—and then they loaded their flechette rifles, cycled through the portside hatch, and quietly went down the ladder.

Wormtown Sally and *Olympus Dreamer* lay side by side upon their retractable berths within Ceres's cavernous spaceport. The docking tunnels had been repressurized after the ships came in. Dock workers and 'bots unloaded cargo and performed routine maintenance on other vessels berthed in adjacent tunnels, but no one was in sight near the two ships.

Peering through the narrow access tunnel leading from *Sally*'s berth to *Dreamer*'s, the four men studied the other ship. A ladder had been lowered from the port side, and fuel lines had been connected to the tank cluster, but the hatches remained shut. The lights were on in the command deck windows and side portholes, yet no one could be seen through them. No signs of exterior weapons; no sentries. If the people aboard were waiting it out, they weren't taking any precautions.

"I guess they thought playing possum was enough," Red said. "That was the first clue we had that we were dealing with amateurs."

They had cutting tools, but Red decided that there was an easier way to get aboard. He removed his armor and all his weapons except for a flechette pistol, which he stuck in his belt just above his butt. Then he rolled up his shirt sleeves, took a pad from a trouser pocket, and sauntered through the tunnel to the *Dreamer*. While the rest of the Crew watched, he went up the ladder and pounded a fist against the airlock hatch until it slid open a few inches and a wary face peered out at him.

"A kid… it was just a kid." Red grinned and shook his head, still not quite believing what he was seeing. "I mean, I was expecting another pro, but this guy looked like he'd just learned how to shave. And totally gullible, too. He completely bought it when I told him I was with port authority and was there to perform a routine inspection."

"That's all it took to get him to open the hatch?"

"Yup, that's it. And as soon as he did…"

If a flechette pistol a few inches from his face wasn't enough to frighten the kid, then the sight of the Crew as they charged from the tunnel must have scared the crap out of him. Red's team had been having fun with the holo projectors ever since they acquired them for covert work; the images they'd chosen for this job were scanned from stuff they'd found in old movies. So Jack Dog looked like a blue-skinned Plutonian from *The Man from Planet X*, Raphael was a claw-handed alien with a protruding brain from *This Island Earth*, and Breaker was the amphibious monster from *Creature from the Black Lagoon*. He was still staring at them with gape-mouthed astonishment as they charged up the ladder, and probably would have surrendered without a fight even if Breaker hadn't decked him with one punch. The kid bounced off the airlock wall and slid to the floor, and the rest was easy.

Ridiculously, stupidly easy. The Crew made their way through the *Dreamer*, rifles raised as they checked one compartment after another. There were three more crew members aboard, and all three were taken by surprise, one at a time. Apparently none of them had anticipated anything like this; they weren't armed, and the guy they found in the head with his pants around his ankles even went down on his knees to beg Jack Dog for his life. It was just pathetic; Jack Dog didn't even bother to hit him, just told him to pull his pants up and stop blubbering.

The *Dreamer*'s captain was having coffee in the rec room with Cosette when the Crew found them. Red expected to find the heiress locked in a stateroom, bound and gagged, possibly ravished, doubtless terrified. Instead, it was as if this was an afternoon tea rudely interrupted. She wore a white silk dress that clung to her in a very fetching matter, silver-streaked raven hair flowing halfway down her back, and she looked very much like a young lady who'd have Cozy as her nickname.

Her reaction surprised everyone. They dropped their squeezebulbs as soon as the Crew came through the door, but while the captain immediately held up his hands, Cozy whipped out a taser hidden in a calf holster beneath her dress. She dropped Jack Dog and was about to take down Red as well before he lobbed a stun grenade into the room. Breaker and Raphael dragged Jack Dog from the room—the taser charge had shorted out his projector, making him appear human again—while Red disarmed the girl. Then he waited until she, the captain, and Jack Dog regained their senses.

The captain's name was Morton, Cyril Morton, and he'd alternated between apoplexy and apology: outraged that his ship had been invaded and his crew beaten up—except for the kid in the toilet, who deserved nothing but contempt—but also embarrassed that he'd been caught so easily. Jack Dog put him down on the floor and held a gun to the back of his head while Raphael and Breaker took the girl and—against her will, protesting angrily every step of the way—hustled her out of the *Dreamer* and back to *Sally*.

Red wanted an explanation for all this. By then it had become obvious that, if this was really a kidnapping, it was the lamest in history. But the Crew couldn't afford to stick around; Ceres port authority might get wind of what had just happened, and Red didn't want to have to talk his way out of a situation he didn't quite understand himself. Besides, the only person he could count on to for the truth about this alleged abduction was its alleged victim: Cosette Trudeau, the heiress to the Lunar Air fortune.

So he went forward to *Dreamer*'s bridge and used a fire extinguisher to batter the instrument panels into junk, thereby making certain Morton wouldn't give them any trouble on the way out. Then he and Jack Dog hurried back to *Sally*, and within minutes they'd disembarked from Ceres and were headed back out into space.

"And that brings me to you," he said to the man seated behind the lights.

"And so it does," replied Mister Chicago.

Pasquale Chicago stood up from his chair and strolled across the darkened room to where Red McGee sat. Red could see him clearly once he stepped into the light: tall and thin, with the white skin and long platinum hair of an albino.

"As I recall," Mister Chicago went on, "you said she'd told you that I'd kidnapped her. Correct?"

"That's right, yes."

Mister Chicago nodded as he reached into a breast pocket of his black tunic and pulled out a cigar. Red shook his head when it was offered to him, and Mister Chicago clipped the cigar with a tiny gold guillotine and let one of his men light it for him. He took his time, knowing it was his to waste.

"I did not," he said at last, exhaling smoke that became blue haze drifting upward into the light. "Fact is, I barely even know *Ma'moiselle* Trudeau. I've had some dealings with her father in the past, yes, but the last time I saw her, she was barely this tall." His left hand lifted slightly, to the height of his waist. "And abducting her would be… shall we say, bad for business?"

Red nodded. Mister Chicago was known throughout the system as an underworld kingpin, a criminal mastermind who'd managed to become virtually untouchable. It wasn't even certain that Pasquale Chicago was his real name. Rumor had it that he'd once been a senior government official in the Pax Astra treasury before fleeing with a considerable fortune for the outer solar system, where he'd established a permanent residence on the asteroid 4442 Garcia. His organization, the Zodiac, had a hand in every smuggling and black market operation between Venus and Jupiter, but Red had never heard of him kidnapping heiresses for ransom.

"That's what I thought," he said. "To be honest, this sort of thing is beneath you."

A wry smile. "It is… and thank you for giving me the benefit of the doubt." Mister Chicago took a luxurious pull from his cigar. "And even if I had, I wouldn't have used men as amateurish as those you describe."

"We didn't think so either, but…" Red hesitated. "Well, we had to make sure you weren't involved. That's why I sent a message requesting a parlay, and you…"

"Invited you to my home. I prefer to discuss such weighty issues face to face, but nonetheless I appreciate your taking the effort to travel all this way."

Red was beginning to relax a little, yet he remained on his guard. While *Wormtown Sally* was docked with 4442 Garcia, he and the Crew were at Mister Chicago's mercy, present hospitality notwithstanding. "Only wanted to make certain that we weren't going to have any misunderstandings."

"We don't, but…" Mister Chicago blew a delicate smoke ring at the ceiling. "Nonetheless, we still have an issue that needs to be addressed. Why did she pretend to be abducted, if that is indeed what appears to be the case? And why did she claim that I was responsible?"

Before Red could respond, he turned away, lifting a hand to his face to gently prod his right cheekbone and murmur something under his breath. A subcutaneous comlink connected him to someone outside the room. "Perhaps we should ask dear Cosette herself," he said, turning to Red again.

A few moments went by, then a door silently slid open and two figures were briefly silhouetted against the light from the corridor outside. The door shut once more, and Cosette Trudeau was escorted into the luminescent circle by another one of Mister Chicago's henchmen. She wore the standard-issue ship's jumpsuit instead of the silk outfit she'd been wearing on Ceres, but she still looked delectable, if nervous.

"Pasquale…" she began.

"Mister Chicago." His pale eyes seemed to darken as they settled upon her. "It's been many years since we met, Cozy, and I'm afraid you've taken advantage of our brief acquaintance. You have much to explain, my dear."

Her slim shoulders fell and she quickly looked away. "I'm sorry," she said quietly, and the arrogance she'd shown Red aboard *Wormtown Sally* seemed to dissipate. "I thought that if… if I managed to make my way out here, you'd…I hoped you'd want me, that's all."

Red stared at Cosette, not quite believing what he'd just heard. Until now, he'd been impressed with her. Smart enough to fake her own kidnapping, courageous enough to take on four armed men with only a taser, wily enough to try pinning everything on the most successful crime lord in space… and why? A foolish crush on a man she'd met once as a little girl?

"It doesn't make sense," he murmured. "I'm not buying it."

"Neither am I." Mister Chicago dropped his cigar—it fell slowly in 4442 Garcia's low gravity, and one of his minions swooped in to snatch it before it hit the floor—and stepped closer, looking her straight in the eye. "Cozy, my sweet, you're not that stupid. Please don't pretend to be. What were you really trying to do?"

Cosette looked up at him again and slowly let out her breath. "All right, okay," she said, no longer contrite and innocent. "I'll admit it… I was just trying to get away from Papa." Her lovely mouth ticked upward a bit. "And make a little money off him, too."

"Ah. I think I begin to understand." Crossing his arms, Mister Chicago regarded her dispassionately. "You staged your own abduction in hopes that I'd willingly accept the blame for it, provided that your father paid the ransom. And what did you expect me to do? Split the money with you?"

A shrug. "I was thinking fifty-fifty."

"Half a million lox?" Mister Chicago closed his eyes, shook his head. "Do you realize just how little a half-million lox means to me? Besides the fact that I'd make an enemy of your father, who supplies me with oxygen along with just about everyone else in the system."

Cosette pouted. "It was just a thought."

"Who were those guys who nabbed you… pretended to nab you, that is?" Red leaned back in his chair. "I'm surprised they were able to get past the bodyguards… you do have bodyguards, I assume."

"I do, but I gave them the night off. And Papa was in Tycho City on business, so I had the house to myself. Except for the servants, and I knew they wouldn't do anything." Cosette hesitated. "The one Breaker punched out in the airlock was a boy I was going with. The other two were his friends. The three of them hired Captain Morton." She looked at Mister Chicago again. "I hope you're not going to hold anything against them. They were just doing what I asked them to do."

"If your friends can get home on their own, I'll leave them alone. Morton will be informed by the Zodiac that his Ceres docking privileges have been revoked. You've never had much difficulty getting men to do what you want them to do, have you?"

A sly grin. "Not really, no." The grin became a coy smile as she inched a little closer. "Are you sure you're not interested in having me, Pasquale? I'd be quite… grateful."

Mister Chicago lay a gentle hand on her shoulder, pushed her back to where she'd been standing. "*Ma'moiselle*, I have plenty of girls and boys to amuse me already. And I'm not in the practice of taking in urchins."

The smile vanished and her shoulders sagged again. "Great. Just excellent. Guess that means I'm going to be dragged home."

"What's so bad about that?" Red was genuinely curious. "You've got it pretty well, so far as I can tell. A private lunar estate, more money than you know what to do with, boyfriends who'd crawl across Venus just to make you happy…"

"Yeah, right." Her eyes flashed in anger. "Do you realize how boring all that is? I can't go anywhere without Papa's bodyguards, and the places I do go are just the same stupid places where the same stupid rich people hang out." She sighed, looked at Mister Chicago again. "You want to know the truth? I didn't particularly want you, either… I just wanted what I thought you would be able to offer me: a life that wasn't so goddamn dull."

Mister Chicago didn't say anything for a moment. Tapping a finger against his lips, he regarded her thoughtfully. "Let me ask you something," he said after a moment. "Captain McGee tells me you took out one of his men with one shot."

"Yes, I did." She glanced at Red. "I told Jack Dog I'm sorry, but I'm not sure he's forgiven me."

"He has… he's just embarrassed you got the better of him, that's all." Red caught a sidelong look from Mister Chicago. "Come to think of it, though… where did you learn to shoot like that?"

"One of Papa's bodyguards trained me. Not that it was Papa's idea, but…as I said, things get dull, and learning how to use a gun is more interesting than fixing my hair again."

"I see. What else did he teach you?"

"Flechette and particle-beam rifles. Hand-to-hand combat. Basic assault and escape tactics." She smiled. "Men like to do things for me."

"Fascinating." Mister Chicago turned to Red. "I think I have an idea."

"And so do I," Red replied.

# # #

Feet propped up on the main console, coffee mug nestled in his lap, Red McGee sat in *Wormtown Sally*'s bridge. Through the bow windows, he saw a lone figure in a moonsuit step through the Trudeau estate's main airlock and, carrying a shoulder bag, begin walking across the landing pad.

"Prime the engines, Raphael," he said. "I think we're about ready to go."

Raphael Coto grinned as he leaned forward in the co-pilot's seat and began flipping switches. Red pulled out his pad and ran a finger across its screen. He smiled when he saw the Crew's current balance at the Pax Royal Bank. Just as he'd expected, *l*1,000,000 had been transferred to their account from the Lunar Air Company. Antoine Trudeau had met his obligations, just as the Crew had met theirs.

Nonetheless, he wasn't *quite* getting everything that he wanted.

A low hum was passing through the hull as Red got up from his seat and left the bridge. His steps took him down a ladder to *Sally*'s airlock. He arrived just it was cycling through. Jack Dog and Breaker were already there; they waited patiently in the ready room as the inner hatch opened and the person who'd left the crater home stepped through.

Cosette Trudeau had already removed her helmet. She dropped her bag on the deck, took a moment to shake out her hair, then pushed her helmet into the rack and began to peel off her suit. "Hi, guys. Thanks for waiting."

"No problem." Red traded a look with Jack Dog and Breaker. Jack Dog was openly admiring the slinky way she was discarding her suit—no one else could make getting rid of pressure gear look so sexy—while Breaker leaned against a bulkhead, arms crossed, studiously unimpressed. "Any difficulties on your end?"

"Not really. Papa's grateful you got me back from those evil men, but he's also pissed that I'm leaving." An indifferent shrug. "What's he going to do? He's been telling me that I needed to find something to do besides hang around here, so…"

"Joining us probably wasn't what he was expecting."

"Life's just full of little surprises." Cozy racked the suit, reached for a pair of stikshoes. "So… do we have another job yet?"

"There's always another job." Jack Dog offered her a hand in putting on the adhesive-soled shoes, and seemed mildly perturbed when she wouldn't let him. "Of course, you'll need to get a holo projector. It's one of those kind of—"

"Way ahead of you." Bending down, Cozy unzipped her bag, felt around inside, then produced a projector. "Got one already. Bought it for Halloween last year."

"Yeah, okay, but you still need to pick a disguise."

Standing up, Cosette ran her fingers across its control menu. "I sort of had one in mind." She grinned. "Ever seen a movie called *Alien*?"

Before anyone could answer, she activated the projector. Red and Jack Dog stepped back in horror, and Breaker nearly bolted through the door.

"Like it?" Cozy asked.

"You're going to fit right in," Red said.

This is one of the saddest stories I've ever written, and one of the most disturbing. But you might not know that unless you knew why.

Many years ago, when I was a junior-high student at a private school in Tennessee, I knew an upperclassman— I won't reveal his name out of respect for his family—who was one of the brightest guys I knew as a teenager. I lost contact with nearly everyone with whom I went to school, but nonetheless I remembered this guy. I don't forget brilliant people I've met, and this kid was sharp.

A few years ago a mutual friend got back in touch with me, and during the course of a long round of email catching-up he told me what had happened to this chap. Something had happened to him after he graduated high school, and he'd begun a long downward spiral that ended when he joined the Heaven's Gate cult. This person, who'd once seemed to be so full of potential, became one of the members who poisoned themselves in an underground bunker in hopes of fulfilling a madman's delusion.

This information deeply shocked me. I've written about religious cults many times—sometimes in jest, sometimes more seriously—but this was the first time I'd ever known someone who'd paid a fatal price for having joined one. And the news couldn't have come at a worse time. Over the past year or so, I'd lost friends and family, and it seemed as if death had become an unwelcome visitor to my life who wouldn't go away. But this was different.

I used to think cults like Heaven's Gate were kind of funny, in a macabre sort of way. I don't any more.

SET THE CONTROLS FOR
THE HEART OF THE SUN

I'm sorry, Matt. I screwed up.

That was the final transmission from the *Jove Zephyr* before it plunged into the Sun. It came as a text message sent via maser, the freighter's last viable means of communication; voice contact with home was no longer possible, since radio signals were scrambled by the magnetosphere. Twenty-seven hours later, telescopes aboard Evening Star in orbit above Venus spotted a brief, tiny flare as the beamship entered the photosphere and was vaporized.

No one thought that anyone aboard was still alive by then, so this last message came as a surprise. Never mind the temperature; the ship's hull couldn't have shielded the passengers from the Sun's intense radiation for very long. So it went without saying that everyone on the freighter was doomed even if they'd turned the ship around... which they hadn't wanted to, until it was too late.

There were a few sick jokes when that last message was made public, but most people didn't find it funny at all; mass suicide is seldom a source of humor. What puzzled nearly everyone was its meaning. Who was Matt, and why did some poor, doomed soul aboard the beamship find it necessary to apologize to him? That question was asked again and again, but no definite answer ever came. As with so many things about the *Jove Zephyr* disaster, it was a mystery wrapped in tragedy.

I know the answer. I'm Matt Garris, and the person who sent the message was Terry Koenig, my best friend. And, yes, I know what he meant. He'd screwed up, all right... and the mistakes he'd made took him on a journey to the Sun.

Terry and I met in the seventh grade. His family had just moved to Beverly, Tennessee, from Cleveland, so he was an unfamiliar face in my classroom when everyone came back from summer vacation. Before the end of the week, he was already in his first fight, when some kid tried to beat his lunch voucher out of him. He would have succeeded, too, if I hadn't stepped in. I was pretty good with my fists, and I've never liked bullies, so I gave the kid the bloody nose he wanted to give new guy, and that's how we became friends.

It soon became obvious that Terry was the smartest kid in school. He sauntered through his classes with effortless ease. Every test received a perfect score, his homework was always completed on time, his projects inevitably made everyone else's look lame. It was like that all the way through high school, with Terry pulling down A's in everything (predictably, the only exception was phys ed; he got a flat F there). I might have been jealous were it not for the fact that there's an advantage to having the class brain as a best friend. I'm no dummy, but I don't think I would've have passed algebra or physics if he hadn't helped me cram for the finals. Math was always a problem for me, but Terry could juggle complex equations the way other kids played video games.

By the time we reached our senior year, it was apparent that he wasn't merely a good student, but in fact possessed an intelligence that bordered on genius. Being the school wizard had its costs, though. Beverly High was dominated by jocks and know-nothings, while Terry was a walking stereotype: tall, skinny, near-sighted, and socially inept. I often played the role of bodyguard, warding off the idiots who'd try to knock off his i-lenses or throw his pad into the toilet.

Truth was, Terry could be his own worst enemy. Like many highly intelligent people, he wasn't very good at the messy business of living. Casual conversation wasn't easy for him—he took things too seriously, and he'd never learned to laugh at himself—and relations with girls was hopeless, but I don't think he really minded; he didn't like talking to people who couldn't keep up with his train of thought, and sex was an unwanted distraction. So it's no wonder that he was picked on so much. It wasn't just that he wasn't normal; fact was, he was downright alien.

All the same, even his enemies grudgingly acknowledged that Terry was destined for greatness. He'd never be a farmer or sell insurance or drive a truck, or have any sort of mundane life. He was going places, and everyone knew it. But I was the only guy who knew what he wanted to do.

Terry wanted to go out into space.

At long last, the human race was leaving Earth. The commercial space industry had finally developed the ways and means to launch payloads cheap, and now the solar system was being opened as a vast and profitable new frontier. Powersats were providing electricity to half the countries on Earth, lunar mining stations had become small towns, and Mars was being colonized. There were even remote outposts in the asteroid belt and the jovian moons. Now the challenge was to build spacecraft which would be faster and more efficient; fusion engines were good, and laser propulsion even better, but—as always—everyone was looking for the next big thing.

That's where Terry set his sights. His ambitions weren't terrestrial at all. He wanted the stars themselves. So it was no surprise that, when everyone else in school was making plans for community colleges or state universities, his application went to MIT. He got in, of course. MIT wanted him so badly, in fact, they offered a scholarship. Naturally, he accepted; his father was a shift supervisor at a local factory, his mother an elementary school teacher. They didn't have a lot of money, but Terry was their great hope, so if he wanted to leave home and go to school in New England, they weren't about to stand in his way.

So while I went off to Middle Tennessee State University, Terry set sail for Cambridge, Massachusetts. We promised each other that we'd stay in touch, and we did… that is, until things began to go bad for him.

During his first semester at MIT, Terry emailed me as regularly as he could. There were often long silences, but I knew why: his coursework was intensive, and there were times when he was simply too busy to drop me a line. Nonetheless we did our best to keep up with each other, and although he often griped about how much work was being piled on him, I could tell that he was happy to be in a place where his intelligence was respected. And when I saw him back home during Christmas break, he was the same brilliant, awkward guy I'd always known.

During his second semester, though, a random accident changed everything. Terry was walking from one side of campus to another, and was about to cross Mass Ave when he was almost run over by a public tram. In his typical absent-minded fashion, Terry nearly stepped off the curb and onto the tram line without looking. He probably would've died right there in the street had he not heard a voice: *watch out!* He stopped at once, and an instant later the tram rushed by, so close that he felt it brush against the front of his parka. Yet when he looked around to thank the person who'd warned him, he saw that he was alone on the sidewalk.

Someone else might have dismissed this as one of life's little mysteries, perhaps an act of his subconscious mind, but Terry didn't. He'd never been religious or had any mystical beliefs, but this strange little incident disturbed his world-view. He'd always been wound a little too tight, and all of a sudden, the rational, cause-and-effect universe he'd always accepted as a given was no longer quite the same. He began to wonder if there was something out there—if not God, then at least a presence, intangible yet omnipresent—that occasionally manifested itself in subtle ways. It was a startling notion, this particular line of thought, and after awhile it began to obsess him.

Until then, his teachers considered Terry to something of a prodigy, a student whose gifts were unusual even for MIT. As the winter semester went along, though, his grades began to slide, his work becoming haphazard and careless. He started skipping classes, sometimes failing to show up for weeks on end. Warnings were given and ignored; classmates became concerned, but Terry rejected their attempts to help him. He told me in his email that he'd begun to suspect that he'd spent his life on a treadmill, pursing goals that now seemed materialistic and empty. After all these years, Terry was questioning the meaning of his existence in a fundamental and very frightening way.

One afternoon, during a lecture, Terry got up and left. He simply walked out of the hall, leaving his pad and t-book on his desk. Everyone assumed that he'd simply gone to the restroom, but he never came back. When his roommate returned to the dorm, he discovered that Terry's dresser drawers were open, his duffel bag missing. Everything else was left behind, including Terry's campus ID; it lay on his bed, purposely discarded.

With that, Terry Koenig abandoned his former life and disappeared.

Terry crashed on a couch in a friend's off-campus apartment for a couple of days, then left the Boston area entirely. It wasn't until his parents got a phone call from the Dean of Students office that they found he'd dropped out of MIT. By then, Terry had cleaned out his bank account and ditched his wristphone somewhere... probably the Charles River, because its GPS signal ended on the Longfellow Bridge.

He told no one where he was going, yet he didn't completely vanish. Over the next three years, I occasionally heard from him. Now and then, I'd find a postcard in my college mailbox, or receive email sent from a public computer. They came from places as near as Chattanooga or as distant as Vancouver; just a few words, telling me that he'd gotten a temp job as a busboy or a convenience store clerk, or that he was living in a flea-bag motel or a homeless shelter.

At one point he was in a commune in Vermont, cohabitating with a number of other spiritual seekers. He got a girlfriend while he was there; he sent me her picture, a doe-eyed teenager with unwashed hair. Another email attachment was a video: shaky, unfocused images of pale November sunlight filtering through bare tree branches, narrated by Terry's rambling, hollow voice: *Time is dying, and autumn is the face of entropy.* He must have been high when he did this, and that alone was disturbing; the old Terry loathed drugs.

No address or job lasted very long; he'd eventually move on, still searching for something he couldn't quite define. He never responded to any of the letters or emails I sent him, so I don't know if he even got them, let alone pay attention to my pleas for him to come home and get help.

This went on for awhile, and then I didn't hear from him again for nearly two years. By then I'd graduated from college, gotten a job in advertising, and had pretty much written off Terry as a high school friend who'd gone off the deep end. I had almost forgotten him entirely when I received a handwritten letter from him. That was when I discovered what had happened.

Terry had joined the Heliotropic Congregation.

Before the *Jove Zephyr* tragedy, few people had heard of them. Which isn't a surprise; fringe cults often don't make themselves visible until they manifest their weirdness in some public way. I can only speculate how Terry met them; it's possible that he might have first heard about the Congregation while living on the commune. In any case, sometime in the last couple of years he'd become a member.

The Congregation was the creation of Dr. Hermann Sneed, a former NASA astrophysicist who'd lost his job when the space agency was dismantled. Somewhere along the line, Dr. Sneed also lost his mind; he became a practitioner of "outsider science"—in this instance, a system of beliefs that merged loony-tunes mysticism with crackpot pseudoscience —and had formed an organization to foster his theories.

According to Dr. Sneed, the galaxy was inhabited by a unseen super-race which existed long before humankind. These extraterrestrials, which he called the Heliotropes, possessed technology so advanced that they'd practically become gods. No longer dependent upon corporeal bodies, the Heliotropes had sent their transcendental spirits into the cosmos, where they searched for worlds where lesser races had begun to evolve. Because the Heliotropes relied on solar energy, they took up residence near stars, hence their name... which, incidentally, has little to do with its dictionary definition.

Because the Heliotropes were benign, they were interested in helping emergent races achieve higher states of existence. Yet the Heliotropes did so in subtle and unseen ways; they preferred to operate in secret, unobtrusively guiding individuals whom they considered to be crucial for the survival of their kind. So someone could be serving an alien master plan without even being aware of it; what might seem to be coincidence or happenstance could, in fact, be the hidden hand of the Heliotropes.

This was total mind-rot, of course, yet there is a kind of person who, for one reason or another, is willing to accept even outright lunacy so long as it sounds possible. It's arguable whether Sneed believed his own nonsense. He demanded that his followers surrender all their possessions to the Congregation and give him their unswerving devotion, so it's possible that money and power may have been his only true objectives. As other charlatans before him have learned, there's a lot of money to be made from preying upon lost, confused people.

Like Terry.

In his letter, he told me that he was living in the Congregation's "spiritual retreat" in South Dakota, where he was assisting Dr. Sneed in his efforts to make contact with the Heliotropes. *I'm happy*, he said. *With my teacher's help, I've found the spiritual clarity that I've been searching for all these years.* He now understood that what happened on Mass Ave was the act of an omniscient force looking out for him, and that he was destined for a role in some great cosmic plan.

As soon as I received the letter, I got in touch with Terry's father. His mother had died a year ago, and although his dad was disturbed to learn what had become of his son, nonetheless he was glad to hear that he was still alive. Terry had invited me to visit him, so we decided to fly to South Dakota and see if we could convince him to leave the cult and come home.

The Congregation's spiritual retreat was a four-acre compound about forty miles west of Pierre, a collection of rusting trailer homes and prefab sheds surrounded by a barb-wire fence; a sixty-foot radio antenna rose from the center of the camp. Terry met us at the gate along with two other cult members. He was almost unrecognizable; even skinnier than he'd been before, his hair was cut close to the scalp while he'd grown a beard that extended halfway to his chest. Like his escorts, he wore shapeless white pajamas and sandals. Eyeglasses had replaced his i-lenses, and he'd apparently never acquired a new wristphone.

Terry wouldn't let us come any closer than the gate, and we were only able to speak to him for about fifteen minutes before the other cultists ushered him away. By then, it was obvious that he now belonged to the cult, body and soul. All Terry wanted to talk about was how wonderful his life had become now that he was with "his family" and that we need not worry about him. The eerie, empty smile on his face never disappeared, not even when his father told him that his mother had passed away. His dad was still trying to persuade him to leave the compound, if only for a few minutes, when someone began to pound a drum from somewhere within the circle of trailers. Terry told us that he had to go—it was time for their mid-day communion, whatever that was—but before he left, I managed to get him to promise that he'd stay in touch, no matter what.

On the way back to the airport, his father and I discussed the possibility of hiring someone to abduct Terry and deprogram him. I think we would have done it, too, if we'd had the chance. We didn't know that we'd never see him again; the next time I heard from Terry, he was aboard the *Jove Zephyr*.

However, he kept his promise.

When ConSpace formed a partnership with the Pax Astra to establish helium-3 mining operations in Jupiter's upper atmosphere, the company built two interplanetary freighters to travel back and forth between Earth and Callisto Station. Next to the He^3 aerostats themselves, this was the most expensive part of the operation. The *Tycho Brahe* and the *Medici Explorer* were immense vessels, each one hundred and eighty feet in length and powered by gas-core nuclear engines; a round trip typically took seventeen months.

At first, this seemed to be an efficient means of getting Jovian He^3 to the tokamaks of Earth, but events conspired to make this otherwise. After the *Tycho Brahe* was lost in the asteroid belt, the *Medici Explorer* became the sole means of cargo transport between Earth and Jupiter. Then political revolution in the Pax Astra resulted in its democratic government being overthrown and a corrupt monarchy rising in its place; one of Queen Macedonia's first acts was the annulment of previous contracts with Earth-based corporations, including ConSpace. And finally, the Pax started making claims to Callisto Station, and threatened to intercept and board the *Medici Explorer* if it came near Jupiter again.

ConSpace originally intended to build two more *Brahe*-class freighters as the *Explorer*'s sister ships. Clearly, a faster vessel was needed to make the Jupiter run unmolested. In recent years, the company had been experimenting with laser propulsion. A pilot program to send beamships between the Moon and the near-Earth asteroid 2010 TK7 had been successful, so it was decided that a new class of freighters would replace the older nuclear spacecraft.

The *Jove Zephyr* was the first of its kind. One hundred and fifty feet long, with a dry mass of five metric kilotons, its principal means of propulsion was a parachute-like solar sail three thousand feet in diameter, suspended by carbon-filament cables from the outrigger spars of the freighter's Y-shaped hull.

The initial idea was to use laser projectors on the lunar farside to send the beamship straight to Jupiter, but then it was realized that these lasers would be much more powerful if their solar collectors were closer to the Sun. So a large powersat was established in a Lagrange-point orbit near Venus. The flight plan called for the *Zephyr* to depart from Earth orbit, deploy its sail, then orient it at such an angle that the solar wind would carry the vessel on a transfer trajectory to Venus. This would be the longest part of the trip, taking nearly six months to complete, but once the *Zephyr* reached Venus, it would slingshot around the planet, intercept the powersat's beam, then be sent on a high-velocity trip to Jupiter. Once the ship left Venus, the transit time to Callisto would be less than six weeks, assuming a launch window during planetary conjunctions between Earth, Venus, and Jupiter.

The *Zephyr* had successfully made its maiden voyage already; its cargo included the equipment necessary to build another powersat in a Trojan orbit near Jupiter for the return trip. As ConSpace figured, the freighter had travelled through the asteroid belt too fast for Pax ships to match course with it. For its second voyage, it was slated to carry passengers along with its four-person crew: eight men and women, recently hired by ConSpace to replace the miners on Callisto Station and who would make the journey in biostasis.

No one at ConSpace was aware that these replacements belonged to the Heliotropic Congregation, or that Jupiter was not their intended destination.

Since its inception, the Congregation had attempted to reach the Heliotropes. First they tried telepathy, gathering in circles to clasp hands and project their thoughts to any astral beings who might be listening. When that didn't work, they purchased a radio transmitter and erected the antenna that stood in the midst of their compound; they used this until the FCC cited them for operating an unlicensed broadcast station and confiscated their equipment.

They even went so far as to go out into the prairie, drench the grass with gasoline in a half-mile-diameter symbol of a triangle encompassed by a circle, then set it afire in hopes that it would be seen from space.

Then Dr. Sneed had a revelation. He had no doubt that the Heliotropes were aware of the Congregation. However, because of their reclusive nature, they wouldn't reveal themselves unless it was absolutely necessary. Therefore, the Congregation's only recourse would be to put themselves in a situation where the Heliotropes would be forced to step in and save them.

To accomplish this, though, the Congregation couldn't remain on Earth. It would have to travel out to where the Heliotropes lived, there to deliberately place themselves in jeopardy and await salvation.

The cult's twelve members agreed—no one ever challenged their leader when he had a new revelation—and so they went about formulating a plan and carrying it out. No doubt Terry had a lot to do with this. After all, he was the member best suited for coming up a scheme to hijack a spacecraft and send it toward the Sun.

It was surprisingly easy for members of the cult to get hired by ConSpace for employment on Callisto Station. Its distance from Earth deterred most off-world job seekers, and the fact that the outpost was being threatened by the Pax Astra made working there even less desirable. The Congregationalists all submitted applications, each and every one under false names and with phony addresses, credentials, and references. Eight were hired, including both Terry and Dr. Sneed; it was eventually learned that ConSpace's computer system had been hacked and all other applications deleted. The four who weren't accepted remained in South Dakota while the others reported to ConSpace's training facility in Texas. Six weeks later, they caught a shuttle to Earth orbit, where they boarded the *Jove Zephyr.*

As passengers, the cult members were supposed to spend the entire trip to Jupiter in hibernation. Yet one of them apparently knew how to reprogram the computer controlling the zombie tanks and change things so that they would be awakened earlier than scheduled, because exactly 180 days after the *Zephyr* departed from Earth, the eight biostasis cells injected their occupants with the drugs that would revive them from their long sleep, and a few minutes later Terry and his companions rose from the tanks and left the hibernation compartment.

We can only speculate what occurred next. Based on the testimonies of the Congregation members who were left behind, though, we have a pretty good idea. The *Zephyr* was equipped with lifeboats, but they were never launched, nor was a distress signal ever transmitted. The captain, executive officer, helmsman, and engineer were most likely asleep in their bunks when the cult members crept down the silent corridors to their quarters, knives in their hands. They probably woke up just long enough to realize that their throats had been cut.

I'd like to think that Terry didn't murder anyone. However, he was doubtless responsible for everything that happened next. No one else would have known how to jettison the sail from its spars, reset the navigation system so that the destination coordinates were now -00.-00.-00, or perform a 180-degree turn and fire the auxiliary engine in a prolonged burst that broke the freighter away from its planned trajectory. In fact, I suspect the entire plan was his idea from the beginning.

The ship's transponder, of course, automatically transmitted telemetry regarding the course change to ConSpace's deep-space tracking network. Within minutes, the communications specialist on duty sent a message to the wayward freighter, requesting an explanation. When no reply was received, she alerted her supervisor, who checked the data and contacted his superiors, and so on down the line until a lot of people had come to the cold realization that something was seriously wrong with the *Jove Zephyr*.

There was no word from the *Zephyr* for several hours after the course-change was detected, then ConSpace received a communiqué from the ship. In a message that was both brief and utterly mad, Dr. Sneed informed the company that the Heliotropic Congregation had taken control of the freighter, that it was now heading directly toward the Sun, and that it would remain on this trajectory until he and his people made the Heliotropes reveal themselves by forcing them to rescue their most devoted believers. *We will stay in touch as we await the glorious moment of first contact with powers greater than our own,* his message said. *Open your hearts... a new era is being born.*

It might have been funny if it hadn't been insane.

You know how the story ends. Most people do; the *Jove Zephyr* hijacking dominated the news sites for months, and since then has become legend. But you don't know what happened to Terry Koenig.

It quickly became obvious that any attempt to intercept the freighter before it reached the Sun would fail. Even if a rescue vessel had been launched from Evening Star, which was then under construction above Venus, it couldn't have rendezvoused with the *Zephyr*; the freighter's velocity was too high, its trajectory too distant. Station personnel could only watch as the freighter streaked past, a tiny comet hurtling sunward.

Aboard the *Zephyr*, though, it seemed as if the Congregation was oblivious to their fate. Judging from the transmissions ConSpace regularly received from the freighter, the cultists were delirious with anticipation; they truly believed that all-knowing, all-powerful aliens would soon swoop in to save them. They sent messages to friends and family, telling them not to worry, that everything would be okay. I heard much the same thing from Terry:

I believe that this is what I've been meant to do, from the moment I was born. I always knew that I had a destiny, but I didn't know what it would be. Now it's all clear. My life has been leading up to this; my moment has come.

Venus is approximately sixty-seven million miles from the Sun; it took the *Zephyr* nearly three months to cross that distance. As the days become weeks and the weeks became months, communiqués received from the ship became less enthusiastic, more worrisome. *When are the Heliotropes going to show themselves? We're running out of food. We're low on water. The compartments are getting warm, and no one is sleeping well. Have you seen anything? Is something coming our way?*

The *Zephyr* crossed the orbit of Mercury, and still there was no sign of the Heliotropes. By then, the messages had become desperate. *The Heliotropes aren't coming! We have to turn back. Can you send a ship to pick us up?* Yet those options were no longer available. The sail had been discarded, and too much fuel had been consumed during the trajectory change for the freighter's engine to pull it free of the Sun's gravity well. Rescue had long-since been ruled out.

The *Zephyr* was falling into the Sun; nothing could change that.

For awhile, there was only silence. When communications finally resumed, it came as text-only messages: *Our provisions have run out. We can no longer enter the bridge. The Heliotropes don't exist. We've killed Dr. Sneed, and the rest of us are contemplating suicide.* More silence, this time even longer. The *Zephyr* had almost reached the Sun's corona when a final transmission was received:

I'm sorry, Matt. I think I screwed up.

No one knew who sent it, or what it meant, except me.

In the end, Terry must have realized how wrong he'd been. He may have even tried to turn the ship around, if he'd been able to enter a bridge that had become a furnace. At some point, though, neither intelligence nor technology can resist the forces of nature. I can only hope that he died before the *Jove Zephyr* was consumed.

As children, we're told not to stare into the Sun. This is common sense, of course, but there's always a temptation to do so, if only to see how long one can look before being blinded. But Terry didn't just stare into the Sun; he threw himself into it. And death was his only destiny.

Poor Terry. Poor damned, deluded Terry.

Some years ago, my friend and long-time editor Gardner Dozois put together a theme anthology with an intriguing premise: take the opening line of a classic work and write a new story from it. When he came to me, I immediately knew which story I wanted to use.

As I said earlier, I love pulp fiction. I'm not a complete Philistine, though: I also enjoy the classics, particularly the works of Herman Melville. I know there's difference between dime novels and the canon of great American literature.

Still, I can't help but think that Moby Dick*'s first line could have been the opening of a Mickey Spillane novel.*

THE BIG WHALE

Call me Ishmael. That's what everyone does, down on the New Bedford waterfront: the longshoremen and wharf rats and sailors who've been away from sea for too long and are drowning their sorrows in a jug of grog. They don't call me unless they're in trouble, though. Trouble is my business. I carry a harpoon.

I'd just returned from a trip to New York. The Bartleby case had been tough, but I got it done. Not that the client was grateful. When I asked him to pay me for helping him keep his job at a Wall Street law firm, he'd said that he'd prefer not to, so I stuck his nose in his ledger book and slammed it shut a few times until he finally coughed up. Never trust a scrivener.

I was pretty wrung out when I got back to Massachusetts. I tried to sleep during the long ride home, but the carriage needed a new set of wheels and by the time the driver put me off in the middle of town, I could have used my spleen as a doormat. If I'd had any sense, I would have gone straight home. Instead, I decided to drop by the office first. I told myself that it was just to check the mail, but the truth of the matter is that I missed the place. For all of its seediness—the stench of cod, the drunks passed out on the sidewalks, the painted women lounging in tavern doorways— the waterfront still has its own bleak, salt-crusted majesty. New Bedford may not be in the same class as Boston, but it's home.

My office was on the second floor of the Customs House, a one-room loft with a view of the wharf. As usual, the door was blocked by a small hill of mail that had been dropped over the transom, most of it bills that would have to be covered by the handful of gold I'd managed to frisk from Bartleby's pockets after I smeared his meticulous handwriting with his face. I transferred the mail from the floor to the desk, and was searching the drawers for the bottle of Jamaican rum I kept stashed in there, when there was a knock at the door. Thinking it was the landlord dropping by for the rent, I told my visitor to come in… and that was when *she* appeared.

The moment I laid eyes on her, I knew the dame was trouble. The beautiful ones always are. A vision in crinoline and wool, her lavender dress covered her from neck down, but as she levitated into the room, I caught a glimpse of a well-turned ankle, the kind of *lateral malleolus* that keeps lonely men awake at night. A lock of lustrous chestnut hair fell from beneath her fringed pink bonnet; I found myself wondering what it might be like to run my fingers through it. Yeah, somewhere beneath three layers of store-bought clothes was a woman with the body of a ship's figurehead. And not a mermaid, either.

"Pardon me," she said, "but are you Mister…?"

"Ishmael. Just call me Ishmael." I beckoned to the chair on the other side of the desk. "Have a seat, will you, Miss…?"

"Ahab… *Mrs.* Ahab," she added, emphasizing her marital status a little more than necessary. If she knew my name, though, then it was a good guess that she also knew my reputation. "And thank you, but I'd rather stand."

She didn't have a choice. Her dress had a bustle in the rear big enough to hide a Navy crew. Not that they'd mind very much. I thought about offering her a drink, but I could tell she was the sort of lady who never had anything more than a dainty glass of sherry once a week on Sunday. So I left the rum in the drawer and refrained from putting my feet up on the desk.

"How can I help you, Mrs. Ahab?"

"I understand you solve people's problems, Mr. Ishmael."

I shrugged. "Depends what they are, ma'am. I can recommend a good doctor."

She frowned. "I don't require the services of a physician. My problem is… shall we say, of a delicate nature."

A high-class dame, all right. I could tell from the way she spoke that she'd had some schooling. Which was good. The ones with class have money. "Perhaps you can tell me about it."

"It involves my husband, Mr. Ishmael... Captain Ahab, master of the whaling vessel *Pequod*. Perhaps you've heard of him?"

I shook my head. "Name doesn't ring a bell, sorry. A lot of ships come and go out of New Bedford, and you can't throw a rock without hitting a captain."

"Certainly you'd recognize my husband if you saw him. He is older than I, his hair and beard already white with age. But his most noticeable feature is his left leg, which has been replaced by a wooden peg from the knee down."

"You've just described half the sailors in town. The other half have pegs on their right legs."

A smile flickered uneasily at the corners of her full lips. "Yes... quite so. Nonetheless, my husband is quite distinctive, not only in appearance, but also by his recent behavior, which has lately become rather strange."

She nervously looked down at the bare wooden floor. I'd once had a nice oriental rug there that had come all the way from China, but I had to throw it out after one of my former clients bled all over it. The room was warm, so I stood up to open a window. From outside came the morning sounds of the wharf: the creak of sail lines, the curses of workers loading and unloading heavy crates, wagon wheels rattling across cobblestones.

"Tell me about Captain Ahab," I said.

"You know how sea captains are, Mr. Ishmael. They're home for only a few weeks, maybe a month or two, then they're off to sea again. Although I wasn't expecting this when I married my husband, I've become accustomed to his long absences. He has accumulated some small measure of wealth from his voyages, which has allowed us to live in comfort."

She wasn't telling me anything I didn't already know. The mansions of sea captains were among New Bedford's most stately homes. They often had so-called widow's walks, and sometimes the lady of the house got tired of standing out there, watching for the sails of her husband's ship to appear upon the horizon. I'd entertained the wives of more than a few captains, in a discrete way that involved entering and leaving through the kitchen door. They were rich, young, bored, and eager for the company of a gentleman who didn't smell of whale oil and blubber.

But Mrs. Ahab didn't fit the type. One look at her solemn brown eyes, and I knew that she hadn't come here to see if I'd scratch an itch. "I take it that his behavior has become unusual even for someone in his line of work."

"Yes, it has, Mr. Ishmael." She shifted from foot to foot, the frilled hem of her bustle whisking the floor like a broom. How she'd managed to climb a flight of stairs in that thing was beyond me. "When he returned from his last voyage, it was obvious that he had changed. And it was not just that he now had a wooden leg, which he told me he'd lost while climbing up a topsail. My husband has always been a serious man, but this time he was aloof, distant. As if his mind was elsewhere." She hesitated. "He's become obsessed with someone named Moby."

"Moby?"

"Yes. Moby... Moby Dick."

"Sounds like a woman." I was thinking of someone I knew with the same surname: Crazy Phil, who hung out in grog shops, raving about things no one could understand. Perhaps Moby was his sister.

"This is what I've come to suspect, yes. I know women aren't usually allowed aboard whaling vessels, Mr. Ishmael, but a sea captain can bend the rules if he so desires. If my husband were to take a mistress..."

"All captains have a mistress, ma'am."

"I'm not talking about the sea!" Her dark eyes flashed. "I'm talking about a woman who is sharing my husband's cabin aboard the *Pequod*. He's going on another voyage very soon, and if he has a... a hussy... who has become his secret lover, I want to know who she is."

I was startled by her anger. Yes, Mrs. Ahab definitely strolled her widow's walk alone. "I understand. So you want me to..."

"Find out who this Moby Dick is, Mr. Ishmael. I don't want the *Pequod* to leave port without knowing whether my husband will have a woman in his cabin."

"My fee is ten dollars a day, plus expenses." That was more than what I usually charged, but she clearly wasn't going to have to pawn the household silver.

"You'll have it, Mr. Ishmael... along with my gratitude, if my suspicions are confirmed." It may have only been my imagination, but something in her eyes hinted that she'd express her gratitude in an interesting way.

That made me smile. "Very well, then, ma'am. I'll take the case."

Mrs. Ahab had just left my office and was beginning to hobble downstairs when the front door slammed and someone started coming up.

A shriek of horror, then the clatter of patent leather shoes running the rest of the way down the stairs. I closed my eyes, shook my head. She'd just met my partner.

"You need to stop frightening people like that," I said as he came in. "We can't afford to lose any more clients."

"Wang dang doodle." Queequeg rested his harpoon against the wall, then removed his beaverskin stovepipe hat and hung it on the rack. As tall and solid as a mainmast, his walnut-brown skin was etched with so many tattoos that he looked like a lithograph. Queequeg was from somewhere in the South Seas—Samoa, Tahiti, Fiji; I was never quite sure—and he was probably too weird for even that place. I guess that's why he came to America; here, he fit right in. He was big and scary, the best goon in New England.

"Yeah, that's our new client. Some looker, huh?" Queequeg shrugged as he sat down and reached into his overcoat pocket for his pipe. "She wants us to see if her husband is cheating on her. Ever heard of some guy named Ahab?"

"Poppa poppa ooh mow mow mow ooh mow mow mow."

"Yeah, I know he's a captain. She told me that already. The *Pequod*'s his tub. What I'd like to know is whether he's knocking boots with someone who isn't his wife."

"Ee ah ooh aah ahh." He lit his pipe, blew a smoke ring at the ceiling. "Ting tang walla walla bing bang."

"Yeah, I was thinking the preacher might know something. He's pretty sharp about stuff like this." I stood up and walked around the desk. "By the way, did you manage to shake down that deadbeat Hawthorne? He owes us some serious bucks."

Without a word, Queequeg reached into his other coat pocket and pulled out a gnarly object about the size of an apple. He handed it to me, and I looked down to see two tiny eyes and a mouth that had been sewn shut. I sighed. No one was going to read a sequel to *The Scarlet Letter* any time soon.

"Great," I muttered. "Just great." I gave the shrunken head back to my partner. "I didn't mean for you to take me literally. A threat would have sufficed."

"Bum bum bubbagum bum bum."

"All right, never mind. Can I borrow your harpoon, at least? I left mine in New York." *Stuck in someone's chest*, I might have added, but didn't. No sense in encouraging my partner. He was bloodthirsty enough already.

"Wamma bamma ding dong."

"Thanks. I'll bring it back." I picked up the harpoon, slung it over my shoulder. "See you later."

"Shaboom shaboom." Standing up, he walked over to a wall cabinet, opened it, and added the head to his collection. I was glad he'd remembered to shut the cabinet the last time he was here. If Mrs. Ahab had seen how he treated clients who didn't pay on time…

The Whaleman's Chapel was located a couple of blocks from the waterfront. You wouldn't think that a church would get much business in that neighborhood—hell, the best whorehouse in town was just up the street—but I guess a lot of sailors wanted to get right with the big guy before they shipped out again, because Father Mappel held services there every morning. I've never had much use for religion, but the preacher and I weren't strangers. He was one of my best sources for what was happening on the street.

Father Mappel was winding up the daily sermon when I arrived. The door was open, so I stood in the foyer. The Whaleman's Chapel looked pretty much like any other run-down, working-class church on the outside, so it wasn't until you went in that you saw that it wasn't the place where your folks dragged you every Sunday. The first time I saw Father Mappel's pulpit, I thought it was pretty clever that he'd had one built to resemble a ship's bow, complete with a rope ladder dangling from its side. It wasn't until later that I learned that the pulpit really was what it looked like. After a schooner ran aground on a sandbar in the Boston harbor, the preacher had it salvaged and towed to New Bedford, then removed its bow and installed it in his church. Pretty impressive, even if it was overkill.

As usual, the sermon was the one about Jonah and the whale, retold in a weird amalgam of Jonathan Edwards-style hellfire-and-damnation and seaman's vernacular that bore only a faint resemblance to the Old Testament version. It was the only sermon I'd ever heard the preacher deliver. I don't think he'd changed his shtick in years. It went down well with the toothless wonders in the pews, though, and they never seemed to mind hearing it again, so the good reverend had never bothered to write something new.

I leaned against the door and watched while he wrapped things up. The offering plate was passed—a handful of coins, along with the occasional gold tooth someone no longer needed—and an off-tune recital of "That Old Rugged Cross" soon followed. The preacher waved a hand in a desultory sort of benediction, then everyone got up and shuffled out the door, either off to work or to the nearest tavern for their own brand of communion.

I waited until Father Mappel climbed down the rope ladder from the pulpit, then I left my harpoon in the foyer and walked down the aisle to meet him. "Nice sermon. Ever thought of buying a new one?"

He'd just bent over to pick up one of the spittoons placed in front of the pews. "Careful, my son," he murmured, standing up to glare at me. "The lord dost not tolerate blasphemy. In the words of the prophet Ezekiel…"

"Knock it off, padre. Save it for the civilians."

He sighed. "Sorry, Izzy. Get carried away sometimes." He bent over again to pick up the spittoon, then grimaced. "Oh, for the love of… can't these guys ever hit the thing?"

"Are you kidding? How many eye-patches can you count when you're standing up there?"

"You got a point." Father Mappel took a seat in the nearest pew. "Man, when I took this gig, I thought it would be easier than fishing. Kind of wish I was still working the lobster boats."

"Naw, you're good at it." I nodded to the offering plate on the altar. "Besides, look at all the tips you get."

"Sure. Two bits a day and all the leftover hardtack I can eat." He ran a hand through what little hair he still had. "So what's on your mind? Don't tell me you're here for confession… guy like you, that'll take all day."

"Funny. Very funny. Ever hear of someone named Ahab? Captain Ahab, of the *Pequod*?"

"Maybe. Name kinda rings a bell." He squinted a bit, rubbed his forehead. "Y'know, I've always got a lot on my mind. Like collecting donations for the widows and orphans fund…"

I fished a couple of coppers from my watch pocket and dropped them in the offering plate, then came back to sit down next to him. "Uh-huh, now I remember. Yeah, I've heard of him. Strange dude, even for this place."

"I know about the peg-leg…"

"That ain't half of it." He lowered his voice. "The captain never set foot in here, but I get his wife in my confessional every Sunday. Man, if I could marry a woman, that's the one I'd want…but from what she tells me, he's been cold-cocking her since day one. I hear about it because I'm always having to give her penance for what she does to make up for it."

"She's on the loose? I had the impression that she wasn't… sort of."

"You're right. She ain't… but that doesn't keep her from looking. She's a walking Tenth Commandment violation, only in reverse. I'm tellin' ya, Izzy, beneath that prim and proper exterior is one very repressed lady. If she ever got a guy in bed, she'd probably break his back."

"She hired me to see if her husband was fooling around. She thinks he is… someone named Moby."

"Yeah, she's told me that, too. But you know as well as I do that women don't go aboard whaling ships… they're just not allowed, period. And believe me, if there was a slut in town who goes by the name of Moby, I would've heard about her. So there's something else going on behind her back, and it ain't no girl."

I was beginning to think that the preacher might be right. Whatever Ahab was obsessed about, it wasn't a dame. But my client wasn't paying me to tell her that her suspicions were wrong; Mrs. Ahab wouldn't be satisfied until she found out who Moby Dick was. "Maybe his crew knows something," I said.

"They might." Father Mappel shrugged. "Their hangout is the Spouter Inn, so you might check there." He paused, then dropped his voice again. "Just be careful of Starbuck, their chief mate. He and his pal, second mate Stubb, are two galoots you want to avoid."

"Thanks, padre. I'll keep it in mind." I stood up to head for the door. "Blessings?"

"Yeah, yeah." He made the sign of the cross. "May the Lord bless you and keep you, yada yada. Now get out of here."

I retrieved my harpoon from the foyer and stepped out into the street. It was almost noon; the first winos would be showing up at the Spouter Inn to get a head-start on their drinking. Some of them might be *Pequod* men. Time to buy a few drinks and strike up a conversation or two.

I hadn't walked a hundred feet from the chapel before someone took a shot at me.

It didn't even come close. The lead ball chipped a cedar shingle off the corner of the tackle shop I happened to be walking past; it missed me by about six feet. A half-second later, I heard the bang of the gunshot from across the street.

Looking around, I saw a little guy with a mean face standing at the mouth of an alley. He'd lowered the flintlock pistol he'd just fired and was pointing the other one at me. If he'd bungled the shot so badly when he'd fired with his right hand, his aim probably wouldn't improve when he fired with his left. I wasn't taking any chances, though, so I dove behind a row of wooden kegs on the sidewalk in front of the shop. I'd barely taken cover when his second shot shattered a window pane behind me. Damned if he didn't get better the second time…

All around me, townspeople were either running for their lives or finding some place to hide. This wasn't the first time shots had been fired in the streets of New Bedford; now and then, a couple of guys would settle an argument this way, usually after they'd had a few pints. The town constable would be here soon, but not soon enough. Whoever that character was, he wanted me dead. When I peered between the barrels, I could see that he hadn't run off, but instead was standing behind a stack of old lobster traps. Probably reloading, which meant that he was carrying only two pistols.

I began to count to fifteen.

There's three reasons why I carry a harpoon instead of a pistol or a musket. First, it looks tough. Second, carrying a harpoon in New Bedford is much less conspicuous than carrying a brace of pistols. The latter means you're looking for trouble; the former means you're looking for a job. My line of work requires a low profile, so it behooves me to appear to be just another harpooner searching for his next billet.

And third, guns are for losers. They can be fired only once before you have to reload, and that means half-cocking the hammer, pouring a dose of black powder into the muzzle, dropping in the ball, packing it down with the ramrod, priming the flash pan with a little more powder, closing the pan, then cocking the hammer all the way. If you don't make any mistakes, the pistol won't blow up when you fire it and leave you picking your nose with a hook for the rest of your life. And if you're really fast, you can do all this in about fifteen seconds.

Takes only a second to throw a harpoon.

When I got to fourteen, I stood up from behind the barrels, raised my harpoon, and waited. A couple of seconds later, the killer stepped out from behind the lobster traps. Since I hadn't returned fire, he probably figured that I was unarmed, hence a sitting duck if I remained where I was, or little more than a moving target if I tried to run for it. He hadn't even bothered to reload his second pistol, that's how confident he was that he'd get me on his third try.

Wrong. Wrong. Wrong.

The instant I saw his face, I let fly with the harpoon. I'd had lots of practice with the thing, so I knew just how to chuck it. There was a look of dumb astonishment on the killer's mug as he caught a fleeting glimpse of what was coming his way, but there was no time for him to duck before it slammed into him. The harpoon's iron barb, which Queequeg kept it nice and sharp, went straight through his chest, entering the solar plexus and coming out through the middle of his back.

I didn't wait for him finish dying before I strolled across the street to the alley. He lay on his side in a red pool that had already spread far enough to enter the sidewalk gutter, and his wide eyes and gasping mouth reminded me of a brook trout that some Indian had just speared. But he was still breathing when I crouched down beside him.

"Hello, sweetheart," I said.

"H-h-h—" he coughed up some blood "—how d-did…?"

"How did I nail you? You made a mistake. You brought a gun to a harpoon fight. Your turn… who are you, and who sent you?"

"St-st-st…" Pink froth bubbled upon his lips "Stubb. S-s-s-sent by sta-sta-star…"

"Starbuck?" I finished, and Stubb managed a weak nod. "Both of you work for Ahab. Did he order you to…?"

A low rattle from somewhere deep in his throat, then a stench as something foul left his body. Stubb sagged against the harpoon's wooden shaft, and that was it. He'd told me enough, though, so I found a couple of pennies in my pocket and carefully placed them upon his unseeing eyes. He'd tried to kill me, sure, but I always pay my informants. At least he'd have something for the boatman he was about to meet.

I'd just stood up when I heard a voice behind me. "St-st-st-stop right th-th-there, Ishma-ma-mael, and p-p-put your h-h-h…"

"Hands up? Sure." I raised my mitts, then slowly turned around. "'Bout time you got here, Billy. What took you so long?"

Constable Budd stood just outside the alley, pistol pointed straight at me. He wouldn't miss if he fired, but I knew he wouldn't. Billy and I went way back, when we'd both served on the same ship in the Navy. He was a pretty handsome guy, with the kind of angelic looks that make girls swoon, but he was a lousy foretopman and had never been able to do anything about his speech impediment. Now he was just a stuttering flatfoot who was never around when you needed him.

"I-I-I w-w-w—" Billy stopped, counted to ten, and then went on. "I was handling another call when I heard about what was happening here. What made you kill this guy?"

"He tried to kill me first. You can ask anyone." A small crowd of bystanders had come out of hiding and was beginning to gather around us. I had no shortage of witnesses. When Billy turned to look around, he saw a lot of heads nodding in agreement with what I'd just said.

"Uh-huh." Billy wasn't completely convinced. "And w-why w-would he do something like t-that?"

"Beats me. I was just defending myself." Ignoring the pistol pointed at me, I planted a foot against Stubb's body, grabbed the harpoon with both hands, and gave it a good, hard yank. The harpoon made a wet sound as it came loose.

"Yeah, I'm s-s-sure that's all you w-were do-do-doing." Billy remained skeptical, but at least he lowered his weapon. "Y-y-you don't t-t-think it has anything t-to do with something y-y-you m-might be working on, do y-you?"

I wiped the harpoon clean on the corpse. "I haven't the foggiest what you're talking about."

"Oh y-y-yes you do." Billy stuck his pistol back in his belt. "I-I-I've t-told you m-m-many times, Ish-Ish-Ishmael... st-st-st-stay out of p-p-p-police b-b-b-business!"

"I'll keep it in mind. Want some advice of my own? You really need to make another appointment with your speech therapist."

Constable Budd cast me a cold glare, but he knew he wouldn't get anything out of me. "G-g-get out of h-h-here. C-come d-down to the st-st-st-station later s-s-so w-ww-we can get a...a...a..."

"A statement. No problem." I shouldered my harpoon again, stepped around him. "C-c-catch you later."

"J-j-j-jerk," he muttered.

Making my way through the crowd, I continued walking down the street. Time to drop by the Spouter Inn and learn why Starbuck had sent Stubb on an errand that would've left me dead if only he hadn't been such a lousy shot.

It was happy hour at the Spouter Inn, which meant that the proprietor had just opened the doors and let the drunks in. If it hadn't been for local ordinances, I don't think Pete would have ever bothered to close up; he probably would have just hired another bartender to handle the graveyard shift, rented cots to the chronics, and mopped the floors every other week. On the other hand, perhaps it's just as well that he gave the regulars a chance to sober up. They'd only come back again the next day, anxious to damage their livers with the nasty swill Pete made from fermented apples and rubbing alcohol. Pete's last name is Coffin. Don't get me started.

It was half past noon when I walked in, yet the tavern had this perpetually lightless gloom that made it seem as if midnight never went away. Sailors and derelicts were sitting around tables, using wooden spoons to slurp up bowls of the reeking foulness Pete called clam chowder; if you ever find a clam in there, please carry it back to the ocean and let it go, the poor thing got lost. The regulars were gathered at the bar, where Mr. Coffin himself was holding court. He noticed me almost as soon I found a vacant stool and sat down.

"Hey, Izzy… I hear someone took a shot at you." He grinned as he spit into a beer stein and wiped it down. "What's the matter? Someone's husband upset with you again?"

One day, a smart fellow is going to invent a rapid means of communication. I'd be willing to bet that it might have something to do with electricity. Whatever it is, though, it won't be half as fast as the waterfront grapevine. The guys at the bar laughed, and I faked a smile.

"Wouldn't know, Pete." I rested my harpoon against the bar. "Why don't you ask your wife?"

More laughter. Pete picked up another stein. "I will, soon as she gets back from giving your sister swimming lessons so she can catch up with troop ships."

"You win," I said, and as a consolation prize he filled the stein with ale and slid it down the bar to me. "Thanks… say, you wouldn't happen to know someone named Starbuck, would you?"

Pete's grin faded. "Over there, corner table. The guy with his back to the wall." He lowered his voice. "Careful, Izzy. He doesn't look it, but he's one tough hombre."

I dropped a silver piece on the bar, then picked up my ale and sauntered across the room, leaving my harpoon at the bar. There wasn't enough room in the tavern for me to use it effectively; besides, the management frowned on customers killing each other. Starbuck spotted me before I was halfway there; although he didn't stop talking to the sailor sitting across the table from him, his dark eyes regarded me steadily as I approached. His sun-darkened skin told me that he'd spent his life at sea, and the way his pea jacket bunched around his biceps was evidence that he'd never been a passenger. Other than that, he looked fairly ordinary... and it's the ordinary ones who are often the most dangerous.

"Mr. Ishmael, isn't it?"

"Just Ishmael. And you're Mr. Starbuck?"

"Uh-huh... and don't forget the mister." He didn't bother to introduce his companion, a muscle-bound pug who couldn't have been anything else but another seaman. Without a word, the sailor stood up and walked away. Starbuck pointed to the vacated chair. "Have a seat."

"I'd prefer not to." A line I'd picked up from Bartleby. The scrivener may have been weird, but he was an expert at the art of passive aggression. "Met a friend of yours just a little while ago. Mr. Stubb."

"Oh? And how is he?" As if he didn't know already.

"Aside from the heart trouble he's been having lately, just peachy."

Starbuck's eyes narrowed, but otherwise his expression remained stoical. "Stubb's a good man. It would be a shame if anything happened to him. I might get upset."

"Really?" I took a swig of ale and put the stein down on the table; I needed to keep my hands free, just in case he tried to start anything. Beneath his open jacket, I could see a big, bone-handled knife stuck in a scabbard on his belt. Starbuck's right hand never strayed very far from it. "If you'd wanted to send me a message, maybe you should've asked someone else to deliver it."

"A message?" Starbuck's head cocked sideways just a fraction of an inch. "Now what sort of message could I possibly want to send you? We've only just met."

"Perhaps a warning to stay away from your captain's wife."

"Mrs. Ahab?" A corner of his mouth ticked upward. "Pray tell, friend Ishmael... what possible interest could I have in the spouse of my commanding officer?"

"If not her, then the woman she'd like to find." I gave it a moment to sink in, but all I could see was bewilderment. "Moby," I added. "Moby Dick."

Starbuck stared at me in disbelief, then suddenly burst out laughing. "Surely you jest! You think Moby Dick is... is a *woman*?"

Only one way to clear this up: lay my cards on the table, let Starbuck know what I was holding. "She does. That's why she hired me... to find the lady with whom Mrs. Ahab believes her husband is having an affair. Moby is a name her husband has frequently mentioned, so..."

Starbuck laughed even more loudly, a hilarious roar that caught the attention of everyone in the room. "Oh, *really*," he yelled, slapping his knee, "this is too much! I mean... my God, when one of my crewmen happened to spy her leaving your office early this morning in a rather furtive fashion, he believed that she might have been having a tryst with you!" He chuckled, shaking his head. "That's why I dispatched Mr. Stubb to... shall we say, attend to you. The captain has always been wary of unmarried men taking an interest in his wife... and you, sir, have a reputation."

"Oh, boy..."

"Yes. One error, compounded by another." His grin disappeared. "But now it seems as if I'm down one crewman, on the very day that the *Pequod* is about to set sail again."

"You're leaving today?" Mrs. Ahab had told me the ship was leaving soon, but not *that* soon. I wondered if she even knew.

"The whales are running, Mr. Ishmael, and the *Pequod* is a whaling ship." His gaze shifted to the harpoon I'd left leaning against the bar. "You're good with that thing. I could use another harpooner."

"Thanks, but I've got a job already."

A malicious glint appeared in his eyes. "You misunderstand me, Mr. Ishmael. I'm not offering you a billet... I'm giving you one." His gaze shifted past me. "Dough Boy...?"

I'd forgotten the sailor who'd been sitting at the table. I was about to look around to see if he was behind me when something crashed against the back of my head. The next instant, I was face-down on the unvarnished floor.

I wasn't unconscious yet. Dough Boy's boot made sure that I was. The moment before it connected with my ribs, though, I heard Starbuck say one more thing.

"Now you'll get to meet Moby Dick," he said. And then Dough Boy kicked me into oblivion.

The creak of oak boards. The mingled odors of salt and fish and sweat. The brown-tinted light of an oil lamp swaying from the rafters of a low ceiling. A narrow bunk that rocked beneath me. As soon as I woke up, I knew I was at sea.

That wasn't my only surprise. I opened my eyes to find a tattooed face hovering above me. "Queequeg... what the hell are you doing here?"

"Iko iko." My partner's black eyes regarded me from beneath his beaverskin hat.

"You signed up? Why would you...?" My headache wasn't so bad that I couldn't put two and two together. "We're on the *Pequod*, aren't we? And you took a billet when you'd heard I'd been shanghaied. Right?"

"A whop bop-a-lu a whop bam boo."

"Yeah, okay... the pay's better, too." I started to sit up, and the sharp pain from my ribs told me that I might be rushing things. Dough Boy had done a number on me. I was in the crew quarters aft of the main hold; there were no portholes below deck, so I couldn't tell whether it was day or night. "Have you seen Ahab? Do you know who Moby—?"

A deck hatch swung open, and I heard booted feet descending the ladder. Queequeg stepped aside to make room for my visitor; a second later, Starbuck came into view. "Very good. You're awake." There was a copper mug in his right hand. "Like some coffee?"

I stared at him. "You abduct me, and then you offer me coffee. You're a real piece of work, Starbuck."

"It's good coffee. Made it myself. And I told you... it's Mister Starbuck to you."

"It's going to be Mister Dead Meat when I get through with you."

"Uh-huh. You and what navy?" He slapped a hand on Queequeg's shoulder. "Your pal here is the only friend you have aboard, Mr. Ishmael. There's forty men on the *Pequod*, and they all take their orders from me. I'd think twice about making idle threats. The captain usually lets me give twenty lashes for insubordination… and you know, of course, that mutiny is punishable by hanging."

Yeah, I knew. Old scars on my back were proof that I was no stranger to a bullwhip, and I'd once seen a sailor do the dead man's jig from the end of a noose. So I accepted the mug from him and took a sip. Not bad coffee, for a creep. "I don't get it. Why did you bring me along? If you've got Queequeg, you're no longer short a harpooner. Hell, he's better than I am."

"He signed up after we brought you aboard. Someone on the dock must have recognized you when Dough Boy and I hauled you down from the Spouter Inn." Starbuck grinned. "We knew that he's your partner, of course… but you're right, he also has a good rep as a harpooner, and we need all the spearchuckers we can get."

Queequeg scowled at him. "Bang shang a lang," he growled.

"What did he say?"

"Don't call him a spearchucker. He doesn't like that." I didn't give him an accurate translation; it was something Queequeg's victims often heard just before he shrunk their heads. "So when are you going to tell me what's going on here? Who the hell is Moby Dick, and why is he so important to Captain Ahab?"

"You can ask him yourself. He sent me down here to fetch you." He stepped back, made a beckoning gesture with his hands. "C'mon now… time to get up."

It wasn't until we came up the ladder that I realized that night had fallen. A cold wind slapped at the mainsails; Orion was rising from the east, and when I looked to the port side, I spotted the Nantucket light house upon the western horizon. The *Pequod* was several miles off the Massachusetts coast, heading north. It must have set sail shortly before dusk; I'd been unconscious for quite a while.

A group of sailors were gathered on deck, eating beans and drinking rum. A guy with an eyepatch sat on a pickle barrel, playing an accordion. All the scene lacked was a talking parrot and some guy in a striped shirt singing "What Do You Do With A Drunken Sailor?" Now I remembered why I left the Navy. Man, I hate sea chanteys.

Queequeg and I followed Starbuck to the aft cabin. The chief mate knocked twice on the door, then opened it and walked in. The captain's quarters were larger than the crew accommodations, of course, but it was still a cold and uncomfortable little room that made the rudest hovel in New Bedford look like a luxury suite. Not that its occupant would probably mind. One look at Captain Ahab, and I knew that he was a hard-boiled egg no one would ever crack.

"Mister Starbuck? Is this our new crewman?" Ahab turned away from the window, the wooden peg of his left leg thumping against the deck. Cool grey eyes regarded from a leathery face framed by a white jaw beard. He reminded me of every bad teacher I'd ever had, the kind who'd break your fingers with a ruler for chewing tobacco in class.

"Yes, sir. Woke up just a few minutes ago." Starbuck unnecessarily pushed me forward, as if I was prisoner being brought before the warden. "Name's Ishmael."

"Ishmael." Ahab stamped closer to me until our faces were only a few inches apart. "Mister Starbuck tells me my wife hired you to check up on me. Is this true?"

"That's pretty much the shape of things. She thinks you're having an affair with a woman named Moby."

"Does she now?" A smirk danced on his lips. He glanced over his shoulder at Starbuck. "Moby Dick is a woman... did you get that?"

"Sure did, Captain. I'm just as amused as you are."

"Indeed." Ahab turned away from me, hobbled over to his desk and sat down. "Moby Dick took my leg, Mr. Ishmael, but my wife would take all my money if she could. I suppose that's why she hired you. If she could prove in court that I'm having an affair..."

"Hold on. She told me that you lost your leg when you fell off a topsail."

"I know. That's what I told her." His eyes rolled toward the ceiling. "If I'd let her know the truth, I would've never heard the end of it. 'You lost your leg to a whale? What kind of idiot loses his leg to a...?'"

"Moby Dick is a *whale*?"

"Of course it's a whale. Have you ever heard a girl named Moby?" Ahab stared at me in disbelief. "The biggest sperm whale anyone has ever seen, and as white as an iceberg. Mean, too. My leg got caught in a harpoon line when we fought it a year ago, yanked it right off. Not that I'm going to tell this to my wife." He sighed and made a talking motion with his hand. "Nag, nag, nag..."

"Might have saved us all a lot of trouble if you had."

"Yeah, well… she wants a divorce that bad, I might just give it to her. When I catch Moby Dick, I'm gonna saw off its head, take it home, and drop it on the front lawn. 'Here's the lady I was having an affair with, bitch. Now gimme a divorce so I can have my life back.'"

"I take it that you're going after Moby Dick for the sake of revenge."

"Revenge is such a harsh word, Mr. Ishmael. I prefer to think of it as aggressive fishing. Anyway, I need another harpooner, and since you took out my second mate, you and your partner are going to replace him."

"Diddy wah diddy," Queequeg said.

"Diddy wah diddy?" Ahab scowled at him, then looked at Starbuck and me. "Can somebody tell me what 'diddy wah diddy' means?"

"He's asking about bennies. Y'know… medical insurance, stock options, retirement plan…"

"Three bucks a week, a cup of rum every day, and a promise to keelhaul you if you ask me that again. But you can have my wife after I dump her, Ishmael. God knows I never slept with the skank."

"So I've gathered." No wonder he hadn't ever been his wife's monkey. He was too weird for sex. At least I had something to look forward to once we got home.

I didn't know it then, though, but that was going to be a problem.

I'll make a long story short. Ahab didn't get the whale. The whale got him.

The *Pequod* spent the next week roaming the waters off Nova Scotia, watching for whale pods making their seasonal migration from the Arctic waters further north. We saw quite a few sperms and right whales, but the captain wasn't interested in any cetacean that wasn't an albino.

In the meantime, Ahab stomped around the poop deck, raving like a loon while everyone else hoisted up sails and battened down hatches and all that other sailor stuff. There was a coffin on the main deck. I don't why it was there, but Queequeg and I used it as a card table while we played poker and waited for this whole stupid trip to end.

Which it finally did, and not well. Seven days after the *Pequod* left New Bedford, the guy up in the crow's nest caught sight of something big and white breaching the surface about a half-mile away. We chased it down, and sure enough, it was Moby Dick. When we were close enough, the captain ordered all the harpooners into the boats. As luck would have it, he picked me to be the bowsman for his boat.

Moby Dick was as big as Ahab said he'd be, and twice as mean. First, he took out two other whalers, crashing straight into them and sending everyone straight into the water. Then he came after my boat. I threw my harpoon, missed, and decided that was all for the day, but Ahab wasn't giving up. When the whale got close enough, he began hacking at it with his harpoon. "From hell's heart I stab at thee, for hate's sake I spit my last breath at thee…" Crazy, but he sure knew how to rant.

The whale had other plans. Moby Dick capsized my boat, and when that happened, Ahab got tangled in a harpoon line. Again. How anyone can let the same thing happen to him twice is beyond me, but the whale was still taking the captain for his own personal Nantucket sleigh ride when it charged the *Pequod*. Moby must have decided that he'd had enough of that damn ship, because he slammed into it hard enough to open a hole in its side.

So the *Pequod* went down, taking everyone with it. Funny thing about Queequeg; he never learned to swim. Nor did anyone else aboard, I guess. All that was left behind was that stupid coffin, which I clung to for the next couple of days, until another ship happened to pass close enough for its crew to spot me.

When I got back to New Bedford, I went to see my client and gave her the good news: she was now a rich widow. She paid my fee, and then she expressed her gratitude in a different way. Father Mappel was right; I could barely walk after I left her place.

After that, I visited a friend of mine, a customs inspector whose office was just down the hall. Herman is a writer, the starving variety. Who knows? Maybe he'll find something useful to do with my story. There might even be a novel in there.

Naw. No one would ever believe it. I mean… a whale named Moby?

Probably the single most chilling event of my lifetime was the Cuban Missile Crisis. Not even 9/11 comes close when you stop to consider the possible consequences if either Kennedy or Khrushchev had made a fatal error. I don't remember it, of course—I was only four years old when it happened—but the more I've read about it, the more I've come to realize that, if things had happened just a little differently during that fateful week in 1962, I would have grown up in a post-nuclear holocaust world... if I'd survived at all.

One of the things that fascinates me the most about the idea of time travel is that, if it ever becomes possible for people to send themselves into the past, we could have chrononauts in our midst right now and probably never know it. After all, a wise time traveler would have to be careful and keep his or her identity a closely guarded secret, for obvious reasons: there's no government in the world who wouldn't give anything to know what happens tomorrow. So we could have people from the future walking among us and never know it... unless they made a mistake.

And if they were discovered? This would raise a very disturbing question: why here, and why now? What is it about this particular place and time that draws the interest of someone from the future?

I don't know about you, but... if I ever met a time traveler, I'd probably run like hell.

THE OBSERVATION POST

Now I'm old, but when I was young I did something which has weighed upon my conscience ever since. In all the years that followed, I've never told anyone about this. Not my late wife or my children or grandchildren, nor any of my friends, not even the priests to whom I've dutifully confessed for all other sins. My actions may have saved the world, but they took the form of betrayal... and worse.

A few months ago, I was diagnosed with an inoperable and terminal form of cancer. My doctor has informed me that, in all likelihood, I'll be dead by the end of the year. Even so, I probably would have taken my secret to the grave, secure in the knowledge that no one would ever learn what I did nearly fifty years ago. That's fine with me. I'm not a hero.

Just the other day, though, I saw someone on the street whom I haven't seen since 1962. Just the mere fact that I spotted this individual has made me change my mind. Perhaps people should know what happened, if only to remind them how dangerous our times have become, and that our deeds will be remembered by later generations.

My name is Floyd Moore. I was 23 years old in 1962, an ensign in the U.S. Navy and a radioman aboard the *Centurion*. The *Centurion* wasn't a vessel; it was a blimp, one of five N-class airships built during the fifties as submarine hunters and later modified to serve as an advance early warning system in the days before the undersea SOSUS network was established.

The Goodyear blimps you see at football games had about as much in common with the *Centurion* as a Chevy pick-up does with a Corvette: same manufacturer, but the similarity ends there. The *Centurion* was 343 long and 108 feet high, and was powered by two 800-horsepower engines. It had a double-decker car with crew space for twenty-one; the bunks, bathroom, galley, and ward room were squeezed into the upper deck above the cockpit, AEW compartment, and engine room. It could stay aloft for over two hundred hours without having to land; its cruising speed was 56 mph, although in a pinch it could reach a maximum airspeed of 80 mph.

When I went through communications training at the Navy flight school in Pensacola, I'd thought I was going to wind up aboard an aircraft carrier, so I was disappointed when I was put on a blimp instead. However, I soon discovered that I liked this job much better. The *Centurion* was based in Key West, so my newly-wed wife and I were able to rent a little beach cottage off-base, and my patrols never took me away from home for more than a few days. Our captain, Roy Gerrard, had been flying blimps since World War II, and the crew was a tight-knit bunch; you could've easily taken us for a group of men who belonged to some club that happened to have its own blimp.

The pleasure we took from our job, though, was tempered by the knowledge that the *Centurion*'s days were numbered. Blimps were obsolete. Planes had already taken over the task of hunting subs, and once the SOSUS net was in place, advance early warning would be taken from us, too. Now that America and Russia were shooting guys into space, there was even talk that there would soon be military space stations. Alan Shepard was a Navy man, and we were proud of him for being the first

American in space, but we were all too aware that his Mercury capsule made a blimp look pretty old-fashioned. Whenever the *Centurion* went out on patrol, we knew that it might be for the last time.

But our mission in the first week of October '62 was rather unusual. Instead of flying up the Atlantic coast to New England and back again, Capt. Gerrard had received orders to go the other way, down to the Bahamas northeast of Cuba, where we would conduct aerial reconnaissance of the passages between the Acklins, Mayaguana, and Caicos islands. We were supposed to be searching for Russian subs, of course—Nikita had lately become a little too chummy with Fidel for anyone's comfort—but we were also to be on the lookout for any freighters or fishing trawlers that appeared to be heading for Cuba.

And we'd taken aboard a new crewmember: Lt. Robert Arnault, a Navy intelligence officer temporarily replacing the j.g. who usually had the same job. None of us had ever met him before; he'd flown in from Washington only a couple of days earlier, and although he tried to be one of the guys, it soon became apparent that he wasn't going to fit in. Capt. Gerrard was still in command, but it was Lt. Arnault who was calling the shots. The skipper's sealed orders had been hand-delivered by the lieutenant and they were the only people aboard who'd read them; the rest of us were in the dark as to what this was all about. Arnault wasn't overbearing—he slept in the same bunkroom and ate the same meals with us, and he could make small talk about the World Series or that new spy movie starring some fellow named Connery—but he wouldn't say a word about why we were here.

You, of course, have the benefit of hindsight. It was at this time that the Soviet Union began a secret operation to arm Cuba with nuclear weapons. They did this because the U.S. had recently placed long-range nuclear missiles in Turkey, and also to prevent another invasion like the one at the Bay of Pigs the year before. So Russian vessels were bringing in medium-range R-12s and intermediate-range R-14s, any one of which could easily reach the American mainland, along with short-range battlefield rockets equipped with low-yield tactical nukes that could be used to repel an invasion.

But the Americans had a mole in the Kremlin, a Soviet military intelligence officer who'd been feeding Russian secrets to the CIA. Colonel Penkovsky was eventually caught and executed, but not before he tipped off the Americans as to what Khrushchev was planning. The CIA didn't have any solid evidence that the U.S.S.R. was sending nukes to Cuba, though, and they would need firm proof before they could take the matter to President Kennedy. So that's why the *Centurion* was watching for Russian vessels sailing to Cuba.

For four days, we orbited Acklins, Mayaguana, and Caicos, maintaining constant surveillance of the passages between them from an altitude of 2,500 feet. We spotted plenty of ships, but only a couple were flying the red Soviet flag. When that happened, we'd descend to 1,500 feet and shadow them for awhile, monitoring their wireless communications and taking pictures that we'd transmit back to Key West via radio facsimile. Nothing about their appearance suggested that they were carrying missiles, though, and their radios would go silent when we were in the vicinity.

We weren't aware that most of the rockets were still on the way. The ships carrying them were still in the north Atlantic and wouldn't arrive in the Caribbean for another week or so. However, the first few R-12s had already reached Cuba, along with a handful of tactical missiles. The R-12s didn't have the range to hit Washington or New York, but they could blow away Miami or New Orleans. Not only that, but Khrushchev had given Castro permission to launch the missiles if the U.S. attacked his country, and Fidel had no problems with nuking the *yanquis*; along with some Kremlin hard-liners, he believed that a first-strike would settle matters once and for all. They didn't know it, but Air Force general Curtis LeMay and many other American counterparts shared the same sentiments.

The world was on the brink of nuclear war, and no one knew it yet. Almost no one, that is.

On the morning of Friday, October 5th, I came down from the bunkroom to take my watch at the radio board in the AWS compartment. As I relieved the radioman who'd handled the overnight shift, I noticed that the dawn sky was an ominous shade of red. For the past two days, we'd been receiving weather reports from Puerto Rico about a tropical storm off the Leeward Islands southeast of our position. As soon as I saw those amber-streaked clouds, I had a hunch it was getting closer.

I was right. No sooner had I sat down than the telex rang three times, signaling an incoming signal. I waited while the message printed out, then

I ripped it off, opened my codebook, and spent the next minute or so deciphering it. Capt. Gerrard had just come downstairs when I handed the decoded message to him.

The captain read it and sighed. "Great," he muttered. "That makes my day." The other officers in the AWS compartment turned to look at him as he went on. "That tropical storm south of us has become a Cat 1 cyclone. It's now called Hurricane Daisy, and its present track has it becoming Cat 2 and turning north-northwest."

"That's coming our way, isn't it, skipper?" That came from our flight engineer Jimmy Costa—"Handsome Jimmy" we called him, because he wasn't—who'd just stuck his head in from the engine room.

"Uh-huh." The captain folded the message and gave it back to me so I could file it. "We're to land at the nearest available field and sit it out." A terse smile. "Glad someone has the common sense to order us in."

Everyone nodded. Back in the thirties, the Navy had lost two dirigibles, the *Akron* and the *Macon*, during storms at sea. No one in the airship corps had forgotten those disasters, but we were always scared that we'd get some dummy in charge of things who thought that a blimp could fly through a hurricane. Lucky for us, a dummy hadn't written our orders.

But we still had a problem: where to land? A blimp doesn't need a runway—it can touch down almost anywhere—but it does require a mooring tower if it's going to be tied down for awhile, which is what we'd need to do if the *Centurion* was going to ride out a hurricane. Key West was too far away; we'd never make it before the storm overtook us. Puerto Rico was closer, but it lay in the direction Daisy was coming from. And the U.S. naval base at Guantanamo Bay was out of the question; Lt. Arnault reminded the captain that our mission orders specifically stated that we were not to approach Cuba under any circumstances.

Our navigator, Harry Taggart, pulled out a loose-leaf notebook and flipped to the list of possible airship landing sites in the Caribbean, and sure enough, he found one: Great Inagua, the larger of a pair of small islands about 50 miles west of Caicos and 55 miles east of Cuba. Only one town, but it had an airfield, and on that airfield was a mooring tower which had been there since WW II. The *Centurion* was on the other side of Caicos; we could easily reach Great Inagua before Daisy came through.

So I sent a telex to Key West informing them of our plans, and as soon as it was confirmed, Phil Bennet turned his pilot's wheel and put us on west-by-southwest bearing for Great Inagua. I called ahead to Matthew Town, and after a half-hour or so I finally heard a Caribbean-accented voice through my headphones. He told me his name was Samuel Parker, and although he was surprised that an American airship was on its way, he assured me that he'd muster a ground crew for us.

The *Centurion* reached the Inagua islands shortly before noon. We passed over Little Inagua, a tiny spit of sand and grass which appeared to have sea birds and wild goats as its sole inhabitants, and came upon Great Inagua, which wasn't much larger but at least showed signs of human presence. Matthew Town was located on the island's southwest corner; as the blimp's shadow passed over its sun-bleached rooftops, townspeople came out to stare up at us. There didn't seem to be much down there: a bunch of houses, a church steeple, a handful of fishing boats tied up at the dock.

The airstrip was primitive, a single runway which looked as if it had been last resurfaced around the time Amelia Earhart disappeared. The mooring tower was located at its coastal end, not far from a couple of small hangars on the verge of collapse. It looked like a misplaced Aztec pyramid, its iron frame rusted black and flecked with salt. Six dark men in shorts and island shirts lounged beside the antique flat-bed truck that had brought them there, smoking cigarettes as they watched the blimp come down; it wasn't until *Centurion* was only twenty feet above the asphalt that one of them tossed away his smoke and sauntered out to raise his hands above his head while his companions trotted over to grab hold of our lines.

The islanders dragged the ship the rest of the way in while one of them climbed a ladder up the tower and snapped a cable hook to the blimp's prow. A diesel wrench then reeled in the cable until the *Centurion* was snugly docked against the tower. Eight of our guys jumped out of the car and helped the local ground crew pull the lines as far as they would go, then used a sledge hammer to pound iron pitons into the sandy ground and lashed the ropes to them. The skipper waited until he was sure the *Centurion* wasn't going anywhere before he ordered Phil to cut the engines.

I joined the Capt. Gerrard and Lt. Arnault as the locals ambled over to greet us, and it wasn't hard to tell that they were amused to have a Navy blimp make an emergency landing in their forgotten little part of the world. In fact, we'd later learn that the only reason why the tower hadn't been torn down for scrap metal was that every year the U.S. State Department sent the District of Inagua a $500 rent check. Among them was Samuel Parker, the person with whom I'd spoken on the radio; besides running the airfield, he also was the customs officer. He made a great show of asking for our passports, which he carefully inspected as if we might be anyone except what our uniforms plainly showed us to be, before he formally shook hands with Capt. Gerrard and welcomed us to Great Inagua.

The wind was beginning to pick up by then. The sky was still bright blue, but a dark wall of clouds had become visible on the southern horizon. We were prepared to spend the night in the blimp, but Mr. Parker wouldn't hear of it. There was a large guest house in Matthew Town which we were welcome to use, and a restaurant across the street was already ready to have us over for dinner.

Capt. Gerrard quickly took him up on the offer; after four days of sleeping in narrow bunks and having canned food for breakfast, lunch, and dinner, some Caribbean hospitality would be a nice change of pace. We couldn't leave the *Centurion* by itself, though, so the captain asked for two volunteers to stay with the blimp. Harry and Phil raised their hands; they'd keep watch on the blimp, and use a walkie-talkie to call for help if the storm threatened to break it loose from its moorings. The rest of us fetched our duffel bags, then crowded into the back of the beat-up truck along with the ground crew, and held on for dear life as it made a bumpy, gear-grinding journey into Matthew Town.

The town looked pretty much like any other small Caribbean port: white-washed wood-frame houses on sand-filled streets, an abandoned prison dating back to the 1700's, a church and a few shops surrounding the town square. The kind of place inhabited mainly by native Caribbeans and a handful of retired British civil servants; there were probably more sea gulls than people. Not exactly a tourist destination. I figured that we were probably the only visitors the town had seen in awhile.

I was wrong.

As it turned out, Daisy only sideswiped the Bahamas. By the end of the day the hurricane turned north and headed for the East Coast; the following day it would dump several inches of rain on New England before petering out over Nova Scotia. As cyclones go, Daisy was something of a wallflower.

There was no sense in taking the blimp aloft again. The crew spent the afternoon in the guest house, playing cards and listening to the Series on the radio as wind-driven rain lashed against the windows. The storm subsided just before sundown, but the winds were still just high enough to make flying hazardous, so Capt. Gerrard decided that we might as well spend the night on Great Inagua and take off again the next morning. Call it shore leave.

None of us were unhappy with the decision save for Lt. Arnault, who seemed nervous about the prospect of missing any Russian freighters bound for Cuba. But the *Centurion* was the skipper's blimp, and he wasn't about to do anything that would unnecessarily put his ship and crew in harm's way. Besides, he reminded Arnault, any Soviet vessels in the vicinity had probably dropped anchor somewhere to ride out the hurricane; they weren't going anywhere either.

The guest house was a two-story inn in the middle of Matthew Town, the doors to its rooms facing outside. The *Centurion* had arrived after what passed for tourist season on Great Inagua, so we were able to take over the whole place. Most of the crew shared quarters, but Capt. Gerrard claimed a room for his own. So did Lt. Arnault, which nettled a lot of the guys; *who does he think he is?* was the general consensus. I didn't care one way or another; I was bunking with Handsome Jimmy, notorious among the crew for his snoring, and so I knew I probably wouldn't get a lot of sleep that night.

The island's only restaurant was just across the street, and as Mr. Parker had told us, the proprietors had been forewarned that twenty-one Navy men would be coming over for dinner. By the time we'd wandered over there, they'd laid out a nice spread: grilled tarpon fresh from the dock, with hush puppies, greens, and the best key lime pie I've ever had. There was a bar in the next room, complete with a pool table and a TV; after we finished stuffing ourselves, we moved over there and settled in for an evening of goofing off.

The regulars gradually filtered into the place, and at first they were put off by the presence of so many uniforms, perhaps afraid that we might be stereotypical American sailors and wreck the joint. But the captain had firmly told us to be on our best behavior, and after awhile the locals warmed up to us. A couple of our guys got a pool tournament going with them, while others gathered at the TV to watch *The Jackie Gleason Show* on a Miami station.

I had just returned to the bar for another beer when I found a young woman sitting there. She was about my age, maybe a year or two older. Women had just started wearing their hair long again, and hers was blond and fell down around the shoulders of her cotton summer dress. She wasn't a raving beauty, but she was pretty all the same, and she was there by herself.

I had no intention of trying to pick her up. My marriage was solid; I was faithful to my wife, and one-night stands had never been my style anyway. It was just that I was tired of seeing no one but other guys, and a pretty girl would be good company for a change. So I walked over, introduced myself, and asked if I could join her. She was a little wary of me, but she nodded anyway, so I parked myself on the next barstool and asked her about herself.

She told me that her name was Helga—no last name, just Helga—and she was from West Germany; I picked up the European accent as soon as she spoke, so the latter was no surprise. She said that she was visiting Great Inagua with two male companions—her cousin Kurt and their friend Alex, an American—and that the three of them were avid birdwatchers who'd come to the islands for its tropical birds. They were renting a house just south of town; she'd dropped in for a drink while Kurt and Alex visited a grocery store down the street.

I told her who I was and why I was there, and she gave me a knowing smile; yes, she'd seen the blimp when it had flown over the island. She was curious about why a Navy blimp would be in the area; our mission was classified, so I told her that it was a routine patrol, nothing more. Even as I said this, though, I became aware of a presence behind me. Glancing over my shoulder, I saw that Arnault had deposited himself on the next barstool.

"Sorry," he said. "Didn't mean to interrupt." He looked at me. "Mind if I butt in, Floyd?"

"Sure. We're just talking." I gestured to the woman sitting next to me. "This is Helga. Helga, this is…"

"Bob Arnault." He raised a finger to the bartender, signaling him for another beer. This was the first time I'd heard him refer to himself as Bob; on the blimp, he was always Lt. Arnault. "You from around here?"

"No." Helga shook her head. "I was just telling Floyd that my friends and I are visiting Inagua to study its birds. There are the loveliest pink flamingos here, and we're photographing them."

"They're staying on the outskirts of town," I added, not wanting to be left out of the conversation. "She says they're—"

"Where are you from?" Arnault asked, ignoring me. "You're not from the States, I can tell."

Helga laughed. "I'm not, but my friend Alex is. My cousin and I are from West Germany."

"Really?" Arnault took a sip from the Red Stripe the bartender had just put in front of him. "Which town?"

"Hannover."

"Hannover! Great place! I was there once, just a couple of years ago. I stayed at a hotel in the center of town, the—" Arnault closed his eyes and tapped a finger against the bar, as if trying to conjure a memory "—I can't remember the name."

"Yes. Of course." Helga turned to me again. "As I was saying, there are quite a number of West Indian Flamingos here. Also parrots, herons, pintails…"

"Y'know. The major hotel in the middle of the city."

"There are many hotels in Hannover." Helga's smile flickered a bit as she gazed past me at him.

"This one was the biggest." He stared at her. "You know which one I'm talking about… don't you?"

Helga's face lost its color, and she pointedly looked away from him. I looked over at Arnault, wondering why he was being so rude. "Lieutenant, we were talking about birds. You can't—"

"Can't what, *ensign*?" His eyes narrowed as he deliberately emphasized my lesser rank. "Talk about hotels instead of birds?" A humorless smile. "I can… but I think it's more interesting that your friend can't give me the name of—"

"Pardon me… is there a problem?"

I turned to see the tall, blond-haired man who'd come up from behind us. His accent was the same as Helga's, and it wasn't hard to guess that this was Kurt. I don't know how long he'd been standing there, but I guessed that he'd overheard some of what Arnault had said.

The lieutenant's face turned red. "Not at all," he replied, a little less sure of himself now. "We were just talking about Germany… that's where you're from, right?"

"Yes, it is." Kurt looked at Helga. "We've bought dinner for this evening, and Alex is waiting in the car. Are you ready to…?"

"Yes. Of course." Helga stood up from the bar stool, leaving her drink unfinished. She glanced at me and smiled. "Pleased to meet you, Floyd. I hope you enjoy your visit here."

"Thanks," I said. "And… um, happy bird-watching." Helga nodded in return, then she stepped past me to join her cousin. Both ignored Arnault as they headed for the door.

But the lieutenant wasn't done with them yet. He waited until the door closed behind them, then jumped off his stool and hurried to the front window. Hiding behind a curtain, he peered outside for a minute or so, then turned to walk back to the bar.

"Lieutenant, what in the world are you—?" I began.

"Listen, Floyd… you didn't really buy that story of hers, did you?" Arnault didn't sit down again, but instead leaned against the counter. "That they're here just to watch flamingos?"

"Sure. Why not?"

"Oh, *really.*" He gave me a disgusted look, then moved closer, lowering his voice to a near-whisper. "Soviet ships in the vicinity of Cuba, and two Germans just happen to be visiting an island near two of the major passages from the Atlantic to the Cuban coast. Kind of a coincidence, isn't it?"

"Maybe it is." I shrugged and picked up my beer.

"And maybe it isn't." He paused to see if anyone was listening in, then went on. "Don't you think it's kind of strange that someone from Hannover can't tell me the name of the biggest hotel in the city?"

"You got me. What is it?"

"I don't know. Never been there." A cunning grin. "But she didn't know either, and that's the point. Oh, she's German, all right, and so is her cousin… if that really is her cousin. The question is, which side of Checkpoint Charlie are they from?"

Now he had my interest. "You think they might be from East Germany?"

"That would explain why she couldn't answer my question, wouldn't it?" He cocked his head toward the room. "I happened to overhear the two of you talking, and when I heard that kraut accent of hers I came over to see what was going on. When she asked you why you're here, that's when I stepped in."

"Oh, c'mon." I shook my head. "It was just a friendly question."

"No, I don't think so." Arnault hesitated. "Floyd, there's a lot about this mission that you don't know, but believe me, there's good reasons why there might be red spies hanging around. And if that's what they are, we need to find out for sure."

All this was just a little too paranoid for me. I knew guys who'd spout John Birch Society nonsense about commie infiltrators at the drop of a red hat, and what Arnault was saying sounded like more of the same. Arnault must have read the expression on my face. "You're going to help me, ensign," he added. "Consider that an order."

"Yes, *sir*." I put down my beer, but didn't get off the stool. "What would you like me to do, *sir*?"

Either he didn't catch my sarcasm or he simply chose to ignore it. "Did she say where they're staying?"

"They've rented a house just south of town. That's all she told me."

"Hmm…" He thought it over a moment. "Well, I caught a glimpse of their car, and there can't be that many red '52 Buicks on the island." He pushed back from the bar. "C'mon… we're going to take a walk and see if we can spot where they've parked it."

Find the car, find the house; the logic made sense, even if the motive didn't. I took a last slug of beer, then reluctantly got off the barstool. "Then what?"

"Then we see if we can figure out what they're doing here." As if he hadn't decided already.

It was dark when we left the restaurant, and there was no one on the streets. The grocery store had closed for the night, as had the few other shops, and only one lonely streetlight illuminated the center of town. There weren't even any sidewalks to roll up.

We didn't tell anyone where we were going or why, and I was just as happy that we hadn't. I didn't want to have egg on my face when it turned out that the lieutenant's communist spies were nothing but some birdwatchers on vacation. I just hoped that we'd get this nonsense over and done with before Capt. Gerrard noticed we were missing.

The sky was overcast, with thick clouds shrouding the quarter moon, but it was easy to see where we were going. A lighthouse rose from the beach south of Matthew Town; every few seconds its revolving beam turned our way, showing us the twigs, branches, and palm seeds that the storm had torn from the trees. After a mile or so we left the town behind and found ourselves on a narrow beachside road, with an occasional house here and there overlooking the ocean.

We had almost reached the lighthouse when we came upon a two-story wood-frame house built on a low rise across the road from the beach. There were lights in the ground floor windows, but the upstairs was dark; as we came closer, we saw a car port half-hidden behind scrub brush and Spanish bayonet. We went a little way up the driveway, trying to walk lightly upon the gravel and broken seashells, and sure enough, there was the red Buick the lieutenant had seen drive away from the restaurant.

Seeking cover in the bushes, we crept close enough to the house that we could peer through a side window. We saw what looked like a dining room. An older man, thick-set and with grey hair combed back from his temples, sat at a table that had been set for a late dinner; I assumed this was Alex, Helga and Kurt's American friend. His back was half-turned to us and he appeared to be talking to someone in another room. We couldn't hear what was being said, but a moment later Helga appeared, carrying a casserole dish in a pair of oven mitts. She carefully placed the dish on the table, then turned around and walked away again, probably returning to the kitchen.

"I don't see Kurt," I whispered.

"If they're getting ready to eat, he's probably downstairs." Arnault pointed to the back of the house. "Let's look around there," he said, and then began making his way through the bushes.

In the rear of the house was a set of outside stairs leading to a small second-floor porch. Without hesitation, Arnault left the bushes and quickly made for the stairs. Reaching them, he turned to urgently gesture for me to follow him. The last thing I wanted to do was sneak into a house, especially when its tenants were there, but the lieutenant wasn't giving me any choice. I swore under my breath, then moved to join him.

The wooden stairs were weatherbeaten and a little rickety; the first couple of steps creaked under our shoes until we put most of our weight upon the railing. We carefully made our way up to the porch, where Arnault stopped to test the knob of the door leading inside. The door was unlocked; he eased it open, revealing a darkness broken only by a sullen blue glow from some distant source. He entered the house and, even though it felt as if my heart was going to hammer its way through my ribs, I followed him.

We found ourselves in an upstairs hallway, with a nearby staircase leading down to the first floor. Closed doors were to either side of us, and straight ahead was another room; its door was ajar, and coming through the crack was the dim light that provided us with what little illumination we had. The light flickered a bit, and I figured that it must be coming from a TV someone had left on.

Unintelligible conversation from downstairs, broken by the scrape of chair legs across a wooden floor, told us that Helga, Kurt, and Alex were sitting down for dinner. I could only hope that they took their time savoring Helga's casserole as Arnault and I tip-toed down the hall, drawn like moths toward the light at its end.

The door made a soft groan as the lieutenant pushed it open, and for a second it seemed as if the voices coming from downstairs had faltered a little. But then Arnault gave a low gasp; I looked past him, and all else was suddenly forgotten.

I was right about the light; it was coming from a screen. Four of them, in fact, arranged in a semicircle upon two wooden desks pulled together to form a shallow V. But they weren't TVs, or at least not like any I'd seen on sale at Sears.

"Holy smokes!" Arnault whispered as he slowly walked into the room. "Willya look at that!"

I was looking, all right… and I was having a hard time believing what I was seeing. The two center screens displayed what, at first glance, appeared to be high-altitude camera images like those taken by a U2 spy plane. But nothing the Air Force or CIA put in the sky had ever produced pictures like these; they resembled photographic negatives, with the colors reversed, but even those colors were strangely accented with unnatural shades of green, red, and blue, making them look like weird cartoons. Although the images were obviously taken from a height, their magnification was much better than any aerial photos I'd ever seen.

And they moved.

On the right screen was what seemed to be a jungle clearing. Infantry trucks were parked in a row at one side of the clearing, with a longer row of tank trucks lined up behind them. Across the clearing was a large shed that might have been a tobacco barn were it not for the flat-bed truck slowly backing up it. A long, narrow cylinder with a cone at one end rested on the back of the truck; the tiny figures of men slowly walked on either side of the vehicle while others patrolled the edges of the clearing, evidently watching the surrounding jungle.

The left screen showed something even more chilling. An ocean harbor, with a freighter docked at a wharf. The ship's cargo hold was open, and a mobile crane parked on the wharf appeared to be raising something from belowdecks. As I watched, the crane moved just enough for me to make out what it was lifting from the freighter: another cylindrical shape, much like the one on the other screen.

"God damn." Arnault's voice was low but hoarse with anger. "God *damn!*" He pointed at the two screens. "That's Cuba, and those are Soviet missiles!"

I barely paid attention to him; I was looking at something else. The screens themselves had caught my interest; they didn't look like normal cathode-ray tubes but instead were as flat as cafeteria trays, with no visible buttons or switches. The screens bookending the middle two were dark, but when I stepped closer, the one on the far left suddenly lit up to display a row of tiny symbols arranged against a background that fluctuated like a small aurora.

On the desktops below the left and right screens were what appeared at first to be a pair of small portable typewriters. There were no rollers in them, though, and when I bent to examine them more closely, I saw that, while their keyboards had the familiar QWERTYUIOP arrangement, the keys themselves were as flat as if they'd been painted on a glass surface, with a double row of buttons above them.

Looking at them, I was reminded of something I'd seen once before: the Enigma code-making machine used by the Germans during World War II. That looked a little like a typewriter, too, but it wasn't. It was a computer. Could this be...?

"I told you so." Arnault was still staring at the two middle screens. "This is a red spy nest. Some sort of observation post."

I ignored him as I glanced behind the desks. No wires or cables; what was the power source? I was still puzzling over that when I noticed a plastic sheet about the size of a notebook page on the left desk next to the keyboard. I picked it up, and almost dropped it again as it glowed with a light of its own, exposing another row of tiny symbols against a shifting background. I experimentally touched one of the symbols; the page instantly changed, this time to show another aerial view: a different jungle clearing, now in broad daylight, with tiny soldiers erecting what appeared to be an anti-aircraft missile launcher.

"This stuff isn't from Russia," I murmured, hearing my voice tremble. "It's not from East Germany either. This is… something else."

"I don't care where it's from. I know missiles when I see 'em…"

"At night?" I pointed to the right center screen. "Look at that truck and those people. They're moving, lieutenant. That's not a still picture… this is happening right now, while we're watching. Do the reds have that kind of…?"

The door creaked behind us.

My heart stopped beating, and I'd just turned around when the ceiling light suddenly came on. I winced against the abrupt glare, but not before I saw Helga, Kurt, and Alex standing in the doorway.

For a long moment, both groups stared at one another in dumb surprise. I flashed back to when I was a kid and my father caught me stealing a quarter from his bedroom dresser; the look on my face must have been the same.

This time, Helga played my dad's role. "Floyd… what are you doing here?" she asked, more shocked than angry.

"Is this the man you were talking about?" Alex's hand was still on the wall switch. Helga nodded, and he glared at us. "You're trespassing," he said, stating the obvious.

"And you're Russian spies!" Arnault snapped, as if a blunt accusation would justify our intrusion.

Alex's mouth fell open, Kurt rapidly blinked, and Helga simply stared at him. Then Helga raised a hand to her mouth, but not quite fast enough to hide her giggle. Kurt and Alex traded a glance, then Kurt's eyes rolled up as Alex tried to control the amused grin that threatened to spread across his face.

"No… no, we're not Russian spies." Alex relaxed a little, letting his hand drop from the light switch. "I assure you, we—"

"Then what's all this?" Arnault jabbed a finger at the screens. "Tell me those aren't pictures of Soviet rockets in Cuba!"

That quickly sobered up the three of them. This was no longer funny. Meanwhile, I felt like I was the only person in the room who didn't know what was going on. "Lieutenant," I asked, "what makes you think the Russians are putting missiles in Cuba?"

Arnault barely glanced at me. "We've received intelligence that Ivan may be shipping nukes to Cuba," he said, not taking his eyes off Helga, Kurt, and Alex. "That's what our mission is… to gather any evidence that the reports are true." A corner of his mouth lifted slightly. "I think we've got all the proof we need right here."

I looked at the screens again. The view of the Cuban harbor was still there, but the image on the center-right screen had changed. It now displayed what appeared to be a beach; in the nearby jungle, an anti-aircraft missile launcher was being covered by camouflage netting. It seemed to be the same shot as the one in the plastic sheet still in my hand, but this time it had the same photo-negative appearance as the earlier images. I realized that they were from an apparent altitude of only a few hundred feet. That was much lower than our blimp could go without being seen, but the people on the ground were apparently unaware that they were being observed.

"Lieutenant, this isn't Russian equipment." I picked up one of the keyboards, held it out for him to see. "They can't even make a decent toaster, for heaven's sake."

"They're pretty good at building rockets!"

"Never mind that. Have you ever seen TVs like those before? Or—" I put down the keyboard, picked up the weird sheet of plastic "—whatever this is? Man, even NASA doesn't have stuff like this!"

Looking away from the three people at the door, Arnault turned his head slightly to examine the equipment on the desks. For the first time, he seemed to notice something besides the missiles. "Those could be aerial photos…"

"At night? At the same time that things are happening on the ground?" A new thought occurred to me. I turned to Helga. "This is… this is from space, isn't it?"

She reluctantly nodded. "We're using satellites, yes… ones far more sophisticated than any your country or the Soviet Union now has. High resolution radar imaging…"

"Don't be too specific," Alex said quietly.

"No, of course not," Helga said. "But Floyd's right. The Soviet Union does not possess technology of this kind, and nor does East Germany." She hesitated. "No one will… at least, not for some time to come."

"Helga…" Kurt cast a warning look at her.

"Let her speak," Alex said. "The truth is no worse than the accusation." He frowned at Kurt. "Besides, this is your fault, for leaving the porch door unlocked. I asked you not to do that." Kurt's face reddened as Alex turned to Helga again. "Go on."

Helga took a deep breath. "We're observers. Not spies, simply… observers. I won't tell you where we're from, other than to say that it's not a place that exists in this frame of time."

"Observers," I repeated, and then I remembered something the lieutenant had said just before we were discovered. "Then… this is an observation post, I guess."

She smiled slightly. "That's a good way of putting it. We established this place for the purpose of watching and recording everything that will occur, or may occur, at this particular point in—"

"What do you mean, 'will or may occur'?" Arnault raised an eyebrow. "Is there something we should know?" Kurt muttered something under his breath that may have been obscene, and Helga went pale as if she'd suddenly realized that she may have said too much. "The missiles," the lieutenant went on. "This has to do with them, doesn't it?"

"It does, yes." Now it was Alex's turn to be both reticent and informative. "There are… certain points in time, shall we say?… when human existence hangs in the balance and its future depends upon the actions of a few. This is one of those occasions. But even so, all the pertinent facts are not always recorded. Because of this, later generations are left to discover how things might have happened differently if the situation had changed even just a little."

"History is malleable," Helga said, "because time itself is not linear. Any deviation, no matter how slight, can have enormous consequences, which in turn can lead to the creation of parallel timelines in which—"

"Look, I don't care about any of that." Arnault was becoming impatient; I'm not sure he even listened at all. "The only thing that matters is that the Russians are stockpiling missiles on Cuba, and those missiles may have nuclear warheads."

Something cold went down my spine. "Is this true?" I asked. "Do those things have nukes?"

"Hell, yes!" The lieutenant regarded me as if I was an idiot. "What would be the point of positioning rockets within sixty miles of our country if they didn't have nuclear warheads?" He glared at the other three people in the room. "Maybe you're not Russians, but that doesn't change a thing. I have to tell my people what's going on!"

He started to walk toward the door. Alex stepped in front of him. "You can't do that."

Arnault halted, looked him straight in the eye. "Don't tell me what I can't do."

"If anyone else learns what you know, it will cause…" Alex hesitated. "Look, I can't reveal to you what's going to happen, but I can say that any changes to this timeline may be catastrophic. If you—"

"Get out of my way." Arnault took another step forward, and Alex raised his hands to stop him. Bad move; the lieutenant had the same training in hand-to-hand combat as I did. Arnault grabbed his arm with both hands, and in the next second Alex was on the floor, gasping in pain from the judo throw Arnault had used on him. Kurt started to move, then froze as the lieutenant whirled toward him. The two men stared at each other, then Arnault stepped over Alex and calmly walked out the door.

Helga turned to me. "Floyd, you can't let this happen."

I was stunned by what I'd just seen, unable to move. "I… I…"

"Floyd… listen to me." Helga rushed across the room to grab me by the shoulders. "What I've said is true," she went on, dropping her voice so that Arnault couldn't hear her. "We've seen the outcome in other timelines. If your president learns too early that there are Soviet missiles on Cuba, it will prompt him to launch an invasion or a preemptive air attack. But he doesn't know how many missiles are already there or their exact locations. And the Russian premier has given his officers in Cuba permission to use tactical missiles against an invasion force, or launch intermediate-range missiles at the U.S. if there's an air strike."

"You know what will occur if that happens," Alex said. Kurt was helping him off the floor; he winced as he massaged his twisted right forearm. "Kennedy will order a retaliatory nuclear strike against the Soviet Union, Khrushchev will respond by launching Russia's strategic missiles…"

"Millions will die." Helga's eyes were locked on mine. "The world as you know it will be destroyed. *We've seen it happen.*"

I was having trouble breathing, and my legs felt weak. From the other end of the hallway, I heard the porch door slam open, Arnault's footsteps trotting down the back stairs. "Why… why can't you…?"

"We cannot interfere." Kurt was apologetic but almost laughably calm, as if he was informing me that I had an overdue book at the library. "No matter what happens, we're prohibited from taking any actions ourselves." He looked at Alex and shook his head. "We've done too much already. When we visit critical events such as this…"

"Go." Helga shook my arms, trying to snap me out of my shock. "For the sake of everyone you know and love… *stop him!*"

I pushed her aside, hurried to the door. I no longer heard Arnault's shoes on the stairs; when I reached the back porch, a passing beam from the lighthouse captured him for a second as he marched down the driveway.

I nearly fell down the stairs in my haste, but the lieutenant had already made it to the road by the time I caught up with him. "Lieutenant, wait!" I yelled, but he didn't stop or turn around. "Just stop, will you? We can't…!"

I laid a hand on his shoulder, and he whipped about to face me. "What do you want?"

"We… we…" I was gasping for breath. "We can't do this. If we tell them…"

"Ensign Moore… *at attention!*"

Training took over. I snapped rigid, back straight, hands at sides, legs together. He stepped closer, so close that I could fell his breath on my face. The searchlight passed over us again, and I saw his eyes only inches from mine.

"Ensign Moore, you are a seaman in the United States Navy. Is this correct?"

"Yes, sir."

"I can't hear you!"

"*Yes, sir!*"

"As a Navy seaman, you are sworn to protect your country. Is this correct?"

"*Yes, sir!*"

"As your superior officer, I order you to fulfill your oath. We will go to the blimp, where you will provide me with the means to send a coded priority message to NAVINT, informing them of what we've discovered! Do you understand?"

"*Yes, sir!*"

"Outstanding." He stepped back, turned away from me. "Follow me."

The ray from the lighthouse passed above us again, and in that instant I saw, on the side of the road, a tree branch that had been knocked down by the storm. There was no hesitation; I knew what I had to do.

I bent over and picked up the branch. It was about the size of a baseball bat and just as solid. I grasped it with both hands and swung it at the back of the lieutenant's head. There was a hollow crack as I felt it connect. Arnault grunted and staggered forward, but before he could react or even turn around, I raised the branch above me, rushed toward him, and slammed it straight down on his skull. He gasped and fell, but he'd barely hit the ground before I brought the branch down upon his head again.

And again.

And again.

The next time the light touched us, I saw that he was dying. He lay face-down in the road, arms stretched out. There was blood all over the back of his head, and it turned the pavement black as it flowed out from under him. I couldn't see his face, but I could hear a rattling rasp as he struggled for his last breath. I raised the branch again, but didn't strike him; instead, I watched as his hands twitched a couple of times, then there was a soft sigh and he was still.

I was still staring at him when Helga touched my elbow. "I'm sorry," she whispered. "I'm so, so sorry…"

I nodded. Then I dropped the branch, went over to the side of the road, and threw up.

History records that only a handful of lives were lost during the Cuban Missile Crisis: the pilot of the American U2 that was shot down over Cuba by a Soviet anti-aircraft battery, and the Russian soldiers who died when the truck carrying them went off a mountain road and rolled down an embankment.

There was another casualty, though: U.S. Navy intelligence officer Lt. Robert Arnault. But he is not counted among the dead.

Helga took me back to the house, where she let me clean up in the bathroom while she washed the bloodstains from my shirt. There was a bottle of scotch in the kitchen; I poured myself a double, no chaser.

Kurt and Alex returned in a little while. I noticed that they'd taken off their shoes and rolled up their pants legs, and that their bare feet were covered with sand. They told me what they'd done with Arnault's body, and how they thrown the branch into the woods and washed his blood off the road with buckets of sea water carried up from the beach. They'd also come up with an alibi; it sounded plausible to me, and we went over it a few times until I had it thoroughly memorized. I had another drink—because I needed it, and also because it was part of my alibi—and then I put on my shirt and left the house.

The hour was late by the time I walked back into Matthew Town; the restaurant was closed, and the streets were quiet. A poker game was going on in someone's room at the guest house, but no one saw me when I came in. Handsome Jimmy was snoring loudly when I let myself into the room we shared, and he didn't wake up as I undressed in the dark and climbed into bed.

It took a long time for me to fall asleep.

Capt. Gerrard woke up the crew up shortly after sunrise, going from room to room to knock on the doors. It was then that Lt. Arnault's absence was noticed; his bed was unmade, and his duffel bag was untouched. Everyone remembered that he and I had left the bar together, so the captain came to me and asked if I had seen him lately.

I told the skipper that Arnault had become interested in a girl we'd met in the bar, and that the two of us followed her back to the house where she was staying with her cousin and a friend. I hadn't wanted to go with him, I explained, but it seemed like the lieutenant had had a little too much to drink, and so I'd gone along to make sure that he stayed out of trouble. Unfortunately, that's exactly what happened; Arnault made a scene when he caught up with Helga, insisting that she come back to the bar with him, until Kurt and Alex threw him out of the house. I'd remained behind to apologize, and ended up staying awhile to have a few drinks. I hadn't seen the lieutenant after that... why, was there something wrong?

Capt. Gerrard called the Mathew Town police and told them that a member of his crew was missing. About an hour later, the police chief came to the guest house with shocking news: the lieutenant was dead, his body discovered on the beach just outside of town. It appeared that someone had beaten him to death, then dragged his body to the waterside. Two sets of footprints in the sand attested to the fact that he'd been attacked by two people, probably while walking back to town; his watch was missing, and although his wallet was found on the beach, there was no cash in it. The police figured that he'd probably put up a fight, and the robbers had murdered him.

Since I was the last person to see the lieutenant alive, I had to repeat my story several times; I'd have to do so again, in front of a Navy board of inquiry charged with investigating the lieutenant's murder. I had my alibi down pat and I was careful never to deviate from it, and so I never came under suspicion. And when the police went out to the house, the three vacationing birdwatchers verified everything that I had said; the lieutenant had made a pass at Helga, and so Kurt and Alex had made him leave, but let me stay awhile because Helga liked me.

The killers were never found, but that didn't surprise anyone in Matthew Town. There was very little crime on Great Inagua, but when it occurred, it was usually caused by one of the Haitian boat people who periodically came over from Hispaniola. That was a common explanation in the Bahamas: whenever there was an unsolved crime, a Haitian was always responsible. The Navy investigation eventually reached the same conclusion; Lt. Arnault had been simply in the wrong place at the wrong time, and the men who'd killed him had only been after his watch and money.

Less than two weeks after the lieutenant's death, President Kennedy learned that the U.S.S.R. had placed nuclear-tipped missiles on Cuba. Over the next nine days, America and Russia played a dangerous contest of wits, each poised to start a war no one could win. In the end, Kennedy and Khrushchev—two men who had seen war first-hand and knew its consequences—managed to persevere over the hawks on both sides to reach a diplomatic solution: in exchange for a promise that the U.S. would cease its attempts to remove Castro from power and respect Cuba's sovereign status, the U.S.S.R. would remove its missiles from Cuba.

The *Centurion* returned to Key West long before that happened. It flew only once more, to watch for Russian submarines off the Atlantic Coast during the crisis. The following month, the Navy decided to ground its blimps for good. So the *Centurion* was deflated for the last time, and its car eventually made its way to an aviation museum in Connecticut. I was transferred to the U.S.S. *Lexington*, where I worked as a communications officer before leaving the service a few years later.

I was given an honorable discharge. The irony of this hasn't been lost on me. But I never told anyone what I did that night, even though it haunted me for years to come.

Did I do the right thing? I'd like to think so, if only because it's helped me deal with my conscience. But something Helga told me that night has stayed with me as much as the murder itself.

History is malleable, she said, *because time itself is not linear*. This implies that there was—there *is*—more than one outcome to the events of October, 1962. Have those alternatives—which Helga claimed to have actually seen—hinged upon what I did or did not do? Or was the lieutenant's death merely an incident that had no lasting consequences?

I'll never know. But there is this:

I'd moved to a small town outside Colorado Springs several years back, and a few days ago I went into the city to visit my doctor. My son drove me there; he's taken care of me since my wife died, and he had a few errands of his own. After I got through at the doctor's office, I walked down the street to a restaurant where I was to meet my son for lunch. My illness hasn't totally bedridden me yet, although I have to depend on a stroller and an oxygen tank to get around.

It was midday and the sidewalks were crowded, mainly with office workers on their way to one place or another. I'd almost reached the restaurant when the front door of an apartment building swung open and a young woman walked out.

It was Helga. Of this, I'm absolutely certain; I've never forgotten her face, even after all these years. And although her hair style had changed and she was wearing a business suit, she hadn't aged a day. It was as if she'd come straight from Great Inagua with only a quick stop at a fashion shop and hairdresser along the way.

She didn't recognize me, of course. I was just a sick old man, bent over a stroller with an oxygen line clipped to his nose. She strolled past me and was gone before I could say anything.

So she's here, in our time. But why?

Consider this: NORAD, the North American Aerospace Defense Command, has its headquarters at Cheyenne Mountain, just outside

Colorado Springs. Since 1966, the Air Force has directed American strategic defense operations from an underground complex deep within the mountain. If a global nuclear war were to break out, this would be one of the first places to know.

Perhaps it may only be a coincidence that I've seen Helga again. Or perhaps it may not. I'm afraid I may live long enough to learn for certain.

CPSIA information can be obtained at www.ICGtesting.com
Printed in the USA
LVOW07s0324130415

434323LV00001B/50/P

9 781627 556347